W9-AWJ-745

Praise for
HOPE RAMSAY and
Welcome to Last Chance

"Happiness is a new Hope Ramsay series."
—**Fresh Fiction**

"Every story by Hope Ramsay will touch a reader's heart."
—**BRENDA NOVAK**, *New York Times*
bestselling author

"The essence of Southern charm!"
—**SHERRYL WOODS**, *New York Times*
bestselling author

"*Welcome to Last Chance* is an impressive start to a charming new series, featuring quirky characters you won't soon forget."
—**BARBARA FREETHY**, *USA Today*
bestselling author

"Last Chance, South Carolina, is a caring community filled with the promise of hope. Come for a visit!"
—**LORI WILDE**, *New York Times*
bestselling author

"Witty, touching, and absolutely delightful—this story has heart!"
—**JOANN ROSS**, *New York Times*
bestselling author

"Ramsay strikes an excellent balance between tension and humor as she spins a fine yarn."
—*Publishers Weekly,*
starred review

"A sweet confection…This first of a projected series about the Rhodes brothers offers up Southern hospitality with a bit of grit. Romance readers will be delighted."
—*Library Journal*

Welcome to
Last Chance

Welcome to Last Chance

HOPE RAMSAY

FOREVER

NEW YORK   BOSTON

This book is a work of fiction. Names, characters, places, and incidents are the product of the author's imagination or are used fictitiously. Any resemblance to actual events, locales, or persons, living or dead, is coincidental.

Copyright © 2011 by Robin Lanier
A Fairytale Bride copyright © 2016 by Robin Lanier
Excerpt from *The Cottage on Rose Lane* copyright © 2018 by Robin Lanier

Hachette Book Group supports the right to free expression and the value of copyright. The purpose of copyright is to encourage writers and artists to produce the creative works that enrich our culture.

The scanning, uploading, and distribution of this book without permission is a theft of the author's intellectual property. If you would like permission to use material from the book (other than for review purposes), please contact permissions@hbgusa.com. Thank you for your support of the author's rights.

Forever
Hachette Book Group
1290 Avenue of the Americas, New York, NY 10104
read-forever.com
twitter.com/readforeverpub

Originally published in March 2011
Reissued: April 2019

Forever is an imprint of Grand Central Publishing. The Forever name and logo are trademarks of Hachette Book Group, Inc.

The publisher is not responsible for websites (or their content) that are not owned by the publisher.

The Hachette Speakers Bureau provides a wide range of authors for speaking events. To find out more, go to hachettespeakersbureau.com or call (866) 376-6591.

ISBNs: 978-1-5387-3203-8 (mass market reissue), 978-1-4555-0062-8 (ebook)

Printed in the United States of America

OPM

10 9 8 7 6 5 4 3 2 1

ATTENTION CORPORATIONS AND ORGANIZATIONS:
Most HACHETTE BOOK GROUP books are available
at quantity discounts with bulk purchase for educational,
business, or sales promotional use. For information,
please call or write:

Special Markets Department, Hachette Book Group
1290 Avenue of the Americas, New York, NY 10104
Telephone: 1-800-222-6747 Fax: 1-800-477-5925

For the steel magnolias who shaped the woman
I have become:
Millie, Annie, Doss, Thelma, Lessie, and Miriam.

Acknowledgments

Thank you to my fabulous critique partners: Robin Kaye, Carla Kempert, and Lavinia Kent. Your help and encouragement over the years have meant so much to me. Also many thanks to my agent and her able assistant, Elaine English and Naomi Hackenberg, for understanding what I wanted to do with these stories, and for helping me bring Last Chance to life. And finally to Bryan, Ramsay, and Susan—I love you guys. Thanks for putting up with me for all these years. I know I can sometimes be difficult to live with.

Welcome to
Last Chance

Chapter
1

One ticket to Last Chance," the agent said as he took Jane's money. "The bus leaves in five minutes."

Jane picked up the flimsy slip of paper and hurried through the Atlanta, Georgia, Greyhound terminal. She found the gate, climbed aboard the motor coach, and sank into one of the plush seats.

She tried to think positive thoughts.

It was hard. She had five dollars left in her pocketbook, a zero balance in her checking account, and bad guys in her recent past. Her dreams of making it big in Nashville had just taken a dive over the cliff called reality.

Thank you, Woody West, you peanut-brained weasel.

The diesel engines roared to life, and the bus glided out of the parking lot heading toward South Carolina, which was not where Jane really wanted to go.

She took three deep breaths and tried to visualize her future the way Dr. Goodbody advised in his self-help recordings. If she could just unleash her inner consciousness through positive thinking, the Universe would give her a road map for success.

That seemed like a good plan. She needed a road map to a better future in the worst way. And where better to seek a new start than a place called Last Chance? She had never been to Last Chance, but the name sounded hopeful.

She sank back into her seat and tried to see the place in her mind's eye. She imagined it like Pleasantville, where the streets were picturesque, the people friendly, and the job opportunities plentiful.

Eight hours later, reality intruded.

The Greyhound left her standing on a deserted sidewalk right in front of a place called Bill's Grease Pit. Fortunately, this establishment was not a fast-food joint but an auto-repair service that doubled as a bus terminal. Both the garage and the terminal were closed for the night.

She looked down the street and knew herself for a fool. Last Chance had exactly one traffic light. The only sign of life was the glow of neon shining like a beacon from a building two blocks down the main drag.

Okay, so Last Chance wasn't Bedford Falls, from the movie *It's a Wonderful Life*. She could deal.

She told herself that where there was Budweiser and neon there was hope of finding some dinner. Although how she was going to pay for it remained a mystery. She fought against the panic that gripped her insides. She hugged herself as she walked up the street, running through her usual list of positive affirmations.

She would get herself out of this mess. She had done it before. And the truth was, she should have read the warning signs when Woody walked into the Shrimp Shack six months ago. If she had read those signs, she wouldn't be standing here today. Well, every mistake was an opportunity to learn, according to Dr. Goodbody.

The bar bore the name Dot's Spot in bright blue neon. It sported a dark wood exterior and small windows festooned with half a dozen beer signs. Jane stood in the garish light cast by the signs, thinking it would be truly awesome if she could walk through that doorway and find Sir Galahad waiting for her. But wishing for Sir Galahad was not positive thinking. Heroes didn't magically appear in southern honky-tonks on a Wednesday night.

Besides, this particular fantasy of a knightly rescue had gotten her into trouble every time she allowed herself to believe it. So she pushed it out of her mind. She needed to focus on manifesting a hot meal and a place to spend the night. Period. She fixed that positive plan of action in her mind and pushed through the front door.

Hoo boy, the place was like something right out of a bad country-and-western tune. Smoke hung over the place and a five-piece country band occupied a raised stage at one end of the barroom. They played a twangy Garth Brooks tune in waltz time. No one was dancing.

The men in the band were, by and large, a bunch of middle-aged geezers, with beer bellies and wedding rings and receding hairlines.

Except for the fiddler.

Jane stared at him for a moment, recognition washing through her. No question about it—there stood another peanut-brained weasel in the flesh. She could tell this because he was a big, powerfully built man with a ponytail and facial hair. He also wore a black Stetson, and a black shirt, and black jeans that hugged his butt and thighs, and a gem that sparkled from his earlobe like a black diamond.

What was that thing? A sapphire?

He was the real-deal, bad-for-any-females-who-came-within-range package. Someone should hang a big yellow warning sign on his neck that said "danger."

Guys like him didn't rescue girls. They rode around on Harleys, and were mean and tough and bad, and got into lots of trouble with the local law. They also had really big shoulders that a girl could lean on, and in a moment of confusion, a girl could confuse one of these bad boys with Sir Galahad, only on a motorcycle.

Good thing Jane planned on rescuing herself, because this guy was like some walking embodiment of Murphy's Law. The spit dried up in her mouth, and her heart rate kicked up. The Universe had just thrown her another curveball.

So she looked away, sweeping the room with her gaze. The rest of the pickings were slim and ran to old men and floozies, and a few obviously married guys in John Deere hats. She might be about to do some serious flirting in order to get a drink and some food, but she would not hit on any married men. That ran counter to her moral code.

She scanned the bar. Bingo. Two prospects, twelve o'clock.

Prospect One wore a dirty Houston Astros hat, his chin propped up on his left fist as he watched the World Series game on the big-screen television. He was devilishly handsome, but the words "hard drinking" scrolled through her mind.

Jane turned her attention to prospect Number Two.

He turned on the stool, and she got a good look at him. He was a smaller-than-average guy, with sandy hair, a widow's peak, and regular features. He wore a blue work shirt with his name—Ray—embroidered above the right pocket. Unlike the other two hunks in the room, this guy wore work boots. He wasn't a cowboy, and he didn't look dangerous at all.

He looked up from his drink.

Okay, he would do. Kindness shone from his eyes. She concentrated on holding his gaze... counted to three... then dazzled him with a smile.

He blinked two or three times like a deer caught in a hunter's sight. But she wasn't a hunter, not really. She was vulnerable, and scared, and hunted herself. And that explained why she was about to do something not very nice—something she would most likely regret in the morning.

The bodacious brunette hit Dot's Spot like the hurricane expected to arrive tomorrow. She wore high-heel boots and a little tank top that barely constrained her assets. Clay Rhodes had never seen her before, which had to mean she'd just gotten off the nine-thirty bus from Atlanta.

She waltzed her butt through the door and captured the attention of every male in the place, except maybe Dash Randall, who was concentrating on the World Series. She stopped just inside the door and gave the place a once-over.

It took all of three seconds for her to look Clay's way, and about fifteen for her to catalog him and move on. But that was all it took for Clay Rhodes to feel the unmistakable pull of lust centering right behind his belly button. Yeah, he could go for some of that, if it wasn't for the fact that he was a responsible, almost middle-aged grown-up, and she looked like trouble on high heels.

He pulled the fiddle down and tried to put some feeling into his harmony line on "Night Rider's Lament," but since he had played this song about five thousand times, it was hard to do.

The little gal distracted him as she scanned the room. It didn't surprise him one bit when her sharp gaze lingered on Dash. The ex-jock was unaware of it, though. He sat at the end of the bar wallowing in self-pity and doing battle with God-only-knew-how-many demons as he watched the baseball game.

The girl was interested, of course. Dash was a fine-looking man, but a woman would have to be nuts to tangle with a guy like that. Clay gave her points when her gaze shifted and moved on.

He pulled the fiddle up to his chin and played the bridge, while Kyle tried his hardest to sound like Garth Brooks. Kyle failed, like he did every night, which was no surprise to anyone.

What happened next, though, surprised the heck out of just about everyone in Dot's Spot.

That girl aimed her laser-beam look at the back of Ray's head and darned if the boy didn't jump like he was some kind of marionette with a nervous puppeteer. He jerked his head around, and disaster struck about twelve hours earlier than expected.

The woman aimed a smile at Ray that had all the subtlety of a Stinger missile, and poor Ray didn't have any defenses for something like that.

Uh-oh.

The song ended, and Clay turned toward Kyle. "Let's cut it short and go to break," he said.

"But—"

Clay jerked his head toward Ray and rolled his eyes.

"Not again," Kyle said under his breath, as he took in the unfolding scene.

"Looks like."

Kyle leaned into the mic and told the crowd they'd be back in ten, while Clay put his fiddle into the hard-shell case that sat atop the upright piano. Then Clay stepped down from the stage and headed toward the bar.

"Clay," Ray said as he approached. "Look, it's April. What do you figure the odds are on that? A million to one?" Ray rocked a little on the bar stool and gave Clay his goofy smile. Eighteen years ago, that grin, combined with Ray's uncanny ability to do math, had made the boy semipopular with the girls at Davis High who wanted to adopt him, or befriend him, or otherwise allow him to do their homework. But that had changed three weeks before graduation.

Clay came to a halt and turned toward the little gal in the white tank top. Man-oh-man, she was something else. Tawny skin and dark eyes with a pair of killer cheekbones and pouty lips that said kiss me quick. She was pure sex on three-inch stiletto heels.

A man didn't get within five feet of this and not lose his perspective on things. Even a half-dead man like himself. The little tingle in his private parts was kind of reassuring, though. It confirmed that he was still alive. Sometimes living in Last Chance, South Carolina, it was hard to tell.

Her pink nail polish was chipped, the neck of her tank top sported a little stain, and the cuffs of her jean jacket were frayed. Her gaze seemed a little guileless, which surprised the heck out of him. He had taken her for trash, but up close she didn't look trashy at all—just a little rumpled and forlorn.

And utterly irresistible.

"So your name's April?" he asked, knowing darn well her name wasn't April. She did look like April, though, which made her hotter than a chili pepper. Hot and forlorn. A deadly combination if there ever was one.

She shook her head. "No…uh…my name's…um… Mary."

Clay went on guard. She was lying. "How old are you, Mary?" he asked.

Her square chin inched up. "Why? Do I look like jailbait?"

Yeah. But he didn't say it out loud. He studied her for a long moment, trying to ignore the sexual rush. She had incredible skin. It looked silky soft, firm and warm. He wanted to touch it.

He forced himself to look into her wide brown eyes. No, she wasn't a teenager. But she was still trouble. He needed to rescue Ray from this woman. Ray could get himself into a heap of trouble if someone didn't do something quick.

Clay turned away. "Hey, Ray, you got a minute?"

Ray ducked his head in that funny little tic that had been there ever since the accident senior year. "Sure. Whatever you want."

Clay jerked his head. "In private."

Ray turned toward the little gal. "You stay right here, April. I'll be back. Don't go anywhere, okay?"

The girl nodded, and Clay got the feeling that she was happy to be rescued. Like she had maybe figured out Ray was playing a few cards short of a full deck.

Clay pulled Ray down to the end of the bar and put his arm around his shoulder. "Listen, Ray, I'm your oldest friend, right?"

Ray nodded.

"Got you fixed up with my uncle Pete at the hardware store, didn't I?"

"Yeah, Clay."

"Bailed you out with my brother Stony that time when you busted up the place?"

Ray kept on nodding.

"Helped you out with Mr. Polk down at the bank when your momma got sick."

"Yeah, Clay, I know all that."

"So you know I wouldn't lie to you."

"No, Clay, you wouldn't ever lie to me."

"Look, Ray, that little gal isn't April."

Ray rolled away, then turned and squared up his body. "She is, too. Look at her."

"April is a photograph of a girl. This isn't her. This is a girl named Mary, who's new to town. I'll bet she came on the nine-thirty bus from Atlanta."

Ray wet his lips. His fists curled up. "Don't you say that, Clay. She's April. *Look* at her."

Clay shook his head. The last person in the world he wanted to fight was Ray Betts. He hated fighting in general, since it messed up his hands. But fighting Ray would be like fighting with one of his brothers.

"Look—" Clay started to say.

"Hey, Ray," Dash called from his place by the bar.

Ray turned and relaxed his hands a fraction. "Yeah?"

"You wanna go down to the high school and shag some balls?"

"Really?" A slow smile filled Ray's face, and Clay breathed a sigh of relief.

In Ray's injured brain, this invitation from Dash Randall was like being asked if he wanted to go hang out with God. Ray loved baseball, and since Dash had once played it professionally, Dash had become one of Ray's personal heroes.

Dash gave Clay a meaningful and surprisingly sober glance. Maybe the rumors were true, and Dash was on the wagon these days. Although why a man on the wagon would spend time in a bar was kind of a mystery. Well, even if it wasn't true, he owed Dash a favor for this.

Dash leaned over and collected an aluminum cane. He stood up, favoring his bad leg. "Yeah, Ray, I mean it. But you'll have to do all the running since my knee isn't up to it, yet. C'mon, I'll even put the top down, and we can cruise over to the Tastee Freeze afterward."

"Gee, Dash, that sounds like fun," Ray said.

Dash winked at Clay as he led Ray out of the bar. Disaster had been averted.

But when Clay turned back toward the little gal, his gut tightened up like a warning. Was she desperate or just looking for some action? He had a feeling it might be a little of both.

And he'd just sent his competition packing.

Two hours later, Jane picked up the little slip of paper and read her bar tab: Six dollars for three Cokes. It might as well have been a hundred dollars. She didn't have the cash to pay it—unless she dug deep in her purse and found a dollar in change and added it to the five-dollar bill in her wallet. Then she would be officially broke.

She should have nursed a single Coke all night. She should have taken steps to get a credit card, years ago. But she hadn't done either of these things. The first because it had been years since she had been this poor. The second because getting a credit card was risky, given her background.

She swallowed the lump in her throat and told herself she wasn't going to cry. Her attempt to find someone seminice to buy her dinner had flopped. There was just the fiddler who had run all the seminice guys off like some kind of reverse bouncer.

That man had spent the last two hours boring a hole in her back with his silver-eyed stare. About an hour ago, she had given up trying not to look back.

Jane could parlay this into something, if she wanted to. But she had to remember that he was not going to rescue her from her current situation. She needed to fix her own life. And, right now, staying away from a bad boy seemed like a good first step.

But then all her other choices were worse. She couldn't sleep in the public park tonight—assuming, of course, that Last Chance had a public park. But even if it did have one, the weather report on the television above the bar said a hurricane was bearing down on the South Carolina coast. It wasn't a big hurricane by Katrina standards, but even so, everyone in the bar was talking about torrential rains starting sometime after two in the morning.

Jane had hoped they might have a hurricane shelter open where she could blend right in, like a refugee or something. But there wasn't any kind of evacuation going on—no doubt because the hurricane was making landfall a hundred miles away near Hilton Head Island. She didn't have many other options in a small town like Last Chance.

Jane stole a glance up at the fiddler, and heat sizzled through her. The Cosmos and her own hormones were against her. She shouldn't do this. This was a mistake.

She turned away and stared down at her bar tab. Behind her, the lead singer signed off for the night. Someone punched up a bunch of songs on the jukebox.

Well, first things first. She needed to pay the bill. She dug deep into her purse, drawing out a handful of pennies and nickels, and started counting. In the background, the jukebox played Tumbleweed's new country single...

> *Feel the rush of my breath*
> *Feel the heat of my hand...*

Heat crawled up her backside as the words of the song suddenly made themselves manifest. The fiddler had snuck up on her. He put one of his ginormous hands on the bar, leaned his big body in, and slapped a ten-dollar bill down on top of her tab like he'd been counting the number of Cokes she'd drunk.

He turned toward her, his unreadable wolf eyes shaded by the brim of his Stetson. "You want to take this somewhere else?" he asked in a blurred drawl. Her insides clutched and burned.

She was close enough to see a network of lines at the corner of his eyes, and little threads of silver in his goatee. He wasn't young. That scared her a little. He was more man than she was used to handling—older and bigger and more dangerous than anyone else in her past.

"Maybe I was mistaken," he drawled in response to her slight hesitation. "I got the idea you might be interested."

Jane looked up into his eyes. A hot, blue flame flickered there. An answering heat resonated deep down inside her. Was this wishful thinking, desperation, or real desire made manifest by her own weakness for guys like this? It was kind of hard to tell.

Her head screamed that going with this guy would be like repeating the mistakes of the past. Getting soaked on a park bench would be better than this. But her body wasn't listening. Instead she gave the fiddler a smile and said, "Cowboy, take me away."

"You drive a minivan?" The girl—Mary, he reminded himself—stood beyond the service entrance to Dot's Spot with her hands fisted on her hips and a semisurprised look on her face.

"Yeah, well, it's practical for hauling around sound equipment and guitars. Disappointed?" Clay said, as he opened the side-panel door of his ancient Windstar and hoisted his fiddle, mandolin, and guitar cases into the cargo space.

The question was rhetorical. She *was* disappointed. Women had a habit of mistaking him for someone else—usually some bad-boy jerk with a Harley who would do them wrong sooner or later. Ironically, most women wasted no time in doing *him* wrong, as if he were the punching bag for their collective disappointments with males in general and bad boys in particular.

He turned around and faced the girl. She had the wrong idea about him. And he wasn't going to disabuse her of it. He was going to take her to the Peach Blossom Motor Court and become that bad boy she was looking for. He wasn't going to apologize to anyone for it either.

He was tired of being a good man.

He was tired of living his life along the straight and narrow.

But most of all, he was weary of being alone.

The girl stepped forward, her body swaying in the lamplight, the gusty wind lifting her hair and whipping it across her face. She tucked the hair behind her ear and gave him a simple smile that curled up the dimples in her cheek. Desire, sweet and warm, flooded through him.

He opened the van's door for her, and she stepped close enough for him to catch the blended scents of cigarette smoke and something spicy like sandalwood or jasmine. Awareness jolted him to full arousal. He felt like a sixteen-year-old with a killer hard-on—the kind that blinded a boy and made him do stupid things. He had to admit he liked that mindless feeling.

She turned in the corner of the door and glanced up at him. She stopped moving, her lips quirking in a clear show of interest. He leaned in, slanting his mouth over hers, pulling her lower lip into his mouth. He tasted cinnamon and the hopefulness of youth.

He fell hard into that kiss and knew he was a goner the minute she responded to him. He put his hand on the flare of her hip and pulled her hard against him.

He was headed straight to hell, with only a short layover at a no-tell motel before the Devil took him.

• • •

The sign said "Peach Blossom Motor Court" in flaming pink neon. Jane had hit rock bottom in her life. The fiddler had checked them in, and she watched through the windshield of his van as he returned with the key in his hand.

He was something, all right. A big man striding across the parking lot on a pair of the pointiest cowboy boots she had ever seen. Yessir, she would probably forget about this low-rent scenario the minute he put his mouth on hers again.

He opened the van door for her and looked up at her out of a pair of eyes that were as pale as a winter day on Meadow Mountain. The fire in those icy eyes burned so hot she felt the flame in the middle of her chest.

He gave her his hand, and she laid her fingers on him. His hand was huge, and warm, and rough, and male.

He helped her down and then shut the door behind her. He leaned his big-boned body against her, pushing her up against the van, his hand sliding down her rib cage and coming to rest on her hip. He was sturdy and hard, and so large that his body shielded her and made her feel safe in some inappropriate way.

How could she feel safe with a man intent on taking her without even giving her his name or asking for hers? But there it was. She knew the fiddler wasn't going to hurt her. The Universe kind of whispered in her ear and told her this would be okay.

She found herself inside the shadow of his Stetson, caught up in the heat of his mouth. He lost his hat, then she lost her mind.

Chapter
2

Jane startled awake, panic folding over her as she struggled to place herself in space and time. Then she heard the soft, even breathing of a slumbering man.

And remembered.

The memories of her frantic trip from Atlanta brought unwanted tears. She squeezed her eyes shut, even before she remembered the fiddler. She had thought her days of running were over.

She needed to get out of here before the fiddler woke up. He was a bad boy, like the bad boys in her past. She had made a huge mistake last night. She had known it was a mistake even before he'd slapped that ten-dollar bill down on the bar.

When would she learn?

Jane pushed herself up on the hard motel mattress and looked over at the digital clock on the nightstand. It was almost eight in the morning.

She rolled out of bed, collected her clothes and purse, and tiptoed into the bathroom. She gave the shower a longing look, but she didn't have time. She ran enough water in the sink to dampen a washcloth for a sponge bath. She brushed her teeth with the toothbrush she kept in her purse for emergencies and pulled her hair back in a long ponytail.

She looked at her reflection in the mirror and almost cried out loud when she saw the mark at the base of her throat.

A little strawberry bruise—tender to the touch—marred the skin right above and to the left of her clavicle. She blinked at it for almost a minute, feeling something hot and cold run through her system.

Last night had been, without question, the most amazing sex she had ever had in her life. And looking at that bruise reminded her that, for a little while at least, the fiddler had managed to make her forget just about everything, including her moral code and her self-respect and even Woody West.

Hoo boy, she needed to get out of here. She was not a slut, but standing there looking at that bruise made her feel like one. How on earth had she let herself do this? Desperation was not an excuse, although it was an explanation.

Jane put on her less-than-clean clothes, squared her shoulders, and opened the bathroom door. She paused a moment, hearing the slow, steady sound of his snores.

She stole into the room, trying not to look at him as she tiptoed toward the door. She got to the corner of the bed and lost the battle.

The feeble light from an overcast day edged the window and gave the room a monochromatic feel. She looked down at him, and in the colorless light, he seemed almost like a fantasy. He was handsome, and male, and big, and strong, and silent save for the deep susurration of his breathing.

She reluctantly turned away and took one step toward the door before tripping up on his blue jeans. They lay crumpled in a heap by the bed, his wallet peeking from the back pocket. She could have his name, at least. All she had to do was look in his wallet.

She knelt on the carpet and took the wallet from the jeans. She flipped it open and stared down at a Tennessee driver's license with a photo of a much younger and more hopeful-looking man than the one curled up on the bed.

Clayton P. Rhodes.

His name was Clayton.

Something tugged at her chest, and she could have kicked herself for succumbing to her curiosity. It would have been better if this encounter had been anonymous.

She clamped her back teeth together and told herself to move on. She was wasting time.

She turned the wallet over, and peeked into the billfold. He had about eighty dollars on him. She could almost feel the Universe tempting her. With that much cash, she could get a bus ticket to a bigger city— Charlotte maybe—where she could find a job waiting tables or working in a beauty shop. She could take care of herself.

It might be easier to find work in Charlotte. She allowed herself to think about it.

Then she rejected the idea. She had stooped to something low last night. She didn't need to add stealing to the list.

She was about to return the wallet to his jeans when

Clayton P. Rhodes captured her wrist in his powerful fingers and bent it backward far enough for it to hurt.

Panic crashed through her. "Lemme go." She tried to twist herself out of his grasp, but the man had leverage and strength on his side.

"No, ma'am," he said in a drawl as broad as a double-wide trailer. He pulled her up onto the bed and then turned on the bedside lamp. They squinted at each other in the sudden light. He had the advantage there, since his eyes were silver and hard to read. Her heart fluttered inside her chest, and she started thinking about routes of escape.

"I'll take that," he said, plucking the wallet out of her fingers.

"Please let me go." She hated herself for begging like that. Guys who got physical scared her.

The pressure of his fingers lessened a fraction. "Honey, didn't anyone ever teach you wrong from right?"

"I wasn't trying to steal from you." Her voice came out as a choked whisper.

"Uh-huh. Then why did you have my wallet in your hands?"

"I just wanted...you know...to know your name." She tugged against his hold, but he wasn't letting go.

"Yeah, well, you could have asked me, and I would have told you my name."

She pulled a little harder, and he released her wrist. But before she could put distance between them, he leaned forward and pulled her purse off her shoulder.

"Hey," she shouted. "Give that back."

He shook his head, then loosened the bag's drawstrings and dumped her possessions onto the thin cotton blanket.

The flotsam and jetsam and loose change of her life spilled out with a jingle and a jangle. How humiliating.

"What are you doing?"

He started pawing through her things. "Same thing you were doing a minute ago."

"Well, stop it."

He ignored her command and picked up one of her self-help cassette tapes. He frowned down at it and read the title aloud: "*Manifesting a Better Reality* by Dr. Franklin Goodbody?"

He looked up at her with one of those male stares that confirmed that men were from Mars. "Little gal, I'd say you need to get your money back for this. You don't believe this crap, do you?"

"You shouldn't laugh at things you don't understand," Jane rejoined, folding her arms across her chest.

"I wasn't laughing. I was pointing out the obvious. What is 'manifesting' anyway?"

"Thinking positively about the things you want so you make them manifest in your life."

"Uh-huh. Sort of like Norman Vincent Peale and the power of positive thinking only without bothering with prayer, huh?"

"What?"

"You have no idea who Norman Vincent Peale is, do you?"

She shook her head. She had obviously failed some kind of test.

He gave his head a weary shake and put the cassette tape back in her purse. He picked up the player and fiddled with it for a moment. "This thing is an antique. And your battery is dead."

She responded by hugging herself and refraining from any explanations about how she couldn't afford an iPod, had bought the tapes secondhand, and had burned up the batteries on the long bus ride from Atlanta as she practiced her manifesting techniques. Somehow all that positive thinking had not turned Last Chance into Camelot, or Clayton P. Rhodes into Sir Galahad.

Dr. Goodbody said that to manifest a better reality, you needed to know what you wanted and the reasons why. Jane had a feeling that manifesting Clayton P. Rhodes was the result of seriously muddled thinking on her part.

"You know," he said, as if they were having a conversation. "I find it interesting that most women will nag a man to death about tracking in dirt and messing up the house, but not a one of you can keep your pocketbooks organized."

"Are you trying to be funny?" she asked, avoiding eye contact and trying to keep the waver out of her voice. "Because it's not working."

"No, I think I was aiming for irony."

She turned her head. He was smiling at her. He had a winning smile, and she wondered why he didn't use it more often. "Irony?" she asked.

He looked back down at her things, reaching this time for her wallet. He hefted it in his large hands as he inspected the green leather with the pink flower embossed on one side.

"Kind of girlish, isn't it?"

She said nothing. It *was* kind of girlish. She had owned it for a long, long time. And even though it was worn out, she had been unable to part with it. It was the last remaining vestige of the life she had left behind in West Virginia seven years ago.

He unsnapped it, flipped it open, and stared down at the ID she had been using for the last seven years. "Mary Smith?" He aimed another disbelieving look in her direction. "Gimme a break. It says here you're twenty-eight. How old are you really?"

She shrugged.

He squeezed his eyes shut. "I swear, if you're jailbait, I'm going to shoot myself right here."

"I'm not jailbait. I told you that last night."

"Maybe so, but you're not twenty-eight and your name is *not* Mary Smith."

"Are you only thirty-four?" she countered, thinking he looked older than the birth date listed on his license.

"Yes, ma'am. I am. And if you're eighteen that makes me almost old enough to be your daddy, which is a thought I find disturbing."

"I'm not eighteen."

"Right. Why am I starting not to believe anything that comes out of your mouth?"

Because you are tapped into the negative energy of the Universe. She wanted to throw it in his face, but she had a feeling he would laugh at her.

He continued to work his way through her wallet, inspecting her Fort Myers Library card and Florida State Cosmetology license. Both bore the name Mary Smith— the name she had been using since she ran away from home. She had been doing okay in rebuilding her life, when Woody came striding into the Shrimp Shack six months ago.

She was such a fool.

Clayton P. opened up the little change purse on the side of the wallet. "What's this?" he asked aloud as he held up her expired West Virginia license. "This is interesting. How many girls carry two driver's licenses? This one says Wanda Jane Coblentz, and it's seven years out of date. Wanda Jane?"

"Yeah, well, your name is Clayton Rhodes, and I'll bet everyone calls you Clay, so don't get so high and mighty, okay?"

He laughed. It sounded like his singing voice. He had a positive-sounding laugh, she would give him that.

"Look," she said. "I would appreciate it if you could forget you saw that license, okay?"

He stopped laughing and shook his head. "Not okay." He glanced down at her photo ID and then back at her. "Doesn't look like you."

"Thanks."

"So you're twenty-four?"

She nodded. "Not jailbait."

He put the license back into the change purse and peeked into the billfold section. "Five bucks, huh? And I don't see any credit cards."

"Okay. You've humiliated me enough now. Can I take my five bucks and leave?"

"And go where?"

"Anywhere that isn't with you."

"That bad, huh?" he said with a little glint in his eye.

"Yeah, well…" She shrugged. What was she supposed to say? She didn't think telling him that he was incredible between the sheets was a good idea under the circumstances.

He dropped her wallet back into her purse, then looked

up at her out of his pale gray eyes. "Look, I'm sorry about last night. I should have asked you if you needed a place to stay instead of…" His voice faded out, and he looked away.

His ears got red. The big, tough guy was blushing. He looked down at her things, picked up her makeup case, and put it back into her purse without rifling through it. Jane scored that as one small victory.

"You know," he said, eyeing the mass of coins that remained, "you probably have close to ten dollars in silver here. You might want to lighten your load."

"Such as it is."

He looked up. "Had to leave Fort Myers in a hurry, huh?"

She didn't answer. It disturbed her to think he'd already figured out half of her secrets. She looked away and heard the sound of change jangling as he pawed through her things.

"Hey, what's this?" he asked a moment later.

She turned, and he was holding up the little necklace that Woody had given her the day before yesterday. A rush of pure hatred ran right through her. "You can have it," she said.

He chuckled at that. "Honey, you should always hang on to your jewelry. No matter what. That's what my momma always says." He squinted down at the little green charm on the gold chain. "What is that, a camel?"

"Yeah. It's a stupid dollar store jade camel, okay? It's not worth anything. I'll bet the chain isn't even gold."

"Uh-huh. He did you wrong, didn't he?" One of his eyebrows arched in question.

"I don't wish to discuss this. I thought this was going to be, you know, kind of quick and anonymous."

"Me, too. But then you decided to steal from me."

"Look, I wasn't stealing. I was just..." Her voice faded out as it occurred to her that if she had wanted something quick and anonymous she would never have looked through his wallet.

"Uh-huh. Like I said."

"Why don't you give me my purse, and I'll leave, okay?"

He didn't respond. Instead, he reached into her bag and pulled out her wallet. Then he placed the little necklace into the change section. He snapped the snap on the change purse and then dropped her wallet back into her handbag. She watched as his big, capable hands scooped up pennies and nickels and dimes and dropped them back into the bottom of her bag. He had almost completed the task when he stopped.

"Well lookit here, isn't that lucky?" He picked up a tarnished coin and angled it toward the light.

"You know the only luck in the Universe is the luck we make for ourselves," Jane said. If only she had believed that before she had come with this guy to a no-tell motel.

"Is that so?"

"Yeah."

"So you don't believe in rabbits' feet?"

She shook her head. A girl with her unlucky track record couldn't afford to believe in charms and such.

"Too bad, because this is a lucky penny," he said.

"What's lucky about it?" she asked.

"It's a wheat penny."

"A what?"

He handed the penny to her. "Look on the back. It doesn't have the Lincoln Memorial on it."

She turned the penny over, and sure enough, it had an unusual back with the words "One Cent" spelled out and encircled by a crossed sheaf of wheat.

She turned it over in her hand and read the date—1943. "So what's lucky about it?"

He continued to scoop up change and return it to her purse. "Well, nothing, really. It's just old. They haven't made wheat pennies since the 1950s."

"Is it valuable?"

He chuckled. "Yeah, it's probably worth one hundred times its face value."

Happiness swelled up inside her until she did the math in her head. "Right. A dollar."

He shrugged. "That's valuable for a penny."

"Yeah, well, it won't buy me a Coke at Dot's Spot."

"You know, the value of things can't always be measured in their price."

She blinked up at him. Was he trying to send a message? After all, if she wanted to be negative about things, he had purchased her for the sum of ten dollars plus the cost of this hotel room. The thought made her heart ache.

"By that look, you don't agree with me."

She shrugged and tried not to feel cheap and dirty. "I'm just blown away that a negative person such as yourself would even consider the possibility of luck as a force in the Universe," she said in a breezy tone.

"Yeah, well, I guess you got that right. So it's not a lucky penny. It's just an old one. Don't you think it's cool that something sixty years old was hiding out in the bottom of your purse waiting to be found?"

Temptation tugged at her insides. Clayton P. Rhodes was a piece of work. But she was not about to let herself fall for his line—even if it was a good line. Maybe one of the best lines she had heard in her life.

"Look," Jane said. "As a gesture of regret for having rifled through your wallet, I'll let you have the penny if you think it's so cool."

"Uh, no thanks, you keep it, since you believe in luck."

Well, that was predictable. "Right," she said, as she slipped the penny into the pocket of her jeans. "So are you going to let me go, now that you've finished humiliating me?"

"I probably should turn you in to the police for attempted robbery."

Fear settled into her belly. "Look, I wasn't trying to steal from you, okay?"

"But then again, explaining stuff to the police might prove a little embarrassing."

She stopped and thought about things for a moment. It *would* be embarrassing—for both of them—since she was new to town and they had spent the night with each other before exchanging names.

"So I'm not going to turn you in. I think I'm going to reform you instead," Clayton P. continued.

"Reform me?" Her voice cracked.

"Not interested in following the straight and narrow, huh?"

She drew herself up and squared her shoulders. "I don't need reforming. Maybe you're the one who needs reforming."

This earned her a little half smile. "You're right on that score. So I guess I'll buy you breakfast instead. And after that, we'll talk about where you go next."

Just who the hell did he think he was, anyway? "What is it, Clayton P., you want to run me out of town like I'm some kind of undesirable? Well, let me tell you one thing, buster, I—"

"Is that what you think?"

"Look, I don't need you to reform me. I may have ended up in this shabby room with you, but that doesn't make me a—"

"I wasn't talking about what happened last night, girl. That was just runaway lust. And I'm sorry I got caught up in it. I was talking about you stealing my money."

"I told you, I wasn't going to steal your money. Why won't you believe me?"

"Because I make it a habit not to believe girls with only five bucks in their pockets who are carrying two forms of identification, each bearing a different name."

He threw his legs over the side of the bed and stood up, naked as the day he was born. The runaway lust made a second appearance.

He was big, and he was built. In every possible way a man could be big and built.

Oh, well, it didn't matter, because Clayton P. Rhodes was not the man the Universe had made for her, even if he was a dead ringer for Michelangelo's David from the neck down. Come to think of it, he was pretty good looking from the neck up, too.

He headed toward the bathroom, her purse still clasped in his hands. "I'm taking a shower. Don't try to leave."

Well, of course she couldn't leave. He had taken all of her belongings hostage.

"I mean it," he said, stopping at the door. "There's a category-one hurricane blowing outside that door. You'll be soaked to the bone inside of a minute."

She cocked her head and heard the sound of rain beating at the windows.

Good grief. The Cosmos really *was* against her.

Clay wiped the condensation off the mirror and gave himself a hard look. He didn't much like the reflection.

That little gal—Wanda Jane—needed something last night, and he'd pretty much failed her. It didn't take a rocket scientist to know she didn't do illicit no-tell-motel sex on a regular basis. She had *not* been faking it.

And she was way too young.

God help him. He'd treated her like some kind of two-bit tramp last night, when it was obvious the girl was in some kind of trouble and on the run. She had only five dollars in her purse.

Instead of helping her out, he'd put her in the place where stealing had seemed justified.

He'd taken something from her last night. He had consumed her like a starving man, and he hadn't given her anything in return, except maybe a momentary thrill. He'd needed the sexual release last night. He'd needed it to find the trigger point for the stuff he'd been holding inside for way too long.

God, how embarrassing. He surely did hope she hadn't heard him when he'd gotten up in the middle of the night. He'd come into the bathroom, taken one look at himself in the mirror, and broken down into tears. He'd cried for

Uncle Pete, who was probably dying, and for Ray, whose life he had screwed up so long ago, and for the career in Nashville that lay in ruins. He'd turned on the shower and tried real hard not to make too much noise while he'd cried himself out like some kind of sissy.

He studied his puffy eyes. He surely did owe Jane a whole lot more than the eighty bucks she'd tried to steal from him. In a way, she'd been a kind of therapy.

Well, he'd make it as right as he could. He'd feed her breakfast and give her enough money to send her on her way once the storm blew itself out.

Then he needed to concentrate on making a change in his life. This encounter was a warning sign, pure and simple. He needed to put the past behind him and start making plans for the future.

He hung his head. He wanted a wife, not a one-night stand. He wanted commitment from a mature woman, not some stupid midlife tryst with a younger woman, even if she was hotter than a chili pepper. He needed to grow up. He needed to settle down. He needed meaning in his life.

He needed to refocus his music career, too, but maybe that was too much to ask. Right now, he just wanted an end to that hollow place in the middle of his chest.

"Today is the first day of the rest of your life," he murmured, looking back up. "Today, you're going to get serious about finding a sane, stable, mature woman to be your wife. You are going to start moving toward the future, instead of wallowing in the past."

He gave himself a hard stare. "You hear me, boy. Needy women are a weakness."

Chapter

3

The waitress at the Kountry Kitchen Dinette wore a salmon pink uniform with a white apron and a little plastic pin that identified her as Betty. She filled up Clayton P. Rhodes's coffee cup and looked down at him with a sweet, unfocused gaze. He missed the look entirely.

Betty didn't give Jane anything like an adoring look. In fact, Betty inspected her the way a narrow-minded, small-town waitress would inspect anyone new—with a look that was one part curiosity and three parts get out of town. Jane recognized this look. Small-town people were not as friendly as the Hallmark Channel or Garrison Keillor made them out to be.

"Meet Wanda Jane Coblentz," Clay said as Betty poured coffee.

"That's Jane for short," she said. The fiddler had insisted on calling her by both her given names, instead of the name she had been using for the last seven years.

Jane had retaliated by calling him Clayton P. This

annoyed him. And annoying the man was too much fun, especially since he had humiliated her this morning and proven himself to be a mule-headed weasel with a pessimistic streak.

Although he *was* resourceful, sort of like a Boy Scout, which was a troubling thought. He'd managed to find her a bright orange plastic poncho in his minivan. Clayton P. apparently took the Boy Scout motto, "Be Prepared," very seriously, since he had a veritable warehouse of stuff in his van, from safety flares to fishing rods. Not the kind of collection of useful items she would expect from a guy who looked like he was bad to the bone.

"Howdy, Wanda Jane," Betty said. "New in town?"

Well, duh. There were no more than a couple thousand souls living in Last Chance. What were the odds that a stranger walking into the Kountry Kitchen for the first time was actually new to town? Probably a dead certainty.

"Yes, I am." She gave Betty a sweet, down-home smile, which the waitress didn't exactly return. "I'm looking for work," Jane added. "You wouldn't happen to have a need for an experienced waitress?"

Clayton P. Rhodes put his coffee cup down hard enough to slosh the contents. The fiddler had already made it clear that he intended to run her out of town as soon as the storm ended. But Jane had other ideas.

"Sorry, we don't have any job openings," Betty said. "But, you know, Dottie is always looking for help."

"Dottie? As in the proprietor of Dot's Spot?"

"Yes, ma'am." Betty did smile then, but it was phony enough to be featured on a piece of forged artwork.

"You're not working for Dottie," Clayton P. announced

as if he had a say in the matter, which he did not. Jane had decided to stay in Last Chance for a little while, because it looked like the kind of small town where Woody and the thugs after him would never dream of looking for her.

"What can I get you, sugar?" Betty asked.

"I'll have the two-egg breakfast," she said, snapping closed the menu. It cost only four dollars. Her mouth watered in anticipation, which was fitting because when she paid the bill she would be officially flat broke.

No, check that, she would be officially in debt because she intended to pay Clayton P. back for the Cokes she drank last night and half of the motel, too. That way she could say she hadn't sold her body for food and shelter. She wrapped her hands around her coffee mug and tried not to look up at him.

"I told you," Clayton P. said in a low voice, once Betty had departed, "I'll give you enough money to get you wherever you want to go."

Well, of course, he didn't mean that. She doubted if he would pay her passage on a cruise to Bermuda, although she was tempted to ask, just to prove her point.

"I want to stay here," she said.

"For goodness' sake, why? This is a dying town."

Jane looked up at him as he frowned down at her. The fluorescent lights gleamed on his dark chestnut hair. He had nice hair, even when he wore it slicked back into a ponytail. But last night, with it falling down around his shoulders, he had looked hotter than Hades. She pushed the vision of him naked out of her head.

"If it's so bad, why don't *you* take your negatory attitude and leave?" she asked.

"Negatory attitude?" His brow lowered, and he looked sour. "What in the Sam Hill does that mean?"

"Dr. Goodbody says pessimism can become a habit, blinding you to the bright side of even the worst disaster. You might try to focus on the positive things about Last Chance instead of the negative ones. And you didn't answer my question. If it's such a terrible place, why do you stay?"

"You didn't answer mine." He didn't stop frowning.

"I'm staying because I have to. It's pretty simple. And I aim to make the best of this disaster, just like Dr. Goodbody says."

"Little gal, you don't—"

"I'm not little, and I'm not a girl, so would you please call me Jane?"

He gritted his teeth. She could tell by the way the muscles jumped in his oh-so-square jaw. "You don't have to stay here, *Jane*. I'll—"

"Forget it. I'm not taking your money, okay?"

He blinked at her for a couple of moments. "Look, if this is about what happened last night, I—"

"Well, of course it's about what happened last night. And I think it would be best, all the way around, if we put all that behind us," she said. "It was enjoyable so far as it went. But we both know it was a big mistake and dwelling on it will unleash lots of negative psychic energy. And at the moment, I'm trying to be positive about the future."

"Good. I'm glad to hear that. So when the storm blows over, I'll stake you to some cash so you can leave Last Chance behind. Trust me, this is not a positive place."

"I'm not taking your money. I told you that already.

Taking your money would make what happened last night even worse than it already is."

"Oh, for goodness' sake, you tried to roll me this morning." He leaned back in the booth, a miserable look on his face.

"No, I didn't. And it seems the only way to make that point clear is to get a job and pay you back for your expenses. That way I won't have anything heavy weighing down my karma, you know?"

"Karma?"

"You know, like a spiritual scorecard. Last night, I slipped, and I—"

"Honey, I owe you something for last night. And I'm sorry about this morning." He sat there looking unhappy. She pitied him, but not enough to take his money. Taking his money would be a big mistake. He would get the idea he owned her or something, and she most definitely didn't want him thinking that. She was independent. She could fend for herself.

Jane reached out and touched his hand where it rested on the Formica tabletop. His skin was warm and a little rough. Touching him reminded her of the way he'd touched her last night, and her stomach clutched.

She withdrew her hand. "Look, I heard you in the bathroom, and it's okay. Whatever got to you last night, I promise I won't tell anyone."

"You heard me?" His voice cracked in alarm.

She shrugged. "I tried not to listen. Honest. But you weren't exactly quiet about it. So anyway, the point is, you don't owe me anything for last night, and you shouldn't feel guilty about your feelings either. Like you said, it was just a case of runaway lust."

His ears got red. It was kind of sexy the way he blushed like that. Clayton P. was kind of sweet for a negative person with lots of emotional baggage. He must have something heavy weighing him down, since he'd gone into the bathroom and cried.

Despite the zinging of her hormones, she could resist him. That was the important thing right now.

He lifted his coffee mug and took a sip, his gaze drifting away from her. They sat in awkward silence for a few minutes while Jane studied her surroundings. The Kountry Kitchen looked like something out of a 1950s family TV show set in some quaint little town where everyone was nice to everyone else. It had polished chrome everywhere, booths and stools covered in red vinyl, a linoleum checkerboard floor, and a gray Formica lunch counter. On this dark and windy Thursday morning, the place was empty, except for a table of old geezers wearing overalls and Country Pride Chicken hats.

That changed a moment later as the front door opened to the sound of an old-fashioned tinkling bell. A big man wearing a plastic-covered Stetson and a full-length, shiny black raincoat stepped across the threshold and shook himself. Rainwater poured off his shoulders and splattered in a big puddle on the floor.

He took off his hat, exposing close-cropped dark hair, graying at the temples. His face had fine, almost perfect features.

The guy took off his raincoat, and Jane realized he was a cop—a big cop, wearing a bulletproof vest and carrying about fifty pounds of weaponry and communications on his utility belt. Barney Fife this guy was not.

The cop hung his coat and hat on a peg by the door

and headed down the line of booths with the coiled grace of a big predator. The radio on his belt made a crackling noise, and his shoes, which looked shiny bright despite the rain outside, had a little squeak to them. He headed right for them.

Fear blew through Jane. What if the thugs had killed Woody and his body had turned up someplace bearing incriminating evidence? What if Woody was into something illegal and not just a gambler with a bunch of sharks on his tail? Negative thoughts of being interrogated about her stupid liaison with Woody West danced right through her mind.

She looked up at the cop and told herself to think happy thoughts, but there was something kind of dead in his green eyes that made all the positive energy inside her condense into a big knot right in her stomach.

"Hey, Stony," Betty said, as she arrived with Jane's two-egg breakfast and the fiddler's biscuits. Betty gave the policeman the same adoring look she had given Clayton P. earlier. The cop was just as immune.

"Hey, Betty," he said in a voice so deep it sounded like it came right out of the center of the earth.

"The usual?" the waitress asked.

"Nope. Just coffee, I've only got a minute. Route 70 is washed out down over to Sweden, and the county needs backup to set up a roadblock. Make it to go, would you, darlin'?"

Betty bustled back to the kitchen, and the cop turned toward Jane. He put his hands on his utility belt and studied her for almost ten seconds without blinking.

Ten seconds is a long time to endure a stare like that. She couldn't look away, so she forced herself to look up into his granite face while she recited the mantra she used every night right before she dropped off to sleep. The mantra was supposed to clear her mind and make it possible for her to manifest self-confidence and positive energy in her life.

"Hey, didn't Momma ever tell you it's not polite to stare," Clayton P. said as he scooted his butt toward the wall, making room on the bench beside him. "Take a load off, bro."

Bro?

The big cop dropped down onto the seat beside Clayton P., and that's when Jane saw the shiny nameplate above his right breast pocket. It said S. Rhodes.

Hoo boy. Unless she'd missed something, the term of endearment coupled with that surname on the cop's chest meant he was Clayton P. Rhodes's brother.

This was not a positive sign.

Clayton P. wasn't nearly the bad boy she had, at first, taken him for. He had a relationship with the local law, which meant he wasn't in trouble with it. More to the point, Clayton P. could turn her in for attempted robbery and get the local law's full attention without too many questions asked.

"Meet Wanda Jane Coblentz," Clayton P. said. "She's originally from West Virginia, and she's just passing through." He gave her a knowing smile, and his silver eyes sparkled with what looked like real amusement.

Oh great, Clayton P. had just handed the cop her entire life story. She hadn't been Wanda Jane Coblentz from West Virginia in more than seven years. And with good reason, too.

She smiled at the cop. He didn't react.

"Stony is my brother. He's the chief of police," Clayton P. said.

Stony Rhodes? Wow, the world had gotten wacky in the last twenty-four hours. She could not be dealing with a couple of guys whose names were Stony and Clay, could she? They probably had another brother stashed somewhere named Dusty.

"Saw your van down at the Peach Blossom last night," Stony Rhodes drawled. "And if I saw it, you can bet your bottom dollar Lillian Bray saw it, which means Momma will know about it before the morning is finished."

Clayton P.'s ears got red again, but he said not one word. Instead, he dove into a biscuit.

The cop looked back up at her. "How old are you, darlin'?" he asked.

Clayton P. nearly jumped out of his seat. "Old enough," he said under his breath.

"Uh-huh," the cop said, and that little grunt conveyed a world of censure. Compared to his older brother, Clayton P. didn't look like a Boy Scout at all. It kind of added to his allure, somehow, which was a development Jane found disturbing.

Betty came back with a large Styrofoam cup of coffee. "It's on the house," she said, handing it off to Stony.

Stony nodded as he stood. He turned to look down at his brother. "I was out to the golf course a little while ago. I'm a little worried about Jesus."

"Daddy and I tied him down yesterday. He should be okay."

Jane almost choked on her bacon. "You tied down Jesus?" she asked, looking from one to the other of them.

"Pardon me, but what, pray tell, was He doing on a golf course? And please do not tell me some old joke about how He was golfing with God."

Stony chuckled, and something changed in his eyes. For a fleeting instant, she could have sworn the chief of police was made of flesh and blood.

He turned toward Clayton P., who was not laughing. "This one's got a sense of humor, doesn't she?" he said as if she weren't sitting there.

Clayton looked up from his biscuits. "It's a statue of Jesus—twenty feet tall."

"On a golf course?"

Clayton P. squeezed his eyes shut and started to massage his temples with his index fingers, like this entire conversation had given him an Excedrin headache.

"It's a minigolf course," Stony said.

Clay dropped his hands to the tabletop. "You know what?" he said in a hoarse voice that conveyed pain, anger, and something else Jane couldn't quite figure out. "I hope it rains so hard today that the ark floats away, Moses drowns, and the whale and Jonah find their way back to the sea."

Jane picked up another slice of bacon and crunched. "There's an ark, too?" she said around the food.

"Life-sized," Stony said. "Golfing for God is our one-and-only tourist attraction."

"Golfing *for* God?" she asked, looking from one to the other of them.

"As opposed to golfing *with* Him," Clayton P. said. "And it's not a tourist attraction. It's the local embarrassment. Unfortunately, our daddy is the proprietor."

The chief gave a little snort. "Amen to that."

"So you have to go, huh?" Clayton asked, changing the subject.

"There's a washout on Route 70. There'll be more before the day's out."

"Let me know if y'all need help. I'll be down at the store," Clayton P. said.

"Probably do a brisk business in batteries and generators once the wind dies down. Will you keep an eye on Momma and the kids?"

Clayton P. nodded. The cop turned and looked down at her. "Wanda Jane, huh?"

"Jane for short."

"You come in last night on the nine-thirty bus from Atlanta?"

She nodded. How did he know that?

He nodded soberly. "Hope you don't intend on doing any damage before you leave."

"What's that supposed to mean?"

He shrugged. "I reckon when a woman with the same name as a hurricane blows into town and maneuvers Clay to the Peach Blossom Motor Court within hours of her arrival, it's a sure sign of trouble." He leaned in. "And I don't like trouble in my town."

With that, he turned on his heel and headed toward the door.

Once he'd left, Jane turned toward Clayton P. "So that was your idea of reforming me, huh?"

"Reckon so."

"Is the hurricane really named Jane?"

"Where have you been the last couple of days?"

"On a bus from Georgia. For the record, though, I think Jane is a stupid name for a hurricane."

"Why's that?"

She shrugged. "A hurricane should be named something exotic like Chantal or Jezebel. Jane is plain. No one takes a Jane seriously. And not taking a hurricane seriously is probably a big mistake."

He looked up from his coffee mug, a strange light in his eyes. Unlike his brother's, Clayton's eyes were not dead. In fact, now that she studied them in the light of day, she could see they weren't gray at all, but the palest shade of green with opalescent flecks in them. Iridescent fire burned in those flecks. That spark of fire had lured her into his arms last night.

Her gaze dropped down to his mouth and got stuck there. She flashed on the memory of his kisses, and she wished for an Alzheimer's moment. Unfortunately, her memory was good and deadly accurate.

"I don't know," he said in his blurred drawl. "I wouldn't exactly call *you* plain."

She dropped her gaze to her half-eaten breakfast. She had been a plain Jane once. She had run away from that awkward and confused girl. In many ways, she was still running.

Clayton P. chuckled, and she glanced up. "Maybe the storm being named Jane is a sign," he said.

"You think?"

His eyes darkened a little, and he looked down at his plate, filled now with crumbs. "You certainly blew into Dottie's last night like a force of nature. I'll give you that." He pressed his index finger onto one of the crumbs and conveyed it to his mouth. Jane watched as his tongue darted out to take the crumb off his finger. Heat flashed through her.

"So," she said on a little puff of air. "Does this burg have a newspaper?"

"Uh, no. Most folks read the *Times and Democrat*. It's Orangeburg's paper. Why?"

"I need to check the help-wanted ads." She smiled up at him as sweetly as she could, which was a good thing, because he suddenly looked like he was about to blow his stack.

"Look, girl, will you wake up? We're sitting on a flat piece of land that's a few feet above sea level. Hurricane Jane may be a hundred miles away, but it's supposed to drop something like fifteen inches of rain on us today. Before the day is out, we'll lose power, half the roads will get washed out, and there will be trees down all over town. No one"—he leaned in—"is going to be conducting job interviews today."

She swallowed hard in the face of these dire projections. "You really are a glass-is-half-empty kind of person, aren't you?"

He closed his eyes, took a deep breath, and let it out. "Well," he said, opening his eyes again and speaking as if she were mentally slow or something. "I realize you like to think positively, but..." His voice rose in pitch. "A hurricane is a frigging natural disaster."

"My ma used to say there wasn't any ill wind that didn't blow some kind of good," she rejoined. "Look on the bright side; maybe the hurricane will take out Golfing for God, although I'm having trouble understanding why you want that to happen. It sounds like Golfing for God is like a national treasure or an eighth wonder or something like that."

A muscle twitched in his cheek. "Golfing for God is a

running joke in this town. It's the kind of place that makes people laugh at me and my kin. And that's something they've been doing for generations."

"Generations?"

"Yeah. My forebears once owned all the land around these parts. The land was part of a big plantation. My great-great-something granddaddy came back from the Civil War and proceeded to lose the farm in a poker game. The story is he left a suicide note penned to the Lord, asking for forgiveness and making a special request that the angels watch over his family, who he left destitute, I might add.

"Anyway, my forebears have been eccentric ever since. My granddaddy built Golfing for God, and my own daddy runs it and claims to regularly converse with angels. Daddy would be heartbroke if Hurricane Jane took out Golfing for God, especially when Hurricane Hugo didn't lay a glove on it."

"Your father talks to angels? Really? That's kind of cool."

"No, it's not. Thanks to Chancellor Rhodes's ill-advised suicide note that invoked the heavenly host, there has always been at least one Rhodes in every generation who has gone off the deep end and talked with angels. It's like a family curse. And me and my two brothers and sister are not going to end up like that if we can help it."

"You really believe this? I would have thought that a negative person such as yourself might—"

"Yeah, I believe there is a strain of serious mental illness that runs in my family. I'm going to rise above it."

"Well, I suppose that's a positive approach. But really,

have you ever considered that Golfing for God was spared by Hurricane Hugo as a sign that the Universe approves of it? I think it's pretty positive to have a pipeline to angels."

"Do you believe in angels? Really?"

She shrugged. "I think metaphorically, being in touch with the forces of the Universe is way cool."

"You are insane. And so is my daddy. I am not going there." He glanced down at her breakfast. "Are you done with that?" he said, clearly changing the subject.

She looked down at her plate. She'd managed to pack away most of the meal, but not all of it. "Yeah. But I wonder if I could get a box. I have a feeling it might be a while before my next meal."

"Don't worry. I'll feed you until the buses are running again. C'mon, let's go."

"Uh, no."

"No?"

She shook her head. "I'm sorry to disappoint you, but this is where we part company."

Clayton P. blinked down at her. "You do realize this storm's going to get worse before it gets better? You can't stay here."

"Why not? It's a free country."

He leaned in. "Because you have no money, no clothes, and no place to stay. Now, get up."

"I'm not budging. You can't make me."

He grabbed Jane by the arm and hauled her to her feet with one powerful yank. His use of force sent fear radiating right through her. She tried to pull away, and he put his face right in hers. "You're a brat, you know that? Someone needs to tan your backside."

"Lemme go," she gasped. She didn't need anyone tanning her backside. Pa had done enough of that when she was young. Every instinct in her body screamed that she needed to run—and run fast.

She pulled against his grip, and he released her. She whirled away, racing for the door like a coon with a bloodhound on her tail. She didn't think about the storm, or the poncho, or anything except getting away from him. A girl on her own needed to run when her instincts told her it was time. She hit the door and pushed through it. A wall of wind and water hit her with the force of ... well ... a hurricane.

Her namesake smacked her upside the head with a fury designed, no doubt, to beat some sense into her addled brains. Hurricane Jane might have blown her all the way to Kingdom Come, too, if it hadn't been for Clayton P., who materialized out of the wall of rain and wind and folded her up in a pair of strong and gentle arms.

He was so enormous that he blocked the wind with his big body and seemed utterly immovable despite the forces buffeting him. "Are you all right?" The concerned look on his rain-drenched face chased away the sudden panic. It also did something to her insides—as if she had just taken a deep draught of something at least one hundred proof. Heat flowed from her belly to every one of her extremities. How could a really big guy who'd just scared her silly make that kind of heat inside her? It was not a hopeful sign. It was scary.

But she nodded anyway, momentarily struck dumb by the strong and benign feel of his hands on her shoulders.

"I'm sorry I scared you," he said above the roar of

wind and rain. The look of contrition on his face seemed genuine. He turned and pulled her with him up the street. As she walked beside him, clinging to his impressive arm, it occurred to her that either Clay Rhodes and the hurricane were in league and out to mess up her life, or the big man was just too darned stubborn to let tropical-storm-strength winds knock him around.

Either way, she had gotten the message: The Universe and Hurricane Jane meant for her to go with him.

Chapter
4

Haley Rhodes sat in her small pink rocking chair in the corner of Granny's kitchen. It was her favorite chair in the whole world. Granddaddy had painted it pink like she'd asked him to, and it was the only chair in the house that fit her just right.

Most times, Granny kept Haley's rocking chair out on the porch, but today it was raining hard on account of the hurricane, so Granny brought the chair into the kitchen. Priscilla, Granny's kitty, had curled up on Haley's lap while Haley listened to Granny talking on the telephone.

"I am certain Clay didn't take a floozy to the Peach Blossom Motor Court, Lillian. I raised my boy to be better than that," Granny said. Granny's voice sounded kind of flat—the way it got when Granny got mad about something. Miz Lillian Bray, who was on the other end of the line, taught Lizzy's Sunday school class.

Haley wasn't sure why, but she knew that spending the night at the Peach Blossom Motor Court was wicked. She had heard Miz Bray talking about folks who had done it. Miz Bray said a good girl never wanted to see the insides of a place like that. Haley wasn't sure what a floozy was, but that didn't sound too good either.

Prissy purred softly. Being a cat, Prissy didn't care what Uncle Clay might have done, but the angel in the corner by the broom closet must have cared something fierce, 'cause she had stopped crying.

Most times, the angel wasn't happy. Instead of being up in Heaven and having wings, like the angels in Haley's Sunday school book, this angel cried—sometimes real loud at night. Haley had named it the Sorrowful Angel. The Sorrowful Angel's crying never woke up Daddy or Haley's big sister, Lizzy, 'cause neither of them could hear her or see her.

Once, Lizzy caught Haley trying to talk to the angel. Lizzy laughed at Haley so bad that Haley had cried as hard as the angel. Then Daddy got mad at Haley and made her go to bed without dessert.

Anyways, ever since then, Haley was careful not ever to try to talk to the angel when grown-ups or Lizzy were around. The angel was Haley's secret.

"Lillian," Granny said into the telephone, "you know good and well that Ike's rheumatism is so bad he can't play organ anymore. I doubt he wants to come out of retirement. I doubt that the members of the choir want him out of retirement either. Besides, even if Clay has slipped a little, whatever happened to the Christian notion of forgiveness?" Granny leaned against the wall and blew the hair off her forehead like she did when she was mad about something. Granny looked real mad right now. Mad and beautiful.

Granny was always beautiful on account of the fact that she owned the Cut 'n Curl. Haley had heard folks saying that Granny was the best beauty consultant in all of Last Chance, and maybe even Allenberg County.

Granny held the phone a few inches away from her ear as Miz Bray talked back. Haley heard Miz Bray's voice hollering on the phone, but she couldn't really make out the words.

Granny took a deep breath and then spoke into the phone again. "Don't you start on Stone. He has nothing to do with whatever you think Clay did last night. You know that as well as I do. And do not lecture me on Stony's absence from church on Sundays. The boy is troubled, and we both know it."

As soon as Granny said Haley's daddy's name, "Stone," the angel took a step forward, like she was really, really interested. Haley was, too, on account of the fact that Miz Bray scared her and also because everyone knew Miz Bray didn't like Daddy much.

Granny said Miz Bray didn't like it that Daddy never went to church like other folks. Granny said Daddy was sad about Momma, and that's why he didn't go to church. Granny said Daddy was mad at God. Haley thought maybe Daddy was mad at God because Momma went to live with Jesus, and that's what made the angel sorrowful.

Haley didn't remember her momma any. But she sure wished she had a momma like all the rest of the kids in second grade. Maybe that's why Daddy was sad, too.

"Lillian, why don't I just go on down to the hardware store and take a look at this so-called floozy and talk with Clay." Granny stared out the kitchen window as she listened. "I promise you I will give you a full report. I'm sure there is a reasonable explanation. Clay is a good Christian man, Lillian. He wouldn't do anything to embarrass the church." Granny paused again as she listened to Miz Bray. "Uh huh, I'll call you right back. Bye now."

Granny slammed the phone down on the hook. "I swear I will tan Clay's backside if what she says is true," Granny muttered. Thank goodness, Granny wasn't smashing any dishes. It was a sign of real trouble when Granny started breaking things.

The phone rang again, and Granny said a word Haley knew good girls weren't ever supposed to say.

Granny picked up the phone. "Oh, hello, Miriam. I've already heard from Lillian."

Haley knew that was Miz Miriam Randall on the phone. Miz Randall was really, really old, and she walked with a cane, but she wasn't as scary as Miz Bray.

"What?" Granny said, like Miz Randall had surprised her.

The angel nodded and almost smiled for a minute, which made Haley stop petting Prissy. The angel never smiled, ever.

"Well, that changes everything, doesn't it?" Granny paused and listened for a moment. She looked a little happier when she spoke again. "Miriam, I am much obliged. I'm going to ride on down to the hardware store and check things out for myself. I'll call you back when I'm done."

Granny hung up the phone much more gently this time. That's when Granny remembered Haley was still in the room. She smiled down at Haley with one of those grown-up looks that meant Haley had been caught listening to something she wasn't supposed to hear.

"Honey, how would you like to go over to play with Betsy Maxwell?" Granny asked.

Haley sighed. Granny wasn't ever going to let Haley see Uncle Clay get his backside tanned. And she wasn't ever going to let Haley meet anyone who had seen the insides of the Peach Blossom Motor Court, neither. And Granny, for sure, wasn't ever going to tell her what the word "floozy" meant.

Haley was stuck. She was going to have to spend a rainy day playing Barbie with dumb old Betsy Maxwell and listening to the endless caterwaulin' of the Sorrowful Angel.

Clay sat on a stool behind the counter at Lovett's Hardware and stared out at the torrent through the crosshairs of the duct tape that crisscrossed the store's plate-glass windows. Palmetto Avenue, Last Chance's main street, looked like a river. The town's single traffic light danced in the wind like a kite. So far, though, they hadn't lost power, and the roof in the one-hundred-year-old building hadn't sprung any leaks.

Ray Betts pushed a broom across the oak floor for the one-hundredth time that morning. Clay and Ray were the only employees who had shown up for work this morning.

Ray had come because it was a Thursday, and he knew he had to work on Thursdays. Clay was there because Ray would come to work, regardless of the weather.

Uncle Pete was in Minnesota at the Mayo Clinic with

Aunt Arlene. Cousin Alex, Arlene's boy by her first marriage, had not deigned to appear. But that was a blessing, because Alex was a jerk.

Alex had returned to Last Chance in August, just after Pete Whitaker had been diagnosed with cancer. Alex figured Pete was going to leave the store to his momma, Arlene, when he died. And since Alex was actually a Lovett—his granddaddy had sold the store to Pete thirty years ago—Alex reckoned on taking over once the cancer had run its likely course.

Alex Lovett had been strutting around Lovett's Hardware like a peacock, acting like he was the designated new boss man. He was getting on everyone's nerves. He'd let it be known that when Pete was gone, he'd make sure Ray was the first person he let go.

So any day Alex stayed home was one more day Clay could avoid losing his temper and knocking Alex into next week. Clay hated fighting. But a fight with Alex was going to happen—sooner or later.

"I checked in on April. She's still asleep on the couch," Ray said, pulling Clay from his sour thoughts.

Clay shifted his weight on the stool by the main checkout. "I told you, Ray, her name's Jane, not April."

"No, Clay, she *is* April."

Clay stared out at the storm and tried not to think about the woman sleeping on Pete's old couch, or the trouble that could easily arise if Ray kept thinking she was April.

He intended to get that woman out of town on the next bus if it was the last thing he did. Then he would move on with his life. He needed a little bit of maturity and balance. He turned toward his oldest friend and asked,

"How many women you reckon there are in Allenberg County?"

"A little more than eight thousand."

Clay grunted. "How you figure that?"

"Because there were 16,658 people living in the county as of the 2000 census, and a little over half of them are female," Ray said, nodding like a bobble-head doll.

Clay laughed out loud. Leave it to Ray to know about the census and be able to extrapolate it into a hard estimate of the number of women in the county.

Seventeen years ago, Ray had been a serious math genius with a full scholarship to Rice University. The accident during his senior year in high school had scrambled Ray's amazing brain. It had messed up his common sense, his ability to stay on track, and his emotional control, but it had left him with this uncanny ability to memorize useless numbers and do complex computations in his head.

"I wonder how many of them are unmarried," Clay said.

"Well, I don't know, but I'd guess there are about twenty-eight hundred women over the age of eighteen and under the age of forty."

Clay shook his head. "I'm not going to ask you how you arrived at that number. I'm going to take it on faith. That is a whole passel of girls, Ray."

"Yeah, but most of them are married."

"So how many of those do you figure are available?"

"Less than twenty percent. But that's a guess." Ray leaned on his broom and looked as thoughtful as it was possible for him to look. "I just thought of something," he said. "Are you interested in white women or all women?"

"Good question." Clay watched the rain falling and thought about Sharie in Nashville. Man-oh-man, he had had a thing for that woman when he was twenty-five. He would marry a woman like Sharie in a heartbeat, even if Momma and Daddy disowned him for it. Sharie had been mature and self-contained and funny and smart and...in love with someone else. Story of his life.

"If we were talking only white women, how many do you figure?"

"Two hundred and ninety four—assuming 20 percent of the females in the county are unmarried."

"You think 20 percent are unmarried?"

Ray shrugged. "I don't know how many are unmarried. The census doesn't publish that."

"Shoot, you'd think with more than two hundred single white females in this county, I could maybe find me one and settle down."

Ray bobbed his head and gave Clay his goofy grin. "You looking for a girl, Clay?"

Clay grunted. "No, I'm looking for a wife."

Ray pushed his broom. "Well, if you want a wife you ought to talk to Miz Miriam Randall. She probably *knows* all the single ladies in the county."

Clay laughed aloud at that one. Miriam Randall, Dash's aunt, was reputedly the best matchmaker in Allenberg County. "I'm not that desperate," he said. A fairly ironic statement given what had happened last night. But then, his need to find a wife had nothing to do with being horny. It was about being lonely. There was a huge difference.

Ray leaned the broom against the counter. "Well, you ought to make a list, then."

"A list?"

"Yeah, you know, a list."

"What kind of list?"

"Hand me that pad." Ray nodded toward a pad of lined paper sitting beside the cash register. Clay handed it over along with a square carpenter's pencil. Ray took the pencil and started drawing lines on the paper. The accident had affected Ray's fine motor skills, and he held the pencil like a first grader, with a tight grip. His lines were kind of uneven, and his face scrunched up with concentration as he worked.

Watching his best friend struggle with something as simple as using a pencil always did something to Clay's insides. He had to look away or get caught up in emotions that knew no limits.

Ray had shared every single milestone in Clay's life. He and Ray had played Hot Wheels on his back porch when they were eight. They had built a tree house in the live oak back of Momma's house when they were ten—the same tree house that Clay's brother Tulane had fallen out of and nearly died.

They had shared their first beers and tried cigarettes down on the Edisto River when they were thirteen. They had drooled over a contraband copy of *Playboy* when they were fourteen. They had gone in together for their first box of condoms the summer they were sixteen.

"Okay," Ray said. "Now let's list all the women we can think of." He paused a moment. "Okay, I've got one. Dottie Cox."

"Oh, c'mon, Ray, she's a little old, don't you think?"

Ray didn't listen. He wrote Dottie's name in the first

column of his list. "Okay," he said aloud. "Now we have to list the things that are good about Dottie."

"Uh-huh. Well, she has a heart of gold. I'll give her that."

Ray scrawled the words "heart of gold" into the second column of his list, followed by the words "great tits."

"Oh, for goodness' sake."

"What? She has seriously nice knockers. Besides, haven't you ever heard that poem?"

"What poem?"

"The one on the Internet about the perfect woman."

"No, I can't say as I have. And, Ray, you spend way too much time surfing the Web."

"Yeah, well, according to the poem, the perfect woman is deaf, mute, loves to have sex, has great tits, and owns a bar. She also *likes* to send her man hunting and fishing."

"That's not a poem."

"Yeah, I know, but it doesn't matter. You gotta admit it sounds like the perfect woman. And if you think about it, Dottie's got several of those traits. I mean she's got a rack on her, and a bar, and Bubba Lockheart says she's one hell of a bass fisher."

Ray wrote a few notes in Dottie's column.

"Will you stop that? Dottie is old enough to be my momma. I'm looking for a woman I can have a family with. And besides, didn't anyone ever tell you it's not nice to objectify women like that?" Although, truth to tell, he and Ray had spent countless hours objectifying women when they were sixteen, and he had certainly objectified Jane last night when she blew into Dottie's wearing that skimpy tank top. In fact, on a scale of one to ten, Wanda Jane Coblentz's breasts rated an eleven.

"Objectify?" Ray looked up, confusion on his face.

"Never mind." Clay looked out at the rain and tried to put the memory of Jane's breasts out of his mind. He failed. "Let's not make a list, okay?"

"No, this is good, but I might need to expand the matrix to account for all the variables. What's bad about Dottie?"

"She's too old."

"Good point." Ray wrote that down, then sucked on the end of the pencil for a moment. "I got another one. How about Betty Wilkins?"

"C'mon, Ray. She's…" He didn't finish the sentence. What he had been about to say would have offended Ray. Betty was sweet, if you went for girls whose entire life revolved around soap operas and *People* magazine.

"Yeah, but Clay, she's got a rack on her. She doesn't own a bar, but she can cook. I mean have you ever tasted her pies?"

"No. And she doesn't bake the pies down at the Kountry Kitchen. She just serves 'em."

"Well, I've tasted her pies at the church social. I think Betty is the best-looking girl in Last Chance."

"Betty is not a girl. Do not put Betty down on that list. Besides, Momma keeps thinking Betty might be right for Stone." Momma was delusional, of course, because Stone thought Betty was dumb as a post.

Ray looked up at him kind of soberly. "You think he's interested?"

"Hell no. But do not put her name on that list."

Ray ignored Clay and wrote Betty's name down. In the good column, he wrote the words "best-looking girl in LC" followed by the words "great tits," and then "great pies." In the bad column, he wrote the words "Stony's girlfriend," followed by the notation that she didn't own a bar and wasn't deaf and dumb.

Well, the dumb part was debatable.

"She is not Stony's girlfriend," Clay said. "I only said Momma and the rest of the church ladies are constantly trying to match them up. But they will fail. In case you missed something, my brother has not yet gotten over the death of his wife. He isn't interested in Betty." Like he would ever be interested in a woman like that. Like he would ever be interested in any woman ever again.

"That's too bad. She's a really nice person, Clay. You should definitely consider her. That's why I put her name down."

"Okay, Ray, let's stop making this list now."

Ray remained undeterred. "I got it, Clay, the perfect female." He bent over his list and scrawled the name *April* into the first column.

"Oh, for goodness' sake, Ray, April is not a real person."

"She is, too. She's perfect, and the best part is she's sleeping up on the couch in Pete's office." He said this like Wanda Jane was Snow White or Sleeping Beauty or something. Like she was waiting there for her prince to come and kiss her awake.

"How many times do I have to tell you, the woman sleeping on the couch is Jane. She's way too young and way too needy to be anyone's wife, and besides, she's just passing through. She'll be gone by Sunday."

Ray shook his head as he wrote. In the "good" column he wrote the words "perfect woman" followed by the words "great tits." In the "bad" column he wrote nothing at all. He looked up. "You know, I'm going to have to ask her a few questions before I can fill this out completely. You think she owns a bar, Clay?"

Clay hauled in a big breath and blew it out, then he snagged the legal pad, tore off the top sheet, and crumpled it up. "Look, my perfect woman is not deaf and dumb, and she doesn't own a bar. It might be nice if she liked to fish, but I could live with a woman who didn't. There are more important things in a woman, you know?"

He dropped the paper into the wastebasket. "Why don't you go dust aisle three, huh?"

Ray bobbed his head. "Okay, Clay. But if you don't want Betty or April, you are stupid. If it weren't for"—he hesitated for a moment, his lips pressing together—"you know...things...I would go for those women myself."

Clay's chest tightened, and he had trouble swallowing for a moment. The accident had robbed Ray of his future and left him just enough so that he knew the difference between what he had been at seventeen and what he was now at thirty-four. Ray still had all the longings of a normal man, and that was a problem. Pete and Clay had impressed upon Ray that he needed to be careful around women.

Ray tried his best, but Clay lived in fear that one day Ray would walk right into trouble that could land him in jail, or worse yet, in some state institution. Ray didn't understand the games women could play, and last night Jane had looked like she might have been a predator.

Of course, Clay's first impression of Jane had been wrong. But there was still a lot about that woman he didn't know. She was running scared, and she was desperate. There was no telling what trouble that could lead to.

He needed to get Jane out of town before the Ray situation exploded into something ugly. That woman was a dead ringer for April, and Ray was likely to forget that April was just a fantasy. Reality and fantasy got mixed up in Ray's head all the time.

"Ray, listen to me. That woman is not April. You stay away from her, you hear?"

Jane curled up on an ancient leather sofa with a Coleman sleeping bag. She was snuggled into a pair of size-thirty-four-waist camouflage pants and an extra-large sweatshirt that said "Get Reel—Go Bass Fishing" across its front.

Clay Rhodes sure did know how to provide for a girl whose clothes had gotten soaked in a hurricane. The man had even provided a supply of double-A batteries for her cassette player, so she could listen to her self-help tapes and try to ignore the little guy named Ray who kept poking his head into the office every twenty minutes.

Clay hadn't poked his head into the office once in the last few hours, which pretty much said it all. The man was avoiding her. He also seemed to think he was responsible for her.

In any event, riding out Hurricane Jane on the lumpy sofa had just reached a new level of tedium when a woman wearing a bright yellow rain slicker and a pair of matching pants opened the door and said, "Goodness gracious, who are *you*?"

The newcomer had a round face with a riot of curls

that had been permed into place. She was carrying a large Tupperware lunch bucket filled with fried chicken.

"Uh, I'm Jane." Jane scrambled to her feet as the woman carefully scrutinized her out of a pair of oddly familiar green eyes. The woman's gaze swept over the sleeping bag, Jane's oversized sweatshirt, and her wet jeans, jacket, and tank top hung over a folding chair.

Something seemed to hang in the balance for an instant, and then the woman let go of a large and genuine smile. "Oh, dear me, I'm sorry, darlin', I must have scared you nearly 'bout to death. Let me introduce myself. I'm Clay's momma, Ruby. I just brought him and Ray some dinner."

Ohmygod, his *mother*! Jane stifled the urge to tug on the neck of the sweatshirt. Heaven help her if the hickey was visible. Oh, crap, hadn't the police chief said this morning that *everyone* in Last Chance was going to find out that she and Clayton P. had spent the night at the Peach Blossom Motor Court?

Did Ruby know?

"So you're Jane like the hurricane?" Ruby asked, pulling Jane away from her tumbling thoughts.

"Yeah, I know, it's a sign."

Ruby's smile got a little wider, and she looked like a former Miss America standing there with her poufy hair and her big smile. "Do you have a last name, sugar?"

"Coblentz."

Ruby blinked. "Is that a German name?"

"To be honest, ma'am, I have no idea. My pa was a coal miner in West Virginia. There were a lot of folks with German-sounding names up there," Jane said, feeling dirty and disheveled in the oversized hunting clothes

Clay had found for her. She gave in to the urge and tugged at her neckline to make sure that little love bite was covered.

"How interesting." Ruby paused a moment. "I reckon that would make you a Lutheran then?"

Jane felt as if she had dropped into the middle of one of those foreign films that never made any sense. There stood the mother of the man she had slept with the night before, wearing a costume that looked like the corporate logo for Gorton's of Gloucester, only she had permed hair, tasteful makeup, and professionally polished fingernails. And this vision of well-turned-out southern womanhood wanted to know if she was a Lutheran.

How did she negotiate this? She didn't think Ruby would understand her own brand of spiritualism.

"Uh, no, ma'am," Jane said.

"No?"

She shook her head. "Not a Lutheran."

"Baptist?"

She shook her head.

"Catholic?"

Jane smiled. "My ma was raised Catholic." She neglected to add that Ma had lapsed pretty much at the age of seventeen when she'd run off and married Pa. She had a feeling Ruby was one of those small-town holy rollers.

"Really?" Ruby paused. "We're Episcopalian. Members of Christ Church. We have a nice group of Baptists and Methodists in town, but no Catholics. For the Catholics, you have to go down to Allenberg. Now, if you were a Baptist, you'd be at Reverend Michael Packard's church, which is right on Palmetto, across from City

Hall. He's such a nice man." She leaned in and spoke conspiratorially. "To tell you the truth, Pastor Mike has a better handle on the Lord than our Reverend Ellis does. But don't you dare tell Lillian Bray I said that. Bill Ellis's sermons are mostly about the wages of sin. I don't know about you, sugar, but a body gets mighty tired hearing hellfire and damnation week in and week out. Don't you think? I reckon the Episcopalians and the Catholics are much the same in that way."

"Yes, ma'am," Jane said. Obviously the slow-talking Clay had not inherited the gift of gab from his mother, who seemed a bit ecumenical to be a real holy roller. Jane relaxed just a fraction.

Ruby plopped the Tupperware down on the desk and unhooked the buckles on her raincoat. Underneath she wore a denim shirt with mother-of-pearl snaps and embroidered roses on the western-style yoke.

"So did you get caught in the storm? Car break down?"

"Uh, no. I came on the bus last night."

Interest of a kind that didn't seem entirely maternal sparked in Ruby's eyes. "The nine-thirty from Atlanta?"

What was it about that bus? That Greyhound had stopped in Columbia and dozens of other places. How come everyone just assumed that she had come from Atlanta?

"Yes, ma'am," she said.

"You got people in town?"

Jane shook her head. Ruby was interrogating her. Whatever she said would be passed along to Ruby's friends in the Christ Church congregation, and her acquaintances among the Baptists and Methodists, too.

Ruby had all the classic markers of a serious small-town gossip. Gossips loved to talk about new people in town.

Ruby looked at her soaking-wet clothes. "What happened, darlin', did the bus company lose your luggage?"

"Yes, ma'am," she said without batting an eye.

Ruby's eyes sparkled with mischief, and Jane had the feeling Clay's mother had the same built-in BS detector as her son. Unlike Clay, however, Ruby didn't argue about this obvious lie. Ruby pretended she believed it.

"So what brings you to Last Chance?"

Well, ma'am, I'm running from half a dozen loan sharks who took my hard-earned tip money and then threatened to beat me up and possibly kill me unless the lying, double-dealing, low-down, rotten, peanut-brained weasel Woody West paid them the twenty thousand dollars he owed them.

She decided Ruby wasn't ready for the truth. "I'm looking for work," she said aloud.

"Do you have any skills?"

Well, yes, she did have some skills. But her resume—and her Florida State Cosmetology license—didn't have the name Wanda Jane Coblentz on them.

She cleared her throat. "I…uh…graduated from Beauty Schools of America in Miami about five years ago, but I never got my license. Actually, I've been working as a waitress for the last few years. I heard there might be something at Dot's Spot." It wasn't the truth. The truth was that she had done a few unsavory things to earn her tuition to beauty school, and once she had gotten her license she worked two jobs—days at the beauty shop at the Best Western resort and nights as a waitress at the Shrimp Shack.

A girl had to work double hard to save two thousand

dollars in tip money. Those hard-earned savings had allowed her to follow Woody's suggestion and go with him to Nashville. Those carefully saved tips were her cushion so she could get herself settled with a day job in Nashville before she started pursuing the dream of becoming a country-and-western singer.

Woody said he would help introduce her to some important people. What a fool she had been to fall for *that* line. Instead, the bad people Woody knew—the ones he owed a lot of money to—had taken her savings as an interest payment on what Woody owed them.

"So," Ruby said, pulling her away from the disaster area that was her recent past. "Do you have any experience with kids?"

"Kids?"

"You know, like babysitting."

Yes, she did have some experience babysitting. But that experience came from her other life. Back when she was a teenager, she had earned almost five hundred dollars in babysitting money that she hoarded just like she'd hoarded her tip money. That money had taken her to Florida when she was seventeen. "Yes, ma'am. I have done a lot of babysitting. When I was younger."

"Have you ever actually done hair?"

Right then, Jane realized Ruby was interviewing her for a job, disproving Clay's negative statements of earlier in the day. Dr. Goodbody always said that a person was not a victim of fate—that a person could make their own luck through affirmative thinking. And look what was happening right here in the middle of a hurricane.

"Yes, ma'am," she said, with feeling. "I worked at a beauty shop in Florida for more than four years."

"Hmmm. Do you have any experience doing nails?"

Jane nodded. "And makeup."

"I take it you don't have anyplace to stay either?"

"No, ma'am." Jane's elation faded away. Who would offer a job to a homeless bum like her?

"Well, then, I reckon that makes you perfect."

"Perfect? For what?"

Ruby's cheerleader smile came out again, and she looked like she was clued in to some big secret. "For the job I have open at the Cut 'n Curl. I own the place."

"The Cut 'n Curl? A beauty shop?"

Ruby nodded. "Now, the job isn't exactly all beauty. I have two grandchildren, aged thirteen and seven, who need watching after school. I really don't like to have them down at the beauty shop when I'm working if I can help it. You know how women can talk, and sometimes they say things I don't want my grandbabies to hear.

"So it's like this. You work the shop until school lets out. Then I need you to keep an eye on the children either at my house or up in the apartment above the shop. You'll have to drive Haley to her ballet lessons on Tuesday, and Lizzy takes flute lessons over to Allenberg on Wednesday afternoons and has band practice on Mondays and Thursdays. I'm assuming you can drive a car?"

Jane nodded. "But I don't have—"

"Not a problem, you can borrow my Taurus. The job pays minimum wage plus any tips you make, and I throw in a studio apartment above the shop rent free."

The Universe had come through for her—a job *and* a place to stay. All that manifesting she'd been doing on the lumpy couch had actually worked. It was amazing. It was a first.

"Excuse me, but do you always hire homeless strangers on the spot like this?" she blurted. Hoo boy, and wasn't that just like her. Something good happened, and she had to question it.

Ruby laughed. "Well, I know, it does sound a little crazy. But that no-account Michelle ran off with Bernard last week, leaving me high and dry without a sitter or anyone to help with the manicures. There are no beauty-school graduates in Last Chance. I've been praying for someone like you for a long time. In my experience, prayer usually works."

Jane opened her mouth and then closed it. Maybe her manifesting techniques were not so good after all. Ruby looked like the kind of woman God might listen to. "I... um... I'll take the job."

"Good. I'm so glad. Now, look, honey, I've got a washer and dryer over at the Cut 'n Curl, and I know you'll feel better once you take a bath, put on your face, and get back into some clothes that don't have camouflage and bass all over them. As an employee of the Cut 'n Curl, I'm going to be counting on you to show your best face every day."

"Yes, ma'am." How she was going to do this with only one outfit remained to be seen. But things were looking up.

Ruby turned toward the door, walked through it, and hollered out Clay's name. "Where in the Sam Hill are you, son? I brought you and Ray some dinner, and I'm taking Jane off your hands."

Clay appeared at the end of the power tool aisle, packing a chain saw. He looked dangerous and competent with that tool in his hand. "Momma? What are you doing out in this weather?"

"Bringing you dinner and checking out the latest news."

"The latest news?"

"Yes. I had a call from Lillian Bray this morning." Ruby smiled sweetly.

Clay's eyebrows lowered. "Momma, I—"

"I left your dinner on Pete's desk. I'm taking Jane over to the Cut 'n Curl so she can settle in."

Clay's gaze narrowed. "Settle in?"

"Uh-huh. Did you know that she has a degree from Beauty Schools of America? She's exactly what I've been praying for, which is a good thing for you, because if she wasn't you'd have been in some serious trouble. Although, to be honest, you're still in trouble. You're going to have to go speak with Lillian, son."

Jane could hardly contain her glee as Clay stood there blinking at his mother like Ruby had just hit him across the head with a two-by-four. Jane pasted a big grin on her face. "See," she said in a bright, I-told-you-so voice. "There *are* people willing to give job interviews in the middle of a hurricane."

"Momma, just what are you playing at? You can't hire this woman. She's—"

Ruby waved her hand in dismissal. "Now, son, don't you go using that word. I heard that word from Lillian this morning, and I didn't like it. All in all, I would rather think that the Lord has sent Jane to us because Michelle ran off last week."

Ruby turned toward Jane, as she started buckling up her raincoat. "C'mon, honey, let's get you across the street so you can wash and dry those jeans of yours. I'm thinking there might be a box of Sharon's old clothes up in Stony's attic that might fit you. Sharon was my older son's wife. She passed a number of years ago in a car wreck. Sharon had such good taste in clothes, bless her heart. I know you'll find something in that box. When the storm blows over, I'll see what I can do about getting it over to you."

And with that, Ruby solved Jane's wardrobe problems. And then, like some kind of immutable force, the woman sailed through the front door of the hardware store, unconcerned about the tempest raging outside, and unaware of the look on her son's face that said there was a storm brewing inside, too.

Chapter
5

The studio apartment above the Cut 'n Curl wasn't much—maybe thirty feet long and twenty wide. It had two narrow double-hung windows on one end that provided a view of Palmetto Avenue and Lovett's Hardware across the street. The windows wore yellow gingham. The sleep-sofa was dressed in a spread of spring green. A couple of green and yellow director's chairs and a battered oak coffee table rounded out the furniture. A Pullman kitchen and basic bathroom occupied most of the back portion of the apartment.

It was homey and clean—even if the décor ran a little bit toward country Martha Stewart—and certainly better than the alternative: the nonexistent village green or another night at the Peach Blossom Motor Court.

Well, Dr. Goodbody always said that when a negative situation arises, the best thing to do was to meet it head-on with a positive plan of action. Jane had done that, and here she was with a place to stay and a job to do. That proved, without question, that she didn't need anyone right now, except her own self.

And a little electricity, which had waited until she was halfway through the dryer's cycle to conk out.

No telling how long it would be before the power was restored. Which raised all kinds of serious issues: like whether the Cut 'n Curl would open tomorrow so Jane could start her new job and start earning a paycheck. And how was she going to afford food if it didn't open?

Although without electricity, the oven and refrigerator in the little apartment were useless, so food was going to be a problem either way.

She needed to stop all this negative thinking. Worrying about stuff she didn't have any control over would make her crazy and sap her energy. She pulled her soggy jeans from the dryer and told herself that things were going to work out.

The sharp ping of a coin hitting the floor drew her thoughts away from her worries. She cast her gaze over the vinyl flooring in the kitchen and watched a penny roll in a crazy circle and spin to a stop. She juggled the bundle of wet clothes and stooped to pick it up. It was the "lucky" penny she had put in her jeans pocket earlier that morning.

Jane put the penny into the pocket of her fatigues and headed off to the bathroom, where she hung her jeans and tank top over the tub to dry. Then she closed the lid on the john, pulled the penny from her pocket, and sat for a few moments inspecting its worn copper face.

It had been minted in 1943—more than sixty years ago. The penny had been in circulation for an entire year before her grandfather was born, and twenty-one years before her own father drew breath.

How many washers had the penny been through?

How many times had some child with grubby hands put this penny into a gum machine? How many times had this penny fallen to the ground and spun like a top? How many times had this penny been lost and found? How many times had someone picked it up and considered it a lucky thing?

But now it was *her* lucky penny. Not that a penny could bring her luck. Luck was manufactured by knowing what you wanted and having a plan for achieving it.

Still, the penny was old and unique and worth keeping. She got up and headed into the main room, clutching the coin in her palm, feeling its familiar round form and knowing some measure of comfort.

She flopped down onto the sofa and dug in her purse for her wallet. She opened the change purse, intent on putting her special penny in a safe place where she wouldn't spend it on some necessity of life, like peanut butter. And that's when she saw the stupid necklace. She dropped the penny in the change purse and pulled out the plastic jade camel.

How lame. She had thought as much when Woody presented it to her several days before with the kind of flourish that said he expected her to appreciate it. She had sort of appreciated the gesture, even if the darn thing was about as cheap as you could get. She should have seen it as a warning sign.

After all, two months ago, Woody had been handing out hundred-dollar tips to her just for singing karaoke at the Shrimp Shack. She had mistaken him for a successful and well-connected man.

Boy, what a fool she had been. He must have been on a winning streak that turned. And when it turned, he'd taken her down with him. Anger boiled in her gut. Unlike the penny, this necklace was not a positive object. She sincerely hoped that she never saw Woody again. Staying here in Last Chance was a good way to make that happen.

Unless, of course, the bad stuff followed her here.

She pushed that thought away as she snapped the change purse closed and put her wallet back in her purse. Then she stood up, walked into the kitchen, opened the cabinet beneath the sink, and dropped the jade camel into the trash can.

"Good-bye, Woody," she said as she slammed the door shut. "And good riddance."

The Universe chose that exact moment to express its approval of this course of action by allowing the sun to make its first appearance of the day. Jane rushed to the windows and stared up into a sky that was changing from gray into a deep, endless Carolina blue.

When the lights went out, Clay sent Ray home from work. Now Ray sat at his kitchen table studying the slightly wrinkled sheet of paper he'd rescued from the trash can at the front of the store.

He needed to help Clay find a wife, because if Clay was married and settled down, then maybe he would stop feeling like he was responsible. Ray hated the way Clay always felt responsible.

He stared down at his list. So far it only had three names on it—in alphabetical order: April, Betty, and Dottie.

He thought for a long time. There were a couple of other names he could add to the list: Lurleen Wallace, who worked for the Sheriff's Department; Amy Swallock, who had a job at the Rexall; Carolyn Mayfield, who ran a little antique shop in the old schoolhouse; and Jennifer Carpenter, who was a teller at the First National Bank and who lived with her invalid mother.

The names on his list had to be a pretty small percentage of the potential pool of marriageable women in Allenberg County.

Ray let go of a big sigh. How was he supposed to figure out which one was the right one for Clay? Clay had made it clear that just rating them by the size of their breasts and whether they owned a bar was pretty immature. And even if Ray's brains were scrambled, he recognized that the Internet poem about the perfect woman left a few variables out.

He needed a better empirical test.

He stood up and went to the drawer in the kitchen where he kept a pad and pencils. He sat down, lit a candle in the deepening afternoon gloom, and started to make a list of the things that would make a woman perfect:

Well, first of all, the perfect woman would understand the geometry of pool and the probability of poker. Although Clay probably didn't care about the mathematical aspects of these games, he did know how to play them. So Clay's perfect woman would have to know how to play them, too. So he wrote pool and poker down on this list.

She would have to love baseball and know the difference between on-base percentage and slugging percentage. Well, at least, she would have to know how to keep score, because Clay loved baseball almost as much as Ray did.

He wrote that down.

She would have to know how to bake a cherry pie, which had nothing to do with math (unless you were trying to figure the circumference of the pie, which would require the use of *pi*). He smiled at his own pun. Still, the pie baking was important. The perfect woman needed to know how to bake.

The perfect woman would not be afraid of Lillian Bray. So any member of the Ladies Auxiliary was out. Not that there were any unmarried members of the Auxiliary, but that was an absolute ironclad requirement. Clay didn't need to be saddled with one of those women. Or any woman who might be inclined to join the Auxiliary. Although, since Clay was an Episcopalian, Ray reckoned that his perfect mate would, at least, have to be Christian.

He wrote that down.

She would have to like more than country music, because even if Clay was an accomplished fiddler, the fact remained that Clay listened to jazz and classical music whenever he thought folks weren't looking. That was going to be a tough one because he reckoned no one in Allenberg County except Clay Rhodes liked that kind of long-haired stuff.

She would have to be willing to relocate, because the entire point of the exercise was to get Clay to move back to Nashville so he would quit hovering over Ray and trying to look after him. He wrote that down. He suspected that finding folks willing to leave Allenberg County wouldn't be all that difficult. The difficult part would be in finding an eligible woman, since women in these parts all seemed to be hot to leave town.

He studied his list for a long time as the gloom outside receded and the storm passed over. He added several criteria and then began writing out the algorithm for determining each potential candidate's overall score on the test—a score he termed the "desirability index." If the electricity had been running, he would have started programming the application directly into his computer, but that wasn't possible.

So he wrote the computer code longhand and would transfer it to the computer later. Now, with that finished, he needed to collect the data.

Ray folded up the original list and stuffed it into his pocket. Then he took the sheets of paper and put them carefully by his computer in the den, where he wouldn't forget them.

The sun had come out, although the electricity was still off. His stomach rumbled. He was hungry. He wondered if the Kountry Kitchen was open.

He smiled at the thought. Betty was probably still on shift. He blew out the candle he'd been using in the kitchen. Then he left the house, forgetting to lock up after himself. He turned left on Oak and walked two blocks to the corner. Then a right on Palmetto Avenue.

Clay knew the exact moment Jane walked into Dottie's place, even though he had his back turned toward the door and his head deep in the music he was playing on the upright piano. The hairs on his neck stood on end, gooseflesh prickled up his back, and his whole body went *zing*.

He missed a note with his left hand and stumbled through three entire measures of "Honky Tonk Moon," losing the meter of the song in the process. The air became thick with charged electrons. He forced himself to concentrate on the piano, but it took almost all of his will not to look over his shoulder to confirm that Jane had arrived.

Then, out of the corner of his eye, he saw her sashay up to the bar on those high-heel boots and ask Dottie about the free hash.

And Dottie, warm-hearted woman that she was, smiled that Amanda Blake smile of hers, ignored Jane's baggy fatigues and shirt, and said, "Darlin', I certainly am handing out free hash. I borrowed Clay's Coleman stove, and I've got two whole cases of that stuff left over from that hash-eating contest we ran last summer. You just set yourself down, and I'll get you a whole plateful. I figure there are lots of folks without warm food tonight, and it's the least I can do."

The bartender turned to fetch the food. Jane hopped up on the stool and turned her head. She looked right at him.

And he, like some stupid sixteen-year-old, turned his head and looked at her. And missed another beat.

Crap.

He needed to get this girl out of town before he took her back to the Peach Blossom Motor Court—or, worse yet, invited her home to sleep in his own bed. Forget about Ray and his delusions about this girl. This woman was dangerous. Clay's body was telling him, in no uncertain terms, that he wanted a second round. And she looked so forlorn in those baggy clothes. Feeling lust for a needy woman could set him back on his plans of finding a real relationship with a mature, straightforward, and self-reliant woman.

He turned his attention back to the keyboard and tried hard not to think about her. He failed.

• • •

Jane was in serious trouble. The Universe might have provided free food and beer, but it required her to sit here at the bar and listen to Clay play piano.

He had skills as a fiddler, but when he sat at the piano, he blew her away. She had heard that piano all the way down the sidewalk as she searched, in vain, for an open grocery or convenience store. The music had drawn her into Dot's Spot more than the sign for free hash.

She listened as he ran through a bunch of country standards. But when he started playing "I've Got Friends in Low Places," it was almost as if he conjured up Ray.

With the opening verse, the little guy sauntered through the doors. He waved toward Clay, then he marched right up to the bar and hopped up on the bar stool next to Jane.

"Hey," he said with a goofy smile and a bobbing Adam's apple.

Clayton P. glanced over his shoulder, watching Ray. That was interesting. It sure did look like Clayton P. thought he was Ray's bodyguard or something. The big question was why.

Dottie worked the hand pump on the keg she'd hauled behind the counter and drew a lukewarm draft that she set in front of Ray. "So," the bartender said as she picked up a dishtowel and started wiping glasses, "where are you from, sugar?"

Yup, this was definitely small-town America. "I'm from Florida," Jane said, not willing to give the whole sordid story of her life and the bad choices she had made.

"She's April," Ray said with a bob of his head.

"Uh, no, Ray, my name's Jane," she said. Behind him, Clay rolled his eyes and shook his head.

"Well, Jane, welcome to Last Chance, home of Golfing for God," Dottie said.

Clay squeezed his eyes shut as if he were experiencing a sudden, swift pain.

"I've heard about that. I'm going to have to get a ride out there just to take it all in."

"You do that. It's good for the economy."

"Hey, Dottie, I got a question for you," Ray said, changing the subject.

"Okay."

"Do you know how to play pool?"

She smiled. "I do, as a matter of fact. Met my late husband playing pool. He was something of a hustler, though. Which is why I don't have a pool table in my bar. I'm afraid it would remind me of him and make me sad. That, and I'm already in trouble with the holy rollers around this town. Bad enough I serve liquor without the inevitable gambling a pool table brings."

"That's good," Ray said bobbing his head, and Jane wondered what, precisely, was good about it. But before she could ask, Ray turned toward her. "You know how to play pool, April?"

Ray was challenged, so she gave him the benefit of the doubt. Besides, it was clear Clayton P. considered Ray one of his friends, and Clayton P. was, actually, a pretty okay guy. "Um, actually, no, I don't know how to play pool," she said.

He stared at her for a long moment, and Jane got the impression that she had somehow disappointed him. "That's too bad."

"Ray, why do you have pool on your mind?" Dottie asked.

"Oh, no particular reason, Dot. Just doing a survey."

"A survey?"

"Yeah. I'm collecting data on the women of Allenberg County."

"Uh-huh. And why are you doing that?"

"Because it interests me." He gave her a speculative look. "Do you know how to play poker, Dot?"

"My late husband and I were both pretty good Texas Hold 'Em players. Donnie was practically a professional before he died."

"That's good, Dottie." Ray turned on his bar stool. "How about you, April?"

"I'm afraid not, Ray. I wouldn't know a good poker hand if it came up and bit me," Jane said.

He frowned. He looked really forlorn. "That's too bad," he said.

"Ray, honey, is this survey about games of chance?" Dottie asked.

"Oh, no, it's a more widely ranging survey than that," Ray said.

"Uh-huh, you got any more questions?" Dot asked.

"Well, yes, I do."

"Okay, shoot."

"Can you bake a cherry pie?"

Dottie snorted. "From scratch or with a crust from the freezer section at the Piggly Wiggly?"

"Hmmm. That's a good question. I hadn't thought about that variable." Ray frowned.

"About what?" Dottie said.

"Whether it's necessary to bake the pie from scratch?"

"Well, using Flako is practically like making it from scratch. I mean you still have to roll the crust," Dottie said.

"Good point. So can you?" Ray asked.

"Of course I can. Donnie used to especially like my peach pie. But peach or cherry, it's all in the crust. For the record, I usually make my piecrust from scratch."

Ray turned on his stool. "How 'bout you, April?"

"Me?"

"Yeah. Can you bake a pie?"

Jane stared down at the little guy. "To be honest, I try hard not to eat pie, because it's fattening."

"But can you bake one?"

"I haven't ever tried, so I don't really know."

"Didn't your momma ever bake pies for you, sugar?" This from Dottie.

Jane didn't want to answer that one. Ma's idea of cooking was running out to McDonald's. "I'm afraid not."

Ray's eyes got round, like he pitied her or something. "Oh, I'm sorry."

"It's okay." But somehow it wasn't okay.

"So can you cook anything?" Ray asked.

"Why is this important?"

"I'm collecting data on the women of—"

"Yeah, yeah, I heard that, but I'm not a woman of Allenberg County. I guess all the women around here can cook, but I'm a call-up-for-carry-out kind of girl. Which is why I'm here eating hash."

"That's too bad, April."

The music stopped abruptly. Jane, Ray, and Dottie all looked over toward Clay. He was glaring back at them, mostly at Ray. "Ray, what are you up to?"

"Nothing. I'm just conducting an informal survey of the women of Allenberg County."

"Well, stop."

"Why?"

"Because you're pestering Jane and Dottie."

"Aw, c'mon, Clay, I'm just working on that problem we discussed today at the store. And besides, Betty didn't mind when I asked her these questions."

Clay's brow lowered into a scowl. "Ray, I told you to quit. Now quit, okay?"

"What problem?" Dot asked. Her gaze shifted from Clay to Ray with the avidity of a bloodhound on the hunt. No one had a nose for gossip like a bartender, unless it was a church lady.

"Never you mind, Dot," Clay said. "Just watch him, will you?"

Clay's gaze shifted and suddenly Jane found herself caught up in the light of those pale wolf eyes. That stare of his was so intense, it practically burned a hole in her middle.

It took almost all of Clay's willpower to tear his gaze away from Jane. Even dressed in baggy fatigues and a sweatshirt, she looked good enough to eat. He flashed on the heat of her skin last night and felt his face burn.

He turned back to his piano. He gulped down a breath and blew it out. He needed to have a long talk with Ray. The boy seemed to be on a mission to find him the perfect pool- and poker-playing woman.

Although why Ray would think he wanted that kind of thing in a woman was beyond Clay's understanding. But who knew how Ray's scrambled brains worked.

Clay put his fingers on the keyboard. He noodled around for a moment in the key of G before launching into a syncopated progression of major seventh chords that took him into a genre of music that was not quite pop and not quite jazz and not quite folk. It was a genre all his own.

Of course, the inability to define a category for many of his own compositions explained his entire life. He, and they, didn't fit. And so, mostly, these songs went unsold, even though they pleased him. Sometimes he thought it might be better to reach a small audience with something true and authentic than to reach for the world.

In a minute, Dottie would tell him to stop putting the customers to sleep with this crap. But right now she was busy welcoming folks to the *One-and-Only Last Chance Hurricane Jane Party*. The news that Dottie was handing out lukewarm beer and free hash had traveled fast. Customers were strolling in, and it was a sad fact that those rednecks and good ol' boys didn't much like this style of music either.

Clay played on, irritated at Jane for being there. And feeling increasingly angry with himself for falling into old patterns of behavior that made him want to take care of her and Ray.

He clamped down on his back teeth and focused on playing, intent on making his audience listen—just this once—to one of his compositions that didn't have a fiddle or a steel guitar part in it, that wasn't some canned Hallmark emotion, but something that required them to think and feel. He closed his eyes, drew in a deep breath, and started to sing.

> *Now I mark the time like a metronome*
> *A single heart, beating on its own*
> *And I keep the time with a watch and chain*
> *From the day you last said my name...*

Jane found herself pulled into the song Clay played. The composition had an arresting tempo she couldn't ignore. Jane counted the beats in her head. He was playing in seven-four time. The musical phrase was subtle and complex, yet it sounded simple. The man was a virtuoso.

Then he started to sing. And the lyrics touched something down deep inside her. They were all about time itself. About losing it, and losing love, and not fitting in. She connected with the message.

Jane watched him as he squeezed his eyes shut and seemed to travel off to some other place—a place of pain and emotion. He was carrying a torch for someone bigtime. He had cried in the bathroom last night, and that could only mean he was seriously hurting about some lost love.

Hoo boy. An emotional man with a poetic streak and a broken heart was about the most seductive thing in the Universe. A girl could get screwed-up notions about rescuing him. A girl just naturally wanted to be the one to introduce him, personally, to happiness and to take care of him.

Which explained why her heart began to race and her lungs started to burn.

Fortunately, Clay ended the song before she burst into tears or did something foolish like start thinking she actually had the power to rescue him or take care of him.

Before Clay could launch into something else equally emotional, Dottie growled at him. "I declare, you know darn well, the folks who come in here want to hear country music, not jazz. Jazz is too complicated for most of 'em." Dottie gave Jane a meaningful look. "Ain't that right, sugar?"

Oh, crap. She was caught between the woman who had just given her free food and the man who had given her a hickey last night, fed her this morning, and blown her away a minute ago. Her entire future in this town might hinge on her response to this impossible question.

Jane pressed her lips together before she opened her mouth and said something destructive like: *Wow, Clayton P., I'm starting to see you as a tortured soul with incredible talent between the sheets who is searching for abiding love. Wanna go back to the apartment above the Cut 'n Curl and see if we can get it on?*

Instead, she shrugged her shoulders.

Clay's eyebrows lowered. "Not a jazz fan, huh?" he said as a little muscle pulsed in his cheek.

Ray turned and stared at her. "Oh, April, that's really too bad," he said, bobbing and shaking his head.

She realized her mistake the minute Ray spoke. She had not affirmed Clay's talent, and she had hurt him in the process. Her noncommittal shrug had been about as negative a reaction as possible, and if anyone needed some affirmation in his life, it was Clayton P. Rhodes.

Jane opened her mouth, intent on fixing the damage by telling him she had enjoyed his song, but he didn't give her the chance. He started playing a series of chords on the piano that didn't sound like country music or jazz.

"Oh, for heaven's sake," Dottie said. "Don't go and start singing hymns on me again. Clay, I mean it..."

In defiance, Clay began to sing "Amazing Grace" in a big voice. Jane noticed the other patrons in the bar shaking their heads and laughing into their warm beers.

"Clay, stop it. You're being a jerk." Dottie gave Jane a woman-to-woman look that Jane understood. Jane needed to do something to turn this situation from the negative into the positive. So she hopped down from the stool, walked over to the piano, and started singing harmony.

Clay looked up at her, surprise etched on his face. She watched a little iridescent fire spark in his eyes, and he smoothed out his playing and singing so they could hear each other and find a blend. And the blend was amazing. His husky tenor filled in all the hollow places of her soprano, and her soprano lent his voice a resonance it otherwise lacked.

As she sang, her consciousness narrowed down to his face, and the sound of his voice, and the sound of her own as she complemented him. In that instant, singing opened a link with the creative force of the Universe, like real manifesting or—Heaven help her—like making soulful, breathless love.

Her synapses lined up and conducted an amazing amount of electricity through her system. It aroused her completely while it sent up warning flares. She needed to stop now. She needed to run away quick.

But she had this awful, sinking feeling as she stared into his face, unable to look away, that it was already too late. With every second the hymn continued, Clay drew her further toward him, like a moth to a flame.

She had to remind herself that this appearance of a soulful connection between them was a sham and lie and a fake. This was a heady illusion of something deep and meaningful brought on by her current circumstances and a night of incredible sex. It was like some kind of flashing danger sign.

But she couldn't look away. She couldn't deny the

buzz that hummed in the center of her being, in her belly and in the deep recesses of her consciousness. Hoo boy, if he asked her, she would agree to another night with him.

Clay ended the song after the second verse, which was a good thing, because she only knew the first verse and had kind of stumbled through the words on the second. In the moment after the last musical vibration and before the smattering of applause, he looked up at her and smiled sweetly.

Her heart lurched sideways in her chest. She ought to run like hell, as far and as fast as she could run. But she didn't, because some force seemed to have nailed her feet to the floor.

"Honey," Dottie called from behind her. "Where did you learn to sing like that?"

"In church," Clay answered for her, never releasing her gaze. He was looking right into her, reading her, and it felt like an invasion of privacy even if his assumptions were all wrong.

"I did not."

"That's good, sugar, because we don't need hymns here. You know anything other than hymns?" Dottie asked.

He leaned closer to her. "You did sing in church, I'd bet on it. In fact, I bet you can hit the high A in the Lord's Prayer."

She squared her shoulders and scowled at him. "I never sang in church."

"Yeah, well, don't sing the Lord's Prayer here, okay? It would be bad for business," Dottie said. "How 'bout some Dolly Parton? 'I Will Always Love You' is my all-time favorite song."

Clay arched an eyebrow in question.

"I don't know the words to that song," Jane admitted. "Do you know 'Whose Bed Have Your Boots Been Under?'"

His brows lowered, and his eyes flashed, and his stubborn streak marched right across his features. "No way I'll let you sing that. That song is wrong for you," he said.

The forces of the Universe released her. His true colors bled through the disguise. He was a stubborn jerk, and she could resist a jerk. In fact, she knew better than to fall for a jerk.

She put her hands on her hips. "Yeah, well, I do that song really well. I sing karaoke every Thursday at the Shrimp Shack. I get *lots* of applause."

Clay's gaze dropped to her chest and the "Get Reel" shirt and then back to her face. "I reckon when you sing karaoke you wear something more like that outfit you had on last night? I'll bet you wiggle your backside, too."

"I don't usually walk around wearing hunting fatigues held up by a length of nylon cord, you know. And I put on a show. That's part of show businesses—the show, I mean."

"That explains it."

"Explains what?"

"Why you get applause."

Fury marched right through her system, scouring her of any desire she might have harbored for this guy. "You are a class-A jerk, aren't you? I try to affirm your talent, and you sit there judging and demeaning mine."

Someone wearing a Country Pride Chicken hat, sitting at the bar, said, "You tell 'im, sister. Anyone can plainly see you got loads of talent."

Clay shook his head and smiled an infernally delicious grin that lit up his face. "Look, Jane, all I meant was—"

"You know, one day I'm going to make it to Nashville, and I'll be discovered. I'm telling you, Clayton P. Rhodes, I'm going to be a star, and you'll eat your words."

The smile vanished from his face. "Honey, I know you believe in wishful thinking, but Nashville is a rough town."

"And what do *you* know about it anyway?"

"I've lived there since I was seventeen. I only moved back here a few months ago. And I'll tell you something, nobody ever just gets discovered, even people with musical talent. And even when you think you've got it made, it can fall apart in an instant."

"Oh, and I don't have *real* talent, is that it?" Clayton had some kind of nerve sitting there calling her talent into question. He had no capacity to acknowledge anyone's talent—certainly not hers, and not even his own. He had a negative outlook on life, and who needed that?

She needed to hang around his negative vibe like she needed another day with Woody West. "Up yours," Jane said. Then she turned on her heel and walked out of the bar without looking back.

Chapter
6

Clay watched Jane march out the door and knew another moment of supreme confusion. He had not meant to make her feel small. He had meant to give her some good advice. Advice she needed if she wanted to make it in Nashville.

"Well, that went well," Dottie said from the bar. "Jeez, Clay, just because you're having a hard time these days doesn't mean you can snap at folks the way you been doing."

"Yes, ma'am," he said on a long sigh. "I didn't mean that the way it sounded."

He moved to the bar, where Dottie handed him a beer. Bubba Lockheart took that moment to connect his iPod to the battery-operated boom box someone had brought along for the Hurricane Party. Predictably, the latest Tumbleweed hit song started playing.

Clay felt something snap inside, and he turned toward Bubba, who had taken a seat at the end of the bar. "Damn it, why'd you have to play *that* stupid song?"

Bubba shrugged. He was already looking halfway wasted. "It reminds me of Rocky," he said.

Well, that was predictable, too. Rocky, Clay's little sister, had broken Bubba's heart into a million pieces a number of years ago. The big man still carried a torch for her, and truth to tell, most of the folks in Last Chance blamed Rocky for the demise of Bubba's potential as a future NFL linebacker. Of course, Bubba was a loser, and Rocky had probably been right to dump him when she did. At least Rocky knew a bad boy when she saw one.

"Bubba, Rocky ain't never coming back. You know that. I know that. The entire town knows that. And my momma is as heartbroke over it as you are. But it's time to move on."

"Right, Clay, I know." Bubba nodded and lifted his beer as the Tumbleweed song played on. There was no mistaking the sarcasm in his voice.

"Clay," Dottie said, "don't take your misery out on Bubba. He's got plenty of his own. And while I'm at it, it was unfair of you to take your sorrow out on Jane, too. As far as I'm concerned, she has a voice like an angel, and I, for one, would not have minded hearing 'Whose Bed Have Your Boots Been Under?' In fact, Clay, you should tell Kyle about that girl. She might bring some real class to the Wild Horses. You owe her an apology."

"Yes, ma'am." When Dottie got to handing out advice, it was best not to argue. Besides, Dottie was right. He did owe Jane an apology, but he didn't feel like running right out the door after her. Instead, he turned toward Ray, who was eating a bowl of hash as if there were no tomorrow.

"You want to explain those questions you were asking Jane and Dot?" he asked.

Ray looked up, his cheeks filled with food. He chewed vigorously for a couple of moments, then swallowed. "I realized this afternoon that the matrix we started didn't have enough dimensions."

"You want to put that in language I can understand? What matrix?"

"You know, the list we started of eligible women. We didn't have enough dimensions on it. So I came up with a list of questions designed to determine the suitability of any woman to be your wife within an acceptable standard deviation."

"Of course." Clay ground his teeth together but held himself back while he counted slowly to ten. "And where did you come up with these questions?" he finally asked when the initial fury had passed.

"Oh, here and there. The questions about games of chance are to determine if she has any mathematical abilities and likes the kind of stuff you like. And, of course, she needs to know how to bake a pie, Clay. You can't hitch yourself up to a woman who can't bake a pie."

He leaned in. "Listen, Ray, you leave Jane alone, and you stop asking women these questions, you hear me?"

"But Clay, I—"

"I mean it. If there are any questions to be asked, I'll do the asking myself. You got that?"

Ray looked up at him. "Sure, Clay. I hear you."

"Good." He took a deep breath. "Well, I guess I need to go find that little gal and apologize for being a jerk, and while I'm at it, I'll apologize for you, too."

He turned, snagged his heavy-duty flashlight from the top of the piano, and headed toward the door. He stopped before he stepped through it and turned over his shoulder, pointing the unlit flashlight at his best friend. "I mean it, Ray, no more questions."

"I hear you." Ray ducked his head a few times like he was nodding.

Clay turned and pushed through the door into the dusky October evening. He found Jane five minutes later, sitting on the bottom step of the stairway that led to the apartment above the Cut 'n Curl. She had her chin planted in her fists.

He had this horrible feeling that she was crying, but he wasn't about to shine his flashlight in her face to confirm it. So he doused the light as he approached, putting them both in the safety of the deepening night.

"Go 'way." She sniffled.

Yup, he hated himself. It was not an unfamiliar feeling. "I'm sorry about what I said back at Dottie's. I didn't mean it the way it sounded."

"Okay. Now get lost."

"No."

Jane looked up at him, and he could almost make out the spark in her dark eyes. "You know, you are a stubborn pain in the butt."

Clay let go of a bitter laugh. "Yeah, I know." He paused for a moment, wondering how to continue. "Uh, look, Jane, the thing is, my life has been crap the last few months." He couldn't speak without a little waver, and it made him feel about five years old.

"Crap? You mean like someone broke your heart or—"

"No, like someone I care about is really, really sick. With cancer and likely to die." His voice didn't waver this time. Instead, it sounded hard and flat and angry. It was so much easier to be angry at Uncle Pete for getting sick than to admit that he was angry about other things: like his broken career or the broken heart that he refused to acknowledge.

"This person who is sick. Is she—"

"He. My uncle."

"Oh."

"He owns the hardware store. He's been like a father to me and my brothers and sister, seeing as my own daddy is...well..."

"What?" Her voice cut through his confusion.

Clay shrugged. He wasn't about to go explaining his complicated and uneasy relationship with his father. "I already told you about my father." He turned to go.

She called him back. "So you're telling me you have father issues and that explains why you're a big, selfish, stubborn, myopic jerk."

He stopped and turned. Suddenly, he wanted to laugh out loud. What was it about this girl that called to him?

"Yeah. I have father issues. And a bunch of other complications in my life."

"Like what? Because my father used to get drunk and beat on my mother. And as for life complications, maybe we could have a contest. Because I'll bet I win. I only have five dollars and assorted change to my name, I'm wearing an oversized 'Get Reel' shirt, and there isn't a store open in Last Chance where I can get a jar of peanut butter. I mean, that's bad, Clay."

He laughed, and the tightness in his chest eased. "I'll concede the point."

"Oh, goody, do I win a prize? Like biggest loser in Last Chance or something?"

"You're not a loser, Jane," he said. "If I gave you that impression back at Dottie's, I am truly sorry. The biggest loser in Last Chance is me."

She looked up at him and cocked her head, and he wished with all his heart that he could see her face. He wanted to sit beside her. He wanted to hold her hand. He wanted to take her up those stairs and make sweet love to her.

"Why's that?"

"Because I'm living here in Last Chance, just waiting for the moment when I snap and start seeing angels like my daddy does. Because my career in Nashville is over and I don't really know what to do next." *Because I'm alone and I'm tired of being alone.* But he didn't say that out loud.

"You had a career in Nashville?"

"Yeah. I was a union-scale side man for years." He didn't talk about Tumbleweed or the rest of it. He didn't want to pour his heart out to this semistranger. "Look," he said, "there's something else I need to say."

"If you're going to invite me back to your place, I think I'll take a pass. I'm thinking maybe you're too needy and high-maintenance, you know?"

He stifled a chuckle. In all his born years, no woman had ever told him that he was needy and emotional. Maybe that was because his exes had all been pretty needy themselves. Or maybe because right now he *was* needy and emotional.

He put his foot up on the first step and leaned toward her. "Can I give you some free advice?"

She drew her knees up and rested her chin on them, the gesture a pretty clear message that she didn't want anything from him. "Free advice is worth what you pay for it."

"Yeah, well, in this case maybe not."

"Sure. Go ahead. I have this feeling there's no way on earth I can stop you anyway."

"I spent years in Nashville, and the thing is… well…"

He paused a moment, trying to find the right words to warn her, to guide her, to give her what she needed to know. It wasn't that he wanted to discourage her. He wanted to keep her from breaking her heart. Nashville was the capital city of heartache.

"I've met dozens of girls like you," he continued. "Girls who've sung gospel in their hometown churches. Girls with pretty faces and killer bodies who *know* in their heart of hearts that one day someone is going to discover them as the next big thing in country music."

"For the record, Clay, I never sang in church, so get that right out of your mind."

"You didn't? Really?"

"No. I sang in chorus in high school. But not in church. Never in church."

"Okay, it's the same deal."

"So you're saying we're all a bunch of dreamers? That we—I—don't have what it takes?" He could hear the pain in her voice, even though she was trying hard to mask it.

"No, that's not what I'm saying at all. I'm saying I've seen dozens of girls who think that singing in church, or chorus, or in karaoke bars is the same thing as being a musician."

"So you don't think I'm a musician?" She was working herself up to angry now, and that was better.

"To be honest and totally frank, no. I don't think you're a musician. But you do have talent."

She didn't say a thing. She raised her head up off her knees and looked at him in the darkness. He could see a sliver of moonlight reflected in her eyes, and he wanted to lean down and kiss her—hard. Instead, he concentrated on telling her the God's honest truth. Because he had this feeling that it was the best thing he could do for her. Giving her the truth would be better than taking care of her, or taking her to bed.

"Honey, when you sang 'Amazing Grace,' it carried me away. Your voice has a haunted quality to it. A sweetness that's all backwoods and mountain hollows and illegal moonshine."

"A mountain voice?"

"Yes, ma'am. The kind of bluegrass voice that would have gotten you right into the Grand Ole Opry a generation ago, before pop invaded the country charts."

"But you said—"

"I said you had talent, and I mean it. And that talent isn't related to your bra size or the firmness of your backside. You have to respect that talent. It takes hard work to break into country music. Years of it, and even then, it's about the longest shot there is in the world. And even when you have the golden ring in your fingers, it can still slip away."

"Yeah, well, I'm a dreamer."

"Okay, darlin', you can dream all you want. But if you want to *do* something about it, then you better know every blessed word to 'I Will Always Love You,' as well as the words to the second verse of 'Amazing Grace.' If you want to make it in Nashville, you need to respect your voice and learn what material is right for you. 'I Will Always Love You' is a standard. It's been recorded by Whitney Houston, Dolly Parton, and LeAnn Rimes. You're not a country musician if you don't know that song by heart."

"Yeah, and I suppose you're just the man who's going to teach me the words, huh?" There was a deep cynicism in her tone that surprised him.

"No," he said firmly. "I'm done with Nashville."

She angled her head toward him. "Why?"

Clay shrugged. He was not about to share his tale of woe about Tumbleweed with this girl. "It's a rough business. And I have obligations here."

She blinked a couple of times, studying him in the dark for the longest time. "I accept your apology," she said after a long moment.

"You do, really?" He was surprised.

"Yes. I'm thinking maybe you're the first person I've ever met who has told me the truth. I mean everyone else just tells me they have a friend in Nashville, and if I'm willing to... well... you know."

"Yeah, I know." He balled up his fists at the idea of the guys who had led her on and taken advantage, including himself.

Clay leaned forward and put the flashlight on the step beside her. "Here, take this. I hate the idea of you sitting alone in the dark."

He backed away, feeling a deep-down longing and a foolish hope that she might invite him to sit with her on that step and let him teach her "I Will Always Love You." Or better yet, let him touch her. He longed for her touch. He could still remember the way she had touched him last night.

But she didn't invite him to stay. She looked down at her feet.

Well, he ought to have expected that, since he hadn't told her what she wanted to hear. And besides, she wasn't what he needed. What he needed was some professional help from Miriam Randall, matchmaker extraordinaire.

Chapter
7

All right, let's try this one more time," Agent Hannigan said as he shoved the eight-by-ten glossy photograph of the Cambodian Camel into Woody West's face. "Where did you stash the necklace?"

Woody stared down at the photo feeling hollow and scared. Freddie the Fence, Woody's employer, was not going to be happy about this turn of events. Freddie was the largest handler of stolen property in the Southeast, and he didn't tolerate screw-ups. Being hauled in and questioned by the FBI about stolen property classified as a screw-up of major proportions.

"I told you," Woody said, looking up at Hannigan. "I never seen that necklace before in my life."

"Who messed up your face?" the cop asked.

Woody closed his puffy eyes. He was not about to explain that he had a thing for playing the ponies and had run up twenty Gs in gambling debts to Carlos the Colombian, a well-known Florida loan shark, who now wanted his money back with interest.

Freddie the Fence would not be amused to learn that Woody was into the Colombian for all that money. And Freddie wouldn't be happy to learn that the Colombian's goons had caused Woody to lose Mary and the stolen property she was carrying. Woody was dead if he didn't find Mary and that necklace, soon.

"Look, you guys," Woody said, trying to sound nonchalant. "You don't have squat to hold me here—unless it's a crime to have a broken nose."

"Woody, Woody, Woody," Agent Wilkes said in a deep baritone. "C'mon, we know you're a transporter for Freddie the Fence. You tell us where we can find the necklace, and we'll cut you a break. Okay?"

Woody looked across the interrogation room at Agent Wilkes. He was a big dude with blue-black skin and a smile as wide as Texas. He was playing good cop.

"I don't have a clue what you're talking about," Woody replied.

Hannigan reached into his jacket pocket and pulled out a scrap of leopard-print fabric. "Okay, so why don't you tell us about these?" He dropped the item onto the eight-by-ten photo of the Cambodian Camel.

Woody stared down at a pair of Mary's thong undies. They were pretty hot, for a nice girl like Mary. Woody was starting to think how maybe he should have tried harder to get into Mary's panties. The leopard print was kind of a surprise.

But the truth was, Woody hadn't brought Mary along on this transport job for the fun of it. Freddie had told him to take Mary to Nashville as part of Woody's cover. Freddie had handed Woody that necklace and told him to give it to Mary and tell her it was for luck. Woody had no idea that stupid thing was worth anything. It looked like a piece of crap from Kmart.

Freddie had also given Woody a plain white envelope that he was supposed to deliver to someone in Nashville. Woody had naturally assumed that the stolen property was in the envelope, not hung around the neck of a hairdresser, who moonlighted as a waitress, with dreams of being a country singer.

Did Mary know the necklace was priceless? That was an uncomfortable thought.

Woody looked away from the underwear. "Pretty kinky," he said to Hannigan. "I took you for a granny pants kind of guy."

"Quit stalling. You know darn well we found these in a suitcase in the back of your car."

Woody shrugged. "So it's a crime to have a suitcase in my car? Since when is transporting ladies' underwear across state lines a federal offense?"

"Who is she, Woody?" Wilkes asked.

"Who is who?"

"Look, we know you walked into the Dew Drop Inn with a woman. Don't be stupid. You're in a lot of trouble. It would help if you could tell us where she went."

"I have no clue." It was the first honest thing Woody had said since the FBI had stormed his hotel room that evening. Mary had ditched him at the Dew Drop Inn right after the Colombian's thugs had shown up, broken his nose, and forced Mary to withdraw two thousand dollars from her checking account to cover the weekly interest on the twenty Gs Woody owed the Colombian.

"Look, you guys, you don't have anything on me. Why don't you just let me go?" he said.

Wilkes and Hannigan exchanged looks that Woody didn't trust. "All right, Woody," Wilkes said. "But if you think for one second you're home free, you need to think again."

He knew that. Only Mary Smith and the Cambodian Camel could get him out of this fix. He had to deliver the goods to Nashville so Freddy the Fence would wire the thirty thousand into his checking account. He had to have that money before the Colombian did something permanently bad to his body—like sink it in the Gulf of Mexico.

Woody looked down at the glossy photograph of the Cambodian Camel. "How much you say this thing is insured for?"

"Several million."

"Holy crap. It looks like something you could buy at Value Mart."

"Yeah, well, it's supposed to be a thousand years old."

Woody looked up at Hannigan. "Really?"

"Yeah, Woody. And don't act so dumb. The Camel was stolen from Oliver Cromwell Jones's collection of Asian artifacts a week ago."

"Asian? Do they have camels in Asia?"

"Don't be stupid, Woody."

"No, sir. I am truly sorry that I can't help you out. Now, if you don't mind, I'd like the keys to my car so I can be on my way."

So I can find Mary Smith, get that necklace back, and pay the Colombian off before he breaks my head.

For as long as Clay could remember, Miriam Randall had worn red Keds and rhinestone-studded eyeglasses that magnified her dark brown eyes and made her look like Mr. Magoo.

Early Friday morning, she sat in a ladder-back rocking chair on the front porch of her Queen Anne Victorian, keeping her eyes on her nephew, Dash, who was keeping his eyes on Miriam's husband, Harry, as the old codger fired up a chain saw and attacked a fallen branch in their front yard. Clay sat on the porch railing keeping his eye on all of them.

"Dash, honey, you tell Harry to stop, now, before he cuts off something important," Miriam directed.

Dash leaned on his cane and gave his aunt one of those looks that said *No way am I getting on the wrong side of Uncle Harry*. At ninety, Harry Randall was the original grumpy old man.

Miriam shook her head and turned back toward Clay. "I don't suppose you could convince Harry to let *you* saw up that branch?"

"Ma'am, I've already made the offer and had my head taken off for it—figuratively, that is," Clay said.

She nodded. "I suppose I should be happy he's too stubborn to let anyone touch his yard. Maybe he'll be too stubborn to die. What do you think?"

Clay's heart lurched sideways. Harry was older than dirt, and no one lives forever—not Harry Randall or Uncle Pete. "I hope so, Miz Miriam," he said aloud.

"Uh-huh, you hope, but you don't have any hope. I can see that plain as day." She pointed a crooked finger at him.

She shifted her weight in the chair. "So what can I do for you, Clay? I got a feeling this isn't a social call." One white eyebrow rose as she gazed at him in anticipation. Miz Miriam might be in her eighties, but those eyes of hers looked not a day over thirteen and full of mischief.

Clay breathed in the scent of the pine needles that the storm had ripped from their moorings. Then he took off his Stetson and looked down at it for a moment. "Ah, well, this is pretty awkward."

Miriam giggled like a little girl. "I declare, Clay Rhodes, are you here seeking professional assistance?"

Clay clamped down on his back teeth. When put in those terms, it sounded pathetic. "You know, I think maybe I'll just—" He started to get up.

"Sit down, Clay. So you're looking for a wife, huh?"

He sat down. "I swear, Miz Miriam, if you tell my momma I will personally—"

"Honey, unlike Lillian Bray, I am the soul of discretion."

He shook his head. "I am a fool, you know that?"

"Aw, sugar, I'm not going to say a word to anyone."

"Then how are you going to come up with a list?"

"A list?"

He looked down at his hat and twirled it around in his hands. "You know, a list of eligible bachelorettes. I'm looking for a mature woman, say thirty-three or so, who wants to—"

"Clay, it doesn't work that way." Miz Miriam leaned forward and snagged the hat right out of his hands. She tossed it on the empty rocking chair beside her.

"What do you mean? I thought matchmakers introduced single people to one another."

Miriam shrugged. "Well, I reckon professional matchmakers do that sort of thing. Amateurs will do that as well, without much success. And then there are those newfangled Internet dating services. But I'm not a professional, an amateur, or a newfangled matchmaker."

He tried not to grin. "So how come everyone in the county says you're the best matchmaker around?"

She shrugged. "Word of mouth?"

He laughed aloud. "No, Miz Miriam, I mean—"

"I know exactly what you mean, son. I'm not senile." She shook her finger at him. "The fact is, I have this reputation, and I don't deserve it. I don't *do* anything."

"You must do something. Momma says you're never wrong."

She shrugged and leaned forward as if she were imparting some great big secret. "Well, see, it's like this. Sometimes I'll see a man and a woman, you know, and it will just come to me that they belong together. When that happens, I'll let them know—directly or indirectly. Mostly indirectly, because in my experience most folks don't recognize their soulmates when they meet up with 'em or are told about it. Mostly folks have to come to understand the truth on their own, I've found."

"Soulmate?" His voice hardened.

"Clay, I don't help people settle. I don't even make matches—the Lord does that. What I do, is help people see the Lord's plan for them."

"Christ," he muttered.

Miriam frowned up at him. "Clay Rhodes, you know better than to take the name of the Lord in vain. Your momma would be ashamed of you."

"Yes, ma'am." He hopped down from the porch railing. "Well, I reckon I best be—"

"Sit down. We are not finished."

"Miz Miriam. I'm pretty sure you haven't seen my soulmate hanging around Allenberg County."

She shook her head. "No, son, I'm sorry. But I've been looking for a long, long time for her."

Clay almost choked as he leaned back on the railing again. "For goodness' sake. You've been looking? For how long?"

Miriam pulled herself up a little straighter in the chair. "Oh, since you were pretty young. I keep an eye out for all the young, single folks of Last Chance. I believe that if I can help the young 'uns find happiness, I just might be able to save this town."

He said nothing. The woman was senile, pure and simple.

"It's been my opinion for some time," Miriam continued, "that your soulmate is not a native of Allenberg County."

"I see." Clay stood up again. He really needed to escape. This had been a dumb idea.

"Sit down and listen," Miriam directed, but Clay remained on his feet, and Miz Miriam continued, "I know what you're thinking. You're thinking that the road to true love is a rocky one filled with heartache and broken dreams. But, son, we never know what God has planned for us. You need to tell yourself that every broken heart is like a sign leading you to the true love of your soul."

"Thanks, Miz Miriam, this has been enlightening in the extreme." He collected his hat.

"Clay, I know you don't believe me, but you never know when the love of your soul might blow in on the nine-thirty bus from Atlanta. In fact, I'd say it's a distinct possibility that the love of your soul will arrive on that bus."

Disquiet settled like a dead weight in his gut. Was the old lady sending up smoke signals, or was she just crazier than a loon? He had this awful feeling that it was the former.

Since Lillian Bray, the chairwoman of the Christ Church Ladies Auxiliary, kept twenty-four-seven tabs on the comings and goings at the Peach Blossom Motor Court, Clay reckoned that just about every member of the Ladies Auxiliary knew he had spent Wednesday night down there with Jane. And since Momma had hired Jane, he figured they all knew she had come on the nine-thirty bus from Atlanta.

Man oh man, those gals were like a bunch of spiders, spinning their web and catching unsuspecting single people. He was in some serious trouble if Momma and Miz Miriam both wanted to match him up with some stranger who showed up on the nine-thirty bus from Atlanta bearing two forms of ID and only five dollars in her purse.

Well, if Jane Coblentz was the best Miriam Randall could do for him, then he might just have to rely on Ray Betts and his survey of the unmarried women of Last Chance.

He cleared his throat and slapped his hat on his head. "Well, thank you for that, Miz Miriam. Y'all take care, now. I'll stop by on my way home from work with a chain saw and take care of that branch out back."

"That's neighborly of you." She smiled like a cherub and winked up at him. "The nine-thirty bus from Atlanta, Clay. You just keep your eye on that."

"What?"

She winked behind her upturned glasses. "You heard me. You just watch the bus, and the Lord will take care of the rest."

• • •

Early Friday morning, Ricki Burrows pushed her VISA card across the counter to the ticket agent at the Atlanta Greyhound terminal, hoping she hadn't maxed it out.

Her heart pounded as the agent ran the transaction. Thank goodness the charge went through, because she didn't actually have enough cash for the fare. Unless she hocked some jewelry or her luggage.

She tried to calculate the net worth of the jewelry and luggage, but the numbers got muddled in her head. Where was Ray Betts when you needed him?

"That's one ticket to Last Chance," the agent said. "Bus leaves in fifteen minutes."

She walked through the bus station wondering just how she had ended up in this place.

Easy answer: She was over thirty, and her boobs had started to sag. Randy had a thing for perky boobs. She should have known Randy would lose interest.

But, really, while having saggy boobs was horrifying, it wasn't nearly as devastating as discovering that your husband of fifteen years had not only left you for a girl of eighteen, but he'd taken all his assets with him—right out of the country.

That was bad.

But then discovering that the assets he had absconded with didn't actually belong to him—well, that was worse.

And having the IRS pretty much seize everything except for her luggage and a few pieces of not-very-expensive jewelry was just about the worst thing that could happen to a girl.

All of which explained why she found herself standing here handing her Louis Vuitton luggage to a *bus* driver.

Her return to Last Chance was going to be ignominious. Well, at least Momma and Daddy were gone. She wouldn't have to crawl home in defeat. Not that she was actually crawling home, or anything.

The only reason to return to Last Chance was to find Clay Rhodes, who was reportedly hiding out there.

Ricki had adored Clay once, even if she *had* broken his heart when she left him for Randy. Well, who could blame her? Randy Wilson was a rich record producer, and Clay was a wannabe.

But Clay wasn't a wannabe anymore.

According to the news on the street, Clay Rhodes was just about the hottest songwriter on Music Row. The songs he'd written for Tumbleweed's first album had taken the group platinum and earned them an invitation to the Grand Ole Opry.

Of course, Clay had missed out on that last bit. Everyone in Nashville knew the sordid story of how Tricia Allen had dumped Clay for Chad Ames, Tumbleweed's lead singer, a turn of events that had resulted in Clay's leaving Tumbleweed just as the band took off on the country music charts.

With all that heartbreak—losing his girl and his band in one fell swoop—Ricki figured Clay would be looking for some comfort. And Ricki aimed to be it.

Because, looking back on her life, she had to say that the only man who had ever treated her with even the smallest amount of respect had been Clay Rhodes.

Ricki wanted him back. She wanted to start over with a man who wouldn't care whether her boobs continued to sag. Besides, if the gossip was right, Clay was racking up a fortune in royalties for the songs on Tumbleweed's first album. It sure did look like Clay had made a success of himself, despite her daddy's predictions to the contrary.

She could kick herself. She should have married him when he'd asked all those years ago. What on earth had she been thinking?

At precisely eleven o'clock on Friday morning, Miriam Randall arrived for her weekly appointment at the Cut 'n Curl. Jane took one look at the old lady, with her white hair carefully done up in crown braids, and wondered why she had bothered to come. After all, the other women who had arrived that morning had all required shampoos, trims, and sets.

Millie Polk sat under a dryer reading the latest June Morning historical romance, *Destiny*. Lillian Bray sat in Ruby's chair, her hair halfway done up in curlers while Ruby continued to work on it. And Thelma Hanks sat in front of Jane, hair coloring on her head, admiring the nail color Jane was painstakingly applying.

"I declare," Mrs. Hanks said in a low, slow, drawl. "I do like this 'Pinkaholic' ever so much better than the 'Girly Pink.' Don't you, Lillian?"

Lillian glanced without turning her head. "To tell you the truth, Thelma, I can't tell much difference."

"Well, it's deeper and has a pearly shine to it." Thelma smiled at Jane. "And, Ruby, I'm so glad you finally got someone who knows how to do nails."

"That was not my doing. The Lord sent her."

"Amen to that," Miriam Randall said as she shuffled in through the door, leaning on her cane. It was almost as if the old lady had timed her entrance in order to say this ridiculous and embarrassing thing.

Ruby, along with Mrs. Polk and Mrs. Hanks, turned toward Miriam Randall, each of them making a little head bob, like court ladies showing deference to their queen. That was kind of confusing, because until Miriam Randall arrived, Jane could have sworn that Lillian Bray was the leader of the pack.

But apparently not. Jane immediately reshuffled the pecking order. These ladies genuinely *liked* Miriam Randall. Lillian, they were scared of.

It was hard not to like Mrs. Randall. She wore red Keds slip-ons, a pair of white ankle socks, a flowered polyester shirtwaist dress in a garishly purple print, and a pair of bifocals that looked like they ought to be on exhibition in a 1950s museum. In short, this newcomer with the incredible sense of timing and the unique fashion sense was one of a kind.

Miriam walked past the appointment desk and ensconced herself in the one remaining seat as if she owned the place. She gripped her cane in a pair of arthritic hands and studied Jane with a pair of inquisitive brown eyes that looked years younger than the rest of her.

"Jane, meet Miz Miriam Randall," Ruby said. "She used to be the chairwoman of the Christ Church Ladies Auxiliary before she retired a couple of years ago. She comes every Friday for a manicure. You can start on her when you're finished with Miz Hanks."

Thelma Hanks said, "Miriam, I'm sure you'll be happy. She's so much better with an orange stick than Michelle ever was."

The little old lady smiled at Jane, and her apple cheeks

plumped up. "So," she said in a girlish voice, "I under-stand you arrived a few nights ago on the nine-thirty bus from Atlanta, right before Hurricane Jane hit."

Jane dropped her gaze to Mrs. Hanks's nails. "Yes, ma'am."

She immediately felt the collective gazes of every one of the women in the shop directed at her. She had a feel-ing they all knew she'd spent the night with Clayton P. at the no-tell motel. It was a mystery, really, why they had decided not to run her out of town on a rail.

Although, she had to admit, Mrs. Bray had not been very friendly to her. But the others all seemed quite interested—too interested, really—in her background.

Mrs. Polk took that moment to pop her head from beneath the dryer and said, "Miriam, I heard Bill Ellis had dinner last night with Jenny Carpenter. Can you imagine? That woman must be ten years older than he is, and she's a Methodist. A Methodist? Please tell me that she's not the one for him."

Lillian snorted. "Don't you worry about Bill. He's only being lured by her apple turnovers. You know how Jenny wins the pie-baking competition every year at the Watermelon Festival."

"That may be, but you know what they say about the path to a man's heart. I like Jenny well enough, but she's too old for Bill. He needs a young wife who can give him children. And certainly not a Methodist. Isn't that right, Miz Miriam?"

Miriam's cherubic smile never wavered. "Well, I'm pretty sure Bill's going to end up with a woman who can cook."

"You can't be serious." This from Lillian. "Not a Methodist, Miriam."

The old lady shrugged. "Lillian, it's not my place to question the Lord's plan. The fact is, Bill Ellis is a man who enjoys a piece of pie from time to time. It's one of his more endearing qualities."

Jane tried hard not to laugh at this. Gossip came with beauty shop territory, like unwanted advances came with waiting tables at the Shrimp Shack.

Last night, Jane had nothing in her cupboard, a limited wardrobe, and no electricity. Now, thanks to Ruby Rhodes, she had groceries and a box of hand-me-down clothes from Stone's late wife. The power company had restored the electricity, allowing her to start her new job. And, by the end of the day, Jane would have some spending money. Ruby had already promised to pay her on a daily basis for the first week while she got herself settled.

The Universe was providing the things Jane had tried so hard to manifest. Of course, Ruby Rhodes seemed to be the author of most of this largesse. And that said a lot about Ruby. Jane could get to like the woman, even if she was a member of the God squad.

Jane finished Mrs. Hanks's manicure just about the time Ruby finished Mrs. Bray's set. Mrs. Bray went under the dryers, Mrs. Hanks had the dye washed off her hair and moved to Ruby's workstation, and Miriam Randall eased herself into the chair across from Jane.

Jane took the old lady's hand in hers. Miz Miriam had surprisingly warm hands for one so old. Her joints were misshapen with arthritis, but even so, her nails bore the evidence of a professional manicure.

She set Miriam's right hand to soaking and began removing the polish and exfoliating and moisturizing her left.

"So," the old lady said in a near whisper. "I hear you come from West Virginia."

Boy, the news did travel fast, didn't it? "Yes, ma'am. Originally. I've been living in Florida the last seven years or so."

"And what brings you to Last Chance?"

Well, there was no real answer to this, was there? She was tempted to tell Miriam that it was none of her business. But that wouldn't stop the old lady from being nosy. "Just traveling around, seeing the South." It was a bald-faced lie, and her cheeks flamed the minute the words left her mouth.

Miriam Randall said nothing in response, but the slight tension in her hands was enough for Jane to know Miriam hadn't bought her line. Jane worked in silence for a while, pushing back Miriam's cuticles.

"You know, sugar," the old woman said, leaning in and speaking in an even quieter voice, "I reckon sometimes it's hard to stay on the right road when you're traveling around. I mean, the road signs can be so confusing at times."

Jane hesitated. What was the old woman talking about? She looked up into those anachronistic eyeglasses. Miriam's dark brown eyes blinked and a little knowing smile hovered at the corners of her mouth. "Yes, ma'am," she said. The customer was always right, wasn't she?

"I mean," Miriam continued. "Sometimes it's just easy to get lost and end up on a road with a lot of potholes and detours."

"Yes, ma'am, it is."

"I reckon Last Chance looks a lot like one of those detours, doesn't it?"

Jane stopped filing and returned her gaze to the old lady. The woman had a real smile on her lips now, and her apple cheeks had dimpled right up. A girlish glint shone in her eyes as well, like she was up to mischief and enjoying every moment of it.

"It's all right, sugar, you don't have to lie," Miriam continued. "I know very well Last Chance isn't exactly a destination spot for young folks."

"No, ma'am, it isn't. But sometimes the Universe takes us places for reasons of its own. It's up to us to make the best of what's handed to us."

Miriam chuckled. "Well, amen to that. But I reckon I would say that the Lord works in mysterious ways."

Jane said nothing to this and went back to filing and listening vaguely to the conversation that Ruby and Thelma were having about a bake sale for the Volunteer Fire Department.

"You know," Miriam said several moments later, "you shouldn't just settle."

"Settle?"

"That's what I said, sugar. You shouldn't just try to make the best of a bad situation. That's settling. The Lord expects more of you."

"Yes, ma'am." To Jane's knowledge the Lord had never expected anything of her. The Lord had been absent from her life, which was just fine with her.

"No, I mean it. You should ask for more."

"More what?"

"More of everything. You should ask for what you want," Mrs. Randall said, and for an instant she sounded like one of Jane's self-help tapes. But that wasn't possible. Miriam was a church lady. And, in Jane's experience, church ladies usually didn't understand the concept of positive affirmations.

"Yes, ma'am," Jane said noncommittally and went back to filing.

"What is it you want, Jane?"

Well, now, that was a zinger of a question. She stopped filing and looked up again. An absolutely avid look had stolen into Mrs. Randall's stare.

"I want what everyone wants," she said.

"And what's that?"

She wanted the bad stuff to take a left turn and leave her life permanently. She wanted a place to hang her hat and call home. She wanted someone there who cared about her.

Oh, yeah, and she wanted to sing. But that was secondary to all the other stuff.

She didn't say all this aloud, though. Instead she shrugged. "Oh, you know, the usual stuff. Health and happiness." She let go of Miriam's hand and turned toward the box of nail colors and spoke before Miriam could pursue the conversation. "Now, Mrs. Randall, what color do you want this week?"

"Oh, I don't care. Red is usually what I get."

"Well, let's see, I've got 'Big Apple Red' and 'Thrill of Brazil.'" She pulled out the two shades.

"Oh, the 'Thrill of Brazil,' by all means." Miriam paused for a moment. "I've never been to Brazil, have you?"

"No, ma'am."

"And that's my point."

"What point?"

"You should be looking for the 'Thrill of Brazil,' sugar."

"Now, Miriam, don't you be telling my new manicurist that she should be taking off for Brazil. She's only just arrived in Last Chance. Let the girl catch her breath before you have her going on trips to foreign lands." Ruby looked up into the mirror. Her reflected gaze looked strangely worried, as if she had taken Miriam Randall's words literally.

"Oh, Ruby. Even Jane knew I was speaking figuratively. Didn't you, sugar?"

"Yes, ma'am."

Lillian Bray stuck her head out from under the dryer. "Did Miriam say something important?" There was a surprisingly eager look on Mrs. Bray's face.

"She just told Jane she should be looking for the thrill of Brazil."

"Brazil, really? You reckon she's going to take a trip soon?" Lillian asked, sounding as if Jane's departure from Last Chance couldn't come soon enough.

"No," Miriam said in a flat voice. "I declare, you ladies have no imagination. I was just telling Jane, in figurative terms, that she shouldn't settle. She should be looking for the whole Sleeping Beauty, Cinderella, Snow White she-bang, right down to the hero on the white charger—you know, like Sir Galahad."

Jane's hand moved involuntarily, and her brush grazed Miriam's cuticle. "Uh, there is no such thing, Mrs. Randall. Now look what you made me do with this foolish talk." She reached for a cotton ball.

"A knight in shining armor?" echoed Lillian Bray. "My goodness, Miriam, you must be slipping. You would have Bill Ellis married up to Jenny Carpenter, who is a Methodist and too old to bear his children. And now you're telling

Jane she should be looking for a Sir Galahad? Lord only
knows what she'll end up with." Lillian gave Jane a narrow stare down her long, pinched nose. She raised one
eyebrow, and Jane felt momentarily paralyzed.

Yup, Lillian Bray knew all about last Wednesday night
at the Peach Blossom Motor Court. That look pretty
much summed it up: A girl like her, who would give herself away cheaply like that, had no possible hope of ever
being rescued by a pure soul like Sir Galahad.

"Well, that's true," Miriam said.

"What's true?" Lillian asked. "Didn't you just say
that—"

"I know what I said, Lillian," Miriam rejoined. "I'm
not senile. The fact of the matter is that the Lord knows
who Jane will end up with. After all, it's the Lord's
plan."

Hoo boy. These church ladies were beyond belief. It
was time to cut this discussion off at the pass.

"Well, thanks for the vote of support, Mrs. Randall,"
Jane said. "But the truth of it is, the whole being-rescued
thing is a fairy tale. I'm smart enough to know not to go
looking for any kind of hero. I can take care of myself.
Now, you need to sit still so I can finish up your nails
without making any more mistakes."

She gave the old lady a friendly but firm stare. Miriam
met it with a knowing smile and a mischievous gleam
in her dark brown eyes. "I know you can take care of
yourself, sugar. The question is whether you can take
care of the crazy hero who's going to come to the rescue,
whether you want him to or not."

Chapter
8

Haley's school was closed on account of the fact that a tree had blown over and busted up the roof. Haley might have felt good about that—after all, Lizzy's school wasn't closed—but when Haley wasn't at school, the Sorrowful Angel would hang around and cry all the time.

That wasn't any fun. And it wasn't much fun spending the morning at Betsy Maxwell's house, either. But that's what Haley had to do, 'cause Granny had lots of customers on Friday mornings and needed to work, and Jane, the new babysitter named like the hurricane, needed to work at the beauty shop, too.

So Haley was stuck with dumb old Betsy until Betsy went to her piano lessons in the afternoon. Thank goodness there wasn't nothing wrong with the piano teacher's house, 'cause Haley didn't like to play Barbies that much, and whenever she was at Betsy's house she had to play Barbies all the time.

Mrs. Maxwell dropped Haley off at the Cut 'n Curl on the way to Betsy's lessons, and then Jane quit doing manicures, and the two of them decided to walk down to the school playground for a little while before they had to go meet Lizzy at her bus stop.

Jane didn't look any different from anyone else Haley had ever met, which was kind of surprising since last night Daddy and Granny had had a big fight about her being a floozy. They had hollered so loud that Haley had heard what they said all the way from Granny's kitchen to the living room, where she had been coloring. Granny kept saying Jane was an answer to her prayers. Daddy yelled back that he didn't believe in the power of prayer and didn't want a floozy looking after his children.

Daddy lost the argument on account of the fact that Daddy was a policeman and had to work a lot of hours, and Granny had said she was going to go on strike if Jane couldn't be the new babysitter. Haley didn't know what a strike was, but she figured it had to be like a lightning strike, 'cause Daddy shut up real quick. Haley was kind of scared of lightning.

So that's how Haley ended up being watched by a person who was a floozy and had seen the insides of the Peach Blossom Motor Court.

It was a red-letter day.

Haley figured this might be the only time she would ever get to figure out some important things. So she looked up at Jane and let her question fly. "What's the insides of the Peach Blossom look like?"

"It looks like any old motel, I guess," Jane answered without even getting mad.

Jiminy Christmas! Grownups never answered questions like that, ever.

"Miz Bray says a good girl never wants to see the insides of that place. Is it scary?" she asked.

Jane laughed and shook her head. "No, it's not scary. I guess Mrs. Bray keeps an eye on the place, huh? I guess that's why she says things like that to little girls like you."

"I don't rightly know, but Miz Bray knows you saw the insides, 'cause she called up Granny and told her. And then Miz Randall called, and Granny got mad."

"What?" Jane stopped walking. "Would you say that again?"

Haley turned and looked up at Jane. She had a nice face. If she was a floozy, then floozies must not be so bad.

"Like I said," Haley began. "Miz Bray called Granny and told her all about how Uncle Clay had been inside of the Peach Blossom Motor Court with a floozy, and how that made Uncle Clay no good to be the organist at church anymore. Granny got really mad about that. But then Miz Randall called and Granny wasn't so mad anymore. And then Granny decided you were the answer to her prayers."

"Because Mrs. Randall said so?"

Haley shrugged. "Don't know." She squinted up at Jane and asked the main question on her mind. "So, what is it about the Peach Blossom Motor Court that turns a person into a floozy?"

Jane looked mad for a minute. And then she turned and headed down the sidewalk. "Come on, Haley, this conversation is officially over."

Haley followed with a determined stride. "Why?"

"Because your question was not polite. No one likes to

be called a floozy. So you'll just need to ask your granny about this stuff...when you're older."

Haley let out a deep breath. "That's what everyone says."

Jane didn't say anything else, and Haley knew she'd messed up her one chance. Jane was mad.

"Jeepers, I'm sorry," Haley said, on account of the fact that Granny always told her to apologize if she ever did anything impolite. Not that she completely understood why Jane was mad or anything. But she kind of liked Jane.

"It's okay," Jane said.

The Sorrowful Angel took a break from crying and nodded like she approved of the apology. Haley took that as a sign and spent the rest of the walk to the playground playing tag with the Sorrowful Angel. Once they reached the playground, Jane sat down on the bench and plugged up her ears with earphones, which put an end to any further conversations.

There wasn't much to do, so Haley made her way to the deserted swing set and took a seat and watched the group of workmen cutting up the tree that had mashed one whole corner of the school, including Miss Jackson's second-grade classroom. The Sorrowful Angel hovered nearby watching Haley watch the men, like maybe the Angel was like a babysitter herself.

Haley pushed herself off and started to pump the swing and sing "Swing Low, Sweet Chariot," which was her favorite thing to sing when she was swinging. A little later, Uncle Clay came down the path, headed for Jane. He had something in his hands.

Haley stopped singing but continued to pump the

swing as Uncle Clay waited for Jane to take the earphones out of her ears. He started talking to her, and jeepers, he talked a long, long time. Jane didn't say nothing; she just nodded. Haley wished she could hear what Uncle Clay was saying. He might be talking about stuff that would explain what a floozy was.

Uncle Clay gave Jane something that looked kinda like a CD player. And then Uncle Clay turned and walked back toward town. Jane started rubbing her eyes, like maybe she was crying, and Haley started to wonder if maybe Uncle Clay had been impolite and called her a floozy to her face, too.

Great, that was all Haley needed, a Sorrowful Angel and a sorrowful floozy. She looked up at the men boarding up broken windows and hammering on the caved-in roof of the school.

Jesus, Haley prayed fervently, *please help me. All this sorrow is starting to wear me down.*

"Look what I found," Haley Rhodes said as she scampered into the sitting room of the little apartment above the Cut 'n Curl. It was late afternoon on Friday, and dusk was settling over Last Chance. Downstairs in the shop, Ruby was finishing Lessie Pontius's weekly wash and set.

Jane pulled the earphones from her ears. "What?"

"Look what I found," Haley repeated as she swung Woody's stupid piece-of-crap necklace in front of Jane's eyes. Recognition rocked through Jane, followed by a shiver of revulsion. How had the kid found *that* thing?

"Can I have it?" Haley tipped her head and gazed up at Jane out of a pair of precocious brown eyes. Haley hadn't inherited her dark eyes or curly blond hair from her pa, that was for sure.

Lizzy Rhodes, on the other hand, was a dead ringer for her pa. She looked up from her book, her green eyes staring daggers at her little sister. "Haley, you know it's not nice to ask for things that aren't yours. Put the necklace back."

"No. You're not the boss of me." Haley stuck her nose in the air and turned back toward Jane. "So, can I have it?"

"Honey, why'd you snoop through my trash?" Jane asked.

Haley gave Jane another innocent-little-me smile. The kid was a danger, really. "Oh, I wasn't snooping, I swear," Haley said. "I was just throwing away the empty juice boxes, and when I looked in the garbage can, I saw the necklace. It's real pretty."

"You pulled that thing out of the trash? Ew." Lizzy wrinkled her nose. "That's gross." Lizzy was the antithesis of sweet little Haley. The teen was going through a serious Goth-libber phase, dressed in black jeans and an oversized T-shirt with the words "Feminist: A woman who respects herself" printed on its front. The shirt was so big and floppy it hid a figure that was somewhere between girlish and womanly.

"Lizzy's got a point," Jane said. "It's yucky to take things out of the trash."

"But it's not yucky. It's pretty. And if you don't want it, can I have it?"

Jane pondered whether it would be good or bad karma to let the child have a necklace jinxed by Woody West. "Why would you want that thing?"

The little girl took a deep breath and began rattling out an explanation. "Oh, I've been wanting a big-girl necklace for *so* long. I even prayed for one, even though I know it's not right to pray for things for yourself like that. But I promised Jesus that I would be good if He would find a way for me to have a pretty necklace like the one Jeremiah Jones gave Liz—oops." The little girl slapped both hands across her mouth and looked at her big sister with terror in her eyes.

Lizzy, who had been sprawled on the sofa, sat up and glared. "How d'you know that Jeremiah gave me a necklace? Have you been spying on me?"

Haley shook her head but kept her hands over her mouth.

"I'm gonna tell Daddy that you've been spying on me," Lizzy said.

Haley dropped her hands, her fear evaporating. "No, you're not."

"Am, too."

"If you do, he'll find out about Jeremiah, and he'll be mad, even if Jeremiah is the cutest boy in seventh grade."

Lizzy blushed a shade of red that rivaled Mrs. Randall's nail color.

Jane had to stifle a smile. "You know, Liz, you ought to think this through. Your pa will probably slap handcuffs on Jeremiah and haul him in for questioning. And he'll probably ground you."

A smug smile split Haley's adorable little face. Lizzy looked like she was ready for fratricide.

"You're going to tell him, aren't you?" Lizzy said in an angry voice. "Michelle, the last babysitter, was always tattling on us to Daddy."

"Me?" Jane pointed at herself and gave Lizzy a *what-who-me?* look. "I don't think so. I have a feeling Chief Rhodes won't listen to a thing I have to say.

"But," Jane continued, lacing her hands together in her lap and trying for her best babysitter-friend-mentor voice, "you ought to be on your guard against any boy who gives you a cheap necklace. Not that getting a gift from a boy is wrong. Just remember what it says on your shirt. You're worth more than a necklace, Lizzy, even if the necklace is made of diamonds."

Too bad Jane hadn't learned that lesson. Wednesday night was the perfect case in point.

Lizzy nodded like she actually understood.

Haley hurled her next verbal bomb into the short silence. "So," she said, "did you throw the necklace away because your last boyfriend was a peckerwood?"

"Haley!" Lizzy sounded totally grossed out. "Mind your manners."

"What? What did I say?" Haley managed to look confused, which only proved that the kid had a future as an actress. Haley was a danger to any adult who came within range.

"I think it was that word you used," Jane said.

"You mean *peckerwood*?"

Lizzy groaned.

"What?" Haley's voice ranged up into the higher registers.

"Not a good word, Hale," Lizzy said.

"Oh. But I heard Cousin Lisa call Jack a peckerwood right before she threw the diamond ring into the Edisto River at the Watermelon Festival last summer."

"Who's Jack?" Jane asked.

"He was Cousin Lisa's boyfriend. But he cheated on her," Lizzy said.

"And when I asked her why she'd thrown her ring in the river, Cousin Lisa said it was because Jack was a cheater and a peckerwood. So, did your boyfriend cheat on you? Is he a peckerwood?"

Jane didn't know whether to be angry or amused. She cleared her throat, determined to act the role of the mature babysitter. "*Peckerwood* is not a nice word. But if you must know, Woody was a low-down, rotten, peanut-brained weasel. And yes, I threw the necklace away because Woody was not a very nice person."

Lizzy giggled.

"What?" Jane asked, suddenly annoyed.

"I was just thinking. Woody the peckerwood?" She sank back into the couch and started to laugh.

Jane tried hard not to laugh with her, because little Haley was watching the two of them like a hawk. The kid was probably putting two and two together in ways that her pa and grandmother wouldn't be happy about.

"So can I have it?" the child asked once Lizzy had regained control of herself.

Well, what the heck, the kid had been manifesting that necklace, and the Universe had caused it to be in that trash can so she could find it. How much bad karma could there be?

"Sure, honey, you can have it."

Haley beamed up at her. "Thanks."

"And you," Jane said, turning toward Lizzy. "Don't let Jeremiah talk you into anything you don't really want to do, you understand?"

Lizzy nodded. "Yeah. I'm not dumb."

"Good. And if you have any questions you don't feel like asking your grandmother, you can ask me."

Haley looked up at her with a mutinous expression. "That's not fair."

"What's not?"

"You said you wouldn't answer my question about what the word *floozy* meant. You told me to ask Granny."

Busted. By a seven-year-old with an infallible memory bank. "Yeah, well, that's different."

"How?"

"'Cause you're a kid," Lizzy said. "When you get to be a teenager, you can ask questions like the ones Jane is talking about."

Haley gave Lizzy a mutinous look, then threw herself into a corner of the sofa where she proceeded to play with the cheap trinket Woody West had given Jane the day that she left Fort Myers hoping to find a better life.

Ha! Ha! Ha!

Jane could almost hear the Universe laughing at her.

Jane stood on her little stairway and looked up at the starry sky. She took a deep breath, filled with the unique aroma of the Deep South—the tangy scent of copper, overlaid with pine and a hint of something sweet, like jasmine.

She hunched her shoulders and closed her eyes and hummed a few bars of "I Will Always Love You." She had learned the words to the song this evening, after Lizzy and Haley had gone home with their grandmother.

She needed to thank Clay for the gift of the portable CD player and the CDs by Dolly Parton and Lee Ann Womack. She had been so flustered when he appeared at the school playground that afternoon that she'd hardly been able to speak. And he'd been kind of stiff and formal. And then she'd gone off and cried after he left. Just enough for little Haley to have noticed.

Oh, well, that kind of awkwardness and emotion was to be expected, wasn't it? She had jumped into the sack with him without even getting his name, and it would seem that everyone in town—even Haley and Lizzy Rhodes—knew about it.

Now that she had listened to Dolly and Lee Ann, she understood what Clay had tried to tell her last night. Their material fit her voice. She hated to admit that the man was right, but he *was* right. He had given her a positive plan to achieve her dreams. That was more than Woody had ever done for her with all his big talk about knowing people in Nashville.

She stepped down the stairway still humming "I Will Always Love You." It was after nine o'clock, and she had decided to head down to Dot's Spot, where she suspected folks wouldn't care if she had ever seen the insides of the Peach Blossom Motor Court.

She would thank Clay to his face, and then sweet-talk him into letting her sing "I Will Always Love You" when the band took a break. She had visualized the entire evening—the good ol' boys and rednecks would be impressed. And Clay would be impressed. And maybe the leader of the Wild Horses would ask her to do another number with them. She had it all planned out in her head, and she couldn't wait.

She left the apartment, walked down the narrow alley between the Cut 'n Curl and the doughnut shop, and was about to turn right on Palmetto Avenue when she heard the unmistakable whoosh of air brakes. She looked to her left, up the street toward Bill's Grease Pit, and sure enough, a Greyhound Motor Coach had just pulled to a stop. She checked her watch. It was nine-thirty.

She watched for a moment as a fabulously platinum woman with a figure like a supermodel stepped down onto the pavement. She wore tight designer jeans, a little cropped jacket fuzzy enough to be angora, and a pair of high-priced high heels with ankle straps that looked like a dominatrix's dream.

Blondie carried a Louis Vuitton handbag and a matching Pullman suitcase. She belonged in this picture the way the queen of England belonged at Wrestlemania. Why would a woman wearing Rodeo Drive chic come to this no-man's-land on a Greyhound bus?

It was an intriguing question. No doubt, Blondie was down on her luck.

Jane stepped into the shadow of the alley for a moment, watching like a voyeur. Forty-eight hours ago, she had stepped off that same bus, feeling that same down-on-your-luck feeling. Would Last Chance be as positive for Blondie as it had been for her?

Blondie pressed her lips together in a grimace as she surveyed the town. It seemed as if the woman wasn't happy to be here.

She began walking toward Dot's Spot, and Jane stepped further back into the shadows to let her pass. When she was more than half a block ahead, Jane dropped in behind her and followed her all the way down the street.

Ricki Burrows Wilson wore sprayed-on jeans, high-heel shoes, and some kind of fuzzy jacket in a puce yellow as she sashayed into Dot's Spot for the first time in almost seventeen years. She captured the attention of every male in the place, which wasn't all *that* surprising, since Ricki had always been able to capture the attention of the opposite sex.

But it was real interesting how fast Ricki lost those good ol' boys when Wanda Jane walked in right behind her.

And Clay, who was trying to play his fiddle and not objectify these two women, felt a little like déjà vu all over again. Hadn't he done this on Wednesday night?

God, his life was in some kind of rut.

Ricki cut a swath through the smoke and the tables and came to stand right in front of the stage looking up at him. She smiled that sultry smile of hers like it had been yesterday the last time they'd crossed paths. Like she wanted to roll back the years and start all over again— before she had smashed his heart into a million bleeding pieces.

He played his fiddle and looked down, trying to figure out how he felt about this situation. The first thing that crossed his mind was that Ricki had just gotten off the nine-thirty bus from Atlanta, and that Miz Miriam Randall had some kind of weird talent when it came to making matches.

And the second thing that crossed his mind was that Ricki was some kind of beautiful. He was not immune to that beauty or to the allure of the past. Was it possible that Ricki was his soulmate?

After all this time?

Well, that would be one hell of a discovery, wouldn't it?

When he was seventeen and ran off with her to

Nashville, he truly had thought she was the love of his life. He'd asked that girl to marry him when he was all of eighteen.

But he hadn't thought about Ricki in a long, long time. And certainly not since he'd fallen in love with Tricia.

God, she looked good. Maybe not as good as Wanda Jane, but good enough for a woman who was thirty-four.

Which made her mature. And that point was punctuated by the fact that Ricki's body was showing a little wear around the edges. Not that that mattered. He was above that kind of immature objectification.

Wasn't he?

She smiled up at him. He smiled back.

"I declare, that's Ricki Burrows," Dot said as she placed a Coke in front of Jane.

"And she is...?" Jane asked, trying not to expire from a lethal dose of curiosity, laced with the tiniest little bit of jealousy. Which was disappointing, because this afternoon, when Clay had given her the CD player, Jane had decided that all she wanted from Clay was friendship—not a repeat trip to the Peach Blossom Motor Court.

So why did she want to march over there and take Ricki by her very straight, very platinum hair and start a cat fight?

"Clay and Ricki were practically engaged back when they were seniors in high school," said the man sitting beside Jane. He was the same guy that she'd seen on Wednesday night—the guy with the Astros hat, the killer blue eyes, and the craggy face.

"I'm Dash Randall, by the way, and I've already heard all about you," he said with a little crooked smile.

"Are you related to Miriam?"

"Yes'm, she's my great-aunt. She's quite happy with her manicure."

"And I'm quite happy with my tip."

"I'm assuming that means the gratuity and not the marriage advice."

She blinked at Dash. "How did you...?"

He waved one large hand. "Oh, everyone knows about my aunt. She's considered the only real matchmaker in Allenberg County. Of course, she will tell you that she never meddles in anyone's business; she just reveals the secret plans of the Almighty." He winked.

Dottie chuckled. "So what did she tell you, darlin'?"

"She told me I should hold out for a guy masquerading as a knight."

"Well, that's a new one. Congratulations," Dottie said.

"Congratulations?"

"Yes, ma'am. What Dash has failed to tell you is that Miz Miriam is not only the main matchmaker in Allenberg County, she is never wrong."

"Never wrong about what?"

"About her predictions. If she says your soulmate is going to be a knight in shining armor, then you'll just have to get used to it, honey."

"You can't be serious."

"Oh, yes, she is," Dash said.

"So what has she predicted for you?" Jane looked up at him. Hard living seemed to be written there in the lines and crags of his face. This guy was certainly no knight in shining armor, that was for sure.

He snorted. "Aunt Mim knows better than to meddle

in my life." He turned and looked over his shoulder. "But she appears to be doing a good job of meddling in Clay's life. Just imagine Ricki Wilson coming back to town, Dottie. It's got the Lord's Plan written all over it, don't you think?"

"Hush up, Dash." Dottie ran a dishrag over the counter before placing another Coke in front of the big man. She looked over at Jane. "Clay and Ricki ran off to Nashville after graduation and everyone, including Miriam, figured Clay would do just like his older brother and marry his high-school sweetheart. But I reckon Ricki had other ideas.

"That girl broke Clay's heart. Ran off with some producer or something. She—uh-oh, trouble…" Dottie interrupted herself in midstream.

Jane looked over her shoulder in time to see Ray Betts come bopping through the door. He took one look at Jane, gave her his goofy grin, and made a beeline toward her.

"April," he said. "You're here."

Jane heard Dash groan under his breath.

"Can I buy you a drink?" Ray asked.

"Um, no, Ray, I already have a Coke." She gave him a careful smile. Jane had learned from Ruby about the head injury that left Ray brain-damaged.

The band went on break, and someone punched up some songs on the jukebox. That Tumbleweed song—"I Gotta Know"—was the first one that came up. Dottie put a beer in front of Ray.

"I declare," the bartender said as she leaned onto the bar with a dreamy look. "That song does something to me every time I hear it. It's about the most romantic thing I've heard in ages."

"Well I guess it's a good thing you like it," Dash said. "Seeing as Bubba Lockheart punches it up on the juke-box every five minutes. But that's only because Rocky Rhodes broke his heart."

"Rocky?" Jane said. "Don't tell me, this is another one of Clay's relations."

"His sister. She left town to go to college and in the process dumped Bubba—hard. Which explains why Bubba drinks too much and is a sucker for every sad country song on Dot's jukebox. I wish my aunt would get to work on him, but Aunt Mim says she has to wait on the Lord, and the Lord hasn't yet revealed what's in store for Bubba. If you ask me, the boy needs rehab first."

"You don't really believe that stuff, do you? I mean about Miriam?"

"Honey, I know it sounds far-fetched," Dottie said, "but what they say about Dash's aunt is true. She has a way of seeing things that is a little strange, if you ask me. Anyway, if she tells you something, you better resign yourself to it. I reckon the Lord is going to hand you a Sir Lancelot, whether you want him or not."

Jane didn't want a Sir Lancelot. All she wanted was a chance to sing "I Will Always Love You" for Clay. She looked over her shoulder just as Clay came down off the stage and gave the blond bombshell a full-body hug.

Heat rose inside her. Was she jealous or just flashing on how it had felt on Wednesday to be in his arms?

Wow, Clay was really snuggled up tight to the woman, wasn't he?

She turned around, disappointment hollowing out her middle. With Ricki over there smooching with Clay in public, Jane had zero chance of sweet-talking him into playing piano for her while she sang "I Will Always Love You." And now that Bubba had punched up songs on the jukebox, her plans for impressing everyone were unraveling like a worn-out sweater.

"Hey," Ray said in a voice that sounded like a child's as he followed Jane's gaze. "Ricki's here. Did you see, Dot? I haven't seen Ricki in seventeen years and three months."

"Yes, Ray, I saw," Dottie said, rolling her eyes in Jane's direction, as if in warning.

"She's perfect for Clay's list," Ray exclaimed with a wide-eyed look on his face. He pulled a piece of wrinkled notebook paper out of his jeans and took a pencil from his shirt pocket. He spread the paper on the bar, tried to press out the wrinkles with his hands, then licked the tip of his pencil and began to write.

Dottie studied the paper with a frown. "Ray, what are you up to?"

Ray looked up with a childish grin. "It's Clay's list."

"What list? And why does it have *my* name on it?"

Ray looked down. "Well, of course it does. You're one of the single white ladies of Last Chance, aren't you? And let me tell you, Dottie, you have scored high on all of the important tests."

"Ray?" Dottie's voice had taken on a dangerous tone. "What's this about?"

"Clay is looking for a wife, and I'm helping him," Ray said.

Jane choked on her Coca-Cola.

"*You're* helping him?" Dash asked as Jane gasped and hoped her beverage didn't end up coming out her nose. Dottie pressed a napkin into Jane's hand as she sputtered.

Meanwhile Dash leaned over, snatched the paper away from Ray, and began to read it, his eyebrows arching and his mouth curving up on one side. "Holy crap, boy, this is pretty impressive. You keep this up, and you'll be giving Aunt Mim a run for the money."

"Dash Randall, don't you encourage him, now," Dottie said, one fist on her hip.

Dash's gaze shifted toward Jane, who had stopped coughing. "I'm sorry, darlin', but your name doesn't appear on this, although your alter ego is here. What's this desirability index mean, Ray?"

"Oh, that's the score each lady gets on my survey." He turned toward Jane. "I'm sorry, April. You are a truly beautiful woman, but I'm afraid your desirability index is kind of low. On the other hand, aside from her age, Dottie is just about perfect, and she owns a bar, too. She gets bonus points for that."

"What?" Jane snatched the paper out of Dash's hand. It was a matrix of columns with names of women in the first column. The second column had comments about their good qualities, the third column comments about their bad qualities, and the fourth column was headed by the words "Desirability Index." Under this heading, each woman had a score. April's score was a three. Dottie's score was a fifteen. Betty Wilkins, the waitress at the Kountry Kitchen, had a score of eighteen with a note that her pies were just as good as Jenny Carpenter's.

Jane handed the ratty paper to Dot, who studied it for a long time with a neutral expression. Then Dottie handed it back to Ray with a gentle smile. "Ray, honey," Dottie said. "Clay didn't actually have anything to do with that list, now, did he?"

"We discussed it," Ray said.

"Uh-huh. He tell you to put Betty's name on it?"

"No, that was my idea."

"I see," she said in a gentle tone. The bartender turned toward Jane. "Well, honey, I reckon you can rest easy since only April's name is on it. Don't take it too personal."

"But she *is* April," Ray insisted.

Jane knocked back the rest of her Coke and turned around to look over her shoulder. Clay and Ricki sat at a table near the stage, with Clay leaning his whole body in toward Ricki, and Ricki leaning right back at him.

It was time to go. Her positive plans for the evening had just gone up in flames, proving that the Universe could and did screw up everything if given sufficient time.

"Well, I guess I better be going," she said, pushing away from the bar.

"So soon?" Ray asked, disappointment in his voice.

"Gotta work tomorrow." She smiled as sweetly as she could.

She turned and headed for the door, only to have Dash Randall call her back.

"Hey, Jane, wait up," he said. She turned, and Dash had already picked up his cane. Oh, great, this guy looked like a cowboy who'd been ridden hard and put away wet. He was a real-deal bad boy and in a whole different league from Clay, who, let's face it, was not really a bad boy at all, seeing as he drove a minivan, played organ at Christ Church on Sundays, and was apparently looking for a wife.

Something of her thoughts must have shown in her

face because the big dude smiled a crooked smile and said, "Don't worry, darlin'. I make it a point to give damsels in distress a wide berth. I ain't about to attempt any rescues, since I am mostly working on my own recovery these days. You are absolutely safe with me. I just need a minute, is all."

"Sure." She turned toward the door, trying hard not to watch Clay and Ricki as their heads got closer and closer together.

When Jane and Dash reached the sidewalk, Dash stopped. "I figured you might want to know about April, since Ray seems to think you're her."

Jane looked up at the big man. "Was April Ray's old girlfriend in high school or something? I mean before the car wreck. I heard all about the wreck today at the beauty shop."

Dash shook his head. "No, ma'am. If you must know, she's Miss April from the *Working Girls Go Wild* calendar from five or six years back. I'm afraid I gave Ray that calendar for Christmas one year, and we haven't heard the end of it. The woman in question is dressed like a firefighter, and she's wearing a pair of suspenders and a fire hat and not much more. No disrespect, honey, but if I were you, I'd take Ray's attention as a compliment."

Jane looked up at Dash and knew a moment of utter humiliation. She swallowed hard. "*Working Girls Go Wild?*"

Dash shrugged. "Don't take offense. He doesn't intend any."

Jane nodded and managed to smile in spite of the fact that her emotions had taken a tumble. "Well, thanks," she said. "I'll be heading home now."

She turned on her heel before he could say another word and before her phony smile faded into tears. The Universe had this way of spitting in her eye at the most inopportune moments.

Just when things were looking up and she was starting to feel positive, up popped the past like a bad penny. She was supposed to blow Clay away tonight by singing "I Will Always Love You." But instead, Clay was in there falling head over heels for his long-lost love, and she was out here wondering how long she might have before the narrow-minded folks in this one-horse town figured out that crazy Ray Betts had it right.

She *was* April.

Chapter
9

At two-thirty in the morning, Clay pulled his Windstar into the driveway of the small house on Baruch Street that he'd been renting for the last few months. It had two bedrooms and a single bath, with a screen porch on the back. It was just big enough for him, his portable piano, and his sorrows.

He unfolded himself from the driver's side, opened the passenger door, and gave Ricki his hand to help her down. As her fingers touched his, a flood tide of memories washed through him. She hopped down from the seat, filling his personal space with her heavy perfume.

Ricki might have arrived on the nine-thirty bus. And once, a long time ago, she might have lit up the moon for him. But tonight, for some reason, he just couldn't help comparing Ricki to Wanda Jane Coblentz. And right now, with Ricki standing there in the van's doorway, he just couldn't get Wanda Jane's scent out of his head. Or the crazy, immature way Wanda Jane had made him feel on Wednesday when she'd stood in that spot, and he'd given himself permission to go to hell and the Peach Blossom Motor Court.

Clay pushed that unwanted memory from his mind and tried with all his might to be positive about Ricki's return. She was, to some degree, the answer to his prayer. She was mature. She had some experience. She was definitely interested in rekindling old flames.

Ricki looked up at him and brushed her incredible breasts against him. He responded in a kind of mechanical fashion, proving that even at the age of thirty-four guys pretty much think with their gonads.

"I do appreciate you putting me up, Clay. I don't have anywhere else to go," Ricki said in that throaty voice of hers that had always given him hot flashes as a teenager. The funny thing was that Ricki, who had fulfilled every one of his teenaged fantasies, was falling short of the mark tonight.

While Jane had made him feel about sixteen on Wednesday.

And wanting to feel sixteen was a sure-fire sign that he'd reached middle age.

"It's okay, Ricki," Clay said, stepping away from her breasts. He yanked open the sliding door and pulled her rolling bag out of the back of the van. He slammed the door and headed up the path without looking back.

He heard Ricki close the passenger door and follow. Her stiletto heels sounded like hammer blows as she strode up the concrete walk. As he slipped his key into the front-door lock, Ricki pressed her hot little body up against his backside. Man, she still felt soft in all the right places.

The woman expected to take up where they'd left off

seventeen years ago. If he was still seventeen, he would probably take her up on the offer.

But he was thirty-four. And his mature brain had kicked in and sent up a number of warning flares. He had let himself go on Wednesday, and that had been disastrous. Ricki was definitely in the running to be his future mate, but that didn't mean he had to sleep with her the first night of her return to Last Chance.

He could wait.

He opened his door and turned on the light. "You can sleep in the guest room," he said.

She wrapped her arms around his middle. "The guest room?"

He turned and looked down at her. She wiggled her hips against him and smiled. "C'mon, Clay, you want me."

"My dick wants you. My brain is being cautious. So you get to sleep in the guest room."

"But—"

"Ricki, I'm not a fool. I know you came here because you have no place else to go. Everyone in Nashville knows what Randy did to you. And I'm truly sorry about it. I'll help any way I can. But—"

"Clay, I still have feelings for you." She pouted, and he remembered exactly how difficult it was to resist her.

"And I still have feelings for you. Some of them are not so happy."

Ricki pressed against his pelvis a couple of times. "And some of them, obviously, are. I'd say you were extremely happy to see me, Clay. We all know you've been nursing a broken heart for almost a year. Is that how long it's been since you got laid?"

He wasn't going to dignify that question with an answer. Besides, it hadn't been all that long, and, really, if he was looking for quickie sex, he would be seeking out Jane right at the moment. Because one time with that woman was actually not nearly enough.

"Ricki, I'm tired. It's two in the morning. I got up early to work at Pete's store. So if you don't mind, I plan to sleep on it. You do the same. As it is, the entire town of Last Chance will be gossiping about us tomorrow morning. And I expect the Ladies Auxiliary will be planning our wedding by late afternoon."

She laughed. "I could help you relax."

"I imagine you could, but I think I'd rather sleep on it, seeing as I'm a grown-up now and not a horny seventeen-year-old."

Clay turned away from his ex-girlfriend. He headed down the short hallway and opened up the linen closet and snagged a set of sheets and some towels. Then he opened the guest-room door. "Bed's in here. It isn't much, just a twin. Here's some sheets and towels. Make yourself at home. I usually shower in the morning. You can have the bathroom anytime in the evening or after I leave for work. Good night."

He tossed the linens on the bed and turned in the hallway, opened his own bedroom door, and gently closed and locked it behind him.

The lock was a kind of insurance. He could easily fall back into a relationship with Ricki. But for once in his life, he wasn't going to just fall into love, or lust, or whatever. He wasn't looking for a good time. He wanted the next woman to be the last woman he would ever make love to.

Clay was just settling down in his bed when the phone rang. At two-forty-five in the morning, a ringing phone could only spell disaster. Why was he so lucky?

He reached for his cell phone and pressed the talk button. "Hello?"

"Clay, this is Cousin Alex." Alex always referred to himself that way even though, technically, Clay and Alex were not related—by blood, anyway. "We have a problem."

"What?"

"Someone's broken into the store and stolen a thousand dollars. I'm calling to let you know that I called Sheriff Bennett. He's going to be coming round your place any minute."

As if on cue, a light shone through his venetian blinds as a car pulled into his drive, its tires crunching on loose gravel. "Why'd you call Billy Bennett, when the store's in Last Chance and in Stone's jurisdiction?"

"Well, Stone's down at the store. He's the one who discovered the broken glass. When he called me, I decided I better call Billy, because it's doubtful that your brother can be impartial."

"Impartial? You have to be kidding me, right? Bill Bennett is your cousin. How does that make *him* impartial?"

"All I know is, one thousand dollars is missing and besides me, Momma, and Pete, you are the only one who knows the combination to the safe. The safe was opened without any sign of being forced."

At that moment, the knock came on Clay's door.

"Alex, go screw yourself." Clay hit the disconnect button and took a couple of deep breaths before rolling out of bed and pulling on a pair of jeans.

Alex was, without question, the biggest a-hole in Last Chance, South Carolina.

It broke Jane's heart to leave the CD player and CDs behind. For some reason those gifts seemed less like charity than the box of old clothes. But she left all of it that morning. She put on her old clothes and walked up the street to the bus stop.

She stood outside Bill's Grease Pit, clutching a one-way Greyhound ticket to Columbia. She checked her watch; it was almost seven. The bus would be here in about five minutes.

She pressed her lips together, feeling the tears fill up her sinuses. She didn't want to leave. But she had no other choice. She couldn't bear thinking about what would happen when Ruby figured out the truth. And her heart wrenched every time she thought about Clayton P. figuring out that she was, in fact, Miss April in the *Working Girls Go Wild* calendar.

She had made a lot of bad choices in her life, starting with the doozy she'd made at seventeen. But she had recovered from those mistakes—at least until she allowed Woody West to sucker her.

And the main way she'd rescued herself was by posing for those photos. She had been eighteen years old, living in Florida, working at a fast-food place, and paying the rent had been a challenge. The only way to move up had been to find a better job, and that required financing her tuition to Beauty Schools of America. So those pictures, unfortunate as they might have been, had financed her future.

She knew the holy rollers in this little southern town

would never understand that. And, Wednesday night notwithstanding, she had a feeling Clayton P. might not understand, either. She didn't want to stick around to face that music. It would be better to leave now.

She looked down the deserted main street and knew a moment of deep longing and regret. A morning haze hung over the town and made it look mysterious and quaint. Last Chance, South Carolina, wasn't very big, and there were a few empty storefronts on Palmetto Avenue, but right then, looking at it through the morning haze, it looked like a safe place. In the last two days, Jane had found kindness here for the first time in a long, long time. She didn't want to leave, but she knew, firsthand, that kindness could turn in an instant. And she didn't want to have to go through that.

Jane swallowed hard, trying to look on the bright side. Her two days in Last Chance had been eye-opening. Thanks to Clay, she had a positive plan for getting herself to Nashville, instead of relying on some weasel like Woody. As soon as she found a job and could scrape together a few bucks, she would replace that CD player she had left behind and buy all of Dolly's CDs. She would learn that material, and she would get a regular gig with a country band instead of singing karaoke.

She only regretted that she hadn't thanked Clay face to face last night or had a chance to sing "I Will Always Love You" for him and the crowd at Dot's Spot. But maybe it was better this way, because Ricki was here now. And anyway, the man had settled down into the back of her mind the way winter settled into the Allegheny Mountains of her home. It would be a long, long time before she gave up his memory.

Chief Stony's cruiser appeared out of the haze and glided up the street in her direction. She had been here long enough to know there were only two members of the Last Chance Police Department, Stone Rhodes and his deputy, Damian Easley. Jane had the distinct feeling neither of these guys ever slept.

The Crown Vic coasted up the street and came to a stop right in front of her. Chief Rhodes got out and strolled around the car, squaring up his Stetson so it shaded his eyes—an unnecessary action, since he wore mirrored sunglasses and the sky was overcast. The firm set of his jaw raised gooseflesh all along her back and arms. This was not a "howdy, ma'am" visit.

"Leaving so soon?" he asked as he came to a halt in front of her and hooked his thumbs into his utility belt.

Jane shrugged. "I decided there might be better opportunities in Columbia."

A muscle twitched in his cheek. "Can I see your driver's license, please?"

Oh, crap. She would have to haul out her expired license and get a lecture from him. Although she didn't think there was any law against waiting for a bus with an expired driver's license. And getting a lecture about her expired license would be better than making him suspicious by handing him the one that said "Mary Smith" on it.

She opened her purse and noted how Chief Stone went on alert. Hoo boy, the guy was bracing himself as if he thought she might be carrying a concealed weapon. His demeanor put her on instant alert. Something was going down here, and she had this awful feeling that it didn't have a thing to do with the *Working Girls Go Wild* calendar.

Jane pulled out her wallet and handed him her license. The chief took off his sunglasses and put the wand through a loop on his shirt pocket. He studied her ID for a long time, and Jane's hands got wet, and her mouth went dry, and her Greyhound bus pulled up.

"Uh, that's my bus," she said. "Can I go now?"

He looked up, his green eyes deadly. "I don't think you're going to make that bus, ma'am." He looked over at the bus driver and waved him off. The Greyhound pulled out in a cloud of dust and diesel fumes.

"Your license is expired," he said.

"I don't drive much," she answered.

"I'm going to have to keep this."

She watched her ID disappear into his shirt pocket. She was in deep, deep trouble, even though she had never done anything illegal in her whole life.

"That was my bus you just waved off, you know. The Greyhound only comes through here once a day. And—"

"You mind telling me where you were last night after eleven o'clock?" he asked.

"I was at the apartment above the Cut 'n Curl."

"Alone?"

"Of course I was alone."

"So you don't have an alibi."

"An alibi for what?"

His shoulders raised and lowered a fraction of an inch. "Someone broke into Lovett's Hardware last night and made off with more than a thousand dollars in cash. It looks mighty suspicious that you're leaving town this morning."

She put her fists on her hips. She was not going to let

this guy push her around. She was innocent, and he'd just fixed it so she had to stay in town another day. "Are you trying to tell me I'm a suspect in a robbery just because I'm standing here waiting for a bus?"

"Ma'am, I'm going to have to ask you to come with me to answer a few questions."

"But that's absurd. I'm not—"

"Please do not make me cuff you, because I will."

The chief was serious. He thought she had knocked over the hardware store. "You think I robbed the store?"

The muscle in his cheek twitched again. "That's a possibility I haven't ruled out yet, but that's not why I'm taking you in for questioning."

He snagged her by the upper arm in a firm grip.

Jane dug in her heels and tried to resist. In the next instant, she found her cheek pressed up to the warm metal of his cruiser's hood and her right arm twisted back behind her back. It happened so fast that she didn't have an instant to get scared or to even feel any pain when Stone Rhodes slapped a pair of handcuffs on her.

"I told you not to resist. Resisting an officer of the law is not a smart move—not for a woman in your position, anyway."

"I have a right to know why you're doing this," Jane said in a voice that was surprisingly calm given the fact that she was terrified.

"Ma'am, you have the right to remain silent, anything you say can be used against you in a court of law…" Chief Rhodes continued his recitation of her rights. When he was finished, he pulled her away from the hood, opened the car's back door, and started pushing her down into the seat.

As the first instant of shock wore off, a million scenarios danced through her head. Woody had been found dead somewhere with her luggage in the back of his Coupe DeVille, and someone thought she had bumped him off. Only then she remembered that the luggage tags didn't say Wanda Jane Coblentz. They said Mary Smith. Maybe Clay had told Stone about the two different IDs.

Disappointment and something like despair hollowed out a place in her middle. She had known this feeling once before, in Lexington, and she had been running from that for the last seven years.

Clay pushed through the doors of the hardware store, then turned around and relocked them. He stretched out the kinks in his back and yawned. That couch in Pete's office was about as lumpy as a three-humped camel.

He needed a shower and a new lease on life.

Unfortunately, there were roadblocks in the way of those needs. He'd have to face Ricki for the shower, since she was crashing in the guest room of his little saltbox house on Baruch Street. Facing Ricki right now seemed like a monumental task.

And as for a new lease on life—well, that was not in the cards. Especially after last night, when Cousin Alex had accused *him* of stealing the thousand dollars from the hardware store.

Why would he do a thing like that? Clay wasn't wanting for money. He didn't even take a salary for helping out at the store. He was doing it for Pete and Arlene—a notion completely lost on Alex.

Well, at least the crisis at the store had saved him from the possibility of having Ricki climb into bed with him.

He wasn't sure he could resist her if she did a thing like that.

But Clay wanted to resist. Ricki couldn't be his soulmate, could she? A soulmate wouldn't run off with someone else, would she?

Well, the crisis at the store had been kind of a good thing, in that sense. It had given him distance from Ricki, in addition to this crick in the neck.

He chuckled out loud. "Shoot," he said to himself as he stretched his back a second time. "I'm starting to think like Wanda Jane, putting a positive spin on everything that happens."

He was hugely disappointed that he hadn't had a chance to talk or sing with Wanda Jane. Ricki, Ray, Dottie, and Dash had all conspired to scare her away before that could happen last night. But she was still here, so there was hope. And if he bought all that crap from Miriam Randall, then Jane was in the running for the position of his soulmate.

An adolescent anticipation clutched his gut. He was looking forward to catching sight of that little gal. And when he saw that dark hair, and those deep brown eyes, and those curves, his heart would do a little dance in his chest. It was going to take a whole boatload of will power not to find some excuse to pop into the Cut 'n Curl just to get a glimpse of her. Yup, soulmate or not, he was definitely in lust with Jane.

Clay turned from the door, and that's when he noticed Stony's cruiser up by Bill's Grease Pit. His big brother was handcuffing some poor soul who was laid out flat on the hood of his car.

Clay's mood improved some more. It sure did look

like Stone had nabbed the bad guy. Maybe his brother
had recovered the money, too, which would be good,
since Lovett's Hardware was holding on by its fingernails. It was comforting to know that Stony was on the
case—making an arrest right there in front of God and
everyone.

Which wasn't exactly a huge crowd this time of morning in Last Chance, but that hardly mattered.

His brother pulled the suspect back off the hood of
his cruiser, and Clay's heart slammed right up against his
windpipe. That wasn't some poor soul his brother was
manhandling. It was Wanda Jane. And this wasn't what
he'd had in mind for his first glimpse of her today.

Something deadly gripped his chest, and he took
off up the street. He arrived just about the time Stone
slammed the back door and locked Jane in.

"What in the hell are you doing?" Clay demanded.

Stone turned, squared his hat, and started walking
around the cruiser toward the driver's side. He said
nothing.

"Stony, answer me."

His brother stopped. "Look, Clay, this isn't your business, so just back off, okay?"

Clay looked down through the car's back window.
Jane was sitting there wearing the clothes she'd been
wearing last Wednesday night. Her face had turned the
color of ashes, and tears streamed down her cheeks.

She stared straight ahead, her hands cuffed behind her
back, looking just like a scared jackrabbit. Clay ducked
down and pressed his hand against the glass. She looked
up at him, visibly struggling against her emotions.

Wanda Jane had to be guilty of something. After all,

she carried two IDs, each with a different name. But somehow, he couldn't bring himself to believe she was a bad person. Down on her luck, on the run, in need of rescue—yeah, he could believe all those things. But she wasn't bad. She just needed some help.

He nodded down at her, trying to let her know he wasn't going to let Stone haul her off without trying to help her out of this jam.

He looked up at his brother, who was standing in the open doorway on the driver's side studying him. "Back off, Clay," Stone said. "We all know you collect needy people. But you don't need this kind of trouble."

"And what kind of trouble would that be?"

"In a word..." His brother's gaze narrowed. "Murder."

Chapter
10

Woody West strolled up to the ticket agent at the Atlanta bus station and prayed to God Almighty that he might turn up some sign of Mary Smith. The bus station was his last chance.

It was amazing how a broad as dumb and naïve as Mary could disappear so completely. In fact, the woman had disappeared so fast and so good that he suspected she might have scammed him. Maybe Mary wasn't as dumb or naïve as she appeared. Maybe she worked for Freddie the Fence, too, and knew from the get-go that the little jade necklace was worth millions.

He hoped not. If that were true, then he was a dead man. The Colombian was losing patience, and the only way Woody could pay off his gambling debts was to find Mary and the necklace and make the delivery Freddie the Fence had hired him to make.

So he'd spent the last twenty-four hours backtracking to the Dew Drop Inn and working his way outward in concentric circles. He'd turned up nothing, except an FBI tail, which he had lost last night around three in the morning. The bus station was a three-mile walk from the bar where he'd last seen Mary. He doubted she had walked all that way in spike heels, but he couldn't rule it out either.

"Can I help you?" the ticket agent asked.

"Uh, yeah," Woody said as he pulled out a creased photograph of Mary Smith—the one from the *Working Girls Go Wild* calendar. Man oh man, that girl had a set on her. Those little teeny-weeny suspenders covered up her nipples, but left everything else visible to the eye. "I'm looking for this woman. I think she might have bought a bus ticket to Nashville or Fort Myers sometime on Wednesday."

The man took the paper and studied it for a moment, his eyes going wide as he took it all in. "Don't reckon she was dressed like this, huh?"

"No, sir, she would have been wearing a little white tank top, a jean jacket, and a pair of jeans."

"High-heel boots? Big satchel of a handbag?"

Excitement clutched at Woody's gut. "Yep, that would be her."

The ticket agent handed back the paper. "You her boyfriend or something?"

"Or something."

"She run out on you?"

Woody dug deep in his pocket and pulled out his last twenty-dollar bill and slid it across the counter. "I'm her brother," he said earnestly.

The agent took the bribe. "Yeah, I seen her. She bought a ticket to Last Chance."

"A ticket to where?"

"Last Chance, South Carolina. I remember because she

was in a hurry, and it was one of the stops on the first bus leaving. She remarked that the place sounded hopeful, and I thought she must be nuts or a little slow on the uptake. Last Chance sounds like a place I wouldn't ever want to visit, even if it were the last place on the face of the earth."

Tricia waited until the ticket agent finished his conversation. She stepped up to the counter until her big belly brushed against the edge. Her belly seemed to be in the way all the time these days.

That thought left a pang of despair in its wake. The baby was in the way of more than just her reach. The baby was a definite roadblock to her happiness.

How could she have been so stupid? How could she have traded in a caring and responsible man for the likes of Chad Ames? Forget the fact that Chad made her heart go pitty-pat, or that the man had lit her up in bed, or that she loved him with all her heart.

All of that was immaterial.

Chad Ames wasn't father material. In fact, he'd said as much to her face last night. He wasn't going to marry her. He wasn't going to settle down with her. He wasn't even committed to taking care of the child he'd fathered.

He was, in a word, the most selfish and immature man she had ever met. He had literally pushed her out of their hotel room in Atlanta, where he and Tumbleweed were performing, leaving her pretty much stranded.

She could go back to Nashville, lick her wounds, and think about suing for child support. Or she could try to fix what she had stupidly broken a year ago. It seemed like fixing the broken stuff was a better plan than going back to Music City.

"I'll take one ticket to Last Chance," she said to the agent.

The man looked down at her. "So what's happening in Last Chance these days?"

"Excuse me?"

"Oh, I don't know. It just seems like there are a bunch of women headed in that general direction. And that seems odd to me on account of the fact that I might sell one ticket to Last Chance every month or so. It ain't exactly a tourist spot, you know?"

She gritted her teeth. "Yes, I know. Can I have my ticket, please?"

"Sure. Bus leaves in ten minutes."

Jane tried to rub away the feeling of the handcuffs on her wrists. She sat in a small, windowless room on a cold metal chair with her hands resting on a gray Formica-topped table. The walls were white, and the floors looked like the same linoleum they used in Value Mart stores—utilitarian and dingy.

Jane was alone. Chief Rhodes had locked her in. In a minute, he would return and maybe then he might tell her who she was supposed to have murdered.

She drew in a deep breath through her mouth and exhaled through her nose. She had been doing her relaxation routine for the last fifteen minutes while endlessly repeating Dr. Goodbody's advice about negative situations. Dr. Goodbody said that obsessing over a problem or trying to wish the problem away was a big mistake. Instead, positive thinking requires a person to be honest with him- or herself and consider alternative courses of action.

The truth was, she had never killed anyone. As for the alternative courses of action—well, she doubted she could break out of prison, and Stone Rhodes was a formidable adversary, so her mind was drawing a complete blank.

Except for the look on Clay's face the moment that he had pressed his hand up against the cruiser's window. That look, if she let herself believe in it, said he cared about what happened to her. Like he was, maybe, the total embodiment of what Miriam Randall had told her she should be looking for.

That scared her silly.

Because the girl inside was hoping that Clayton P. would come busting in here like Sir Galahad. She could just imagine Clay rescuing her from this mess and carrying her off to some castle where he would sing love ballads to her.

Yeah, right. Like that was ever going to happen.

The door opened with a little squeak, and Chief Rhodes strode in. He wasn't wearing his hat, although his short hair bore the unmistakable indentation of his Stetson, as did the skin of his forehead. He'd lost his utility belt, too. But he was still packing heat and still wearing a bulky Kevlar vest.

Which explained why the room had been air-conditioned into something that resembled wintertime in Juneau.

The chief took a seat and dropped a thin manila folder on the table. Then he reached into his shirt pocket and pulled out Jane's West Virginia driver's license.

"Okay, Mary, suppose we start with a simple question. Where'd you get this?" He held up the license and then placed it on the tabletop in front of her.

A tense little laugh burbled out of her. Forty-eight hours ago, his younger brother had rifled through her belongings and concluded that her name was *not* Mary. Obviously, Clay had better police instincts than the chief.

"You think this is funny?" the chief said.

Jane sucked in the frigid air and hugged herself, trying to find some warmth in the cold room. "I got the license in the usual way."

"The usual way? Were you looking for identities online? Did you buy it from someone?"

She stopped laughing. "I hate to tell you this, Chief, but most folks go down to the DMV and apply for their licenses. Didn't you know that?"

He pressed his lips together. It wasn't a friendly look for him. "Do not get cute with me. I'm onto you."

"I got the license at the DMV."

"Uh-huh." He leaned back in his chair and pulled a piece of paper from the folder. "If you think I believe that, then you need to think again. There is no way in hell you are Wanda Jane Coblentz."

He slid the paper across the table. Jane recognized it as the missing flyer that had dogged her heels for years. It featured her eighth-grade school photograph—not because she'd gone missing in eighth grade, but only because her parents couldn't afford to pay for a high-school yearbook head shot.

Looking down at her young face was never much fun. She always wondered where that little girl had gone off to. She had traveled a long way down life's road since this photo had been taken. She'd hit more than her share of potholes and taken way too many detours into blind alleys on the road of her life.

Jane worked to suck back the tears. On some deep level, she mourned that little girl. That Wanda Jane *was* missing. She had died a long time ago.

She refused to meet that pain head-on. She had been running from the memory of the girl she once had been for the last seven years.

"All I can say is thank the Lord for laser hair removal," she said in a shaky voice. "That unibrow was not attractive, was it? They ought to have a law prohibiting any photographs of a person between the ages of thirteen and seventeen. It's an awkward age."

She looked up into Stone Rhodes's stony face and knew that the man had zero sense of humor. "You know," the chief said, "you have an attitude problem. This is not a joking matter. That little girl, right there, has been missing for seven years, and her folks are tore up about it. And the police in Lexington, Kentucky, are certain she was murdered not long after she ran away."

It didn't seem possible, but the temperature in the room dropped a few more degrees. A cold sweat trickled down Jane's back as she thought about Ma and Pa and her two little brothers. How on earth had the police in Lexington come to the conclusion that she was dead?

She was a runaway. That was true. She already knew Ma and Pa were looking for her. The Center for Missing and Exploited Children had been trying to locate her for years. She had seen her own face a dozen times on milk containers and bill stuffers. The photo was always the same: that eighth-grade graduation photo.

She had always been grateful for this fact, because it was amazing how people could look right past those milk container photos when they showed a thirteen-year-old girl with heavy eyebrows and a bad case of acne. She no longer resembled the girl in the flyer.

She put the flyer down on the table and leaned in. "As you can see, I am alive. So can I go now?"

The chief wasn't moved by her statement. "So tell me," he asked. "How are you acquainted with Joseph Andrew Hamil?"

She hugged herself harder as it occurred to her that the police always referred to the notorious by their full names, like Lee Harvey Oswald or Mark David Chapman. Not that Joey was all that notorious. But the boy had been a peanut-brained weasel, for sure.

It was a sad commentary that Joey was the *first* peanut-brained weasel in her life—the bad-boy hero she had mistakenly expected to rescue her from Seth, West Virginia, and her dysfunctional family. Instead, Joey had dumped her in a hotel in Lexington the minute reality came knocking.

He had done her a big favor. She had learned how to take care of herself, thanks to Joey. She had managed for seven years until Woody came waltzing into the Shrimp Shack throwing hundred-dollar tips around and talking about his musical connections.

Jeez, when would she learn?

Jane didn't want to talk about this. She had done nothing illegal that night in Lexington. Not that the same could have been said of Joey. But she wasn't Joey's keeper.

And clearly Joey had not been hers.

She pushed the shameful memories back, just like she fought her tears. She didn't have to tell this story. She wasn't guilty of anything except terminal gullibility.

"What do you want to know about Joey?" she said on a sniffle.

"So you know him?"

"Sure, I know him. We were classmates at Sherman High School in Seth. We were in chorus together. He was one heck of a guitarist, too, and if he hadn't been such a complete screw-up as a human being, he might have made it in Nashville. But, unfortunately, the guy was a loser."

A little muscle pulsed in Stone Rhodes's cheek. "So what is it, Mary, you have a thing for musicians? Do you cruise through small towns picking them up and then rolling them for cash? For the record, my brother is not a rich man, despite his recent successes."

Wow, this was personal with the chief. Stone Rhodes was doing more than his job. He was looking out for his little brother. She gritted her teeth and decided that she wasn't going to say another word.

He waited a long moment for a response, then he heaved a big, disgusted sigh. "Look, Mary, I'm about to haul your butt down to the county and have you thrown in jail. There is a detective up in Lexington who is pretty hot to have you extradited up there for interrogation. You are in serious trouble. I'm trying to help you out before the higher authorities tie my hands."

Right. He was trying to play the roles of both good and bad cop. She leaned forward in her chair and spoke. "Okay, Chief, I guess I'm going to exercise my rights and ask for—"

A commotion in the outer office interrupted Jane's words. An instant later, the door swung open, revealing a man who looked like he had just stepped off the greens at Augusta National. He wore a yellow V-necked sweater over a white Cutter and Buck golf shirt. A pair of cream-colored slacks and saddle shoes with soft spikes completed his ensemble.

"I'm here to see my client," the man announced. He looked down at her out of a pair of sparkling blue eyes hidden behind horn-rimmed glasses. "Wanda Jane, I presume."

She nodded. This was manifesting at its finest, because she had been on the point of requesting an attorney. And *bingo,* one appeared as if by magic. The Universe was her friend.

Although it occurred to her that the Universe might have had a helping hand in the form of one Clayton P. Rhodes. That gave her a sense of hope.

She could fall for a guy like that, especially since he had a few additional talents, like fiddling and other stuff between the sheets and, after all, Miriam Randall had told her to ask for more.

"Oh, for goodness' sake, Eugene. You do divorces and family law. You don't know squat about criminal defense. Get out of here. Go back to the country club. I'm trying to do my business," Stone said.

Family law? Okay, so Clay had to move in a hurry and Eugene was the only lawyer he could find on short notice in a town like Last Chance on a Saturday morning. It didn't negate the fact that Clay had taken steps to rescue her.

Eugene drew himself up. "Stony, I've been retained to represent Ms. Coblentz, and you know very well you have to let me talk with her. So why don't you take ten?"

Stony's ears got bright red. "Did Clay hire you?"

"That's none of your business."

"He did, didn't he?" The chief pushed out of his chair

and strode toward the door. "You have exactly five minutes before I return and continue with this interrogation." He slammed the door behind him.

Eugene took a seat, and Jane noted that the man wasn't carrying a briefcase or even a writing implement. She wasn't sure how much faith she ought to put in him. "Don't mind Stony, honey," he said in a drawl that didn't sound quite as deep as either Clay's or Stone's. "He's got lots of personal problems these days that weigh heavy on his mind. He lost his wife about five years ago and has never recovered."

"Family law?" she asked.

He smiled. "Best divorce attorney in the county. Clay sent me down here in a hurry. Said he didn't believe you actually needed a criminal attorney."

"I think maybe I *do* need a criminal attorney."

"Well, let me be the judge of that. My name's Eugene Hanks, by the way. I believe you met my wife, Thelma, at the Cut 'n Curl yesterday. So what's all this about?"

"Chief Rhodes believes I murdered myself seven years ago."

Eugene laughed out loud. "Is that so?"

She nodded. "You see, I ran away from home when I was seventeen, and I changed my name for a lot of reasons that aren't important. But anyway, he says the police in Lexington think I was murdered, and he says he's going to force me to go to Lexington to be interrogated by some detective up there who has this theory that I'm dead. Can he force me to do that?"

"No."

"Is it breaking the law to live under an assumed name? I mean, I pay my taxes and make contributions to Social

Security. I just don't choose...I mean I haven't until recently chosen to use my real name, because my face turns up regularly on milk cartons."

"Does it?"

She nodded. "But people don't recognize me because it's a terrible picture and I had my eyebrows fixed."

"I see." Eugene cleared his throat. "Honey, I'm glad you're paying your taxes, but if you aren't using a legitimate Social Security number, that's a problem. As a legal matter, you probably want to formally change your name, and I can certainly help you do that."

"Oh. Can they put me in jail for living under an alias without doing it legally?"

"Well, the Social Security Administration won't be too pleased, but if you've been paying your taxes and can prove you are a U.S. citizen, then I think we can negotiate something. In any case, I don't think jail time is in your future for that."

"I swear to the almighty power of the Universe that I did not murder myself in Lexington, Kentucky. Isn't there some way I can prove that I'm myself and that I'm alive? What about DNA? I've seen those shows on TV. I'll let the chief swab my cheek."

Eugene laughed again. "Wait here one minute. I'm going to have a word with Stony and see if we can clear this up."

He stood up just as the sound of more shouting came from the outer office. Ruby Rhodes came bursting into the room, her oldest son hot on her heels. The chief didn't look happy, which was nothing new.

"Lord a'mercy, child, are you all right? I heard you got arrested right there on Palmetto Avenue in front of God and Clay and everyone else," Ruby said, giving her oldest child an annoyed look.

"Momma, you need to leave now," Stone said.

Jane had to bite the side of her cheek to keep from laughing when little Ruby Rhodes whirled around and looked up into the face of her giant-sized son. "Don't you dare tell me what I need to do, Stonewall Ezekiel Rhodes. I have a right to know what my employee and tenant has been charged with. Just arresting her is bad for my business. But I'll bet you didn't even think of that, did you?"

"Momma, for heaven's sake, don't put your nose in something that will hurt you. And besides, I do not want this woman babysitting my children. I have made that abundantly clear to you. Speaking of the girls, where are they?"

"Well, I had to run them up to their riding lessons this morning because you took a notion to work today. Stony, Saturday is the day you get to spend with your girls. You know darn well it's my busiest day at the shop. And if you don't want Jane watching your girls, then I reckon you'll have to be running them here and there to their activities yourself, because as of this moment I'm going on strike."

The chief's ears were flaming red now, and the color was spilling over into his cheeks. "Momma, this isn't the time or the place."

Ruby turned back toward Jane. "Are you all right, sugar? I heard he slammed you upside the hood of his car. I'm so ashamed of him, really. He hasn't been the same since Sharon died, but that's no excuse for him manhandling you."

"I'm fine," Jane said. "He scared me but he didn't hurt

me." And that was the honest truth, because the chief hadn't even bruised her. And that was saying something, given the fact that his younger brother had put several bruises on her all in the name of passion.

"Momma, you have to go now. Don't make me manhandle *you*," the chief said.

Eugene cleared his throat. "I do believe we have a case of mistaken identity here."

"No," Stony said. "We have an unsolved murder. The police in Lexington believe Wanda Jane Coblentz was murdered there about seven years ago by one Joseph Andrew Hamil. Until Mary, here, showed up with Wanda Jane's driver's license, the detectives working the case had nothing to go on except a crime scene at a hotel room and some blood evidence, but no bodies."

Jane felt something hitch in her chest and she sank her face down into her hands. "Oh, God," she moaned. "How could that be? I cleaned the room."

"Jane," Eugene said sharply. "Not one more word."

"Sugar," Ruby said as she rested her hand on Jane's shoulder.

"They found blood in that room, and they found Wanda Jane's DNA there," Stony said grimly. "Joseph Andrew Hamil left Seth, West Virginia, with Wanda Jane Coblentz the day before she was supposed to graduate from high school. That evening, Hamil shot a convenience store clerk in Lexington, putting the man in a wheelchair for the rest of his life. The authorities captured Hamil within half an hour of the shooting, after a high-speed chase. The next day, when they realized he was involved in Wanda Jane's disappearance, they went to the hotel room and found it stripped clean and totally empty. The bathroom lit up when treated with Luminol, and they found Wanda Jane's DNA at the scene."

"Do not say one word, Jane," Eugene said.

Jane tightened her jaw. "No one was killed in that room," she said.

"The evidence says otherwise." The chief's voice was firm and strong and righteous.

"Stony, don't be a jerk," Eugene said. "There are dozens of reasons why Jane's blood might be in that room. The police never found her body, did they? So don't jump to conclusions just because Jane Coblentz decided not to go home and was last seen in the company of a known criminal."

"Joey was not a *known criminal*," Jane said. "He was just a kid in a bad situation who made a wrong decision. We were trying to get to Nashville."

"He had drugs on him and a .45-caliber handgun when he was apprehended," Stone said.

Ruby squeezed Jane's shoulder. Jane had no idea that Joey had been into drugs. How gullible could a girl get?

"So you admit you were his accomplice," Stone said.

Jane shook her head. "Accomplice in what? Running away from home? Believe me, I *am* Jane Coblentz. I thought Joey loved me. I thought we were going to Nashville to make it big in country music. I was seventeen and trying to escape an abusive father. I was also pretty stupid."

"Yeah, well, you'll forgive me if I don't believe you. You don't look a lick like that girl's photograph or even the photo on the license, which could have been doctored in any case." The chief snagged the missing-person poster off the table and handed it to Eugene.

Eugene studied the photo for several long moments, then handed the flyer off to Ruby, who blinked down at it and then said, "Honey, I'm so glad you did something about that eyebrow."

"Oh, for goodness' sake, Momma, you can't believe that—"

"I don't know, Stone," Eugene interrupted. "That's an image of a little girl. You can't say positively that it isn't a photo of this woman."

Ruby leaned over and whispered in Jane's ear. "Did that boy beat you up, sugar? Is that what happened?"

Jane didn't respond to Ruby's question because she didn't want to lie. Joey had never laid a finger on her in anger. She wouldn't have tolerated that.

"I think we can solve this with a DNA test. My client has agreed to provide DNA," Eugene said.

"Okay, then, but I'm keeping her locked up until I get the results. The way the state labs work it'll take the better part of a week."

"Oh, for Heaven's sake, Stone, don't be an idiot." Ruby's voice was flat and firm.

"Look, Stone, you can't hold this woman. I'm pretty sure you don't even have a warrant. I'm sure she would agree to stay in town until this issue can be resolved."

Ruby squeezed her shoulder again. "Honey, you promise you won't try to run away again, won't you? I don't know why you were trying to leave. I know you probably got the wrong idea about Ricki. You just put her right out of your mind. The Lord will find a way, girl. Just remember that."

A way for what? But Jane didn't have the courage to ask that question aloud.

Chapter
11

Clay watched through the windows of Lovett's Hardware as Momma walked Jane up Palmetto Avenue and down into the alley between the Cut 'n Curl and the doughnut shop. Momma deposited Jane at the apartment, then came down the stairs and opened the beauty shop.

He hung there for a few moments, knowing it was best not to go running across the street and up those stairs. He'd handled this maturely, without storming the police station or picking a fistfight with his big brother. Momma and Eugene had taken care of things.

Clay ought to go down to the Kountry Kitchen and get some coffee and biscuits and calm the hell down. Or go home and make some breakfast for Ricki and have a mature conversation with her about whether she wanted children. He sure ought to turn his back on that woman across the street. Because she *was* trouble. A woman didn't get slapped into handcuffs unless there were some unsavory things in her past.

He ought to turn his back on her.

Only he couldn't.

Clay headed across the street and took the stairs two at a time, knowing this was a true sign that he had fallen back into old, worn-out, bankrupt patterns of behavior.

Jane opened her door when he knocked.

She looked like hell, with a red, puffy nose and swollen eyelids. One look at her and his whole body reacted with lust and longing and relief and something much deeper that spread through his bloodstream like an intoxicating drug.

Christ almighty, he wanted to take care of this woman. He wanted to pull her into his arms and hold her tight and tell her it was okay to cry her eyes out.

But he was finished collecting needy people.

Wasn't he?

Except, of course, Ricki was holed up at his place, and she had breezed into town on the bus needing a place to stay and a shoulder to cry on, and clearly, a bed to warm.

So Clay hooked his thumbs in his belt loops and started to wonder why the hell he hadn't gone to the Kountry Kitchen for biscuits in the first place. He stood there staring at Jane feeling like a class-A jerk.

"Hey," he said lamely.

Her lips twitched, and he had this feeling that she wasn't finished crying. He squeezed his fists around his belt loops to keep from reaching out to comfort her.

She cleared her throat. "So," she said in a forced tone that he figured was supposed to sound light and breezy. "I guess I owe you for the lawyer. I—"

"You don't owe me squat," he said. His voice didn't sound good. It came out flat and angry, and she jumped a little bit.

A little piece of his heart broke away and a lump the size of a pecan lodged in his throat. He didn't want to make her jumpy. He started again. "I mean, I only paid Eugene a dollar. Just to make it legal and official, you know. So he could keep your secrets because of attorney–client privilege."

Secrets? God Almighty, he didn't want her to keep any more secrets. He wanted a full confession right now so he could know the true extent of her culpability. Maybe then he could walk away and go make Ricki some breakfast.

"A dollar?" she asked.

He nodded. "Yeah. Eugene owes me a favor on account of the fact that my little brother and I fixed his roof last January after an ice storm."

She nodded while her mouth trembled. "So I guess you want some answers, huh?" she said, looking like a little girl who needed a big hug.

Clay leaned harder against the door frame and pretended his feet were super-glued to the landing. *Darn straight, I want answers.* "Nope," he said aloud, and knew himself for the ultimate fool.

She blinked. "No?"

"If you want to tell me about it, I'm happy to listen," he managed to say between suddenly numb lips. "Otherwise it's none of my business." Which was true, but hadn't he made it his business the minute he called Eugene?

Something changed in her face, and he got the feeling either he'd surprised her or he had screwed things up again. He hoped it was the former, but he had this awful feeling it was the latter.

Maybe she *wanted* to make a full confession.

Maybe she needed somebody to care.

Well, he could do that. He cared a lot.

"Do you want me to make it my business?" he asked.

She bit her bottom lip and shook her head. It was a pretty weak denial. But he was a pretty weak man.

He pushed away from the door frame and unhooked his hands from his belt loops. The minute he cupped her jaw in his hand, he knew he'd burned all his bridges. There was no way back across this river.

The heat of sexual awareness flowed through him. He pulled her head into his chest, and she sagged against him as he held her up. His anger dissipated; his frustration disappeared; his doubt evaporated. He cupped the back of her head, the texture of her hair silky against his palm, as he drew in a deep breath, filling his head with her spicy scent. Every fiber of his being told him this was the right thing to do, although somewhere in his head he knew he was making the same mistake he always made.

Why had the Lord given him this talent? He'd been holding up women for a long, long time, and he was pretty good at it. But it wasn't the same as love or commitment. A man couldn't build a future on this.

In a minute, she would cry. And he'd let her get snot all over him. And, fool that he was, he would confuse her neediness for the real deal.

And in six months—a year tops—she'd meet some exciting guy with a Harley, and she'd leave. The women he had cared for over the years had all left him for guys on Harleys. And when he asked why, they all told Clay he was the best friend they'd ever had. They would say they needed more than a friend.

Just then, Jane pushed away from him. "I'm sorry, Clay," she said in a hoarse little voice. "I guess I'm feeling pitifully grateful at the moment. Thank you for sending Eugene. And thank you for not pushing me for answers. And thank you for the CD player. And thank your mother for the food and the shelter when I needed it, even though I have a policy about not accepting charity." She swallowed hard. "You're a good man, Clay Rhodes, from a good family. But I think it might be best if we left it there, okay?"

He stared down at her, completely nonplussed. The woman was bypassing the crying jag and the six months of great sex and moving right to *Gee, Clay, you are a great friend.*

His heart was safe. She wasn't going to break it.

So why the hell did it hurt to breathe?

"Uh, it's okay. If you ever need someone to..." His voice faded out. If she ever needed someone to what? Tell her secrets to? Cry on? Love? Sleep with? Just exactly what?

Jane stepped back and sniffled. "It turns out I'm going to be staying in Last Chance for a while, until your brother is satisfied that I'm really Jane Coblentz. It apparently takes a little time for DNA testing. So I need to go downstairs and get to work. It's almost nine, and a beauty shop gets kind of crazy on a Saturday. Your ma gave me this opportunity, and I don't want to disappoint her. She's been kind to me."

"DNA testing?"

She shrugged. "I guess some of this *is* your business, since you sent Eugene. Your brother doesn't think I'm Jane Coblentz."

"Why would he doubt who you are?"

"Because I ran away from home when I was seventeen, and I haven't been Jane Coblentz since the first time

I saw my face on a milk carton and realized my folks wanted me back. Some yahoo cop in Kentucky thinks I was murdered. He doesn't have a body, of course, since— to quote Mark Twain—reports of my demise have been greatly exaggerated. I understand the FBI is interested in making sure I'm myself, too, since I'm officially missing and that makes it all a federal offense."

"Are you telling me my stupid brother arrested you for killing yourself, and the FBI wants to find you even though you don't want to be found?"

Jane nodded and managed a little smile. "Something like that, yeah."

"And the only reason you're in this fix is because I discovered that you weren't Mary Smith that day the hurricane blew into town?"

She nodded again. "Uh-huh."

"Oh, God, Jane, I'm so sorry."

She shrugged. "Serves me right for rifling through your wallet that morning." She folded her arms across her chest. The defensiveness settled stiffly on her shoulders.

"Oh, crap," he said on a puff of air. What a jerk he'd been. That morning he'd pawed through her purse, he'd been feeling incredibly guilty and confused. She had the misfortune to be in the way when he'd lashed out.

"Look, Clay, you didn't know," Jane said quickly. "And God knows you've been trying to atone for Wednesday night and Thursday morning for days now. I forgive you. I don't blame you. In fact, well…" She hesitated for a moment, controlling the wobble in her voice. He wondered if she might break down. She didn't.

"I should have refused your offer that night," she finally said. "I'm the one who acted like a slut."

"You are not a slut," he countered. The by-now-familiar guilt tugged at his insides.

"Let's just put it behind us, okay? We made a mistake on Wednesday. We don't need to compound it. I'm trying to get my life in order, and I've decided that for once I'm going to do it on my own. It's a good thing, in a way, that you found that old ID. I'm okay with it. And, for the record, I don't need to be rescued."

He clamped his back teeth together. She was lying through her teeth. If ever there was a soul in need of rescue, she was it. She was the poster child for abandoned and down-on-your-luck waifs. But she was also smart enough to recognize the difference between passion and compassion, need and love.

When he didn't respond, she added, "I have to go to work now, but I did want to tell you how much I appreciated the Dolly Parton and Lee Ann Womack CDs you lent me."

He jammed his hands into his back pockets. She was sending him away. He was getting a first-class brushoff.

He ought to feel some sense of relief. He could go home and rekindle the flame with Ricki. And wasn't that something he had fantasized about a million times? But instead of feeling excited about his future with his old flame, Clay felt this huge gaping hole in the middle of his chest where Jane had just blown him to kingdom come. He wasn't used to getting turned down by females in need.

Clay didn't want to leave, so he opened his mouth and said the first thing that came into his head. "You have a nice voice."

That got him an inkling of a smile. "Thanks," she said.

"I learned all the words to 'I Will Always Love You.' You were right about that song."

"Why don't you come down to Dot's Spot and sing it tonight?" he asked, trying to regroup and figure out if this was what the next move ought to be.

Jane's smile widened and hit him upside the head and made him weak in the knees. "I'd like to come down to Dot's and sing."

That's when he realized he had been fooling himself for the last twenty-four hours.

He wanted this woman, and not so he could take care of her, or be her friend. He wanted to lay her down in the grass somewhere and make hot, hard, sweet, endless love to her.

The sudden desire exploded inside him and blew away every possible objection his feeble mind could conjure up. Oh, yeah, she was too young for him, too smart for him, too unstable, and too New Age. She had baggage and secrets and demons, and she was probably engaged in something illegal. And to sum it all up, the woman had been so badly hurt she had run away from home at the age of seventeen and didn't want to go back even though her parents were looking for her. She had major-league trust issues that would make a sane and stable relationship with her impossible. She didn't even trust herself to have a crying jag on his shoulder.

The woman was hell-bent to rescue her own self. Without any help.

And that made her one of a kind.

Oh, yeah. And she was beautiful and built and Clay wanted to touch her all over. He wanted to feel her hands on his body. Jane Coblentz was seriously hot and seriously determined and seriously screwed up.

It was a killer combination.

Clay pulled his hands out of his back pockets and took a tentative step toward her. "Jane," he said on a half-whisper as he cupped the back of her head in his hand, embracing the heat and lust and want that flooded his system. He pulled her up into a hard, wet, possessive kiss in which he allowed himself to explore the heat of her mouth for about fifteen seconds—long enough to enjoy it, but short enough not to scare her too much.

Then he let her go and put his hands back in his pockets and tried to catch his breath as he said, "Okay. I'll see you at Dottie's tonight."

Clay turned away before Jane could chew him out or give him grief or otherwise ruin the absolute best moment of what had begun as a terrible day.

Chapter
12

Saturday at the Cut 'n Curl had not been fun. By nine o'clock, just about everyone in town knew all about how Jane had been arrested. Back in West Virginia, she would have been ostracized by the end of the day. But much to Jane's surprise, Ruby Rhodes stood by her, and in Last Chance, that clearly counted for something.

Even so, between dodging nosy questions and doing nails, Jane had found it impossible to keep her mind away from the hot memories of Clay's mouth closing over hers. And every time she thought about his invitation to sing at Dot's Spot, her stomach would pinch and her pulse rate would spike.

Was it fear or anticipation?

Probably both. Jane decided the Universe was trying to send her a warning. She needed to respect her own self, like the message on Lizzy's T-shirt yesterday. She was going to stay home and hide from Clay and his talented mouth and fingers. She intended to take a bath and read a good book.

She stood in the back of the Cut 'n Curl perusing a small bookshelf that contained a selection of well-thumbed paperbacks that Ruby lent out to her customers free of charge. And since Jane didn't have an Allenberg County library card, this bookshelf would have to provide the night's entertainment.

Only trouble was the books all had garish covers and words like "desire" and "passion" in their titles.

"This one's real good," Ruby said, pulling a book from the shelf entitled *Her Knight of Temptation*. It featured a semiclad woman with big flowing hair in the arms of a bare-chested man wearing a sword belt and gauntlets. A stone castle loomed over them in the background.

"Is all you have romance?" Jane asked.

"Afraid so. I keep a supply of 'em for the customers since you can't find any of these books down at the library. I'm afraid our regular librarian, Nita Wills, looks down her nose at these books. But then I reckon Nita never did have much luck with love."

Jane took the book from Ruby's hand. She stared down at the cover. Ruby was trying to tell her something. "Are you recommending this because it has the word 'Knight' in the title?"

Ruby let go of a little laugh, and then she reached out and touched Jane's hair. "I declare, girl, you have such beautiful hair. Why do you always wear it up in a ponytail like that?"

"Uh, because it's easy. And to tell you the truth, I figured I was just going to be on a bus today."

Ruby looked deeply into her face. The compassion in Ruby's eyes scared the crap out of Jane. "Yes, I do realize, and I'm trying to figure out why you were running away from us," Ruby said.

"Do I have to answer that question?"

"No, darlin', you don't have to answer any question you don't want to answer. That's one of my rules. One day, though, I'm hoping you'll realize I'm your friend."

Jane looked down at the book and pursed her lips. "Well, I guess it won't rot my mind too bad. I'll just remember to tell myself that most men out there are not knights ready to rush in and rescue a girl. Mostly men are interested in one thing."

"Hmm. Well, you're probably right about that," Ruby said. "And as long as they're interested, I figure a girl ought to enhance her assets. You know what I mean?" Ruby gave Jane a wink and then took her by the arm and led her to one of the shampoo sinks.

"Um…uh…" Jane momentarily lost the ability to speak.

"Honey, you need a makeover. I know you got rid of that unibrow, but you need to do something new with your hair. I'm thinking a few layers to bring out the curl." Ruby maneuvered her into the chair and plucked the paperback from her hand.

"Now, you trust me, don't you?" Ruby asked.

"Uh, yeah, I guess, but I don't—"

"Good, then lean back. I'm going to make you beautiful. Not that you aren't already very nice to look at. But I know exactly what to do with your hair to make you irresistible."

"Uh, but I don't want to be—" Jane found herself being gently forced back into the chair.

Ruby started the water, and before Jane knew what was happening, Ruby had doused her with almond-scented shampoo and was working up a professional lather.

"Of course you want to be irresistible. Well, not to everyone, mind, but just to the right one, you know what I mean?" Ruby said.

"Uh, no."

Ruby started rinsing. "Now, Jane, don't you try to fool me. We both know where you spent Wednesday night. And I know you were leaving town because Ricki arrived on the bus last night. But you can't just give up the field like that."

"Give up the field?"

"Yes, you know exactly what I mean. And besides, after the way Clay came to your rescue today, calling Eugene and me and everything, you have to admit that he's kind of living up to what Miriam told you to be looking for."

Ruby wrapped a towel around Jane's head and brought the seat back up.

"Okay, now come on over to my station and let's see what we can do."

"Uh, Ruby, I don't really want to change my hair, and I don't think chasing after Clay is a good idea."

"Of course it's a good idea. What woman wouldn't want to snag herself a sensitive songwriting hero?"

"Well, I . . ." Jane's voice faded out.

"Come on now, let me help. I'm just going to put a few little layers in your hair and give it some highlights. It would look so nice feathered around your face a little. It would make it look fuller, you know."

Oh, yeah, she knew. Ruby was going to do her hair like she used to wear it when she posed for those photos.

"I mean, I know the Farrah Fawcett hairdo has kind of gone out of style," Ruby rattled on, "but we can give it a twenty-first-century take that will be modern and sexy and drive Clay crazy."

"Uh, Ruby, I don't think I want to—"

"Drive Clay crazy? Honey, don't kid a kidder. And I'm giving you permission. That boy's been moping around here for months ever since that woman did him wrong, and I think you're good for him. I really do. He needs to quit worrying about Ray and the store, you know, and start worrying about his own self."

"He does?"

"Oh, yes."

"But what about the Peach—"

"Honey, put that out of your mind. I know y'all started out a little fast, but you wouldn't be the first ones to do that sort of thing. I hear the Peach Blossom is doing a very nice business."

Jane sat in Ruby's chair while the hairdresser started combing out her hair. Jane watched Ruby in the mirror for a long moment. "Are you saying I have your blessing?"

Ruby looked up at her. Their eyes met in the mirror. "I have a feeling about you. And yes, you have my blessing. Clay needs to get over Tricia and quit worrying about Pete and Ray. And you just might be the ticket."

"What about Ricki?"

Ruby sniffed. "That woman broke his heart a long time ago. I am not pleased that he's let her sleep in his guest bedroom. At least, I hope he was telling me the truth about that."

"She's not the one he's broken-hearted over?"

"Oh, no. He's broken up about Tricia. She's the one he wrote the song for."

"What song?"

"Oh, you know, the one they play on the radio all the time. The Tumbleweed song."

"Clay wrote that song? The one Bubba Lockheart always plays down at Dot's Spot?"

"Well, I don't go down to Dot's. But if it's the one with the words about loving more than needing, then that's the one."

"He wrote that song?"

Ruby started cutting her hair before Jane could stop her. "Yes, he did. And he's made some money off it, which is a positive sign. But excuse me for being uncharitable toward that woman. I declare she dumped Clay for that Chad Ames, you know—Tumbleweed's lead singer. Clay didn't even fight for her. Instead he quit the band and came back here with the lame excuse that he wanted to help my older brother, Pete, with his hardware store, on account of the fact that Pete's got lung cancer. If you ask me, he came home to lick his wounds, and he's going to end up here trying to be Ray's keeper.

"Now, don't get me wrong. I would love it if Clay would move back to Last Chance, but he's got to do that for the right reasons, you know. Because he wants to, not because he's hiding out or because of some kind of wrong-headed sense of responsibility."

"Uh-huh." Jane didn't nod, because Ruby had her head pointed down and locked into position while she snipped away at her hair.

"The way I see it," Ruby continued. "I do respect Clay for wanting to help Pete, but I don't think coming back here and hiding out and pretending he doesn't have talent is a good career move for him. And while I'm proud of him for his songs, I'd just as soon see him happy as see him having to suffer heartbreak after heartbreak so that he can write those sad country songs."

"Uh-huh." Jane found herself suddenly more interested than she wanted to be. Ruby was really dishing the inside story, and Jane was lapping it up.

Ruby let go of Jane's head and she looked up again, studying Ruby in the mirror. "But the chief thinks I'm—" Jane started.

"Oh, never mind him. He doesn't like strangers. I want to see him happy, too, but he's going to be a much harder nut to crack. He loved Sharon, but she died. Stone's heartbreak is much deeper than Clay's. Clay gets heartbroke pretty easy. I reckon all he needs is a good woman with a big heart and a good head on her shoulders. But Stony...well, he feels things just as deep, but he never shows his feelings."

"You think I'm a good woman?"

Ruby looked up with a big smile on her face. "Oh, honey, I know you're a good woman. I have that on the highest authority there is."

Jane didn't ask what authority that might be. It could be the Universe, or it could be...

Well, it was probably Miriam Randall, who appeared to be someone who regularly messed around with people's lives. All day long, people in the shop had been talking about Miriam and her matches. It really looked like both Ruby and Miriam were trying to tell her that Clay was a Sir Galahad ready to swoop in and rescue her from her life.

Which was something she already knew.

And that's why she had decided not to go to Dot's Spot tonight, because all in all, Clay was starting to look too good to be true. And when guys started looking like that, it was a danger sign pure and simple.

Ruby continued with her work. An hour later, Ruby and Jane studied Jane's reflection in the beauty shop mirror. The transformation was complete. Jane looked...

Hot.

Ready for action.

Available.

And exactly like Miss April in the *Working Girls Go Wild* calendar, only with her shirt on.

"Oh, honey, I think he's going to like this. Now, you need to go get yourself dolled up and put on that little huckleberry blue T-shirt that Sharon liked so much when she was alive. Then you get your butt down to Dot's place and you sing that song for Clay."

"What song?"

"The one you've been humming all day. You know that old Dolly Parton song from the movie with Burt Reynolds."

"'I Will Always Love You'?"

Ruby grinned. "Yeah, that's the one. You go down there and sing that for Clay and we'll see what happens."

Just thinking about that made Jane's insides flip-flop. She knew better than to listen to Ruby. Clay was a danger she ought to be avoiding. But she knew right then she wasn't going to stay home with *Her Knight of Temptation*. She was going to go down to Dot's Spot and actually experience temptation firsthand.

Jane waited until nine-thirty before she headed down to Dot's Spot. By the time she hit the alley beside the Cut 'n Curl, her heart was hammering so hard she could hear it in her ears.

She wondered, not for the first time, if this was a case

of being nervous about singing for Clay or just being wound up at the thought of seeing him again. And then there was the fear that he would take one look at her poufed-out hair and Sharon's tight jeans and think she was trashy. She didn't want to be trashy. Not to Clay.

Jane had reached the sidewalk and started to turn up the block toward Dot's Spot when she heard the familiar and unmistakable sound of air brakes. She looked in the opposite direction toward Bill's Grease Pit, and, sure enough, the nine-thirty bus from Atlanta was discharging a passenger.

This time, the lady was brunette and wore her hair back in a ponytail. She couldn't have been less like Ricki if she tried. She had an all-American-girl look to her, right down to the blue calico maternity dress and the gently faded jean jacket that didn't close up the front anymore. She wore running shoes, and carried a small, generic rolling suitcase and leather shoulder bag.

The woman stood for a long moment under the streetlight as the bus pulled away. Jane felt a strange kinship with her. The woman looked lost and forlorn. She stared up the street and absently blew her bangs off her forehead, then wiped a tear from her cheek.

Jane ducked back into the alley and fought the urge to go over to her and ask her if she needed help. Jane wasn't in any position to offer help. Besides, seeing that big belly on the woman brought back memories that she didn't want to deal with.

Not tonight with Clay waiting for her.

She stood for a long time and waited until the woman started walking down the street. And then, as if the Universe was laughing at her, Jane realized that the mother-to-be was headed toward Dot's Spot.

Jane fell in behind her and followed at a distance as she made her way up the street. Hadn't this happened yesterday? Jane didn't have a good feeling about this.

Ricki looked like she might burst into tears in the next three seconds, and Clay had to grip his Budweiser bottle to keep from doing what he usually did when some woman sprang a leak. But reaching out for her would be a foolhardy move, since the only reason Ricki was tearing up like that was because of what he'd just said.

"How can you suggest a thing like my working for Dottie Cox?" Ricki said in a husky voice.

"Well, I heard Dottie is looking for help." He picked at the label on his bottle, avoiding eye contact. "And, based on what you've told me about Randy, it sure does look like you need a job."

"I can't believe you think I should work for Dot Cox." Ricki sounded outraged now.

Irritation prickled his skin, and he looked up at her, feeling practically no sympathy whatsoever. His lack of feeling surprised him, since Ricki's cheeks were glistening with tears.

"Why won't you work for Dottie?" he asked, leaning forward. "I work for her on Wednesdays, Fridays, and Saturdays. What's the matter, Ricki, her money's not good enough for you?"

"You don't really work for Dottie," she countered. "You perform with that awful band, and for the life of me, I don't understand why. You don't need to work for Dot Cox any more than you need to work at the hardware store. I know this for a fact."

He peered at her through the perpetual haze that

hung over the tables at Dot's. "Ricki, are you back here because you think I'm some kind of success?"

"Well, of course you're a success."

Clay pressed his lips together as disgust washed right through him. Yep, Ricki was looking for a meal ticket, and she figured he was it, just because a few songs on an album had netted him some royalties.

Oh, if she only knew.

He was tempted to tell her that songwriters were working stiffs just like other guys, only songwriting didn't pay nearly as well as most other jobs. That might send her away.

He studied her face, and he couldn't help but compare it to Jane's. And that irked him, too. That little gal had this way of popping up in his brain every five seconds like some lame advertisement on the Internet. And here Jane was, popping up, and demanding his attention, and making him see just how pitiful Ricki was as a human being.

Ricki wanted a handout, for sure. Jane—who had breezed into town with only the clothes on her back— would claw and kick and scream before she let anyone give her a handout.

Ricki was only too happy to use tears to ensnare him. Jane didn't even _want_ to cry on his shoulder.

He was wound up tighter than a drum waiting for that little gal to come walking into the bar on her high heels. He was about ready to explode from random, pop-up thoughts of taking her out back and...

Oh, yeah. That would be fun. Immature, crazy, way out of bounds. But fun.

He swallowed hard and looked back down at his beer bottle.

"So you're saying that if I don't get a job you're going to throw me out on the street?" Ricki whined.

He let go of a long sigh and looked up again. "No, Ricki, I'm saying that you're going to have to move out—sooner rather than later. Have you forgotten how this town gossips? Right now, I don't need my momma or the Last Chance Ladies Auxiliary sermonizing every time I show my face anywhere. I play organ on Sundays now, and they are watching every move I make. So you need to get your own place, and for that, honey, you need a job. I'll go talk to Dot for you, okay?"

"No, it's not okay. I can't believe you're ready to throw me out, after all we've been through together."

He decided it was best not to touch that last line, because they had been through different things. He had gone through hell; she had gone shopping with Randy's credit cards.

Clay pushed up from the table. "Ricki, you can't stay at my place. I didn't ask you to come back here. I don't want to rekindle any old flames. And I'd be much obliged if you would get out of my house as soon as possible. I should have never offered my spare bedroom. I should have known you'd move in and try to manipulate me into something I don't want anymore."

"But where will I—"

"That's your problem."

"But—"

He shook his head. "I'm not rescuing you. You hear me? Not after what you did to me all those years ago. Do you think I'm so pathetic that you can just waltz right back into my life like nothing ever happened? Like you didn't break my heart, ruin my career, and go get married to someone else?" A flood of anger and resentment ran right through him as he finally said the words that had been percolating in his head all day.

He pressed his lips together before he said anything else that might be ugly. He turned away. And practically ran right into Tricia Allen, the other love of his life. Or, more precisely, he ran right into Tricia's belly, which was swollen with child.

In all the times that he had dreamed of running into Tricia, he had never imagined her being pregnant. Clay gazed down into Tricia's familiar face with its porcelain skin, freckled nose, and bow lips. Those lips had once driven him crazy.

Oh, yeah, this face had been the inspiration for dozens of love songs, including "I Gotta Know," which currently topped the country charts. He had never planned on looking into that face again, although God help him, he'd wasted almost a year of his life hoping to.

Tricia was teary-eyed, too. She wore one of those long flowery dresses that he had always thought were kind of shapeless. She sure did fill out that dress in a way that she had never filled out any of her other flowery dresses. She had to be a good six or seven months pregnant.

"Tricia," he said, feeling like someone had taken a hot poker to his insides. "How's Chad?"

The tears spilled over and got caught in her long, dark lashes. "He threw me out," she said in a little, broken voice that made him cringe. "I'm here to acknowledge that you were right about him. He's a complete jerk."

Tricia didn't wait for any response from Clay. She took three steps toward him and fell into his arms.

And wouldn't you know it—Jane chose that precise moment to come walking into the bar, wearing sprayed-on jeans, high-heeled boots, and a little blue T-shirt that left nothing to the imagination. Her hair wasn't in its usual pony-tail. Instead she wore it down but kind of teased up and big.

Real hard lust hit him like a Stinger missile, and it had nothing to do with Tricia.

Especially since Tricia didn't fit in his arms the way she used to, what with that big belly on her. And for some odd reason, he didn't feel at all comfortable with her sob-bing on his shoulder like that. She was getting snot all over one of his best T-shirts and doing it in front of Dot Cox, the Wild Horses, Ricki, and most important, Wanda Jane Coblentz.

Who stood there studying him like he had just done her wrong. God, she looked good enough to eat tonight. It was kind of amazing, but with her hair teased up big like that, Jane looked a whole lot like Miss April in that calendar of Ray's. And Miss April was hot—really hot.

No doubt this sudden surge of lust was another manifestation of his current life confusion. A part of him didn't want to grow up.

Jane studied the back of Tricia's head for a long moment. Her lips narrowed, and a look of deep disap-pointment crossed her face. She didn't say anything. She just stepped around them and headed for the bar.

Clay looked down at Tricia, feeling his own over-whelming sense of disappointment. "What are you doing here?" he asked, just as Ricki jumped up out of her seat and put her fists on her hips. Clay glanced her way. If looks could kill, Ricki was loaded with a quiver of poi-son darts. He decided to ignore her. Maybe she would go away so he could concentrate on the ex-girlfriend who was pregnant with someone else's child.

Tricia sniffled and looked up at him with a tear-stained face. "I came because you've always been my best friend, and I didn't know where else to go after Chad kicked me out of our hotel room in Atlanta. I came on the nine-thirty bus."

Well, of course. That explained everything.

"Clay, unhand that woman." This came from Ricki, who seemed to think she had some hold over him by virtue of the fact that she occupied his spare bedroom. Which, of course, begged the question of where he was going to stash Tricia.

He was mulling through this conundrum when the honky-tonk's doors opened with a louder-than-average bang, and Stony strode in accompanied by his deputy, Damian Easley. Each of them was armed to the teeth, wearing their Stetsons low on their foreheads and bearing grim expressions.

The din of conversation ended sharply, like this was a scene in some spaghetti western. It was unusual, to say the least, for Stony to set foot in Dottie's, much less to come with his deputy. Clay tensed, wary as a coon with a hound on his tail. Something unpleasant was about to go down.

Clay released Tricia and started in Jane's direction. He wasn't about to let his older brother haul her back to jail. Enough was enough.

But Jane wasn't Stony's focus. Instead, the chief stepped right up to Ray and glared down at him with a grim look. "Ray," Stone said, closing his fist around the boy's right biceps.

"Huh?" Ray looked up at the chief with his goofy grin.

"You're under arrest for grand larceny. You have the right to remain silent…" Stony began to read Ray his rights.

Clay forgot about Ricki and Tricia and Jane, turned on his heel, and took three steps toward his older brother, something kind of violent rising up into his throat. "What the hell are you doing?" he asked, his voice coming out raw and angry.

His brother stopped droning and looked up at Clay with pity in his eyes. The last thing in the world Clay wanted from his older brother was pity. His brother had given him a lifetime of looks like that—every time Clay got his clock cleaned on the playground, or when some woman cut out his heart and ate it for breakfast. God damn it, what made Stone that much more of a man than him anyway?

It sure didn't take a man to wear a badge and gun and use his government-issue combat training to run innocent people like Jane and Ray into jail.

"Clay, this isn't the time," Stone said in that deep-down, always-in-control voice of his.

"What'd Ray do?"

"Just stand aside and—"

Something that had been brewing inside Clay for a long time—maybe since Tricia dumped him or maybe since Uncle Pete had been diagnosed with lung cancer—took that moment to break. And when it broke, it snapped, clean through, like a bone under stress.

In the following seconds, Clay lost himself inside a rage so deep and so wide and so vast that he launched himself at Stone intent on hurting him…bad. It took the combined force of Dash Randall, Bubba Lockheart,

Damian Easley, and all the members of the Wild Horses to pull Clay off.

When they finally separated Clay from his brother, Clay had done what he'd wanted to do all day, from the moment Stone had arrested Jane. He had put his fist right through his big brother's face.

And, boy howdy, he had sure messed up his big brother's good looks. Stone's perfect blade of a nose was bloodied, and his cheeks were bruised, and he was going to have a couple of big fat shiners on him.

"Shit," Stone said as Dottie hurried over and handed him a dish towel filled with ice from the bar. "What the hell is the matter with you?" He applied the ice to his rapidly swelling nose.

Clay said not one word. He just tried to get away from the boys holding him so he could go another round.

"I ought to haul you in for assaulting an officer of the law," Stone continued.

Clay tried to get his right hand free, but Damian was stronger than he looked.

"Momma would have my ass in a sling if I put you in jail. So you listen up." His brother had the temerity to point one bloody finger at Clay's chest. "Ray stole the money from the store. I gotta haul him in. I don't have any choice."

Stone wiped blood from his nose, snagged Ray by the arm, and turned around toward the door. He took three paces, then turned and said over his shoulder, "And I swear, Clay, the next time you come at me like that I'll put you right on your ass, and break a few bones just for fun. And don't you think for one minute I won't, either."

It gave Clay a little mote of satisfaction that he'd managed to wound his brother's pride. It was the first time he'd ever managed to do that. It was also likely the last, because Stone *would* put him in the hospital, or jail, or maybe both, if he ever picked another fight with him.

Clay took a deep gulp of air as sanity returned. It was then that he looked down at his right hand and saw the torn and bloody knuckles. He had this feeling as he watched the knuckles swell up that holding a bow wouldn't be possible for the remainder of the night.

Not to mention trying to play piano while Jane sang, which he had been looking forward to all afternoon.

Crap. He hated fighting. It always messed up his hands. And this time, it might have messed up his relationship with Stone, whom he loved, even if the guy was frequently a raging idiot.

That's when the shame hit him, followed by this hollow feeling of hopelessness and grief. If he didn't haul his butt out of that room quick, he was going to embarrass himself in front of everyone. And the thought of Jane seeing him cry made him feel like a jerk. Real men didn't cry.

So Clay turned in his tracks and marched himself right out the service door to the alley without looking up or meeting the shocked looks on everyone's faces.

Chapter

13

Dash Randall started to follow Clay from the room, but Dottie intercepted him before he reached the door. The bartender didn't say a word. She just blocked Dash with a hand on his chest and shook her head. And that's when Jane saw something in both of their faces that made her heart squeeze in her chest and her stomach flip-flop.

There wasn't a soul in that bar who didn't care about Clay Rhodes. She could see it in their faces. Like they all knew his pain. Like they all understood his compulsion to look after Ray Betts. Like they all knew Clay would be embarrassed if anyone tried to help him out.

And just like that, Jane understood. The Universe and Ruby Rhodes had not sent her down to Dot's Spot this evening to be rescued or tempted. No, indeed, the Universe had something else altogether in mind.

Dash and Dottie returned to the bar, and the remaining members of the Wild Horses took the stage and started playing an old Hank Williams number short one fiddler. Ricki and the pregnant woman who had just arrived on the nine-thirty bus sat down at the same table and stared at the door to the alley like they had no clue what to do next.

Jane turned away from them and headed to the bar to speak with Dottie. "Can I have a cup of ice and a towel?" she asked.

Dottie gave her a long, hard stare. "What for...?"

"Clay needs ice for his hand. I was going to take him some."

"I'm sure he does need ice, but I also know he sure doesn't want you to see him cry."

"I'm sure he doesn't. Which is why I'm giving him a few minutes while I get ice for him," Jane said in a voice that sounded firm and filled with positive energy. "Tonight he needs someone to lean on instead of always being everyone's rock. I think you know that." She nodded toward the table where Ricki and the mystery woman sat glaring at each other and the back door.

Dottie nodded back. "You know, Jane, you are my kind of woman." The bartender filled a large paper cup with ice and put it on the bar.

Jane picked up the ice and reached for the clean dish towel Dot proffered. But before Dot released the towel, she said, "Don't you hurt him." She rolled her eyes toward the women at the table. "He's been hurt before, and I'm telling you, he's one of a kind."

"Don't you think I know that?"

Dottie's mouth narrowed. "I sure hope you do."

Jane found Clay in the parking lot behind the bar. He stood with his palms braced on the hood of his minivan with his head hung low. A street light illuminated the scene, but even in the feeble yellow glow, Jane saw the muscles in his back straining against the dark fabric of his T-shirt.

Heat flowed through her when she put her hand on his back, between his shoulder blades. His T-shirt was sweat-dampened, and the solid feel of his spine and muscles beneath her hand unleashed a torrent of hormones.

Leave it to the Universe to put a man like this in her path. He might be what she had been looking for all her life—a real hero. Or he might be a huge mistake.

"Why did you come out here?" Clay asked in a low and husky voice.

"I brought some ice for your hand."

He made a noise that might have been a laugh, but it was devoid of positive energy. He rolled his head in her direction and gave her a stare that was hard to read in the dim light. "Man, you are something else, aren't you? Tell the truth. You really came out here looking for explanations. But I'm not interested in explaining."

She poured the cup of ice into the dish towel. "Let me see the hand, Clay," she said in an imitation of the no-nonsense voice she'd heard Ruby use with her children and grandchildren.

Clay responded appropriately. He turned around and leaned on the front quarter panel of his van, holding out his hand.

Jane took his hand in both of hers. His palms were warm and rough, and the feel of his skin sliding across hers made the breath hitch in her throat. His knuckles were bruised and abraded. The hand was swollen, but it didn't look as if he had broken any bones.

"Well," she said as she placed the icy towel over his knuckles. "This confirms it."

"Confirms what? That I'm some kind of out-of-control jerk?"

"No, that's not it. But it does confirm that your brother's head is harder than your knuckles. And that's saying something."

She looked up at him. He'd lost his hat somewhere, and the street light glimmered on his beautiful hair and the smile that ghosted his lips. Her heart stumbled in her chest. She could love this man. But loving him would be crazy.

After what seemed like an eternity, he pulled his hand away from hers and steadied the ice on his knuckles. "Yeah, well, thanks for the ice." He looked away.

"I'm not afraid of you, Clayton P. Rhodes." It was a lie.

"No?" he whispered.

"No," she whispered back. And to prove the point, Jane reached up behind his neck and pulled his head down toward her. He resisted, but after the second tug, he leaned forward and brought his forehead to rest on her shoulder. She inhaled him then: the scent of sweat and laundry detergent and secondhand cigarette smoke from the bar.

He leaned there for maybe half a minute, before he straightened. "I seem to be acting like some kind of freaking teenager these days. And I hate being so out of control. But I have to say something important—you are not what I need, Jane. I'm sorry to say that, but it's true."

"What *do* you need?" she asked, feeling the hurt of his words prickle along her skin and settle heavily into her heart.

He pushed up from the fender, the move violent and sudden. "I don't know what I need," he raged. He

punctuated the point by hurling the towel and the ice
against the brick wall. It hit with a slushy *slap*.

"Shit." He stood there, his back to Jane. He was
breathing hard, his hands clenched into fists. "I guess I
need to control my temper for starters."

"That would be good. But get this straight—until I
know you're okay, I'm not leaving you alone. I don't
need to be your lover, Clay. I'd like to be your friend."

More lies.

"You want to be my friend?" He looked at her over
his shoulder.

"Yeah."

He stared up at the streetlight for a long moment.
Then he turned and faced her. He continued to hesitate, as
if he were weighing the pros and cons of saying anything
else. When he finally spoke, his voice sounded tight. "I'm
stuck in my life, Jane. You need to know that."

"And what does that mean?"

"It means I'm having a midlife crisis, and *you* are
one of the symptoms. And meanwhile, the past is coming home to roost, and every time I think about changing
myself, the people in this one-horse town remind me who
and what I am."

She leaned her fanny against the fender, folding her
arms across her chest. She told herself he was just trying
to pick this fight because he was angry and wanted to
fight with someone—anyone. So she decided not to fight
him at all. "Who exactly are you?" she asked.

A bitter laugh escaped his lips. "I started out my life
as a fat boy with a violin whose only friend was a math
geek. And I've ended up a failure with a violin whose
only friend is a math geek with a damaged brain."

"A fat boy? I don't think so. You're a big man, but you aren't fat."

"Yeah, well, I was short and fat as a kid." He went back to studying the streetlight like it held the answers for him. "I didn't put on any growth until I was sixteen, and then I grew like a weed. And as for being a failure—my brother, Tulane, has just signed a contract with Ferguson Racing to be a NASCAR Sprint Cup driver; Stone is nearly 'bout the most well-respected man in Last Chance; and my little sister, Rocky, got herself a full ride to the University of South Carolina and parlayed her education into a job running Senator Rupert Warren's Columbia office."

"Clay, I hate to say this, but it seems to me that you are stuck in a vicious cycle of negative affirmations."

He turned an angry gaze on her. "Would you stop with the Pollyanna routine? If you want to be my *friend*, you're going to have to quit with the glass-is-half-full crap. I'm telling you right here, right now, the glass of my life is half-empty, okay?"

"Okay. But for the record, you are not the only one who suffered through teenaged angst. You have to stop calling yourself names. That kind of thinking won't help you get unstuck in your life."

"Do you ever stop with that bull? You don't know squat about my life."

"That's true, I don't. So tell me, is being stuck in your life the reason you unloaded on your brother?"

"Ah, I knew you would get around to asking that question sooner or later."

"You don't have to answer it if you don't want."

"No, I reckon I will," he said on a soft sigh. He came

forward and leaned into the fender beside her. He crossed his arms like a barrier. "Like I said, the folks in Last Chance will always see me as that fat boy with the violin who ran off to Nashville, failed miserably, and then came back. And if you want to know why I decked my brother, it was because I could see all that in his eyes, and it pissed me off."

"I'll bet."

"I'm not even sorry I did it."

"Good, you shouldn't be sorry for the way you feel. Hitting is wrong, but feelings are feelings."

"You sound like a kindergarten teacher."

"Yeah, well, you're acting like a preschooler."

"Thanks. So you think I should go use words and apologize, huh?"

"Only if you feel like it. It's okay to be pissed off at your brother, Clay. He's so easy to dislike."

That earned her a chuckle. "That makes you just about the only person in town who doesn't think he walks on water."

"For the record, I'm mostly here validating your feelings. Although, to be honest, your brother is not one of my favorite people, especially after what he did this morning."

He rolled his head so he could look at her out of the corner of his eye. "So you gonna tell me what *that* was all about?"

"I already told you about his theories. Are you trying to change the subject?"

"Uh-huh. And I'm doing that because I don't need anyone to validate my feelings, and I don't like being told that I'm acting like a preschooler. I'm trying real hard to get a grip on my feelings and act like a man."

Jane turned and faced him, leaning her hip into the fender. "I'm not buying your lame excuses. If you don't like it in Last Chance, it's time to move on."

"You mean like running away? Like what you did when you were a kid?"

Oooh, he was good. "That's one way to look at it," Jane said. "Or you could say you're moving on. You need to decide whether spending the rest of your days managing a hardware store for your ailing uncle and looking after people like Ray Betts will make you happy. You need to decide if maybe being a musician and going back to Nashville to play country music is what you want. And then there's the choice of going someplace like New York or L.A., where you could be the singer-songwriter that you want to be, but are too afraid to try."

"Wow, that's a lot of things on my 'to do' list. And, by the way, I thought you said you didn't know much about my life."

She shrugged. "I work in a beauty shop in a small town. You hang out there for a day and you pretty much get the full story on everyone."

"I see. And you're qualified to tell me what to do with my life because..."

"Well, it seems to me that you weren't shy about telling me what to do with *my* life. I think you told me on Thursday that I needed a positive plan for my life, and that singing karaoke and shaking my backside was not enough to get me into the Grand Ole Opry."

"Touché." He pushed himself away from the fender and turned to face her. "Look, I need to go bail out Ray. Would you do me a favor and tell Ricki that she needs to make nice to Tricia and let her sleep on my sofa?" He started to step around the van toward the driver's-side door.

Jane pushed away from the fender and followed him. "That woman is Tricia?"

Clay stopped in his tracks and turned, his features unreadable in the dim light. "You know about Tricia?"

She shrugged. "I heard about her at the beauty shop." A million new worries coursed through her head. That woman in the bar was pregnant.

He answered her unasked question. "Don't worry, it's not my baby. But I'm thinking she came here hoping I would rescue her."

"And you make a habit of doing that, don't you? And you go around making yourself responsible for everyone and everything."

"Is that what you think?"

"It's what I know, Clay. It's what I see with my own eyes. It's what I hear all the time in the gossip at the beauty shop. You rescued me on Wednesday. You gave Ricki a place to stay last night. And now this pregnant woman shows up and cries on your shoulder."

"I didn't rescue you on Wednesday. Let's get that straight. I took advantage of you on Wednesday."

She waved away his argument. "Okay, but you definitely feel responsible for Ricki and that other woman. And you look out for Ray all the time. Why do you feel responsible for him?"

A little muscle played in his cheek, but he said nothing.

And that's when it hit her, like the proverbial bolt of lightning or like some lame animated lightbulb above her head. She put all the puzzle pieces together—everything she'd heard down at the Cut 'n Curl suddenly added up and made sense.

"Oh, crap, you were driving the car the night Ray got hurt, weren't you?"

"You just won't give it a rest, will you?" Clay said, his voice sounding raw. He stood there looking vulnerable and angry and lost.

She walked the three paces that separated them. Then she wrapped her arms around his neck and pulled him back down to rest against her shoulder. He didn't resist so hard this time.

He was a big man, but she was strong enough to hold him up. She didn't think of herself as being strong, but she realized that all of the bad stuff that had happened to her over the last seven years had prepared her for this moment. He didn't need a lover right now. He needed someone to reflect back a new and different image from the one he was used to seeing in the mirror. And *that* was why the Universe had sent her to this place.

"What happened?" Jane asked.

He didn't say anything for the longest time. And then he inhaled and straightened up, his arms resting on her shoulders, his hands laced behind her neck. "It was senior year, two weeks before graduation. The Davis High baseball team had just won the state championship on the strength of Dash Randall's bat, and Ray and I were following the team bus on the way back from Columbia. And from out of nowhere, this pickup truck crosses the dividing line. It almost took out the bus, and I had to swerve." His lips pressed together. "The guy was toasted. I mean three sheets to the wind."

"Oh, Clay..."

"I know it wasn't my fault," he said tightly. "In my head I know that, but in my heart, I keep beating myself up for yanking the wheel to the left instead of the right. I replay that moment over and over again."

"Aw, honey." She reached up and touched his face, the texture of his goatee sliding under her fingers. Her body flashed hot, even as her mind told her to keep it friendly.

"Ray's body took the brunt of the collision, and he wasn't wearing his seatbelt. I walked away without a scratch. If I had turned the wheel the other way. If he had buckled up. If I had insisted that he buckle up..."

Clay captured her hand and brought it to his mouth. The feel of his soft, warm lips against her palm made her insides tense. He put her hand back on his cheek and leaned into it slightly. "I ran off with Ricki after high school mostly to get away, but when she dumped me for Randy, I came back for a time. I realized there was no getting away from what had happened. So I got Pete to give Ray a job at the hardware store before I headed back to Nashville to try a second time. Even when I was away, I kept tabs on Ray to make sure he got what he needed, and Uncle Pete helps me. But now with Pete so sick..."

His voice faded out, and he leaned his head into her so that they were touching forehead to forehead. "Bad stuff seems to happen to me more than your average guy. You should keep that in mind," he said.

Jane didn't have the heart or the courage to explain to him that he was a piker when it came to bad karma and bad luck. When it came to that kind of thing, she was the absolute queen of the Universe, which was the reason why the Universe had sent her here to listen to his story and tell him it was okay.

"So I guess you have to go rescue him now, huh?"

He nodded. "Yeah."

His hands played down her back and came to rest at the curve of her hip. He pulled her closer so that the contours of his thighs pressed against her. She wanted to melt right into him. Maybe he'd been fat once, but there wasn't any part of the man's body that wasn't rock hard now.

"I'm sorry, Jane," Clay said. "I wish I could tell you I had honorable intentions. But that's not the case. I just want you. Bad. I just want to lose myself in you, even though it's probably a huge mistake. That's how I felt on Wednesday. And I still feel that way. It's a case of runaway lust, and I'm weak."

He leaned down and captured her mouth. He was probably right about this being a mistake, but she opened up for him just the same. The rush hit her head and her heart and her core and her sexual places and almost buckled her knees. And then, just to punctuate the point, Clay linked a series of moist wet kisses down her jaw and into the hollow of her neck right to the place where he'd given her the hickey on Wednesday.

Jane had gone to great lengths to hide that love bite, but she did nothing to stop him from working that place against her neck. Instead, she found the elastic that held his hair back and pulled it free. His hair tumbled around them. He pressed himself against her—all hard bones and soft hair. His mouth worked at her neck, and little by little, Jane lost the ability to think rationally.

Oh, yeah, this was all about hormones and chemistry. Hot, dangerous, forbidden chemistry. The kind of experiment that ended up with something being torched or blown to smithereens.

"Lord a'mighty," he said against her neck. "You drive me crazy. All I can think about is pushing you upside the van and, well..." His hands made a slow circuit of her breasts and then moved to her shoulders. She was ready for his next move, knowing that what he wanted—what *they* wanted—was less than what either of them needed.

"But I'm not going to do that," he said in a deep and husky voice. "And not because you have some misguided notion of wanting to be my friend, either. That's BS, Jane. We are not going to be each other's friends, and we both know it."

Her heart sank—and soared. "It's because you think I'm bad for you, isn't it? A mistake," Jane said.

"No, that's not the reason," he replied. And her heart took flight again. Oh, Lord, being with him was like riding a roller coaster.

"Then why?"

"Because the next time I get naked with you, I'm not going to let myself think too hard about it. In fact, I'm going to let myself enjoy the ride. And when we have sex again, you are going to scream my name out loud."

"Oh." Her voice strangled in her throat because the fire in his eyes told her he intended to do what he said. She wanted it, too. Just the way he said. Even though her heart kept saying she wanted more than just *that* from him.

"And I'd go for it right now, but I'm kind of in a hurry. I gotta rescue Ray," he said, sealing the deal. She understood where she stood with him. She was just the girl he had the hots for. The one he wanted right now because he was in the middle of a life crisis.

"Okay," Jane said, but it wasn't okay. She swallowed hard, trying to keep the disappointment at bay.

"Look, tomorrow is Sunday and that gets kinda busy," he said in a tight voice. "I'll give you a call, okay?"

She didn't know how to respond to this. It was the classic line guys gave when they had to think things over. It was okay. She needed to think things over, too.

So Jane said nothing. He took it for assent, which was typical of most men. Then he let her go, climbed into his van, and fired that baby up. He left her standing there in the dust as he pulled out of the parking lot going faster than was altogether necessary.

Behind her, Ricki and Tricia opened the door to the bar and strode out into the alley together. They were both mad as hell—at each other, at her, but mostly at Clay, who was leaving them all in the dust.

The sound of the jukebox carried out into the night. Bubba Lockheart had punched up that stupid Tumbleweed song again, and the lyrics hit Jane upside the head and made her dizzy.

> *Do you love me more than need me?*
> *Baby I gotta know*
> *'Cause if it's just needing, then*
> *I gotta go.*

Chapter
14

Thelma Hanks's voice came over Clay's cell phone as he punched the gas in his POS Windstar and peeled out of Dottie's parking lot. "Oh, Clay," she said into his ear. "I heard about Ray. Eugene is already on his way to the sheriff's office."

"Someone called him already?" he asked.

"Yes, they did, about ten minutes ago."

"Who?"

"I don't know, honey; I didn't take the call."

Clay hung a right onto the state highway that led to Allenberg and thanked Thelma for the information. Then he hit the disconnect button on his phone and tried hard not to think about the conversation he'd just had with Jane. But his brain was not obeying his command these days. So he immediately began rehashing the entire scene.

It was a wonder the woman hadn't hauled off and slapped his face, given that he'd tried three or four times to pick a fight with her. For some crazy reason, he counted her restraint as a positive. She was pretty darn mature for a twenty-something. And then he realized that he was counting positives, and that annoyed the heck out of him.

He just needed to rescue Ray, and then he could try to figure out exactly what to do about Jane. He sure as shooting wasn't going to go looking for a quickie with her without thinking everything through two or three times. That was the mature thing to do, and come hell or high water, he intended to behave maturely from now on.

Fifteen minutes later, he walked into the fluorescent brightness of the Sheriff's Department's squad room. His brother leaned on the reception desk filling out paper-work. One look at Stone's face affirmed Clay's resolve to be grown-up from here on out.

Stone's nose would never be the same. It was lying over on its side, and the skin beneath both of his eyes had turned a shade of purple as dark and plump as the figs on the tree in Momma's backyard. Stony hadn't changed his shirt, and the blood spatter down the front made some-thing roil in Clay's stomach.

The guilt and remorse clutched Clay's middle and canceled out the momentary triumph he had felt during the fight. "Oh, Lord help me, Stony, I'm…" His voice got kind of wobbly, and he had to stop or lose it in front of his big brother. That would be just too humiliating for words.

"'S okay. It's just my nose."

Clay chose to read the expression on his brother's face as a smile, even though it was a whole lot less than that. "Yeah, but—"

"You were due." Stone shrugged.

"No, I was…" Clay's voice faded out with his confusion. What was he, exactly? Upset? Outraged? Enraged? Out of control? Just what *was* he? He didn't have a clue anymore. So he stood there feeling like a jerk.

Stone put his pen in the pocket of his ruined shirt and took a couple of steps forward. "You were due. You've been like a pressure cooker for a long time, since all that trouble in Nashville. And Uncle Pete's getting sick hasn't helped none. Not to mention that a-hole Alex showing up throwing his weight around. You were due, big-time."

Clay bit the inside of his cheek to keep from asking the suddenly urgent question about when Stony might be "due" for a breakdown. Near as anyone could figure, Stone had shed zero tears for his dead wife in almost five years. So when would Stone allow himself a breakdown? Probably never. Stone was made like a rock in more ways than one.

"I'm sorry, man," Clay said. The words were a pale substitute for the things he wanted to say about all the issues that lay between them—jealousy for sure, and sorrow that was too deep and too wide for brothers to talk about unless they both were drinking beer and sitting in a bass boat somewhere far away from public scrutiny.

"Apology accepted," Stone said.

"So I guess Eugene is here bailing Ray out?" Clay asked, breaking eye contact as he scanned the deserted squad room looking for Ray and Eugene.

"I don't think anyone's getting bailed out tonight, Clay. Ray confessed to stealing the money," Stone said softly.

"What?" Clay's gaze panned back to his older brother.

Stone put a steadying grip on Clay's shoulder. "Look, I know this is hard for you." Stone's voice had that mature and rational quality to it that Clay hated. His brother was so perfect sometimes.

Stone squeezed his shoulder. It was more than a friendly gesture. The touch told him that Stony cared about him, forgave him, loved him even. And that made Clay feel worse. He shucked the touch away. "Ray confessed? Why'd he do that?"

"Because he's guilty."

"Oh, for crying out loud, Ray didn't take the money."

"We found it in his locker at the store," Stone said.

"So?"

"So that's incriminating."

"Right. C'mon, Stone, if Ray took the money, why would he leave it in an unlocked locker? And why would Ray steal from the store? I'm pretty sure Alex set this whole thing up. Alex wants Pete to fire Ray. Alex figures he'll be in charge once Pete kicks the bucket. He also says Ray is a money-losing proposition. I'll bet you a hundred dollars Alex stole that money himself, just to get Ray in trouble."

Stone squeezed his puffy eyes closed for a moment. When he opened them again, he gave Clay a somber look. "You can't go around saying stuff like that without evidence. I'm sorry, but the evidence points to Ray taking the money. He doesn't have an alibi, and the patrons at Dot's put him on Palmetto Avenue about the time the crime took place. He had opportunity. Besides, Ray said he did it, Clay."

"What? Why would he—"

"My guess is Ray was lashing out at Alex. But maybe

not. Maybe he just had some other wild-ass notion. Who knows what goes on in his head?"

"Oh, for chrissake, you can't blame him just because—"

"Stop it. You've always got an excuse for him. And that's admirable. But you're not his keeper. Ray isn't stable. And what happens to him if Pete dies, God forbid? Are you going to stay here and look after him the way Pete's been doing all these years?"

"You know good and well that Ray would never—"

"It's got to end, Clay. For your own sake. It's got to." Stone took Clay's shoulder again and gave him a little shake. "And now it has. He needs to be put someplace where he won't hurt himself or anyone else."

"So let me get this straight," Clay said, his voice inching up with his ire. "I'm supposed to sit back and let the state put Ray in jail even though I know he didn't commit this crime? And sitting back and letting that happen is supposed to help me move on with my life?"

"C'mon, Clay, do you have to twist everything up?"

"I'm not twisting anything. I'm just saying Ray is innocent. I don't give a rat's behind what he said to any damn sheriff's deputy or even to you. And I'm sure not going to stand here and let you throw him in jail."

"I'm not going to throw him in jail, you idiot." Stone's voice increased a notch.

"Then what?" Suddenly, for the second time that evening, he found himself standing toe to toe with his older brother, wishing the guy would just get out of his way.

Stone took a breath and blew it out like he, too, was fighting for control. It was uncanny the way Stone could swallow down his emotions so quick.

"Look," Stone said a moment later in a voice that was rational and calm. "Eugene is talking with the county prosecutor to see if they can negotiate a deal where the state drops the charges if Ray goes into a state home or halfway house. We've got social services on standby. Eugene does this kind of thing all the time. He might not know criminal law, but he knows how to deal with people like Ray."

Clay's heart twisted in his chest. "Y'all want to commit him to a state institution? That's worse than putting him in jail."

"It is not. It's what Ray needs. It's what *you* need. His momma's gone. Pete is sick. And even though Aunt Arlene says the folks up at the Mayo Clinic have given her some hope, the fact remains that people don't recover from lung cancer most of the time.

"Look, Clay, it's the only solution to this problem. And it's been inevitable. You just haven't been willing to admit it."

"I can't believe this," Clay raged. "Ray didn't do anything wrong. Arresting him for this is the stupidest thing on the face of the earth. The only thing stupider was arresting Jane this morning. You know, you don't have to be such a tough guy just because you used to be a homicide detective in Tallahassee. You could start behaving like the small-town cop you're supposed to be. You could start—"

"Look," Stone cut him off and pointed a finger at his chest. "First of all, stealing a thousand dollars is a serious offense. Unfortunately, even though the money has been recovered, Alex Lovett is not willing to let the issue slide, and he's been all over Sheriff Bennett to get justice on this."

"Alex doesn't own the store, Stone. Not yet, anyway. Maybe not ever. Pete can't stand Alex."

"It doesn't matter. The county has pulled rank on me. You know how tight Alex is with his cousin Billy. There isn't much I can do."

"Jeez, Stone, I—"

"And"—his brother pushed his finger deeper into Clay's sternum—"if you think Mary Smith is innocent, then you need to quit thinking with your dick. They found Jane Coblentz's blood in a hotel room in Lexington, Kentucky. Her last hours were spent with a strung-out junkie who went on a crime spree, shooting up a convenience store and putting some guy in a wheelchair for the rest of his life. I'm telling you, Clay, that hotel room had been stripped of its bedding and all the towels. The bathroom had been scrubbed, as if someone wanted to erase the evidence. But they missed some blood, and they didn't know about Luminol. Jane Coblentz is dead. And that woman you think so highly of has the dead girl's driver's license."

All the wind left Clay's sails. "Blood? What are you talking about?"

"Momma didn't tell you, did she?"

"Tell me what? What blood are you talking about?"

"Look, Clay, I don't want to ruin any budding romance here, but you need to know the facts. Why don't I get us a couple of coffees and I can fill you in on all the details? By the time we're finished, you'll have a different view of the situation. And maybe by then, Eugene and the prosecutor will have worked out some kind of deal to get Ray out of the county lockup and into a halfway house."

• • •

It was almost three in the morning before Clay made it home, exhausted, emotionally drained, and longing for a few hours of shut-eye before he had to haul his butt out of bed and play organ at Sunday services.

Ray was in the custody of social services and likely to end up permanently in a halfway house. Clay had failed to rescue him.

Worse than that, Stony wasn't nearly the idiot Clay had figured him for. His brother had some pretty damning evidence that suggested Jane was guilty of something terrible. Jane Coblentz might not be Jane at all, but some other person. Maybe someone named Mary.

He didn't want to believe it, but when Stone laid out the facts, there were only a few conclusions he could draw.

Clay didn't want to feel disappointed, but he did. He needed to get some sleep, and get a grip, and regroup, and try to figure out what his next move needed to be. One thing *was* clear. He needed to get over his midlife crisis, put that little gal out of his head, and focus on the important stuff: saving Ray from a state-run institution and finding a nice girl to settle down with.

Clay stumbled through the door of his little bungalow, intent on falling into bed and finding oblivion. But the Almighty had another plan for him.

He hadn't gotten three steps into his tiny living room before he tripped over something that wasn't supposed to be there. He landed hard on his hands and knees.

"Crap," he muttered, as he remembered that his exes were cohabitating in his small house. Obviously they had decided to rearrange not only his life, but his living-room furniture as well.

"Clay, is that you?" A sleepy voice murmured in the darkness. Tricia was sleeping on his sofa.

The lamp on the end table snapped on, blinding him as he pushed himself off the floor.

"Oh, God, I'm so sorry. I shouldn't have left my suitcase open like that."

Clay turned around. Tricia looked like crap. Her eyes were puffy, and her nose was red. She had obviously been crying herself to sleep.

He stifled the urge to pull her up into his arms and pat her back and offer a Kleenex. Instead he just studied her for a long moment thinking ugly thoughts.

Like it served her right.

Like he had cried himself to sleep only a few million times after he caught her and Chad humping like bunnies in the back of Tumbleweed's tour bus.

Like he'd given up his dreams for this woman who had pretty much burned all her bridges when she'd told him he had never satisfied her in bed the way Chad did. He ought to put her out onto the street. Only he couldn't. Because he still loved her.

Maybe not like he'd loved her a year ago, but he loved her just the same. It was a feeling he would probably never lose. He kind of loved Ricki, too. Or at least the memory of her when they were both seventeen and chasing a dream.

Tricia sniffled. He felt himself weaken.

Why did stuff like this always happen? A woman would cry, and it would twist up his insides. Like he needed to do something about it when he was in the presence of a distressed female. He stared hard at the glittering tears in Tricia's eyes, but this time the only thing that crossed his mind was how Jane had come out to the alley earlier that night and given him a place to rest his head.

He couldn't think of any other woman who had ever done that for him. It had felt so good resting his head against her shoulder. It had felt as if that little gal had enough strength to actually hold him up for a small space of time.

Neither Tricia nor Ricki could have managed that. They didn't have such strong shoulders, he reckoned.

"Oh, Clay, what am I going to do?" Tricia dissolved into sobs.

He crossed the carpet and sat down on the couch and took her into his arms. It felt good to have her there. Not mindless and out of control like having Jane pressed up against him. Just nice. The kind of nice he was looking for.

Tricia blubbered against his shoulder. The feel of her, even rounded in pregnancy, kind of turned him on. Not the way Jane turned him on down in his sexual parts. But in a manly way that had more to do with being a good person than being a rutting bull.

He could get used to this. He could be happy with Tricia in his life.

He could go for having babies, too. He wanted a family. He wanted a whole passel of kids. And Tricia would make a good momma, too.

There was only one bad thing about this scenario.

Tricia was crying over someone else.

That pretty much made this a nice fantasy. But it wasn't real. Even if he wanted a mature and stable woman to marry, he also wanted that woman to love him. It wasn't enough for him to love Tricia, and Tricia just to need him in return. He wanted more than that.

He didn't want to settle. He wanted the whole she-bang: the mature, stable woman, the marriage, the kids, and love, too. In short, he wanted his soulmate. And he just wasn't certain she had arrived yet.

The next nine-thirty bus from Atlanta came on Monday. So maybe there was still hope.

Haley Rhodes touched her new necklace to make sure the little camel was showing. Granny said the little green charm looked pretty against the yellow of Haley's Sunday dress. Granny said it had been nice of Jane to give her the jewelry.

Of course, Granny didn't know that the necklace had belonged to Jane's peckerwood boyfriend or that Haley had dug it out of the trash. Haley knew better than to tell Granny the entire truth of how she had sweet-talked Jane into giving her the necklace. Besides, she liked Jane and didn't want to get her in trouble. Jane was way more interesting than the last babysitter.

Like for instance, in addition to maybe being a floozy, Jane didn't go to church, just like Daddy. Jane must be angry at God, too.

Haley sat on a folding chair in the fellowship hall, her feet tucked up under her as she sipped on a cup of apple cider. She was keeping an eye on things, which was hard because the Sorrowful Angel was being a poop-head.

The Angel was hovering across the room at the long table where Miz Randall sat, instead of hanging around near the doughnut table at the opposite corner where Jeremiah Jones and Lizzy were standing. Haley needed to have eyes in both sides of her head to keep track of both the Angel and her older sister. She really kind of wanted to spy on Lizzy and Jeremiah, but Haley needed to keep an eye on the Angel, too.

And then there was Uncle Clay, who *had* come to church and played the organ just like always. Right now, the Sunday school teacher, Miz Bray, was giving him dirty looks from her place by the coffee station. Granny said Uncle Clay was in big trouble on account of the fact that he had broke Daddy's nose.

Daddy had two black eyes.

Daddy said Uncle Clay had apologized, but Granny said that wasn't enough. Granny said Uncle Clay was acting like an idiot. Daddy kind of agreed about that and blamed Jane for the way Uncle Clay was acting. Granny didn't seem to think Jane was to blame.

Anyways, Granny was really mad this morning about Uncle Clay, so Haley was staying out of her way.

Haley gave up watching Lizzy, and instead, she watched Uncle Clay. He said something to Miz Bray and smiled at her. But the Sunday school teacher didn't smile back. Yup, Uncle Clay was really in the doghouse about breaking Daddy's nose, even though Miz Bray didn't even like Daddy that much.

Uncle Clay left the coffee station with two cups in his hand. He headed toward Miz Randall. The Sorrowful Angel watched him, like maybe she was mad at him, too.

That was interesting. Why would the Angel be mad at Uncle Clay? Haley needed to find out. So she hopped down from the folding chair and skipped in the direction of Uncle Clay, Miz Randall, and the Angel, trying for all she was worth to look like she was just playing around like all the other bored kids, instead of moving in so she could hear what the grown-ups were saying.

• • •

Miriam Randall took the Styrofoam coffee cup from Clay's hand and blinked up at him from behind her rhinestone bifocals. "Busy night?" she asked.

Clay sank down into a hard-backed folding chair and watched his niece as she skipped past the table. Miriam looked at him expectantly, and he was suddenly at a loss for words. Clay leaned back in the chair and shut his eyes. He could fall asleep right here.

Miriam took a noisy sip of her coffee and then spoke. "So it appears to be raining single white females around here, doesn't it?"

Clay opened his eyes and leaned forward, bracing his elbows on his knees. "You wouldn't have anything to do with that, would you?"

Miriam giggled like a little girl. "Honey, I'm good, but I'm not *that* good. I can't make women fall from the sky—or arrive on the bus from Atlanta. But the Lord, well now, the Lord has a way of answering prayers. I have been praying for you, if it's any consolation. It does appear that the Lord has answered our prayers in a big way. He sure has given you a wide range of choices."

"You think?"

Miriam nodded. "Oh, I know, honey." She shifted her gaze across the room to where Ricki, who was dressed for church in a little pink designer number that made her look like go-to-church Barbie, was working the room like the flirt she had always been. Ricki was cruising for a place to stay, and by the look of things, Dash was interested in signing up.

"She's getting pretty cozy with my nephew." Miriam's voice didn't sound too pleased.

"Not his soulmate, huh?"

"Most definitely not. You need to tell Ricki to keep her hands off."

"Right. Like Ricki listens to me."

"Honey, if you want to marry that girl, you're going to have to find some way to keep her."

"Miriam, you can't be serious. Ricki isn't *my* soulmate, either. And you know it. She's only interested because she has this misguided notion that the royalties from Tumbleweed's first album have made me rich."

"They haven't?"

"No, ma'am. I'm comfortable, but not rich. Not even close to rich if you measure by Dash's standards. Baseball pays better than songwriting, believe me."

She gave him an enigmatic smile, then shifted her gaze toward Tricia. "So maybe it's the girl behind door number two. And this one has the advantage of coming ready-made with that family you've been hankering for. Sometimes the Lord is magnificent in the way He answers our prayers."

Clay gritted his teeth. Chad Ames was a class-A jerk. How could anyone walk away from Tricia and the baby she was carrying?

"Yeah, Miriam, she's got it bad for someone else." Clay swept the hall with a pair of eyes that burned from lack of sleep. And alighted on Betty Wilkins, who was dressed today in a yellow dress with a sweetheart neckline that showed off her cleavage. Her dark hair was piled high, and her makeup was a little on the heavy-handed side, but the woman looked comfortable in her own skin. Okay, so maybe she wasn't so smart. But she was sweet, and she was built.

"You know," Clay said aloud, "right now Betty

Wilkins looks like the best choice of the lot. At least she's steady and—"

"Honey, Betty is not for you," Miriam said in a flat voice. "And you know this, so don't fool with me."

"You're sure she's not the one?"

"No, honey, she didn't come on the bus. And besides, she's already spoken for."

Clay blinked at the erstwhile chairwoman of the Ladies Auxiliary. "You're serious, aren't you? About the bus, I mean."

Miriam patted his hand. "Of course I am, honey. I never joke about these matters. When I told you that your soulmate was not living in Allenberg County, I was being completely honest."

"So who has spoken for Betty? Please don't tell me it's my older brother."

Miriam snorted. "No, it's not your brother. Stone still loves Sharon, and there isn't any more to say on that score. I've told your momma that, but of course, she wants to see her oldest learn to love again. Quite frankly, I'm skeptical that it will ever happen. The Lord has been silent about your older brother for quite some time."

"Well I guess that's semigood news, since I'm not sure I want Betty Wilkins as a sister-in-law."

"Well, you can relax. She's meant for someone else."

Clay leaned in, not averse to sharing some gossip, himself. "Who is it?"

Miriam shrugged. "Not for me to say, Clay. I told you I'm not a gossip."

"Much." He leaned back in his chair. "I just hope whoever he is isn't using her, you know what I mean?" Betty was too sweet for her own good.

"You are a good man, Clay Rhodes. And no, Betty's beau is not taking advantage of her. He is, in fact, her soulmate. He just hasn't figured it out yet."

Clay sighed deeply.

"Now, that was a sorrowful sound. You have no reason to be that sorrowful, boy."

"No, ma'am. My best friend is in a state institution, my mother is not speaking to me on account of the fact that I messed up my brother's face, and I've got two women living in my house with me, one of them divorced, and the other an unwed mother.

"Add to that the fact that my cousin-by-marriage is a jerk, and my father, who swears he talks to angels, expects me to eventually take over the management of his miniature golf course devoted to the Lord. As you can see, my life is a picnic."

"Yes, but the Lord is doing His best to answer your prayers."

Clay blinked down at Miriam. "What, by sending a steady stream of women on the nine-thirty bus from Atlanta?"

She shrugged, her eyes lighting up like the sparkly rhinestones in her glasses. "You have to admit, three in the space of five days is pretty extraordinary, seeing as nobody ever comes to Last Chance these days."

"Oh, so you're including the third one—the one who isn't here today because she isn't a Christian."

"Oh, I wouldn't say that, honey. Your momma says the girl has a deep faith in something that might be the Almighty. She just doesn't realize that's what it is."

Clay leaned in. "Trust me on this, Miriam, Jane is not a Christian, unless we have taken up the concept of karma and manifesting better realities. And besides, I know you ladies know all about what Jane and I did on Wednesday night. So in addition to not being Christian, Jane is not what y'all would call a sweet little thing."

"I don't think she's fallen *that* far, honey."

Obviously the town gossips had not yet heard about that hotel room in Lexington, but it was only a matter of time.

"For the record, Clay, Jane did my nails on Friday. The girl's got a gift."

"Yeah." *Like for crime.*

"Yeah? That's all you have to say? Jane has a wonderfully positive outlook on life, son. And she's a strong woman. She's learned how to take care of herself, and she's determined. That's something."

"I think I'll just wait to see what comes on Monday's nine-thirty bus. Jane is kinda young for me." And kind of crazy. Not to mention the walking embodiment of trouble. And her name might not even *be* Jane.

"Well, that's true, I guess. Jane's not exactly the mature woman you were looking for."

"No, Miriam, I don't think so," Clay said, feeling a little hitch in his chest because he didn't want to think the worst of Jane. He kept thinking about the things they had talked about last night. He'd been ugly to her, and she just came back for more, like some kind of punch-drunk fighter—or a remarkably strong and mature woman.

"And she's running from something, isn't she?" A little frown folded into Miriam's brow.

"Yes, she is. And I have a feeling it's not very nice," Clay said.

"Well, of course, it isn't nice," Miriam said with a little sniff. "People don't run away from nice things, do they?"

Chapter
15

Sunday started off clear and semicool. Jane opened the windows and let in fresh air touched with the bite of autumn. The October breeze lifted the curtains, and restlessness stirred inside her. It had been a while since she'd experienced the turn of a season. When she was young, autumn always brought this restlessness on, as if she were a migratory bird that needed to hit the skyway for warmer climes.

She tuned the kitchen radio to a country station, and the sexy tones of that stupid Tumbleweed song filled her ears as she stared down at Palmetto Avenue, watching folks go to church.

She listened carefully to the words because Clay had written them.

> *Do you love me more than need me?*
> *Baby I gotta know*
> *'Cause if it's just needing, then*
> *I gotta go*

Here in my heart
Where I'm not so damn tough
I want you to love me
Needin's not near enough
Do you love me?
Or just need me.
Baby, I gotta know.

Hoo boy. Her pulse rate kicked up a beat or two. It would be easy to fall in love with a man sensitive enough to understand the difference between wanting and needing and loving. But was Clay that guy? Or had he just written a song with some good words?

That was a dangerous question. Maybe she had been looking for the wrong thing all these years. Maybe the best a girl could hope for was a simple man like the narrator in the song. Not a hero, just a guy who wanted to be loved.

Yeah, like there were really men like that in the world.

She knew it wasn't a positive thought. But love songs weren't reality, either. Songs were bought and sold like everything else. And pinning her hopes to a song lyric was like wishful thinking.

Songs were not real life.

She needed to quit dreaming and concentrate on the real things in her life. Like getting out of Last Chance before she slept with Clay Rhodes a second time. Because sleeping with Clay would be a cosmic mistake.

Jane knew that. Clay knew that. End of story.

There was a bus to Columbia tomorrow morning at seven-thirty. She was going to be on that bus, and she didn't care if Chief Rhodes viewed her departure as jumping bail. He'd learn soon enough that his theories about what happened in Lexington were all wrong.

Jane walked into the kitchen and snapped off the radio. She needed to concentrate on what she wanted out of life, not some fantasy. So she picked up a piece of notebook paper resting on the kitchen table and scanned the lyrics to "I Will Always Love You."

She took several deep breaths and concentrated on relaxing the muscles in her neck and jaw. Then she reached for her "head voice" and worked on supporting it deep down in her diaphragm just the way her high-school music teacher had taught her.

She began singing a cappella. That was better. When she sang, she could keep her loneliness and her disappointment at bay and channel her deepest fears and desires and emotions into the song itself.

Clay was still trying to get Miriam's words out of his head as he pulled his Windstar into a parking spot right in front of the Kountry Kitchen. He stepped out into a bright October day, but he had no energy to enjoy the weather. All he could think about was sleep. And since he had no intention of going home and getting caught in a cat fight between the hormonal Tricia and the desperate Ricki, he intended to nap on the couch in Pete's office.

Clay was heading up the street toward the hardware store when he heard music, and it entered his ears, and knocked around his brain, and messed up his mind. He stood there planning to turn right and slip his key into the lock on the front door of the store, but instead he turned left and looked up at the open windows above the Cut 'n Curl.

The wind lifted the yellow gingham and carried the sound of Jane's voice to him. Like a Siren of old, she beckoned him toward shipwreck. The sound pulled and tugged at him, reminding him that there was a bed in the apartment above the Cut 'n Curl, and, more important, a pair of arms that would hold him tight. He wanted to rest in the circle of Jane's arms, like he'd rested against her last night.

Clay wanted to follow the music. But danger lay in that direction. Jane was trouble. Stone had made that pretty clear last night, and Clay already had too many things to worry about.

He forced himself to turn right and slipped his key into the hardware store's lock. The wind blew, and the sound of Jane's voice carried. He stopped and rested his head against the cool of the windowpane and listened. She had learned that song real well. Her phrasing was perfect. When she got to the words about how she wasn't what he needed, he yanked the key out of the lock and turned around.

Shoot. Who said she wasn't what he needed? He needed that girl like a starving man needed bread. He needed her in a way he'd never needed anyone in his life.

But he also cared about what had happened in that hotel room in Lexington. Something terrible happened there. He needed to know the truth.

He hurried across the street and took the fire escape steps two at a time. Then he stood there on the other side of the door listening to her sweet, sweet voice. Man oh man, she could sing. And when she sang, it was like the sound of angels.

He waited until she finished the song, and then he pounded on her door like a madman.

Jane nearly jumped out of her skin when someone pounded on the door. Her first fear was that Woody had found her, and then she saw Clayton P. Rhodes silhouetted against the shirred curtains. It was not a calming sight.

Jane opened the door a crack and peered out at him. He stood there on the landing looking like some cross between an ice cream sundae, something the cat dragged home, and the big bad wolf. She wanted to eat him up, open her arms and take care of him, and slam the door in his face and go cower in the bathroom.

"I'm sorry," Clay muttered. "I...uh...heard you singing, and I..."

"Did you get any sleep last night?"

"Nope. Not one wink."

"Were you able to rescue Ray, at least?" Jane asked, forcing the conversation in that direction just to remind herself where she stood in his list of priorities.

He shook his head. "Nope. I didn't accomplish that, either. Ray confessed to the crime. His lawyers and the prosecutor are arguing now about which group home to send him to." His voice wavered a little, and she watched the tendons work in his neck. He was at the end of his emotional rope. She tried not to empathize too much with him on that score.

She failed.

"But I know he didn't steal that money," Clay said in a grim voice. "I just need time to figure out how to prove he's innocent."

The man had complete faith in his friend. Her throat

got tight thinking about that. What would it be like to have someone to watch her back like that?

And the sheer seduction of that thought made her firm her resolve. She needed Clay to back off. She needed to back off. Someone was going to get hurt, and Jane didn't want to be the one. "I'm sorry, Clay, but—"

He put his hand on the door and pushed back on it, forcing her to step deeper into the room. "Here's a news flash for you: For some reason I can't explain, I believe in *your* innocence, too. Let me in."

Jane pushed back on the door. "My innocence? Jeez, Clay, thanks. Last night you told me I was a mistake you were about to make, and now you think I'm innocent. You need to get your—"

"Listen to me, for once! I don't believe you killed anyone in Lexington. I just want to know the truth. And then I want to crash on your couch. And after that, I have a long agenda of stuff that I want, starting with your body."

"No," Jane said, a wave of real fear washing through her. She pushed harder on the door, trying to push him out of her apartment—out of her life.

"No?" Clay pushed back. He gave her a boyish grin that melted a little piece of her heart. He was in flirt mode now. She hated him for turning on the charm like that.

"Letting you in would be a dumb idea," Jane said.

"Why? After the kiss last night, I thought you were hot for me. I'm hot for you, Jane. I admit it. I'm weak."

"You're the one who said it would be a mistake. I concur."

"Yeah. So why'd you chase me out into the alley last night? Why'd you bring ice for my hand? Why'd you kiss me back?"

"Temporary insanity."

"Okay, you win. Let's be friends."

"Friends?"

"Uh-huh. Friends. You can tell me the truth, I'll forgive you, and then I can crash on the couch."

"Don't you have a home to go to somewhere?"

"Yeah," he said in a tired voice. "I've got two ex-girlfriends living at my house. My mother is not speaking to me because I broke Stone's nose. That leaves either your couch or the lumpy sofa at the store. For obvious reasons, your couch sounds way more comfortable."

Okay, she could resist this. "Gee thanks, Clay, you really know how to court a woman. And about those women. What are you going to do about Tricia?"

"I have no idea. She wants me to be her child's daddy, seeing as the biological father is an a-hole. But, you know, it's not my kid."

"Well, that shouldn't matter, if you love her."

"Maybe not. But in this case, she's in love with the jerk who got her pregnant, and that kind of ruins it for me, ya know? But she says I'm her best friend, and we should get married."

"Gee, Clay, didn't I hear from Ray that you had a list and were looking for a nice wife?"

"This is the man who thinks your name is April. You shouldn't listen to him."

The fact that Ray knew she had posed for those photos was precisely the reason she should listen to him. Ray might be a little weird, but he was smarter than people gave him credit for.

Jane inched her chin up. "I'll listen to Ray if I want to. And I saw his list. It had all these women on it, and my score—or to be more precise April's score—was low. I seem to have failed most of his tests."

"Jeez. You saw that stupid list? Look, I've given up on that plan. It's not working out."

"No?" She pushed back but didn't budge the door an inch.

"No, it's not. I've decided to follow Miz Miriam's plan instead."

She went cold. "What did Miriam Randall tell you?"

"I take it from your tone of voice that you have learned all about Miriam and her predictions."

"I have. The old lady told me I needed to hold out for a knight in shining armor, and you don't look like one of those. So in a way, I'm following Miriam's plan. She told me to ask for more and not to settle."

"She told you that?"

"Yes, she did." Jane pushed back on the door.

Clay met her resistance with relentless pressure of his own. He was going to get through this door. The only question was whether he was going to walk through it as her lover or her friend.

"Well," he said, "Miriam told me that my soulmate would arrive on the nine-thirty bus from Atlanta. And that makes you a possible candidate for my soulmate. Miriam says this is all part of the Lord's plan."

"The Lord's plan?" Her voice squeaked.

"Yes, ma'am. But if I understand Miriam correctly, she seems to think the Lord's plan is the same as the Universe's plan. Although I'm not entirely sure on the absolute theology of this, on account of the fact that I haven't had that much sleep."

"Miriam Randall told you that she understands

about the Universe?" Jane let the door go, and Clay stepped right into the apartment and closed the door behind him.

Oh, crap, she'd let him in, and she wasn't certain whether he'd come as a lover, or a friend, or some horny guy, or some honorable man bent on rescuing her.

"Well," Clay said, looking down at her out of bleary eyes, "I don't rightly know. But she is of the opinion that you haven't fallen far from the Lord."

The minute the words left Clay's mouth he realized his mistake. Jane whirled away from him and made a beeline toward the bathroom. If she ever got to that door, she'd lock herself in, and he'd never get another opportunity to break down her barriers.

Of course, he wasn't quite sure why the barriers had appeared. Last night, he could have sworn the woman was hot for him. But the temperature in this room was approaching absolute zero.

Oh, crap. He needed to face the fact that he had a crazy, mixed-up, reckless, and immaturely romantic urge to take care of Jane, and not because she was running from something ugly. Down deep he had this feeling— this crazy hope, really—that Jane might want to take care of him right back. And that crazy hope led him to the unfounded conclusion that if the two of them could get the taking-care-of-each-other thing down, nature would take care of everything else.

So Clay chased after her, and because he had longer legs, he caught up with her before she could reach the bathroom to lock herself in.

"Whoa, now," Clay said as he grabbed her upper arm,

making sure he didn't grab it too tight, or too hard, or in any way that she might find threatening.

But grabbing Jane was kind of a threat, and she tried to escape his grasp. He had to use both hands on her shoulders and yank her around so that he stood between her and the bathroom door.

"No," Clay said looking down into her face. "You don't get to run away from me. Or lock yourself in the bathroom. Not after last night, you don't."

"Nothing happened last night, unless you count the fact that you told me I was a symptom of your midlife crisis."

Shoot. He'd forgotten those stupid things he told her last night when he wanted to push her away. Instead, he had gotten swept up into a mind-blowing kiss that almost carried him right back to the Peach Blossom Motor Court.

Obviously, she hadn't forgotten the stupid things he said. Women were like that. They had memories like steel traps.

"Look, I'm sorry about what I said last night, Jane. I didn't—"

"Oh, yes, you did mean it. Now let me—"

"Okay, so maybe I did mean it...sort of...at the moment I said it. But that was then, and this is now, and..." He stopped speaking before he dug himself all the way to China.

"And what?" Jane demanded.

"Look, the last eighteen hours have been kinda rough on me, you know? I'm confused. I'm dazed. I'm sleepless. I said stuff last night to push you away, but I didn't want to push you away. You should have realized that the moment I broke down and kissed you. Okay?"

Her shoulders relaxed a fraction, and he thought he'd better clear the air entirely. "And then I went off to the police station and talked to Stone. What he told me confused me some more. Jane, what happened in Lexington? I gotta know."

Her shoulders stiffened again. Something real bad had happened in Kentucky. He was afraid of learning the truth.

"You gotta know?" she whispered and then let go of a bitter-sounding laugh. She looked up at the ceiling, purposefully avoiding his stare.

"Jane?" He gave her little shake.

She responded by trying to twist away from him. "It's not important. The past isn't important. Just leave me the hell alone, okay? I don't gotta tell you anything, because we don't have any kind of relationship unless you count one night at a no-tell motel."

"No, I'm not going to leave you alone," Clay said, softening his voice. He reached up and stroked her temple, her silky skin warm under the pad of his thumb. The touch ignited his libido. He wanted to be her friend, but his body kept pushing him the other way. He forced himself to think about the things Stone had said about the hotel in Kentucky. It helped, but not entirely.

"Darlin', look at me," Clay said.

Jane shook her head and closed her eyes.

"Darlin', you can't carry this alone."

"Yes, I can," she said in a strangled whisper.

"No, you can't."

"I told you. It's not important."

"Are you worried about what I might think?" he asked.

Jane opened her eyes and stared up at him. He'd hit the mark.

"Baby, I promise you," Clay murmured, "I won't think less of you if you let me share this burden."

Jane made a little noise and then shook her head. "You can't make that promise, Clay. You don't know."

"Did someone die in that room, girl? Tell me the truth."

Her body tensed, and his heart sank. Someone *had* died in that room.

"Who, Jane? Who died?"

She said nothing. She hardly moved. It was like she had shut down or given up or something.

"Jane?"

She took in a deep breath and let it out. He could almost feel her marshaling her strength, and he found himself rooting her on.

"Innocence and Faith," she said in a wobbly voice.

That threw him for a loop. "What happened, darlin'?"

Muscles tensed in her jaw as she fought against tears. She collapsed into his chest. She didn't cry, though. She just let him hold her up, as if she was drawing strength from him.

It felt right to have her in his arms, and not just because she was a woman in need and he was a sucker for needy women. It felt like coming home. Like Miriam Randall knew what the hell she was doing sending him to her. Because hadn't that old lady sent him here precisely to find out what Jane was running from? Like his holding Jane up was part of some plan the universe had set in motion.

But maybe Clay was getting carried away. He always got carried away. He needed to remember that someone had died in that hotel room, and Jane had been there when it happened.

"Jane? What happened in Lexington?"

She let go a shuddering breath. "I wanted to call her Faith."

"Who?"

"The baby I lost in that room."

His stomach clenched. Oh, Lord.

"How pregnant were you?" he asked. His voice sounded ragged to his own ears.

"Four months."

"Jane, you didn't—"

She pushed back and looked up at him with this ravaged look on her face. "I didn't kill my baby. She was born too soon. And I don't understand why the Universe let that happen."

A rush of relief wrapped up in deep affection washed through him as he pulled her into his arms and made soft noises against her temple for a couple of minutes.

"Honey, I'm sorry about the baby—" he began.

"I told you I wanted to call her Faith," she said emphatically.

She had named her lost child Faith. He didn't want to delve too deep into the psychology of that.

"Darlin', this is nothing to be ashamed of."

"You don't understand." Jane pushed back and ran the palm of her hand over her cheek, knocking away tears she still refused to cry. "The point is I got myself into trouble and then I decided to run away with Joey instead of facing my parents with the truth, and because of me,

Faith died, and Joey went to prison, and some guy up in Lexington is in a wheelchair for life. I'm bad news, Clay. I'm bad luck and bad karma, and Mrs. Randall is wrong. The Lord has never been on my side."

Okay, Clay was confused now. He'd been working himself up to hearing about some heinous murder, and now she was talking about some guy in a wheelchair. "Baby, you want to slow down and try that one again, because I'm working on no sleep here and my brain's not functional."

"Look," she said, turning around and putting her hands on her hips. "I got pregnant. I didn't tell my folks because I was afraid my pa would beat the crap out of me for it, or maybe haul off and shoot Joey. Instead, I ran away with Joey. And when we got to Lexington, I started having cramps and that's when Joey found out I was pregnant. He wasn't happy to learn that. So he dropped me off at a sleazy motel and left me there. He said he was going to find a doctor. Only he didn't come back. And the next morning...after I...lost the baby...I turned on the television, and I saw where the law had chased Joey down after he'd shot someone."

Her voice petered out, and tears leaked from her eyes. Clay reached for her, and she ducked. "I've always believed Joey robbed that store to get money for a doctor."

"That wasn't your fault," Clay said, feeling a sudden connection with her that went so deep he could feel it in his bones. He understood what it was like to feel guilty about something that wasn't really his fault.

"No?"

"Honey, it wasn't your fault that this Joey guy shot someone instead of being smart and dialing 911."

"I should have told him the truth before we ran away. He freaked out when I started bleeding."

"So he dumps you at a sleazy hotel and runs off and knocks over a convenience store? Nice guy."

"I drove him to it."

"You did no such thing. The cops in Kentucky think this Joey guy killed you, don't they?"

Jane nodded.

"I seem to recall Stone saying that this jerk was some kind of junkie."

"For the record, I had no idea Joey was into any drugs. I'm not sure your brother has all the facts right."

"Look, honey, Joey dumped you in that hotel room and never intended to come back. When he found out you were pregnant, he got the hell out of Dodge and stopped off at the convenience store on the way out of town."

Jane closed her eyes. "Okay, so he was a weasel. But don't you see? Bad things like this happen to me all the time."

Clay shook his head. "This has nothing to do with bad karma, Jane. Listen to me. Seventeen-year-olds can do some real bone-headed things—like not calling 911 when it's the smart thing to do, or running off with losers instead of going home and telling their parents they made a mistake. I'm pretty certain your folks would have understood. Why didn't you go back home?"

"There was no reason to. I was done watching Pa beat on Ma, and I changed my name so the law couldn't find me. I felt responsible for what Joey had done."

Jane stood there looking pitiful, and Clay hauled her

back to his chest where she belonged. She didn't resist. It felt good to have her there, warm and alive against him, her curvy body under his hands.

And it felt good to have this Lexington mystery solved. Jane hadn't done anything wrong. She was just torn up with guilt over her baby and things that were beyond her control.

"Faith would be about Haley's age," Jane said in a shaky voice. "I just don't understand why the Universe didn't want her to be born." Her voice petered out, and he hoped she would break soon. He had a feeling that she had given that baby a name but had never cried for her.

"When I left that hotel room, I promised the Universe I would give something up if I could just get away from the past and start over. So I gave up the idea of going to Nashville. Instead I skipped out on the hotel bill and used almost all of my money to buy a ticket to Miami because it's warm there and I'd never seen the ocean."

Clay brushed his hand across her cheek, and she leaned into his touch. He wished he could take away her pain. He promised to hold her hard, and steady, and true when she let go. "Why did you give up the idea of going to Nashville? Honey, you have a pretty remarkable singing voice."

Jane shrugged. "I guess I figured everyone in Seth, West Virginia, knew I wanted to go to Nashville. I just figured I could disappear in Miami. I wanted so desperately to disappear."

The words came out as a sob. And that's when Jane finally broke down, and Clay pulled her hard against him.

Then it hit him. Jane didn't need to be taken care of. She had been managing on her own for a long time. What she needed most was forgiveness. And time to grieve for the children she had lost: the baby named Faith and the young girl named Wanda Jane.

Chapter
16

Jane opened her eyes and knew that the world was a different place than when she had fallen asleep. Time had moved on. Long afternoon shadows hung in the corners of her room, and the little slice of sky framed by her windows had gone from bright blue to magenta.

She wasn't alone anymore, either. Clay had curled himself around her, and they lay together, fully clothed but nested like spoons. His left arm wrapped around her middle, and the rise and fall of his breathing was steady and regular against her backbone. They had been sleeping together like this for hours.

For a moment, before she woke up—before she thought too deeply about what had happened this morning—it seemed as if the world had moved on without her. As if she were in a warm, safe place where the bad stuff couldn't ever get in.

Jane closed her eyes and tried to evade consciousness. But the burn behind her lids reminded her of her breakdown earlier in the day. And, imperceptibly, the safe feeling began to ebb away.

She sucked in a deep breath, filled with the scents of the autumn afternoon and Clay Rhodes. The man smelled like a Boy Scout—one part Downy, two parts Ivory Soap. Clean and basic.

She wanted him on every level a woman could want a man. But she couldn't have him on all those levels.

Not without telling him everything about how she left Lexington on a bus to Miami. About how she had been homeless for a while, and about how she pulled herself up. He needed to know about the pictures she'd posed for, too—the ones that had paid for her cosmetology classes. He also needed to learn about how she had finally moved to Fort Myers, where she had gotten things together for a while until Woody the weasel had walked into the Shrimp Shack throwing around his money and reminding her about her lost dream of singing country music.

Once Clay heard about those naked photos, and her poor choice of a boyfriend in Woody, he would politely excuse himself and take this safe feeling with him when he left. Jane needed to remember that her time with Clay was not going to be forever. No matter how much she wanted it to be.

She snuggled deeper into his arms, impressing a memory of how it felt, banking that feeling as a hedge against the future when she would be alone again and on her own.

Clay responded to her movement by tightening his hold on her waist and by a small, but unmistakable, upward flex of his hips.

Sweet, hot, liquid desire trickled through her. They were fully clothed, of course, but there was no mistaking the fact that Clay was not entirely asleep. Part of him was waking up. Fast. And the rest of him was coming along for the ride.

With returning consciousness, his sturdy deadweight transformed itself into coiled muscles and male energy. He flexed his hips again, much harder this time and with much clearer intent. At the same time, his left hand, which had been resting against her abdomen, dipped under the hem of her T-shirt and made a slow but steady slide up her rib cage to the underside of her breast.

He was putting on a move. And, hoo boy, it was a good move. It made her kind of breathless with anticipation, because he didn't grope her breast or anything like that. He kind of teased her with a touch that was almost there but not quite. The man had fire coming from his fingertips.

Her nipples hardened, and Jane settled herself more firmly against his pelvis. He made a little gruff noise that sounded halfway between a purr and a growl.

He lifted his head from the pillow and drew her hair to one side. He leaned back down and pressed a small, moist kiss on the nape of her neck that produced gooseflesh all over her body.

Not satisfied with this, the man made a wet trail from her nape to the hollow of her neck, while Jane forgot how to breathe and concentrated, instead, on cocking her head to give him better access to her skin.

Clay moved in until he found that spot right at the base of her neck that he'd bruised last Wednesday. He hit that same spot, and she went haywire, like he had already figured out that was her main erogenous zone. She squirmed against him and he pressed himself harder against her.

Jane had to start breathing again, but when she

exhaled she made a little, unladylike noise. This elicited a chuckle from him. A cocky male sound that made her think that maybe this particular Boy Scout had earned the sex merit badge.

That thought pulled her out of the safe feeling. She needed to see his face. So she twisted in his arms and looked up at him, hoping that her puffy eyes wouldn't turn him off. She wondered if maybe she'd made a big mistake making eye contact with him. Maybe his brain would take over, and he would reconsider what he was doing.

But he wasn't turned off. In fact, his eyes were on fire, dancing with hot silver flickers of amusement and desire.

The Boy Scout wasn't interested in asking her any more questions about her past. At least not right at the moment. He seemed happy to let things progress down this road without having any kind of long-winded conversation with her.

Clay also didn't seem in any hurry to get to the end of the road, either. He seemed content with the current state of play, and focused on the journey and not the destination.

She ought to let him take her on down that road. It looked like it might be fun.

But she couldn't do it. Maybe with some other guy she didn't care about. But not with Clay.

She had fallen for Clay, and she didn't want to do this kind of thing with someone who hadn't fallen, too. Jane wanted more than his kindness and his friendship and his desire. She wanted the real thing. It was time for the Universe to make it happen for her. She must have telegraphed her sudden change of heart in some way, because she saw it mirrored in his face.

The little smile left his lips, and he exhaled deeply. But then he surprised the hell out of her by pushing himself up and reversing their positions, so that she was lying with her back to the mattress and he was above her, his big body blocking every path of escape. He looked down at her, and the spark in his eyes had not diminished one bit. His gaze made her skin burn hot all over.

That look was an affirmation.

Hoo boy, the guy was doing the same thing that he'd done this morning. Pushing back and pushing back until she gave in. He was so good at that. He was so stubborn and bullheaded and so...

"Baby," Clay said in this deep, husky voice, "I want to make love to you."

It was one of those *duh* statements. Like the size of the erection he kept rubbing against her hadn't already told her what he wanted to do.

Only wait, the guy hadn't said he wanted to have sex with her, or screw her, or do her, or any of those words he'd used before.

He'd said he wanted to make love to her.

Her heart twisted in her chest. Maybe she needed to listen. Words mattered.

Clay tucked the hair behind her ear and continued to stroke her face, his fingertips generating an incredible heat.

She should push him away. She should get on the next bus. She should run, run, run before she got hurt. Before he learned all her secrets and found out she wasn't the woman he was looking for.

"I am so sorry for the stupid things I said last night.

I want you to know that I'm here because I want to be," he said.

He kissed her then, so softly. Just a brush of his mouth on hers. Jane reveled in the feel of his lips, the male texture of his goatee against her cheek and chin. Desire bubbled through her. She was losing this battle. She wanted him so bad.

He lifted his head. "Look at me, Jane," he said.

She opened her eyes and got lost in his gaze. It was sultry and hot and full of a yearning that she'd never seen before in any man's eyes.

"You are *not* a symptom of my midlife crisis. I want to make that clear. I was being a jerk last night. I was trying to talk myself out of what I was feeling," he said.

"And what were you feeling?" Jane asked.

His sudden smile revealed a dimple and a few dozen crow's-feet at the corners of his eyes. "It wasn't just what I was feeling. It was the way you make me feel every time I get near you."

"Oh?" Her heart squeezed in her chest. "How's that?" Her voice sounded strained.

He ran the back of his finger across her cheek. It felt so nice the way he was petting her. Not groping her or forcing her or anything like that. His touch was so amazing. No one had touched her that way—ever.

"Like a man."

"What?"

"Like a man. Like a man's supposed to feel, I guess. I can't explain it. I just know it's sexual. It's incredibly sexual. And yet it's not sexual at all. It's confusing as hell, to tell you the truth. It's like getting caught up in a hurricane or some other force of nature. It's hard to fight this feeling, because it's kind of addicting. It feels incredibly good when I go with it."

"Oh."

Clay leaned forward and rested his forehead against hers. "I'm doing a piss-poor job of explaining this, aren't I?"

Jane said nothing because there was this knot in her throat and she wasn't sure she could make her voice work. He thought she was like a hurricane? Was that a good thing or a bad thing? Didn't hurricanes usually create major disasters?

On the other hand, being a force of nature was sort of an affirmation. Wasn't it?

Maybe she should stop fighting it and go with the flow. Didn't Dr. Goodbody always say that it was better sometimes to make a bad decision than to make no decision at all? He said that drifting through life would never help anyone realize their deepest dreams.

Jane suddenly realized the Universe and Clay Rhodes were going to let her decide. The decision might be a disaster, or it might be the smartest thing she ever did in her life.

Either way, it was fish-or-cut-bait time.

"Make love to me," Jane said. "I want you to make good on the promise you made last night."

Clay's lips pressed against her forehead. "And what promise was that?"

"That you're going to make me scream your name out loud."

He smiled against her skin. "Oh, yeah, that promise. Okay."

"Okay?" Her voice kind of squeaked.

"Yeah. Okay. It would be my absolute pleasure to make that happen."

Clay raised his head and looked down at her. Jane could see the little tic of his pulse right at the nape of his neck. He was turned on. And they hadn't even gotten naked yet.

Wow.

Double wow. Because every female place in her body was aching with a deep-down need for him. Like he was some kind of force of nature himself. And together they were like the yin and the yang. Male and female. Positive and negative.

And the Universe had laws about opposites like that. Nobody could fight the laws of the Universe. They were built right into the nature of things. They were immutable.

So she quit fighting it and let go. Clay's mouth came down on hers, and it was like Wednesday all over again, only ten times better.

Clay knew by the wild feeling down in his chest that he had gotten through some kind of barrier Jane kept around her heart. That wild feeling was so intoxicating that he felt like he might lose it before even losing his pants. He'd forgotten what it was like to make out with a girl and feel out of control.

Her mouth was perfect. Jane was soft and hard in all the right places, and he was certain he had fallen right into Nirvana. But then she took his tongue in her mouth and sucked on it kind of hard. Suddenly, kissing her wasn't enough. He wanted her mouth on every other part of his body. He wanted to get his mouth on every square inch of hers. But for that, they were going to have to lose the clothes.

He looked down at her and lost the ability to breathe for a moment. "I want to get naked," he said on a tight breath. It was a pretty inarticulate thing to say. But at least the words were brief and honest.

Jane blinked once, and her mouth curved up in an eloquent smile. "Me, too," she whispered.

Well, that was all it took. They were out of their clothes inside of thirty seconds.

Dusk had just about fallen, and the light in the room was kind of hazy and soft and purple, and Jane's body looked like it had been crafted out of Tuscan marble by Michelangelo himself. She was perfect.

She came back into his arms, against him skin to skin as they lay down together. He reached for her breast, and it fit perfectly in his hand. It felt heavy and soft and the nipple pebbled up against his palm. Just touching it took him back to that crazy place where he didn't have to think about anything.

And then Jane sabotaged all his plans for going slow when she trailed her fingers down his chest and over his hip and took him into her hand and touched him like she knew the way he liked to be touched.

His brain kind of narrowed down, and all he was capable of comprehending was the tension she created inside his body with the slide of her hand. This went on for some time until he had to pull her hand away.

"Uh, you need to quit that now," he said in a rusty voice.

"Oh?" She looked up into his face with a devilish spark in her eyes.

"Yeah," he said, pushing her onto her back. "It's my turn."

He went back to the spot at the nape of her neck, because he knew that turned her on, and he wanted to give her pleasure. So he went after it, and she squirmed against him, and he felt himself tumbling down into desire so deep he was pretty sure he would drown in it. But what a hell of a way to go.

Oh, sweet Jesus, Clayton P. Rhodes had talented fingers. It probably came from playing piano and violin all those years. Jane opened her eyes and looked up at him. The smirk on his face was so damn cocky and so masculine, and so sultry, and so...

Clay stopped teasing her with his finger, which was probably a good thing, because otherwise she just might have lost it before they got to the main event.

He moved in and kissed her again. And his kiss made her feel like she was the center of his universe—like the young girl she'd once been. It felt like a first kiss. Like a never-before-been-kissed. It swept her away.

She wanted him, now. "I want you, bad," she said. The words were not eloquent, but Clay understood her meaning.

He held up one finger. "Hold that thought, darlin', I need to find a condom," he said.

"Oh, man, I don't think I..."

Clay grinned. "Not to worry, I'm prepared."

He rolled half off the sofa-bed and reached for his pants. He pulled out his wallet and found a little foil packet in one of the inside pockets.

"Just like the Boy Scout you are," she said.

Clay turned back toward her with a little frown, and Jane had this horrible feeling she had ruined the moment. "Is that how you see me?" he asked.

"I meant it as a compliment," she said.

His gaze narrowed. "You did?"

Oh, yeah, she did. It occurred to her that a Boy Scout was probably the best thing a woman could ask the Universe for. A Boy Scout was better by far than Sir Galahad. White knights had a tendency to go thrashing about the countryside for long periods of time, crusading and bashing people, or jousting with one another to see who was the top guy on the block.

Boy Scouts were much handier. Not only were they always prepared, honest, thoughtful, and patriotic, the average Boy Scout could rescue people, perform first aid, and forage for food in the wilderness.

And Boy Scouts could build fires. Big, big fires.

"Yes," she said. "I meant it as a compliment. I have a thing for Boy Scouts. Especially the ones who have mastered the art of fire building."

His eyes flashed. "Fire building, huh?"

"Yeah. Fire building."

Clay tore open the foil packet and covered himself. "Yeah, well, the thing about building a fire is that you always have to take a few safety precautions."

"Uh-huh. I know. And I'm sure glad you were prepared."

He lay down beside her and pulled her back into his arms. "Me, too," he whispered into her ear.

And then he was pushing his way inside her, and it felt so right. Like some balance had been restored to the Cosmos.

Clay rocked against her and took her up, and up, and up, and up, and up. And then she shouted his name out loud, and she unfolded like one of those pyrotechnic starbursts that filled the sky on the Fourth of July. And oh, how she burned like fireworks, until she was nothing but ash, buoyed up by a midsummer breeze that floated her along for miles before depositing her, ever so gently, back on solid ground.

It was much later that it occurred to her that the windows were open and that anyone walking on Palmetto Avenue would have heard her scream his full name, including the middle initial, P. And that made her smile, and it made her hot, and she wondered if it might be possible for him to make that happen a second time.

Chapter
17

Ray lay in a hard single bed in a dark room in a strange house. He tried not to feel panicky. He had figured *pi* to the seven hundredth decimal, but this trick for lulling himself to sleep hadn't worked.

He was scared. He wanted to go home.

What had he done? It had never occurred to him when he had staged the robbery at the store that they would put him in a place like this and treat him like a dummy. He wasn't stupid. He was just a little mixed up. He had expected to go to live in Stone's jail. So that Stone could watch out for him when Alex decided to fire him. And then Betty and Clay could get on with their lives.

But things had gotten really confused, and they put him here in this strange place instead of Stony's jail. And he hadn't counted on that. He hadn't counted on missing the hardware store, or Dot's Spot...or Betty, either.

His chest burned with the thought. He was going to hell. He had had a thing for Betty Wilkins since he was twelve and she was fourteen and started growing those incredible tits.

Betty had been seventeen and he had been fifteen when she finally let him touch one. She'd let him go all the way with her that same year—a secret he'd kept even from Clay. And man oh man, Betty had always made him feel like his head was scrambled, even before he bumped it on the windshield of Clay's Dodge.

Ray had kept his thing for Betty secret back then, for a lot of reasons. Betty was older than he was, and she was...well...not the smartest girl he'd ever met. But she was as sweet and hot as one of his momma's homemade blueberry pies. She could play pool and poker and loved baseball and could bake like nobody's business. Betty had turned him on and embarrassed him at the same time.

Now the tables were turned. He was much dumber than she was, even though he could do math in his head. They had put him in a home for stupid people.

And that bothered Ray.

But it didn't bother him as much as knowing that he would miss her. He was going to miss the way she would sneak over to his house with her basket of fried chicken and squash casserole. He was going to miss having sex with her. He was going to miss the little notes she left in the morning with the little heart-shaped circles over her i's.

Ray was going to miss holding on to her at night and listening to her tell him that it was okay for them to be together. And he didn't have to worry about Lillian Bray or the holier-than-thou members of the Ladies Auxiliary saying that he was too dumb to be in love. And he was going to miss the way Betty made him feel—like he was whole and complete and worthy of something more than what he was.

Ray curled in on himself, feeling miserable and alone. This is what he deserved for the way he had treated Betty when he was seventeen and had won the scholarship to Rice University.

He had to let her go. He had to get out of her way, and Clay's way, too, because his friend was on the point of making some big mistakes all on account of the fact that Clay still felt guilty about that car accident.

Ray would endure. He would keep thinking about *pi*.

Which he did for a long while, until he heard a noise that wasn't just the settling of the strange house. Someone was tapping on his window.

Ray sat up in bed and looked at the window that dominated one wall of his little cell of a room. He squinted in the dark.

Betty Wilkins was on the other side looking in. How she managed this remained a mystery until he opened the window and realized she was standing on an extension ladder that didn't look too steady.

"How did you know this was my window?" he asked.

She smiled that sweet smile of hers. "I snuck in earlier, disguised as a cleaning lady. I saw your name on the door, but you weren't in the room. So I told a big lie about needing the key to the window lock so I could clean the outside of it. It's amazing how people look right past a person wearing a uniform sometimes. It's hard to get good help, these days, you know?"

"Sure, Betty, but—"

"C'mon, let's go. I'm springing you."

"But Betty, that's not—"

"Hush, now, I'm not going to take no for an answer. I've got my car, and my life savings, and a bunch of maps that will get us to Vegas. C'mon, now, you're going to make an honest woman of me if I have to drag you kicking and screaming to the altar. And I'm making it clear right now, I want a preacher dressed like Elvis."

"But Betty, I stole that money from Clay and I—"

"Ray Betts, you get your butt out of that room, you hear? That had to be the stupidest thing you have ever done. I'm only glad you left that money where folks could find it. And don't you think I don't know why you stole that money and then allowed yourself to get caught. You thought you were a burden to me and Clay. Well, I'm telling you right now, Ray Betts, you are not a burden to me. I can't speak for Clay, of course, but as far as I'm concerned, Clay needs to move on with his life."

"But Betty, I—"

She stepped up one more wobbly step and stopped his protest by giving him a kiss that rearranged his gray matter once again. "Don't you like me, Ray?" she asked.

"Uh, yeah, Betty, I like you a whole lot."

"So are you saying you would rather be in jail than with me?" Her voice wavered a little, and he hated the idea of smiley-faced Betty crying over anything, especially him.

"Don't cry," Ray said. "I thought if folks like Lillian Bray ever found out about us they would send me away to a bad place, especially since Pete is sick. Everyone says he's going to die. And Alex aims to fire me from my job when that happens."

"Oh, so taking the money and getting put in jail or being sent to a place like this is the answer?"

He thought about that for a minute. "I guess I screwed up."

"Yes, you did. But it's okay, darlin', because you did it for the right reasons. Now, you better come on. Because if we get caught, I'm going to jail. And you don't want that to happen to me, now, do you?"

"No, Betty."

She backed down the ladder, and he watched her in the pale light of a full moon. It shone bright on the swells of her breasts, and the sight of them made him feel a little dizzy.

Big-breasted Betty had just rescued him from a bad place. And that was pretty cool, because Betty Ann Wilkins had the best tits in all of South Carolina—maybe even the Universe—and she had a higher Desirability Index than any other woman in Last Chance, South Carolina.

Clay watched Jane sleep. The light in the little room faded from black to gray with every breath she took. Dawn was breaking outside the windows, and he ought to be getting up and heading home to take a shower and do battle with Tricia, Ricki, and the entire legal system of South Carolina.

He checked his watch. It was after six.

Clay curled a lock of Jane's hair around his index finger. Suddenly, evicting the ex-girlfriends and rescuing Ray didn't seem all that important. He looked down at this remarkable woman and felt the change inside him, right there in the center of his chest.

Jane had captured his heart. There were no two ways about that. Still, on some level, his brain was screaming that things were happening too fast. There were still lots of things he didn't know about her.

But he didn't care right now. Right now, she made him feel like a real man. A man in every possible way. And he didn't want to give that up.

Clay leaned forward and pressed a little kiss to her forehead and watched her sleepy eyes flutter open. She'd been through hell, and somehow it hadn't touched the goodness in her soul. He watched her come to full consciousness, knowing that he was the first thing she would see today.

Miriam Randall was so right. She wasn't at all what he had been looking for, or even what he had expected. She was so much more. And it was amazing, really, how close he'd come to missing out.

Now, looking down at her, he found himself mentally filling in the cells in Ray's stupid spreadsheet. On the plus side, Jane had a voice like an angel and a body made for sin. She saw the positive in every situation, and she was great with kids.

On the negative side, there was that little matter of why she had turned up in Last Chance with only the clothes on her back and five dollars in her pocket. But aside from that, Clay was hard-pressed to find anything wrong with Jane Coblentz. He had a pretty good idea of some of the things she probably had done in the last seven years—just to survive. He was pretty sure he could forgive her for just about anything.

He was a forgiving man, at least when it came to Jane. He wasn't feeling magnanimous toward his ex-girlfriends. But the difference was that Tricia and Ricki had hurt him. Jane hadn't hurt anyone.

Jane Coblentz had to be the first woman who had ever called him a Boy Scout at the beginning, as opposed to throwing that label at him like an epithet on the way out the door. And that made him feel so good he could hardly contain his joy.

"By that canary-eating grin on your face, I guess you had a good time last night," Jane said in a sleepy voice.

"Yes, ma'am." He placed a kiss on her forehead.

"I guess it's time to come back down to earth, huh?"

"I've got a better idea."

"A better idea?"

"Yeah."

"What?"

"Marry me."

"*What?*" The smile on her face disappeared. It occurred to him that, perhaps, the disappearing smile was a danger sign. But he was committed now, so he forged ahead.

"Yeah. I thought we could throw some clothes in my Windstar and head for Vegas. Find ourselves one of those chapels where the judge dresses up like Elvis. I figure if we drive straight through, we could be husband and wife in a matter of days."

"You want to get married by an Elvis impersonator?" Jane rolled away from him and sat up. The blanket fell to her waist and gave him a killer view of her breasts. His body responded in a completely adolescent and predictable manner.

"Yeah, well, if you prefer we could get Reverend Ellis down at Christ Church to do the job."

"You're teasing me, right?"

Clay sat up beside her and pulled her into his arms. She didn't come willingly. "No," he said to the top of her head. "I'm not teasing. I want you to be my wife, Jane. And besides, if we're going to sleep together in this town, being married is practically a requirement."

She pushed away. "For heaven's sake. Please don't."

"What?"

Jane stood up, turning her back to him. By the set of her shoulders, he got the impression that she wasn't too pleased with him. This was not going the way he thought it would. Maybe he'd missed something. Maybe he'd been thinking with his pecker and not his head.

Jane headed off in the direction of the bathroom. "You're insane. You don't even know me. I met you less than a week ago. Getting married right now is not going to happen."

Clay followed her, but he wasn't fast enough. The bathroom door slammed, and he heard the *snick* of the snap lock. Shoot, she'd managed to lock herself in the bathroom after all.

He got up and leaned into the door frame. "Jane, let me in."

She didn't say anything, but a few moments later, the toilet flushed. He waited until the water quit running.

"Jane?" he said.

"Yeah," she said through the door. He wasn't sure, but he had a feeling he'd made her cry.

"Open the door."

"No."

"I really do want to marry you."

"Yeah," she said in a voice that sounded lost and unhappy. "So I guess I got myself on your list, after all."

He stood there blinking at the door and realized his mistake. He'd forgotten to tell her he loved her. Instead he'd started with the marriage part, and then he'd justified it in a pretty stupid way, too. "Uh, Jane, open the door, would you please?"

"No."

"I'm not going to leave until you open the door."

"Guess you'll be stuck here for a while, then."

"Jane, please, I have something important to tell you, but I'm not going to say it to a locked door."

Silence beat like a ticking clock for several moments. But then the door opened, and she stood there wearing a pale yellow dressing gown. She had her arms folded across her chest, and a mutinous look on her face.

"Jane, I—"

"What about Ray?" she asked, interrupting his big pronouncement, bringing him back down to earth. "Are you just going to run off to Vegas and leave him high and dry? And weren't you the one who said on Saturday that you can't run away from your life? Because, excuse me, this proposal of marriage sounds a whole lot like a not-very-nice proposal from some guy who's almost middle-aged and is terrified that his not-very-successful life is at a dead end."

Wow. Low blow. Serious low blow. And it hurt because it was dead-on.

Clay stood there naked as the day he was born, looking at her, wanting her, needing her, and terrified that he was never going to actually get her.

"Honey, I'm sorry. I didn't mean to hurt you. I guess I got things kind of out of order. Because in case you missed it, the main reason I want to marry you is because I—"

At that moment, trouble came knocking on the door,

like it usually did. And in this case, it took the form of his older brother. And Stony didn't exactly knock.

"Clay, are you in there?" Stony bellowed as he banged his fist on the door.

Crap. Stone's timing couldn't have been worse.

Clay held up one finger. "Hold that thought one moment, honey, while I dispense with this interruption." He turned his back toward her and snagged his boxers from the floor. He stepped into them and opened the door.

His brother stood out there on the landing with the glow of dawn over his shoulder. His nose was less swollen than it had been night before last, but it was never going to be as straight as it had been. His shiners had started to fade to green and yellow. Clay felt sorry about what he'd done. He was going to have to make it up to Stone one of these days.

But maybe not today. Because Stone was looking pretty serious out there. No doubt his big brother was not happy about finding him shacked up with a woman he thought was some kind of criminal.

Stony's icy gaze missed nothing—not Jane standing at the bathroom door, or the tumbled sheets, or the condom wrappers on the carpet, or even the Oscar the Grouch boxers Clay had thrown on yesterday morning because he'd been at the absolute limit of clean laundry.

The boxers got a hint of a smile. Maybe because Stone remembered that the underwear had been stuffed in the toe of Clay's stocking last Christmas. Or maybe it was because Momma had stuffed a pair of Grinch boxers in the toe of Stone's stocking last Christmas, too. Momma had a way of getting her point across that was sometimes irritating as hell.

Stone's smile vanished. "You're in big trouble, boy, you know that, don't you? And if you think for one minute I'm going to save your sorry butt, you better think again." He leaned into the door frame and his utility belt creaked. Stony was not fooling around.

"Uh, what trouble would that be?"

"Shoot, Clay, did you think the authorities wouldn't figure it out? My God, you left your ladder there for the forensics team to dust. I'd say the chance of finding your prints on that ladder are about one hundred percent."

"Uh, you want to rewind that, Stony, 'cause I'm trying to figure out which ladder you are talking about and why the forensics team would be dusting it for my fingerprints. If this is your idea of a joke, or some lame attempt to save me from Jane, then *you* can think again."

Stony blinked at him for a moment and then shifted his gaze to Jane, something changing in his face. "Has he been here all night?"

"It's none of your business," Jane said, and Clay could tell she was as pissed at Stone as she was at him. She had good reason, too. Boy, what a couple of losers they were.

"It is if you're his alibi." Stone shifted his gaze back. "Although I have to admit that she's a pretty unreliable alibi, given her criminal past."

"Alibi for what?" Clay asked.

"So you're telling me you had nothing to do with Ray escaping from the halfway house last night?"

"He escaped?" A boatload of guilt hit Clay. If Ray had escaped on his own, then he was out there by himself, probably scared and lost. And what had Clay been doing?

"Get your clothes on," Stone said, "because in about five minutes Sheriff Bennett is going to be here to haul you in for questioning. And I'm telling you, if the sheriff decides he wants to charge you for being an accessory to a jailbreak, there isn't much I can do to help you out. But I can haul you in first and buy a little time."

"You're serious. You're going to arrest me?"

"Nah, just bring you in for questioning. If you tell me where Ray is, I'll go easy on you."

"I don't know where Ray is. Maybe you and the sheriff should be searching for him."

"We are. Have been all night. You would have known this if you had been home. But you weren't home, and that looks mighty suspicious. According to Ricki and Tricia, you haven't been home since yesterday before church. And then we found your extension ladder leaned up against the halfway house up in Orangeburg."

"*My* ladder?"

"Uh-huh. The one with your name etched on the third step."

"Stone, Daddy borrowed that ladder on Friday morning. He was using it out at the golf course on account of the fact that Jesus sustained some damage during the hurricane. You can ask him."

"Yeah, well, I already did. And it isn't at Golfing for God now. Someone took it up to Orangeburg. My guess is that someone is you. So don't play stupid with me, okay?"

"I didn't help Ray escape," Clay said, feeling the pit of his stomach drop and his heart rate kick up. Was it possible that Alex was trying to frame both of them? Jesus H. Christ, he was in trouble here because the county sheriff was Alex's first cousin on his daddy's side.

"He's been here since about noon yesterday," Jane said from right behind Clay. It made something hitch up in Clay's chest to know that Jane had come to his defense.

Stone gave her a skeptical look. "That would be eighteen hours?" His gaze swept over the bed and the little foil wrappers, missing nothing. "Was he with you the whole time?"

"No, he went out around ten o'clock. He was gone for about half an hour."

"Only half an hour?"

"Look, Stone, I went out and got some burgers and stopped in at the Rexall for a few things. Amy Swallock was at the checkout, and I'd be willing to bet she would remember me and what I bought. In fact, I have this feeling that most of Last Chance is going to know I was at the all-night Rexall last night buying a king-sized box of rubbers."

Stone shook his head. "Get dressed, Clay. I don't know whether to bring you in for being a criminal or just an idiot."

"I'm telling you I didn't—"

Stony held up his hand. "I believe you. But I doubt Billy Bennett will, since Alex is on a tear about this. Just put your clothes on, okay? I need to figure out how I'm going to stop the sheriff from arresting you."

"You mean my alibi doesn't count?" Jane asked. God bless her sweet little heart.

Stone looked at her. "I doubt Billy Bennett would take your word once he speaks with the detective up in Lexington. And, honey, you can count on him doing that if you come forward as an alibi witness. Because when you put the name Wanda Jane Coblentz into the system, it lights up like a Christmas tree. My guess is that Billy would slap your butt in jail faster than I can say Jack Robinson. He doesn't have to worry about staying on Momma's good side like I do."

"Oh, for Heaven's sake, Stone, she's not a murderer."

"Get your clothes on," Stone ordered.

His big brother was in full-out police chief mode, and there was no deterring him. "Okay, I will, but can I have a private moment, please?"

Stone leaned his body into the door frame. "Nope. The sheriff is going to be here in two minutes, and you don't want him to see you wearing those boxers, boy. Trust me on this. They'll be laughing all the way to Orangeburg."

Clay shook his head and turned back into the room. Jane was standing there looking kind of pitiful and forlorn and angry and hot all at once. So much for a romantic and soulful morning after.

He took her by the upper arm and walked her farther into the room. He leaned in and gave her a quick kiss on the lips. "Honey, I meant what I said earlier. I intend to marry you, and I'm not going to take no for an answer. And it's not because I'm thirty-four and ready to take a wife. I've been looking for a wife since I was twenty. I'm the marrying kind, I guess. And it's taken me fourteen years to find the right girl, and I'm not about to let her get away. The fact is I—"

"Clay, would you hurry it up, please. The sheriff has just pulled into the parking lot with his lights flashing."

Jane's eyes got wide. "You better go with Stone."

Clay kissed her quick. "Don't you run away, now.

Because I intend to finish this conversation tonight. You understand?"

Jane nodded.

Clay turned and collected his pants from the floor. He stepped into them and zipped the fly just as Billy Bennett swaggered up the stairs and started reading him his rights.

Chapter
18

Well, that settled it. Mary Smith had to be working with Freddie the Fence, or maybe with someone in competition with Freddie. And from the look of things, the cops were closing in on her.

Woody pulled the brim of his ball cap down around his ears and rustled the Monday morning paper as he watched the police cuff a big dude with a ponytail. They stuffed him into the back of a Crown Vic cruiser and hauled him away.

Woody was sitting at a table in the front of the Kountry Kitchen that gave him a great view of the main drag and the second-floor apartment where Mary was supposed to be staying.

He didn't recognize the guy the cops arrested, but it had to be a big bust because both the local police and the county sheriff had arrived on the scene. The cops must not have figured out Mary's connection to the heist of the Cambodian Camel, because they hadn't arrested her. Of course, knowing Mary's MO, it was possible she had already blown town.

Although the yokels around here insisted that Mary was living up there above the beauty parlor and using an alias. Woody prayed Mary hadn't handed off the Camel to the guy who had just been cuffed and stuffed. He needed that necklace and pronto. He might have shaken the FBI, but the Colombian's goons were still on his tail. He had run out of time to come up with the twenty Gs he owed. He needed that necklace, now. His life depended on it.

"Hey, Fred, where the heck are my eggs?" an old codger wearing a Country Pride Chicken hat yelled back to the short-order cook. The waitress had failed to show up for work, and the woman who had been pressed into service about an hour ago had obviously never worked a day in her life.

"Ricki," the cook yelled to the platinum blonde who was leaning over another table, displaying her cleavage. "Quit talking to Dash and come pick up the orders. I swear, I'm gonna kill Betty. I surely am."

"Hey," the old codger yelled, as the waitress scurried to get the order. "You check Betty's number? I mean, when was the last time Betty didn't come to work?"

"I can't remember," the cook said. "And yeah, I called her cell phone, and I called her at home. I didn't get an answer."

"Shoot, we ought to call Stone and get him to investigate. Ain't like Betty not to show up for work."

"I already called the police. Damian said Stone was busy, on account of the fact Ray Betts escaped from that halfway house the state put him in. Damian said he would swing by Betty's place, though, to make sure she was okay."

"Ray escaped. Really?"

"Yeah, and I heard Clay was the one who sprung him loose. Kinda puts the chief of police between a rock and a hard place, don't it?"

"Now, that ain't true, Fred," a woman at the counter said.

"What ain't true? Stone being in a sticky situation or Clay being guilty of springing his best friend from the hoosegow?"

"There is no way Clay Rhodes sprung Ray from that halfway house." This from the guy who was flirting with the waitress named Ricki.

"How you figure that, Dash?"

"Because Aunt Mim heard from Amy Swallock that Clay was down at the all-night Rexall buying condoms at about ten-thirty last night. And according to Thelma Hanks, who called up this morning before the sky was even light, Ray escaped from that halfway house between ten and eleven o'clock. Aunt Mim figures Thelma should know since her husband is Ray's attorney. The way I figure, there ain't no way Clay could get up to Orangeburg and do that job and still be buying rubbers at the Rexall at ten-thirty. And besides, why would a man be buying rubbers at a time like that? To my mind, the more interesting question is who, precisely, is Clay Rhodes keeping company with. I'm willing to bet it's—"

The waitress named Ricki dropped the tray of orders that she was carrying, and Woody didn't catch the name of the woman who was shacked up with the man named Clay. But that didn't matter, because at that moment, Mary Smith walked out onto the landing of the fire escape that led to the second floor of the Cut 'n Curl beauty parlor.

• • •

What was it about the Universe anyway? One minute it seemed hell-bent on making every one of Jane's wishes come true, and the next it was putting all kinds of obstacles in her way. Jane stepped out onto the landing and watched Sheriff Bennett and Stone drive off in opposite directions. She hugged herself, trying to figure out whether she was angry or scared or...well, joyful.

Joyful seemed to be the right word for that little tickle of a feeling deep in her chest. Clay had asked her to marry him, which had thrown her for a real loop there for a moment. It had made her angry, before she realized that Clay was serious about it.

And unless she had missed something important, the man had been right on the brink of making some kind of declaration of his feelings. Was it possible that the Universe was about to grant her deepest wish?

Having Clay love her would be about the best thing in the Universe, because she had fallen hard for him, too. He was the sweetest man she had ever met. She actually wanted to take care of him. She had a long list of things she wanted to do for him and with him and to him: like sew him a shirt, even though she didn't know how to sew, and cook him dinner, even though her idea of cooking was heating up a Lean Cuisine in the microwave. She also wanted to sing with him and make love with him until her strength was gone.

Maybe, if her luck held, Clay would even forgive her when he learned that she was April the pinup girl. She sincerely hoped so. Because tonight, after they cleared up this mistake with the sheriff, she would have to tell him the whole, unvarnished truth, not only about those naked photos, but also about Woody and the loan sharks.

Jane hugged herself and looked up at the morning sky. The weather had turned. Yesterday's bright blue sky had given way to ominous clouds that presaged more rain—as if Last Chance needed more rain after Hurricane Jane had dumped five inches in a day and a half. The clouds made her feel uneasy. Like maybe her hopes for forgiveness and understanding were unfounded.

She told herself there was no reason to feel jumpy. She had not killed anyone. And Clay was not responsible for Ray's escape from the halfway house. Clay would forgive her after she explained how she had used the money from those photos to better her life.

Jane fixed those affirmations in her mind and turned back into the apartment just in time to pick up the ringing telephone.

"Honey, I surely hope I didn't wake you up," Ruby Rhodes's voice came over the line. Jane wondered what Ruby might have to say if she learned where her son had been last night. Would she approve?

Ruby would probably approve—wholeheartedly. And that was, maybe, the biggest affirmation of all. Hadn't Ruby told her that she should go for it with Clay? And then there was the fact that Jane was Clay's alibi.

"No, ma'am, I'm awake," she said.

"Thank the Lord. I need a huge favor from you, honey. The elementary school is still closed because of the hole in the roof, and Haley flat-out refuses to go to Betsy Maxwell's again. Would you mind looking after Haley for a little while? An emergency has just come up."

Jane was pretty sure she knew what the emergency was. Ruby was about to storm Stone's jailhouse to spring her middle son from the jail. "Just Haley?" she asked.

"The middle school is open, thank the Lord. Are you decent?"

No, not even close. "Yeah, I'm decent." She glanced at the mess in her apartment. She needed to move fast to clean up.

"Be there in fifteen, tops."

Jane had just stepped out of a speed shower when she heard the knocking at her door. "Coming," she hollered as she pulled on a pair of jeans and a T-shirt that used to belong to Sharon Rhodes. The shirt was faded pink and said something on the back of it, but she didn't have time to read the words.

Jane had cleaned up the obvious evidence of last night's activities, but she'd have to keep her eye on Haley to make sure that child didn't do any more trash-can snooping. She had a feeling Haley had a future in law enforcement or journalism—especially the kind that involved discovering the real juicy dirt and exposing it.

She raced to the door and pulled it open...

Her worst nightmare stood on the other side.

Woody the weasel, aka Woody the peckerwood, didn't wait to charm his way through the door. He used the brute force method. Inside of five seconds, the man had her pinned to the wall. He didn't look like he'd shaved in a solid week, and his jaw was covered in ugly bristles that detracted from his movie-star looks. He didn't smell too good, either. His Reyn Spooner Hawaiian shirt—the one with the bright orange birds of paradise on it—had a ketchup stain right on the front.

"Where is it?" Woody demanded, tightening his fists on her arms.

Jane didn't answer. Her throat seemed paralyzed by fear. The Universe had, once again, crapped all over her rainbow.

He slammed her hard against the wall. "I asked you a question, damn it."

"Where's what?" she asked, her voice wobbling.

"Don't play dumb with me," he bellowed and gave her another violent shake.

No one was going to rescue her from this. Even worse, in a few minutes, Ruby and Haley would come walking through the door and into this disaster.

Jane couldn't allow that.

That thought brought an odd clarity to her mind. She inhaled deeply and reached for her calming mantra. Then she told her racing heart to slow down, and she forced her mind to work against the fear. She needed to get Woody out of that apartment, and the only way to do that would be to play along with him.

"Okay, Woody," she said in a surprisingly calm voice. "It's not here."

"You gave it to your contact, didn't you? Who are you working for? Did you and Freddie double-cross me? Or did you double-cross Freddie? Because if you did, honey, your life is toast. I mean Freddie doesn't mess around with people who double-cross him. You know?"

No, she didn't know, but she needed to play along. "Look, I handed it off, okay?" It would be nice if she understood what she was supposed to have handed off and who Freddie was, although she had an idea that Freddie was not a legitimate businessman.

"Where is he now?"

Where is who, and what are we talking about? Every

ticking second felt like a blow to her middle. *Think, think, think, Jane, don't panic.* "In Bamberg," she said, because it was the only place she could think of. She had no idea where Bamberg was, exactly, only that it was another little town in the next county over.

Woody looked down at her, and she could almost see the cogs turning in his weasely brain. He shook her again, and she bit her tongue. The salty iron taste of blood filled her mouth.

"You're lying," he said, then he backhanded her across the face.

The sting of the slap stunned her for a moment. But not as much as what happened next, because Woody pulled a small handgun out of his pocket and put the barrel right up against her temple. He pinned her to the wall by encircling her neck with his left hand.

"Where is it?"

"Woody, I swear, I don't know what you're talking about," she said in a whiny voice that telegraphed her fear. She could feel her body going cold. It was hard to breathe.

Suddenly, her brain didn't want to think about anything except that she was going to die before she ever heard Clay say the words "I love you." And before she could say them back to him.

Woody squeezed her throat. "I'm talking about the goddamned Cambodian Camel. For chrissake, Mary, what did you do with it?"

The Cambodian Camel? "Are you talking about that piece-of-crap necklace you gave me?"

"Don't play dumb, Mary."

"Uh, Woody, I threw that piece of junk away. It's probably in the landfill by now." Unless, of course, Haley was wearing it around her sweet little neck.

Hoo boy.

"What?" He lowered the gun and stared down at her with an incredulous look. But he still had her by the neck. "You threw it away? You couldn't possibly be that dumb. You gave it to that guy they arrested this morning, didn't you?"

She almost laughed aloud. "No, honest, Woody, I didn't give it to that guy."

"You're lying." He pulled her away from the wall and began dragging her across the floor toward the kitchen, where her satchel purse rested on the table. "Dump it out," he directed.

She did as she was told, and he pawed through the contents of her purse in much the same way that Clay had pawed through them last Thursday morning. He picked up her green leather wallet with the flower on it. "Open it."

She opened the wallet and dumped the contents of the billfold and change purse, which consisted of about thirty dollars and one 1943 wheat penny. Woody picked up the thirty bucks and stuffed it in his pocket. He ignored the penny.

Jane didn't.

When the penny hit the Formica tabletop, Jane almost lost whatever shred of composure she still possessed. All she could think about was the day Clay had found that penny and put it in her hand. And ever since then, her luck had changed.

So she picked up the penny and pressed it in her fist like it was a talisman. And since Woody saw it as only a penny, he didn't give her any crap or otherwise shoot her head off for picking it up.

She squeezed that lucky penny and winged a prayer skyward—not to the Universe, but to the God of the Christ Church Ladies Auxiliary. She prayed to *that* God to keep Clay and Haley and everyone she cared about in Last Chance—even Stone Rhodes—safe from the menace she had brought down upon them. And just for good measure, she asked God to please, please help her out of this jam.

Woody gave her another head-rattling shake. It reminded her that she had never actually had any kind of relationship with the Almighty, and if she wanted to be rescued, she was going to have to do it for herself. Right now. She needed to get Woody out of this apartment before Ruby and Haley got there.

"Am I going to have to turn this place upside down?" he hissed in her ear.

"No," she said firmly, willing herself to be calm, to invest her voice with authority and to lie like hell. Jane was a terrible liar, but she bucked herself up and sold her lie with all the straight-faced conviction of a politician running for election. "It's not here. We put it in a safe place."

"Where?"

"In Columbia. In a safe-deposit box at the First National Bank." She was extemporizing, and she hoped there *was* a First National Bank in Columbia.

"I don't see a safe-deposit box key here. Where's the key, Mary?"

Oops—that was a major hole in her story. She thought fast. She just needed to buy a few minutes, and Haley and

Ruby would be safe. "The key is hidden outside of town. The tenth hole at Golfing for God." She said the first thing that came to mind.

She had never been to Golfing for God, of course, but she knew it had a tenth hole depicting the birth of Jesus. Friday afternoon, Haley and Lizzy had given Jane a complete run-down of all the holes at Golfing for God, starting with Adam and Eve and ending with the Resurrection. "The key is hidden in the manger with baby Jesus," she added for good measure, remembering how Haley had described the crèche scene, and the angel that looked over it.

"Golfing for God?" Woody sounded skeptical.

"It's a roadside attraction about three miles outside of town on Route 321. I'll take you there."

"Okay, baby, but I swear if you're lying, I'm going to knock the crap out of you and strangle you for good measure."

Jane tried to think positively about this turn of events, but it was kind of hard. She had convinced him to leave the apartment and save Ruby and Haley. That was a good thing. On the other hand, she figured she had less than an hour to live.

"Okay, baby, let's go. The Colombian's goons are on my tail, and I need that necklace quick. You understand me?" He didn't put the gun away, but at least he stopped pointing it at her head.

Woody snagged Jane by the upper arm, put the pistol up against her spine, and half-dragged her to the apartment's door. She tried to quell her fears with the thought that her lie had worked. In five minutes—maybe less, depending on where Woody had parked his car—they would be gone, and Haley and Ruby would be safe.

He opened the door, and they headed down the metal fire stairs. And with a predictability Jane had to admire, the Universe took that moment to throw another monkey wrench into the works. Ruby Rhodes had already pulled her Ford Taurus into the alley, and she was just getting out of her car.

Clay's mother stood by the open car door and looked up at Jane, taking in the disheveled, unshaven, Hawaiian-shirt-wearing Woody West.

"Run like hell," Jane yelled. "Get Stony, quick."

Ruby hesitated for one instant. And that little hesitation proved utterly disastrous.

Chapter
19

S o if this is all settled, can I go, please? I've got some unfinished business to attend to," Clay said to Stone and Sheriff Bennett. They had just corroborated his alibi with Amy Swallock, and both law officers were looking somewhat chastened.

Apparently Betty Wilkins was missing, and folks were putting two and two together and coming up with a larger number than four. So Miz Miriam had worked some kind of magic and matched up Betty and Ray. It had to be some kind of miracle.

A commotion in the outer office interrupted the interrogation, and Clay reckoned it had to be Momma arriving to the rescue, right on schedule. She probably had Aunt Arlene and Uncle Pete in tow, seeing as the two of them were supposed to have returned from Minnesota yesterday. He had a feeling Uncle Pete would not be amused with Alex.

Clay was feeling especially smug and looking forward to completing his conversation with Jane just as soon as he could hotfoot it back to the Cut 'n Curl.

But instead of Momma and Uncle Pete charging in, Deputy Chief Easley poked his head into the room. "Uh, Stone, we got us a problem out here."

"It's not my mother?" Stone asked.

Damian shook his head. "No, it's a couple of guys from the FBI, and they have a warrant for Jane Coblentz's arrest, but the warrant says Mary Smith on it. And y'all won't believe this, but Mary Smith, aka Jane Coblentz, just happens to be the girl in that pinup photo we found in Ray's locker—you know, from *Working Girls Go Wild*."

Clay exploded from his chair. "What in the hell are you talking about?"

Stone stood up, too, and grabbed Clay by the shoulder before he could rush out into the reception area and confront a couple of G-men and get himself into real trouble.

Damian shrugged. "They got a copy of that pinup photo. They say the woman in that photo is Mary Smith, and they believe she's involved in some kind of jewel heist. It sure does look like our Jane."

Sheriff Bennett made a beeline for the door. Clay made to follow, but Stone yanked on his shoulder.

"Lemme go, Stone. Quit being a jerk. I love that woman." Clay tried to twist away, but Stone pulled a move on him that put him down on his backside looking up.

"You're the one acting like an jerk," Stone said. "Just cool your head for five minutes and let me see what this is all about. And as for loving that woman, shoot, boy, you've known her for what, four days? Gimme a break." He pointed down at Clay. "You stay here, or I'll have to break one of your bones, and I really don't want to do that."

Stone let Clay go and turned his back, which Clay took as a sign of filial trust. That and the fact that Clay knew Stone would probably break one of his bones if he made any sudden moves.

So he didn't. He just lay there feeling like someone had put a hole right through the middle of his chest.

And that's when the radio dispatch in the outer office went haywire with the news that someone had been shot in downtown Last Chance.

Jane tried hard not to let fear paralyze her. It sure did look like this was going to be her last day on earth. She told the Universe that she was okay with that. Just so long as both of them worked together to make sure that nothing bad happened to little Haley Rhodes.

The Universe, as usual, had a different plan in mind. Or maybe there was no pattern in the Universe. Maybe life was just random.

That was a frightening thought, but one Jane didn't have time to dwell on. She was too consumed with gut-wrenching guilt over what had just happened to Ruby. Clay's ma should have run like the wind, but she hadn't run. She had frozen for one instant—just long enough for Woody to raise his pistol and fire a round at her.

Ruby went down and didn't make another sound. Then Woody hauled Jane down the remaining stairs and shoved her right into Ruby's Taurus. The keys were still in the ignition.

Jane figured things couldn't get any worse, until she spied Haley curled up into a tiny little ball on the floor of the backseat. The sight made her sick and dizzy with fear.

Luckily, Woody hadn't seen the child. And Haley, bless her heart, had the presence of mind not to say a word or whimper or otherwise give herself away. Which meant the seven-year-old was smarter than your average child. Or maybe she was merely scared to death.

Jane figured it was probably a little bit of both. That thought made her heart rate spike, and her throat close up, and her world tilt sideways on its axis. How could the Universe do this to Haley and Ruby? They didn't deserve this.

Woody pulled the car out through the alley and turned right on Palmetto, heading south in the direction of Golfing for God.

"Where the hell is this place?" Woody said as he floored the Taurus and broke every speed limit in town. Jane didn't reply. Instead she prayed that Damian Easley and Stone Rhodes were paying attention, like they always did. A minute went by without any sirens sounding. Obviously, God and the Cosmos were still not listening.

Her chest felt so tight she was having trouble breathing. Time was running out on her. Jane looked up at the big dark cloud that had filled the sky and knew she would probably never see the sunshine again.

"Woody, you need to think things through," she said around the knot in her throat. Her voice wavered, and she hated herself for her weakness. She gulped down air and continued. "You're in big trouble now. That woman you just shot was the mother of the police chief."

"Shut up, you're just trying to confuse me." He looked at the rearview mirror. "Shit."

Jane looked behind her, and sure enough, a dark Cadillac had pulled in behind them. It had Florida tags.

This was not a good sign.

"I'll bet those are the Colombian's goons back there, baby. They want their money, and I don't have it. The Cambodian Camel is the only way I'm going to survive. So you better not be lying to me, you understand?" Woody brandished the gun.

"Have you thought of reasoning with those men?" she asked in a voice that sounded much stronger than before. It was funny how her heart was still hammering, but her head was clearing. The main thing she needed to focus on right now was getting Woody away from the car. She sure hoped Haley had the presence of mind to stay put and go unnoticed.

Woody stared over at her and then back at the road. "Those goons don't reason, you should realize that by now."

"But I know where the necklace is." *In the backseat, you idiot, around the neck of a terrified little girl.* Jane tried to think of some way to get that necklace and use it as a bargaining chip without letting anyone know Haley was back there, but there was no real hope of that. So she kept talking.

"Slow down, Woody, that's Golfing for God right up there on the left," she said. Maybe Haley would be smart enough to leave the car and hide once Jane got Woody away from it. Jane prayed a little harder to the God who never listened. *Sweet Jesus, help that little girl.*

Right then, the skies opened up. A veritable sheet of water fell down from the heavens and pummeled the windshield with a deafening roar. The road vanished from view before Woody could put on the wipers. Woody slammed on the brakes.

And since he had been doing eighty in a car with tires that Ruby Rhodes had been nagging her husband to replace for the last six months, he went into a skid.

The car slid sideways, and the certainty of death scrolled through Jane's mind in slow motion. She was going to die, and there was nothing she could do about it.

But Woody surprised her. He turned into the skid, and the Taurus twisted over the wet pavement, tires squealing. Woody cut a perfect doughnut right there on Route 321.

In some corner of her mind, Jane started to feel hope. Maybe she wouldn't die—at least not in a car wreck. The gray, rain-soaked scenery flashed sideways across the windshield, but Woody had the skid under control. It would be okay.

Only in the next instant, as they completed the 360-degree skid, a large Country Pride Chicken truck materialized out of the rain coming right at them in the opposite direction.

The truck swerved to the right across the Golfing for God parking lot. Jane watched with a kind of detached fascination as the chicken truck plowed head-on into the twenty-foot statue of Jesus Christ at the golf course's entrance. The statue, already weakened by hurricane-force winds, toppled sideways in slow motion and landed right in front of Ruby's Taurus. The Savior bounced and cracked on the blacktop as it hit.

The impact knocked the breath right out of Jane as her seatbelt snugged down and the airbag deployed. Pain and pressure flared across her shoulder and hips, and in some surprised part of her mind, she realized, even before the sound of bending metal died away, that she would survive this crash.

As the car jarred to a stop and the airbag deflated, all Jane's rattled brain could absorb was the sight of dozens of chickens, flying feathers, and the raucous sound of clucking.

Then her brain remembered that chickens were not the only ones in peril. Haley was on the floor in the back, not protected by a seatbelt or an airbag. A new wave of fear and remorse washed through her.

Instinct took over then. She gave one glance over at Woody. A gash had opened in his head, and he was bleeding pretty badly, but she felt no remorse for him.

Jane unbuckled herself, opened her door, and stepped out into a torrential rain that soaked her to the skin. She opened the back door of the Taurus, just as a *crack* of lightning struck.

She jumped, and the flock of newly released chickens screeched. The little hairs on the back of her neck and along her arm danced. That lightning had hit way too close for comfort.

Jane forced herself not to worry. She had to get Haley. She had to make certain the little girl was okay.

She found the child down on the floor of the Taurus and hauled her out into the rain. The seven-year-old had a scrape across her head and the beginning of a bump on her right temple. She was breathing, but she wasn't entirely conscious. She gave a little moan as the water hit her face.

Jane almost raged out loud and pumped her fist at the tempest and the Universe. But she didn't have time for that.

The Cadillac with Florida tags pulled into the parking lot, and four big guys got out of it. In unison they reached into their suit jackets.

In that instant, Jane's plans became pretty simple and basic. She needed to gather up that baby and run like hell.

Stony's cruiser shot up Palmetto Avenue with the siren going and lights flashing. Clay raced it on foot, dodging raindrops, as he headed toward the Cut 'n Curl. Dodging the rain soon became as impossible as dodging the truth.

Damn Jane Coblentz and damn his big brother and damn his rotten luck. Why did bad stuff always have to happen right when things were starting to look up? For one split second this morning, he'd had this feeling like God or some benign force had reached down and touched his life. Everything had been perfect.

He was in love with Jane. And Ray, it would seem, had escaped in the arms of the curvaceous Betty Wilkins.

And then Damian Easley had opened that door, and everything unraveled.

Pain burned in Clay's chest, and it wasn't just from running like a crazy man, frantic to get to his mother, who, according to the county dispatcher, had been shot.

No, his chest burned with all kinds of emotions: hurt and disgust and deep, deep disappointment.

Lightning streaked across the black sky, and with the crackle of electricity, his emotions distilled down to fear. Fear that his momma might be dead or dying. Fear that his niece might be dead, too. And absolute terror that Jane was responsible.

Clay wasn't strong enough to handle this. He could feel his emotions bubbling up through his system, torn between loyalty to his family and Jane Coblentz, jewel thief and pinup girl.

Why would the Lord send him a woman like this to love? He wanted to settle down somewhere and raise a couple of kids with someone he could grow old with. He wanted a simple life. Clay didn't really want to go back to Nashville. Truth be told, there were a lot of positives to living in Last Chance, where everyone cared about him, even if everyone also seemed to have their noses firmly poked into his business.

Clay huffed and puffed his way down the alley to the Cut 'n Curl's parking lot. The scene looked like something right out of a television cop show. Cop cars and ambulances were converging on the scene with their sirens going and their lights a bright-colored smear against the rain and the tears filling up Clay's eyes.

He backhanded the water from his eyes and then elbowed his way through the throng of cops to get to his momma. She sprawled on the wet pavement, blood pouring from a wound in her right temple. Stony was on her right side holding her hand tight. Seeing Momma's blood all over Stone's hands and the wet pavement turned Clay's fear into fury.

Clay slid down to his knees beside his big brother and leaned over Momma. An EMT, kneeling on the other side of her, held a bandage to the wound on her head. The EMT screamed above the roar of the storm that they needed to make room for his partner. Clay didn't budge. He was paralyzed by fury and grief and about a dozen other emotions he couldn't name.

Momma's eyelids fluttered.

The EMT shouted that she was conscious.

She looked up at Stone with a glazed, unfocused look. "Jane," she whispered and blinked in the rain. Clay could see her trying to focus on Stone's face, but her pupils were dilated unevenly. "A gun…Haley's in danger." She closed her eyes, and the color drained from her face.

"She's going into shock. Get the hell outta here, Stone," the EMT bellowed.

But Clay's brother seemed a million miles away. Someone had to bring him back to reality. Clay stood up and grabbed Stone by the arm and hauled him out of the way. "Get a grip," he said into his brother's ear as he pulled him away from the scene.

Stone turned violent. "You asshole," he hissed through his teeth. "I told you she was trouble. Did you listen? She shot Momma."

"No, she didn't," Clay replied, certain of the words. He was also certain that whoever shot Momma was here because of Jane and because of that little necklace he'd seen in Jane's purse last Thursday morning.

"Damn it, Clay, can't you see the truth when it's right there in front of you? That woman is no good."

Clay wanted to argue the point, but he knew better. He wanted to believe in Jane's innocence, but his mother was lying there bleeding while the EMTs worked, and Haley was missing, trapped in a hijacked car. One couldn't refute such irrefutable evidence.

Loving Jane wasn't going to work out.

Then Stone turned toward the cops converging on the scene. "Did anyone see Jane attack my mother? Did anyone see which way that woman went?" he asked.

Chaos answered. Lightning hissed above them. The streetlights went out, and an explosion of static crackled over the police radios as dispatchers began to call in an astounding number of weather-related disasters.

To hear those radios, one might think Armageddon had arrived in Allenberg County, South Carolina. Power lines, telephone lines, cable lines, and just about every form of mass communication except radio was down. The Edisto had flooded its banks, washing out the bridges north of town, with additional high water being reported along Route 70 east and west of town. It was almost as if God Almighty had set up a series of roadblocks to ensure there that were no routes of escape for Jane Coblentz. No routes, except 321 South.

That's when the county dispatcher informed everyone that a Country Pride Chicken truck driver had just used his CB to call in an accident on Route 321 South. One of Country Pride's trucks and a tan Ford Taurus had gotten tangled up with Jesus down at Golfing for God.

Chapter
20

Jane hugged Haley to her side and was encouraged when the child hugged her back and settled herself onto Jane's hip like a little monkey. Like a *heavy* little monkey.

Jane took off down the waterlogged gravel path leading to the golf course. Ahead she could see a darker blur against the beating rain that looked like a life-sized Ark. Okay, maybe not life-sized, but at least as big as a barn.

She almost laughed aloud because the rain was so heavy it looked like it might flood the entire area. She wondered if the Ark was seaworthy.

Jane was losing her focus. She needed to stay sharp, because one look behind her told her the bad guys had not given up the chase. A wave of adrenaline hit her system, causing her heart rate to spike and her stomach to drop. She was in flight mode now. Running for her life.

"Haley," she shouted into the child's ear.

She got a grunt.

"Is there a phone in the Ark?"

Silence.

· "Is there a phone in the Ark, honey? You gotta tell me."

"Uh. I think so. In Granddaddy's office." The child's voice sounded dreamy and sleepy, like she'd suffered a serious head injury.

Hoo boy. If Haley suffered irreversible damage, Jane would never forgive herself. She prayed a little harder to the Universe to show her the way.

"Is your granddaddy here?"

"Uh, no. He was still eating breakfast when we left."

"Great. I could have used some help, especially from his angels," she muttered as she picked up her pace. Her thighs and lungs burned. Heading for the Ark was the best plan she had. Maybe the door wasn't locked, and she could get to that phone before the bad guys got to her. Maybe she could stash Haley in a safe place.

One quick glance at the bad guys behind her told her that the Ark was out of range. Woody was almost on her, with the school of four loan sharks only a few paces behind him.

The situation was hopeless. She couldn't outrun these guys, even without being weighed down by Haley. Maybe she could find a place to hide in the wooded area that grew on the right side of the path.

Jane swerved to the right and down into a little gully that was ankle deep in water. She splashed along for a few steps, then ran up the other side onto soft ground covered in fragrant pine needles. Above her, Carolina pines swayed in the ferocious wind.

Lightning whizzed through the air. *Crack*. The sound was sharp and deafening, and Haley screamed.

Jane stumbled to one knee, pain jolting up her thigh.

The unmistakable odor of ozone filled her nose as she struggled back to her feet, only to be knocked flat by a secondary explosion ten times louder than the lightning strike.

Haley screamed again. Jane cried out, too, as the breath left her body. Through the rain and wind, heat flashed against her back.

Jane struggled to inhale against her bruised diaphragm as she looked over her shoulder. The scene could have come right out of an action movie. The lightning had hit something explosive—maybe the propane line for the tiki torches that lined the path. Whatever it was, the explosion had blown the tiki torches sky-high and transformed the path into a corridor of fire.

Jane didn't have the time to ponder how anything could burn like that in a raging downpour. Woody had followed her up into the woods and had managed not to be barbecued.

And so, apparently, had at least three of the four bad guys on his tail.

Jane pulled Haley back onto her hip and started running again. The girl was awake now and weeping about being afraid of lightning.

"It's okay, Hale; just think about your Grandfather's angels, okay?"

It was lame, but maybe the kid would buy it. Jane scanned the terrain in front of her. There wasn't any place to hide. She needed to get to the Ark and find the telephone. She swerved left and headed toward the golf course. She could see the brighter green of fake turf ahead.

She stumbled through a stand of azaleas. To get to

Golfing for God from this direction, she would have to wade the looping carp pond that ringed the golf course like a moat. The pond came complete with lily pads and fish, and probably snakes and other creepy crawlies.

Jane put the thought of snakes out of her mind and splashed through the knee-deep water. She clambered up onto hole number four, featuring a bunch of oversized, blue-green fiberglass frogs. What frogs had to do with God was a mystery to Jane—probably because she was more than a little vague on her Bible stories. These particular frogs spat water at each other in short bursts and streams. Anyone who missed their first putt was going to get wet.

She ran down the fairway, the frogs shooting at her like amphibian water artillery. She took a sharp right onto the path that led to the Ark.

And that's when the earthquake hit.

Well, it wasn't exactly an earthquake. But the ground did kind of shake, and there was this funny grinding noise audible even above the raging wind and the pounding rain and the crackle of the burning tiki torches.

She ran harder, past statues of David and Goliath—a story she actually knew. But with each step, the noise grew louder until it crescendoed with a sharp series of *pops* followed by a roar that sounded like a freight train. All of this was punctuated by male shouts of surprise.

"Look," Haley said in her ear. "You were right about the angels. The Sorrowful Angel and her friends are smiting them just like in the Bible." The girl's voice sounded dreamy.

"Huh?" Jane looked over her shoulder. She didn't see any angels.

Instead, one of the fiberglass frogs lost its head. It popped off and shot skyward, and then the water it had been spitting turned into a raging torrent. In quick succession, the remaining five frogs similarly converted themselves into open fire hydrants, spewing water so hard that it knocked down Woody West and one of his assailants. The entire scenario gave a new meaning to the term *water hazard*.

But the scene gave Jane no comfort because little Haley was hallucinating about angels, and it was all Jane's fault for suggesting it. There was no way Stone Rhodes would ever forgive her for this, even if she lived through it.

Jane kept running, putting distance between herself and the two bad guys who had managed to bypass the frog hazard.

Jane swerved left, past Jonah's whale. Then she scrambled up a little rise where another, smaller statue of Jesus stood with open arms. Noah's Ark stood behind this statue.

Noah's boat was not built for sailing. It was more of a barn. A pair of wide doors were built into its side, and several wooden-fenced corrals occupied a space to one side of the structure. Jane recognized a cattle barn when she saw one. She also recognized the sounds that were, at that moment, emanating from deep inside.

Another bolt of lightning hissed overhead, followed immediately by a crack of thunder. This storm was right overhead, not miles away. And that probably explained why the panicked cattle took that moment to kick down the barn's door. Suddenly she came face to face, or more properly face to horn, with a large brown bull.

"Mamie," Haley said in greeting to the horned beast, who had a pair of mild brown eyes and looked more like a Texas longhorn than an actual bull. "Follow the Sorrowful Angel and her friends," the little girl said. "Get the bad guys."

Haley pointed toward one of the putt-putt holes that featured a tower that sort of looked like the Leaning Tower of Pisa, only without the lean. Jane had no idea what Pisa had to do with God, either.

Mamie followed Haley's orders impeccably and charged. She also possessed leadership qualities, because she took the entire Golfing for God herd with her. The herd was not that large: It consisted of just one llama, a billy goat, two sheep, and a bunny rabbit.

To be honest, the bunny rabbit wasn't up to stampeding and scurried off in the opposite direction, but the goat made up for the bunny's cowardice by making a beeline toward one of the men in black. The goat took him out with a single blow.

Jane put Haley down on her feet and looked down at her. She had a huge bump on her forehead, but her eyes looked clear. "Are you dizzy?"

Haley shook her head, and Jane felt relieved.

"Honey, go hide in the barn and stay there, you hear me?"

Haley looked up at her with this odd look. "Don't worry, Jane, the angels are here. They won't let anything bad happen to us."

The relief vanished. Haley was seriously hurt. "Just hide in the barn, honey. With the angels, okay?"

Haley shook her head. "No, the angels are smiting the bad guys just like in the Bible. They're busy; they can't hide with me right now." With that pronouncement, Haley scurried toward the black maw of the Ark's doors. Jane watched her run, feeling the weight of the whole world on her shoulders. Stone Rhodes was going to murder her—or at least lock her up for life.

Jane turned toward the office door but didn't get very far because something deep in the earth gave way and the ground shook again. And then a geyser of water shot up through hole eighteen, right at the feet of the second statue of Jesus. In fact, it looked as if the fiberglass statue, with its outstretched arms, was willing the water up through the golf hole.

And since it was hole eighteen—the hole where the establishment collects your golf balls so you can't cheat and play another round—the geyser was not composed entirely of water.

It was, in fact, loaded with multicolored golf balls. It streamed forth like some kind of supercharged bazooka that shot those babies skyward with an aim that was pretty darn remarkable and not at all random.

Haley stopped and turned, and the two of them stood speechless as every single one of the bad guys—even the ones who had been burned or drowned or taken out by the stampede—got brained by one of those balls just for good measure.

Haley laughed aloud, and it was a joyful sound. "Jiminy Christmas! The Sorrowful Angel sure has a good throwing arm, doesn't she?" she said.

"Who?" Jane asked.

"The Sorrowful Angel."

Jane swallowed hard and looked up at the sky but didn't see any angels, sorrowful or otherwise. Instead, the heavens were in the process of folding themselves up. That was about the only way she could describe what she saw. The black clouds were disappearing as if some hand or power were sucking them dry.

Blue sky was breaking out all over.

And so were the sirens.

In the next thirty seconds, the entire combined police forces and fire departments of the towns of Last Chance, Denmark, and Olar, not to mention various county authorities, converged on Golfing for God and took the bad guys into custody.

Stone Rhodes led the charge.

The chief of police covered ground fast, and when he got to Jane and Haley, he fell down on his knees in front of his child and hauled that little girl up against his chest like his entire life depended upon it.

Jane felt like a voyeur watching the chief lose his composure. There were tears running down his craggy cheeks, and he looked bad. Real bad.

Even though Stone was big and macho and capable of looking after himself, a person would have to be blind not to realize how much he loved his family and why he worked so hard to keep the bad guys out of Last Chance.

Jane hugged herself against a cold that seeped into her bones and made a mockery of the bright sunshine breaking out all over the place. A lump lodged in her throat, and guilt settled on her shoulders. She would never understand the Universe. If she had gone somewhere else, Ruby and Haley would still be all right.

At that moment, Clay came dashing through the wreckage like the U.S. Cavalry. She watched him approach with a mixture of hope and fear and overwhelming relief. She had thought she might never see him again.

She could count at least that blessing.

He came to a stop, breathing hard, and gave her one soulful look that said it all. Things had changed between them.

His actions punctuated the point. Clay didn't pull her into his arms and profess his love, like Stone had just done with his child. He didn't reach out and give her the warmth she needed. He just looked at her as if he were trying to figure out what he was supposed to do next. As if he were weighing the pros and cons and thinking things through, instead of acting on them.

His lips tightened. For one instant her hope soared and then it crashed. Clay turned away. It was over.

He presented his back as he squatted down and squeezed Stone's shoulders for a brief moment. There was a world of love in that touch. Jane ached for it.

Clay hung there beside his brother, listening to Haley babble on about the Sorrowful Angel and studying the scrape on her head. Then it was like he made a decision.

He stood up and yelled for an EMT.

One of the medics who had just arrived detached himself from one of the bad guys and hurried up. He started examining Haley. Stone took that moment to look up at Jane, murder in his deep green eyes. Clay didn't turn back toward Jane until the EMT and Stone took the child to one of the waiting ambulances. There wasn't murder in Clay's eyes, only a deep sorrow that made Jane want to weep.

He stood there, his waterlogged Stetson shadowing his face. She wanted to throw herself against his broad, sturdy chest. She wanted that safe feeling back, but she wasn't going to find it there anymore.

"You all right?" he asked.

No. She wanted to wail the word. But she didn't want to show her weaknesses. She didn't want Clay to rescue her. She wanted him to love her. She wanted a love that could overlook even this, but that was more than anyone could ask. So she just ignored his question and asked one of her own. "Is Ruby...?" She couldn't finish the sentence.

Tears gathered in his eyes but they didn't spill over. "She's bad. It's a head wound. But she's still alive, if that's what you're asking." His voice sounded kind of dead.

Jane's stomach clenched, and her heart twisted. Ruby Rhodes had been kind, and this is how she had repaid her. She closed her eyes and winged a little affirmation to the Cosmos on Ruby's behalf. She doubted that the powers of the Universe would answer her. She had lost her faith in manifesting. She had lost her hope, too.

"Look, I know what I said this morning, but..." Clay started, and his voice faded out.

Jane opened her eyes, her heart shattering. "I'm not going to hold you to that," she managed to say. "We both know I'm not what you want," she said, paraphrasing the words to "I Will Always Love You." She *would* always love him. But right now, she needed to run—and run hard.

Clay nodded like he understood. "I gotta go. They were taking Momma up to Orangeburg. Getting up there's going to be a problem, seeing as the road's all flooded."

Jane took a deep, shaky breath. Her world was coming unraveled. She had just cheated death, only now death seemed such a small hurt compared to this big hurt inside her heart.

"I'm so sorry," she said.

She looked away so she didn't have to watch him turn his back. She stood there alone with her sadness and her guilt and her fury at the Universe.

"Mary Smith?" a deep, no-nonsense voice asked a moment later. Jane's trip to the very bottom was not finished.

She turned and faced an African-American man with a grim face. He reached into his suit jacket and pulled out a leather case and a shiny FBI badge. His name was Bernard Wilkes.

Clay still stood there, behind the G-man. The look on his face sent another wave of sorrow and regret running through her. He was thinking the absolute worst. Well, so be it. She didn't want a man who always thought the worst of her. She wanted someone who could see the bright side of things. Someone who would support and forgive her, no matter what. Someone who would have her back when the bad stuff arrived.

She shifted her gaze back to the federal agent. "I've gone by that name," she said. "But my real name is Wanda Jane Coblentz." It was time to accept who she was.

She couldn't blame anyone else for all the bad things that had happened to her in the past. She wasn't a victim of bad luck or mean people. She was a victim of her own mistakes. It would be terrific if Clay could understand that, but he couldn't. Not with his mother lying in some hospital with a gunshot wound that was, at least in part, her fault.

Jane would learn from this experience. She would pick herself up and move on. It was what she did best.

The FBI agent spoke again. "We need to ask you a few questions about the disappearance of the Cambodian Camel."

Clay pulled his Windstar up to the curb, opened the door, and stepped out into a suddenly warm and humid day. A glorious autumn sun beamed down on him, making his wet clothes cling, but failing to warm him.

He kept thinking about the look on Jane's face as the FBI hauled her away. His heart kept telling him that he needed to quit worrying about what was true or untrue about Jane and just go after her. He couldn't shake the feeling that he'd failed her in some awful way.

On the other hand, Momma was shot and possibly dying in a hospital up in Orangeburg. Haley was traumatized and talking about angels. Clay didn't think he could forgive her for either of those things. He didn't need to be running after the woman who was responsible for what had happened.

Right now, he needed to focus on getting some dry clothes and getting himself up to the hospital.

He stepped into his living room, and the sight of Tricia's suitcase and purse lined up like they were ready to go reminded him of every other heartache he'd ever suffered. And to make it worse, Chad Ames, a-hole of the century, had decided to pay a social call.

"Man, what the hell happened to you?" Chad asked as Clay entered his home. The lead singer for Tumbleweed sat on the sofa in the living room looking handsome. With his spiky bleached hair and soul patch, Chad was the hottest heartthrob in country music. And as usual, he was operating as if the world revolved around him.

He sat with one leg cocked up over the other, his arm around Tricia with her head resting on his shoulder. A pile of Kleenex littered the coffee table, and by the look of things, there had been a major scene played out between Chad and Tricia that had, at least for the moment, ended amicably.

Tricia was asleep.

Well, that was a good thing. That loose end was tied up nice and neat and tidy. Clay didn't have to worry about having to settle for something comfortable instead of passionate. He could settle for nothing at all.

That thought hit him like a punch to the gut.

Clay wondered where Ricki might be. Maybe the woman had taken the hint and hightailed it back to Los Angeles. That was a good thing, too. He didn't want Ricki, either.

You want Jane, his heart said. *You can't have Jane*, his head rejoined; *she's a criminal*. Every time that thought crossed his mind, his chest constricted and his gut burned.

"Great timing as usual," Clay said in a barely civil voice, then turned his back on Chad and Tricia as he headed toward the bathroom at the back of the house.

"Hey, man, wait up."

Clay stopped midway down the hall, ready to punch Chad if the guy pushed him too hard. Right now, he didn't even care about messing up his hands. He just wanted to hit something, hard, and Chad looked like a good target.

Clay turned and watched Chad disengage himself from Tricia and lay the sleeping woman out on the couch.

The singer sauntered down the hall. "I just wanted to say thanks."

"Thanks? For what? Letting you steal my woman and my band and—" Clay stopped in midstream. This was an old hurt. He was almost over it. He had other, much bigger hurts right now.

"Hey, look," Chad said. "It doesn't have to be this way."

Clay let go of a cynical laugh. "Oh, yes, it does. But for the record, I'm glad you're here."

"Really? So you're ready to reconsider and come back? We could sure use—"

"Are you insane? I meant that I'm glad you came to get Tricia. I'm glad on her account."

"Oh, that." Chad shrugged like that didn't matter much. "Look, the thing is, everyone in Tumbleweed feels bad about what happened. Fact is, we wouldn't be where we are today without your songs. It—"

"You mean you wouldn't be where you are without 'I Gotta Know.'" If he could bottle up this hurt and turn it into lyrics, he might end up as a success at something. Isn't that what Jane had told him on Saturday night? Country music was made for sad love songs, and he had plumbed the depths of human heartache.

"The songs are good, Clay, that's what I mean. But more than that, there's no reason you had to walk out. Everyone wants you back. Our new fiddler hasn't worked out, and there's a place for you in the band, man."

Something deadly coursed through Clay. Chad Ames was a hanger-on. And so were Tricia and Ricki. They came into his life when they needed him and left when the need disappeared. Tumbleweed had been Clay's band.

He'd been the one to hire Chad as a lead singer. Boy, the guy had *cojones*.

"Is that what this is all about? Is that why you came back here? Are you more interested in getting me to write a few more songs than you are in Tricia?"

"Look, Clay, this is a good deal for both of us. It's not like you haven't made some money on the songs Tumbleweed recorded. And, hey, it would make Tricia happy, you know. She says you're still her friend. And I figure with the baby and all, it would be better if you were around."

Clay lost it then. He let all the emotions that had been building up through the morning explode. "You are a supreme asshole," he bellowed. "You take a look at that woman over there. She's carrying your baby. She loves you for some reason I cannot fathom, and there's no reason why you shouldn't love her back. What she feels for you is whole and pure, and she's going to give you a miracle. And instead of taking Tricia off to a preacher and marrying her and making sure she feels like the center of your universe, you let her come to me? And now you're saying you're ready to share her with me just to get a few hit songs. Oh, my God, *that* is just *wrong*."

Clay turned his back on Chad and stalked down to the bathroom at the end of the hall and slammed the door. He stood there shaking for a solid minute.

Why the hell couldn't he have a love like that? Why did he have to fall for all these screwed-up people? Why did he have to be in love with someone who was a criminal?

Aw, crap.

Clay sat himself down on the lid of the commode and

hung his head in his hands and waged a ten-minute battle with his emotions. When he'd managed to regain control of himself, he took a quick shower and placed a call to the hospital that netted him no information about his mother's condition. A half hour later, after cursing Chad Ames out a second time, he was back in his Windstar, dry-eyed and heading north toward Orangeburg with a hole in his chest where his heart used to be.

Chapter
21

Jane sat on the hard chair under the bright fluorescent light. She wore a Day-Glo jail jumpsuit that was several sizes too large. Someone had given her a cup of coffee and a blanket. She was still cold, even though she was no longer wet.

She had made a full confession to FBI Agents Hannigan and Wilkes during the car ride from Golfing for God to the Allenberg County jail. She made a clean breast of everything. Not just the location of the Cambodian Camel, but a blow-by-blow description of her life for the last seven years.

They had recovered the necklace from Haley before the EMTs left for the hospital, and they had listened with avid interest about Joey Hamil and Woody West and the stupid things Jane had done in her life.

Then they had brought her here and left her alone so she could ponder the Universe and her place in it. During this time, Jane concluded that she sucked at manifesting change in her life. She decided that when they got around to booking her, she would destroy Dr. Goodbody's tapes. They were not particularly useful.

While she was waiting, she also did a lot of thinking about Clay. She decided that she would always hold the memory of the last twenty-four hours close. She would let herself remember that for one instant, she had been on the point of having a remarkable man tell her he loved her.

She sniffled and shivered as a single tear left her right eye and trickled down her cheek. She was too depressed to wipe it away.

Her morose thoughts were interrupted by Agent Hannigan, who entered the room carrying a bundle that looked a whole lot like the soggy clothes she had given up for this ugly, oversized jumpsuit with the words *Allenberg County* stenciled on the back.

He sat down across from her. "Turns out you were right about the necklace you gave to Haley Rhodes."

"Huh?"

He shrugged and gave her a warm smile that had his Irish eyes sparkling. "Turns out the necklace is, in fact, an item that you can find at any Value Mart. It's not even gold."

She blinked at him for a few moments as her brain processed this. "Are you telling me Woody the weasel went on a crime spree over a discount-store necklace?"

He nodded, and a little blush crawled up his face. "I'm afraid so."

"And just exactly how did he get the idea that this necklace was valuable?" She was warming up a little bit. A dose of healthy anger percolated down in her belly. Ruby Rhodes got *shot* over a piece-of-crap necklace? It was too awful to even consider.

Hannigan cleared his throat. "Well, ma'am, I'm afraid the FBI gave him that idea. We had gotten a tip from a reliable source."

"I see."

"Turns out our Miami Office has recovered the real Cambodian Camel."

"Do tell. And where did they find it?"

"In a vault deep beneath Oliver Cromwell Jones's compound in Palm Springs. Seems the old goat was a little strapped for cash and stole it himself."

"Say that again?"

"For the insurance, you know. Apparently, Jones faked the robbery and then passed a forgery to Freddie the Fence, who runs one of the largest high-end stolen property rings in the country. Freddie was probably in on the scam, and being a wily kind of guy, he arranged to have Jones's fake transported to a buyer in Los Angeles."

"Los Angeles? So what does that have to do with Woody and the necklace he gave me? We were going to Nashville."

"Well, see, Freddie was fed up with Woody. Near as we can figure, Woody's gambling had become a huge liability for Freddie, so he set Woody up. Gave him a fake Cambodian Camel, told him to give it you, and then we think he was the one who provided the anonymous tip that my partner and I followed."

The anger was really making her hot now. She shrugged off the blanket. "You mean Woody only asked me along because this Freddie guy wanted me to wear the necklace?"

"It looks like that's what happened. At least that's what Woody says. Woody was a decoy, designed to keep us off the scent. And by having us pick up Woody, Freddie also allowed the Colombian's goons to take care of Freddie's little problem."

"Woody works for Freddie the Fence?"

"'Fraid so. There is no honor among thieves, Jane. That's for sure."

"I see." But she didn't see at all.

"If you want my advice, you'd do a whole lot better if you avoided jerks like Woodrow Arnold West and Joseph Andrew Hamil in the future."

"So you checked out the whole Lexington thing, huh? Are you going to arrest me for Jane Coblentz's murder?"

"No, ma'am, I'm not. Jane Coblentz isn't dead."

Jane blinked a few times. "You believe me?"

He nodded. "Seems the Last Chance chief of police has a DNA report that proves you are Jane Coblentz. And your story about the miscarriage squares with what Hamil told authorities years ago."

"And no one believed him back then?"

"No one had reason to believe him. You gave the impression of being a pretty responsible girl until you ran away."

"So what happens now?" she asked.

"You're free to go, although I'm pretty sure the state of South Carolina and the federal government are both going to want you as a witness at Woody's trials."

She nodded. "I'd like nothing better than to put that peckerwood away."

"Well, I'm sure that will happen. But look on the bright side: Maybe you'll luck out, and the state will negotiate a plea bargain, and we can put this sorry and embarrassing situation behind us."

Sorry and embarrassing? Is that what he thought?

Woody had shot Ruby right there in the parking lot of the Cut 'n Curl. That was not sorry or embarrassing. That was a disaster. It was something she would regret for the rest of her life.

And a piece of cheap jewelry from Value Mart was the reason Ruby might be dead.

Hannigan cleared his throat. "Look, it's going to be all right, Jane. The worst is over, and we appreciate the way you cooperated with us. Sheriff Bennett says you can keep the jumpsuit since your clothes are soaked. But I wanted to make sure you didn't lose this."

He put a copper penny down on the Formica tabletop and pushed it across the surface with his index finger.

Jane stared down at the 1943 wheat penny, as her anger transformed itself into a grief so deep she could hardly breathe.

She should have told Clay and Stone that there were bad guys on her tail. She should never have taken a job babysitting Stone's kids. That was just dumb, and neither of those men would ever forgive her for it.

She stared down at that penny through a smear of tears. She would keep it with her for the rest of her life as a reminder. What had Clay said when he found it? Oh, yeah, that it was something special hiding out in plain sight. That its worth was not measured by its value.

She reached for it, and took it into her palm, and squeezed it. When he'd said those words, he'd been halfway talking about her.

"So where'd you find it?" Hannigan asked.

She looked up at him. His tone had been more than casual. "Why?" She sniffled back her tears.

"Because if it's real, it's worth a great deal of money."

"If it's real?"

He grinned. "You have no idea, do you?"

She shook her head.

Hannigan folded his arms and leaned on the table. "I do a lot of stolen property work, and we come across cases all the time involving rare and valuable coins. I'm not much of an expert, but if that's an authentic 1943 copper penny, it's very rare and valuable. The U.S. wasn't supposed to make any copper pennies in 1943 because copper was needed for the war effort during World War II. All of the pennies struck in that year were supposed to be made of steel. Only a mistake was made, and an unknown, but small, number of copper pennies were made. If it's real, that penny is worth thousands of dollars."

"You're kidding, right?"

"No, ma'am, I'm not kidding. But here's the catch. People fake 1943 pennies all the time. The usual methods are to put a copper coating on a 1943 steel penny or to alter the eight in a 1948 copper penny. I used a refrigerator magnet to see if your penny was steel. It's not. So it's not copper-plated. It appears to be real copper. You should have someone appraise it."

"A refrigerator magnet?"

"Yeah. A magnet can pick up a steel penny, but it won't pick up a copper penny."

She opened her palm and looked down at the penny and almost laughed. It might be a rare and precious object, or it might be a bad penny. But that wasn't right. It wasn't a bad penny. It was the penny Clay had found in the bottom of her purse last Thursday morning. It was her good luck charm.

That made it priceless. Worth more than the value of the thing itself. Like a MasterCard commercial.

"Thanks," Jane said in a shaky voice.

"There's just one more thing," the agent said.

"Yeah?"

"I've been meaning to ask you about that shirt."

"Huh?"

Hannigan nodded toward Sharon Rhodes's pink T-shirt that lay in a soggy pile on the table. "I guess it's your lucky shirt, huh?"

She didn't really know what he meant by that, so she unwadded the T-shirt until she could read what was written on its back. Two angels, standing with wings outstretched, framed a verse from Psalm 91:

> *No evil shall befall you,*
> *Nor shall any plague come near to your*
>   *dwelling,*
> *For He shall give His angels charge over you,*
> *To keep you in all your ways.*

Her vision blurred with tears. What was the Universe trying to tell her? What was Hannigan trying to tell her?

"Look, Jane, don't beat yourself up over Woody," Hannigan said. "The fact is, you saved that little girl's life today...you were her guardian angel in a really tight spot. That's probably why she's coping with the trauma the way she is."

Jane blinked away the tears. "Uh, Agent Hannigan, do you know how Ruby Rhodes is doing?"

He shrugged. "She's in the hospital up in Orangeburg with a head injury. I don't know the details, but the county is watching it closely. That woman dies and Woody's up for murder, instead of just assault and kidnapping."

"Oh, God, I need to go there."

"If you want, I can give you a lift."

She closed her eyes as the monumental truth settled into her head. She didn't have anywhere else she wanted to go. And Miriam Randall had been so right. Jane needed to ask for more.

"I really need a lift up there," she said in a tiny voice.

She had to apologize to Stone and Clay and the rest of the Rhodes family. For once, she had to face the mistakes she had made.

Then she had to fight for what she wanted. That was the point. Running away had never solved anything in her life. She *had* saved Haley. And she had tried to warn Ruby. She wasn't a bad person, even though bad things had happened.

She was worthy of Clay's love. She needed to make that statement right out loud—like the biggest affirmation of all. She needed to rescue herself.

Clay stepped out of Ruby's hospital room, making a place for Tulane, his younger brother, who had just driven down from Florence. Since Momma was in the critical care unit, they only allowed two family members at a time, and Daddy was one of them. Daddy hadn't left Momma's side, even though she hadn't regained consciousness yet.

Clay walked down the hall to the waiting room, where the family and a few of Momma's church friends kept vigil. Stone and his children; Clay's little sister, Rocky; Aunt Arlene; and Uncle Pete had all come up here to wait. Reverend Ellis had come along with Thelma Hanks and Miriam Randall, to sit with the family and do whatever was needed. Clay knew good and well that the rest of the Ladies Auxiliary were back in Last Chance cooking up more than enough food to feed everyone for the next month. There was nothing like a life-and-death emergency to bring out the banana pudding and squash casserole.

Clay sagged against the wall for a moment trying to find the positives in this awful situation. There were a few that came to mind. Woodrow West had turned out to be a lousy shot, having only grazed Momma's head. Bobbi Lee Andrews, who worked at the doughnut shop next to the Cut 'n Curl, had seen Ruby go down and immediately called for help. The flooding that blocked the road from Last Chance to Orangeburg had lasted all of fifteen minutes, so the EMTs had been able to get Ruby to the hospital fast.

Even so, the .45-caliber bullet had knocked Momma back, and she'd fractured her skull in the fall. The doctors were guardedly optimistic, despite the brain swelling. They said her EEG and CAT scan looked good.

But the scenario reminded Clay of the night Ray hit his head on the windshield of Clay's old Dodge. The doctors were optimistic then, too, only Ray hadn't come out of that in one piece.

How was he supposed to feel guardedly optimistic? What the heck did that mean, anyway? He felt weary and used up...and alone.

He pushed away from the wall and found himself a seat on one of the hard waiting-room chairs between Stone on his right and Miriam Randall on his left.

His older brother had shed his uniform, and his puffy shiners made the rest of his face look pale and sallow. Stone had lost all composure this afternoon after Haley started babbling about angels. Stone might be "due" for a breakdown, but Clay didn't like the idea of Stone losing his composure. Stone was supposed to be a rock. Now Stone sat with Haley in his lap, holding her with a death grip—like if he let her go something bad would happen to her.

Unfortunately, something bad had already happened to her. Haley sported scrapes on both knees and a purple bruise on her noggin. The doctors said the little bruise wasn't much to worry about. However, they had suggested Haley needed the services of a psychologist to help her over the trauma of the experience. Haley had always been scared of lightning, and they figured she had seized upon the idea of angels as a coping mechanism. Lord only knew, she had heard enough talk around the dinner table about Daddy and his angels. Apparently, Haley had invented a few just to help her through what must have been a terrifying situation.

Of course, angels had not rescued Haley from the criminals Jane had brought to Last Chance. The very lightning that Haley feared had been responsible for everything that had happened. The lightning strike had exploded the propane tank, and that set off a cascading series of events that ended in the complete failure of Golfing for God's water management system.

Stone had tried to explain the situation to his young daughter, but Haley didn't really understand the engineering.

Clay looked away from Haley and tried not to think about what she had endured. Instead, he became uncomfortably aware that Miriam Randall was scrutinizing him with a pair of wise and knowing eyes.

Boy, he was a dunce. How could he have ever misunderstood the things Miriam had said to him yesterday at church? Obviously, Miriam didn't think Jane was his soulmate. How could his soulmate be a criminal?

"There's one thing I don't understand," Miriam said suddenly, into the silence that hung in the room.

"What's that?" Thelma Hanks asked.

"The floods. Have you ever heard of a fifteen-minute flood?"

Thelma shook her head. "No, can't say as I ever have."

"It was the angels," Haley said in a surprisingly chipper voice.

"It was not," Lizzy said in a defiant voice. Lizzy slumped in a chair on the other side of the room, as far from Stone as a person could get. The thirteen-year-old and her father had a stormy relationship, and the kid was going through a real obnoxious teenager phase.

Lizzy leaned forward and gave her little sister a snotty look. "Just get off the angels, okay? Nobody wants to hear it. They all think you're crazy."

"Lizzy, don't be ugly," Thelma said in that church-lady tone of voice. "Your granddaddy talks to angels all the time."

Lizzy folded her arms across her chest and looked away from Thelma. Thank goodness, she had the good sense not to challenge authority, for once. Clay felt terrible for the kid. She'd already lost a mother at a young age. And now this. He couldn't imagine what losing her grandmother would do to Lizzy. Clay read the fear in Lizzy like she was an open book. He wanted to tell her everything was going to be okay, but he didn't believe that.

And he wasn't going to lie. Not to Lizzy.

Clay's throat clogged and he had to swallow back his own fear.

"Well," Miriam said in her little-old-lady voice, "I don't think Haley's crazy. Don't you believe in angels, Lizzy?"

Lizzy rolled her eyes. "Yeah, sure I do. In the Bible. But not at Golfing for God in the middle of a thunderstorm."

Haley squirmed out of her daddy's arms and scrambled down onto her feet. She turned toward Clay and leaned her little hands onto his knees. His skin warmed under her touch.

Haley stared up at him for a long, uncomfortable moment. She wore a pink T-shirt with the words "Girls Rule" across the chest, and she looked dangerous and adorable. All Clay could think was thank God she was whole and in one piece.

"They were beautiful angels," Haley said, looking up into his face with her big, innocent eyes. "They had white wings, and there were boy angels and girl angels, and they were all around us. Some of them protected us, and the rest smited the bad guys. The Sorrowful Angel was the one who smited them hardest of all. She was really, really angry."

"Haley, stop it," Stone said in a low voice that sounded near the breaking point.

She leaned in toward Clay, something lighting up her face in a preternatural way. "The Sorrowful Angel is here all the time, but the rest of them came when Jane called 'em. She said it would be good if they could come and help out, and they did." Haley whispered this last bit, so that her daddy wouldn't hear what she said.

Clay stared down at the child. "What?"

Haley nodded her head once, and then she turned around and went back to her father. She climbed up into his lap, and for the life of him, Clay got the feeling that the child was comforting the adult, not the other way around.

Miriam took that moment to touch his hand. Her fingers were cold, and her ancient skin felt papery, but there was something alive in that touch.

"Innocent faith is such a wonderful thing," she murmured. "It can move mountains, sometimes."

And that's when enlightenment hit him, like a hammer blow to his hard head.

Oh, crap. He was an idiot.

He stood up. "I gotta go," he said, looking down at the old woman.

Miriam smiled up at him like an angel herself. "I was starting to think you were never going to figure it out, boy. For a sensitive man, you sure are boneheaded."

Oh, yeah, he sure was.

The only thing Jane had done today was save Haley's life. Even if she hadn't summoned angels, that woman had run half a mile with Haley on her hip. Maybe she had brought trouble to Last Chance, but she hadn't done that on purpose. Trouble had followed her. And Clay knew how it felt to have trouble follow you.

She deserved another chance.

And anyway, he loved Jane. He believed in her. She was the center of his universe just like Chad was the center of Tricia's universe. He wasn't going to be stupid like Chad. He was a better man, by far, than that jerk.

Why hadn't he seen this before?

He knew the answer right away. He'd been too busy looking at the bad things that had happened to see the good things. He'd made the mistake he always made. He forgot to count his blessings. He'd lost faith.

He was never going to do that again. If Jane had taught him one thing, it was that. There were positive things coming out of this disaster. All he had to do was look for them.

He was blessed. He had the good fortune to love a woman who could summon angels, even if they were just figments of a little girl's mind.

She was his true love, not just some shadow of a love that he was going to settle for. This was a gift, not a complication. Love came straight from the higher powers of the Universe, and sometimes love was hard and painful. Love came from God Himself. You didn't look a gift horse like that in the mouth. You accepted it.

And just like that, the hole in his stomach disappeared, and the emptiness in his heart filled up, and he knew that it would take more strength to walk away from Jane than to love her, even with all her imperfections. And with that knowledge came the understanding that he was no longer alone.

He turned on his heel, intent on getting himself back to Allenberg and the sheriff's office. Jane needed his help more than Momma did. He would be guardedly optimistic about Momma, but in the meantime, he needed to rescue Jane before she got it in her head to run away again.

Clay headed down the hallway to the elevators and that's as far as he got, because the elevator opened, and like some apparition that he had manifested through his own sheer will, out stepped Wanda Jane Coblenz, wearing an ugly orange jumpsuit and carrying a plastic bag that said "Allenberg County Jail" on it.

She looked like a hollow-eyed criminal in that getup, but there was determination in the set of her shoulders and a dry-eyed look on her face, and the handcuffs she'd lately worn were conspicuously absent.

"The FBI let you go?" Clay said and almost winced. This was not the way he wanted to start this conversation. But he couldn't help feeling a little cheated. The woman was either Houdini or she had rescued herself—again.

"I've been cleared of all charges. Clay, I'm so sorry, but I had no way of knowing Woody would follow me here. I just wanted to get away from him and the loan sharks who were hounding him. Those guys took everything from me. All my money and my pride and…"

Her voice began to shake, but she was not crying this time. "Look," she continued, "I know you don't want me here. I know you probably hate me, but I came to apologize. To you and to everyone."

"Oh, baby." He reached out to caress her cheek. Her skin felt so wonderful under his hands. "Why would you apologize? None of this was your fault. We're all grateful that you protected Haley the way you did."

Jane opened her mouth and then closed it. Something relaxed in her face and her body. "I was coming here to fight for you," she said.

"And I was heading out to the police station to rescue you," he replied.

"I don't need to fight, do I?"

"No, and it's clear I don't need to rescue you." Despite his worry about Momma, he felt the smile hit his lips. It felt so good to smile in the face of uncertainty.

"I love you," Jane said.

"I love you back."

Clay stepped close enough to smell her shampoo and feel the heat coming off her body. Awareness jolted through him. It was like his body was tuned to hers or something. There was no doubt that she was the one for him. He reached for her with both hands, and she came into his arms like a lover and a friend. It felt like home with her there. Like it was meant to be.

"How's Ruby?" she asked against his chest.

"She's got a skull fracture. But it could be worse. I'm guardedly optimistic."

"Really?" He heard a mote of amusement in her voice.

"Yes, ma'am. I've decided I'm going to look on the bright side, for once."

"Is she really going to be okay? The police made it sound like she might die." Her voice cracked.

"Oh, honey, she's not going to die. The doctors made that clear. But it's a head injury, and you never know how that might affect her. But even the docs are guardedly optimistic."

She sank into his chest then. "Hold me," Jane whispered. "Don't ever let me go. When I'm in your arms, it feels safe."

"I promise you I won't let you go, ever again."

At that moment, Daddy came running down the hall from Momma's room. "She's awake, y'all, she's awake," he said, his voice wavering with joy and relief.

Elbert came to a stop by the waiting area and looked down the hall toward the elevators. He cocked his head the way he sometimes did. "Are you Jane?" he asked.

"Yes," she answered. "Are you the guy who sees angels?"

He laughed. "I am. I'm Elbert. And I'm really glad to see you here. C'mon, Ruby wants to talk to you. You were the first person she asked after. Get your butt down this hall, girl." He turned and practically sailed back down the hall toward the ICU.

Something eased deep inside Clay's chest. His optimism had not been misplaced. It was going to be okay. Everything was going to be okay.

The Christ Church Ladies could sometimes be annoying, but they were a force to be reckoned with. In the days that followed Woody's crime spree, the ladies mobilized like an army. They descended upon Ruby and Elbert's house like reverse locusts bearing casseroles, fried chicken, coleslaw, potato salad, banana pudding, and two chocolate cakes. They took care of Elbert, until Ruby came home a week later.

Neither Elbert nor Stone and his family could eat all that food. So, the overflow ended up filling Clay's refrigerator at his little bungalow on Baruch Street, which was a good thing because Jane was not a very good cook.

She had moved in with Clay, ceding her apartment above the Cut 'n Curl to Ricki Wilson, who was waitressing down at the Kountry Kitchen on account of the fact that Betty and Ray had absconded to Las Vegas to get married.

The ladies were pretty shocked about that one. Which was good, because it gave them something else to talk about besides the fact that Jane was living with Clay without the benefit of marriage.

Clay was ready to haul her down to the preacher, but Jane wanted to wait at least six months. Clay agreed that was probably a sane and sober thing to do. And during that period, they were going to see what happened with Uncle Pete's health, and think about whether they wanted to go back to Nashville or whether Clay wanted to explore his options as a songwriter, here.

Clay really didn't want to go back to Nashville. Which was okay with Jane, because she was realizing that she had a lot to learn about singing.

Like right now, standing up on this stage at Dot's Spot with the Wild Horses behind her. This terrified her.

It wasn't the same as singing karaoke. She had to rely on her voice, instead of all the hip shaking she'd done back in Fort Myers. She clutched the mic and looked out through the haze.

Dash Randall sat at the corner of the bar watching ESPN on the muted television, drinking a Diet Coke and battling his demons, as always. Bubba Lockheart sat next to him, already unsteady in his seat.

Dottie, wearing a chartreuse tank top that displayed her cleavage, was handing out beers and advice to the good ol' boys and Country Pride Chicken workers from behind the bar.

This was a really tough audience. She understood that now. And she understood that singing for an audience like this was part of paying her dues.

She glanced at Clay, who stood beside her, his fiddle under his chin. He gave her a steady, heartwarming look out of his big gray eyes. She drew strength from that look.

He expected her to stand up on her own feet when she

was on stage. But he was there for her and would rescue her if she lost her way or forgot the words. He was an unbelievably patient teacher.

The band struck up the opening bars and she hit her first cue right on time. Then she breathed in for the next phrase and gave it all she had.

"I will always love you," she sang and put her heart and soul into the words. Which was easy, because no truer words had ever been sung.

Keep reading for the bonus short story, "A Fairytale Bride," the start of Hope Ramsay's Chapel of Love series.

Melissa Portman is fighting a losing battle when it comes to saving her grandmother's store—and selling the historic building may be her only option. Yet when a handsome stranger wanders in one day, she wonders if her very own fairytale is just beginning...

FOREVER

Chapter
1

Jefferson Talbert-Lyndon turned up his jacket collar and hunkered down in an easy chair by the front window of Bean There Done That, the trendy coffee shop in downtown Shenandoah Falls, Virginia.

He fired up his tablet, connected to the coffee shop's Internet, and scanned the headlines from the *Washington Post* and several cable news networks. Things had not improved since he'd left New York a week ago.

Jeff was still being pilloried by the president's political party for a series of articles he'd written for *New York, New York* about Joanna Tyrell-Durand, the nominee for the Supreme Court, and her husband's and brother's illegal lobbying on behalf of various oil and gas interests.

Jeff's stories had relied on information from Val Charonneau, a well-known climate-change advocate and one of Jeff's longtime friends. But it turned out Val's source of information, which included printouts of several damning e-mails, was the unreliable Helena Tyrell, the nominee's soon-to-be-ex sister-in-law.

So what had appeared to be a career-making scoop had turned into the blunder of the century, featuring a philandering husband and a vengeful wife. The embarrassment reached critical mass last week when Brendan Tyrell filed a defamation suit against *New York, New York,* and on the same day, Jeff's father, Thomas Lyndon, the US ambassador to Japan, issued a statement saying that Jeff was a lifelong screwup who had no business trying to be a journalist.

Jeff had resigned from the magazine the next day and headed out here to the wilderness of the Blue Ridge Mountains in order to escape the carnage he'd unloosed on himself and his career.

He turned his tablet off. He needed to move on. But toward what?

If he wasn't a journalist and a writer, then who was he? The man his mother wanted him to become? The CEO of the Talbert Foundation?

He couldn't think of anything he wanted to do less than managing his family's money.

He returned his gaze to the picturesque town beyond the window. Despite the chilly spring rain, the town reminded him of a Norman Rockwell painting. The wrought-iron light posts lining Liberty Avenue were hung with American flags, in honor of the upcoming Memorial Day celebrations. Several of the storefronts were draped in red, white, and blue bunting.

His eye was drawn to the store across the street—a used bookshop called Secondhand Prose—which wasn't draped or decorated. Instead, like independent bookshops everywhere, this one had flyers for upcoming community events and a large orange "Help Wanted" sign taped to its front windows. The store reminded him of his favorite bookshop in Park Slope. He found himself smiling.

Until his gaze snapped to the dark-haired woman dressed in a blue raincoat and carrying a blue umbrella, standing at the corner in front of the shop.

What the hell was Aunt Pam doing in downtown Shenandoah Falls on a rainy Friday morning? Her husband, Mark Lyndon, was a US senator. Didn't they live in DC most of the time?

Oh, wait, the Senate had probably adjourned yesterday because of the holiday. Crap. He'd lost track of time up in his cabin. This was bad.

Aunt Pam was the only member of the Lyndon family, besides his father, who would recognize him on sight. Pam was the only family member who had remained a friend after his mom and dad's messy divorce. Although Jeff had a bunch of Lyndon cousins, he'd never met most of them. He'd visited the family compound at Charlotte's Grove only once in his life, when he was fourteen. That year Dad had been posted in Washington instead of someplace foreign.

Aunt Pam crossed the street and swept into the coffee shop as only Aunt Pam could—like she owned the place.

Jeff leaned his elbow on the table and planted his face in his hand. He stroked the patchy, one-week's growth of scruff on his face. He didn't have a lot of faith in his disguise.

He needed to get out of here. If Pam knew he was hiding out in Dad's fishing cabin, she'd tell Mom, and Mom would come running. Even worse, Pam would invite him to stay at Charlotte's Grove. Jeff couldn't think of anything more excruciating, especially after what Dad had done to him last week. Jeff might have Lyndon in his hyphenated name, but he'd never, ever been a member of Dad's family.

Jeff waited until Pam's attention was focused on the barista behind the counter. It was now or never.

He stood and scooted out the front door, then loped across Liberty Avenue, but had to wait for the traffic on Church Street before he could cross. The rain pelted him as he waited for the light to change.

Pam must have ordered black coffee because she came out of the coffee shop when he was halfway across Church Street.

He needed to hide. Now. He headed for the used bookstore, collar up, head down. A little jingle bell rang as he pushed through the front door.

Jeff loved the way old bookstores smelled, and this bookshop had a lot of old books on its shelves that gave the place the aroma of bookbinder's glue and dry paper.

Jeff turned toward the window, intent on Pam's whereabouts, and discovered a cat tree, complete with a cat, sitting in the front window. The cat was gray and regarded Jeff with a pair of cool, amber eyes.

"Hello," he said in his most cat-friendly voice as he ducked down and glanced through the dusty window. Where was Pam going?

The cat arched its back and hissed.

"Shhh," he hissed back at the cat. Oh, good. Pam had gone into the real estate office across the way.

The cat growled.

"Sorry," Jeff said as he backed away.

He ought to leave the store, but the thought of going

back to the solitary cabin on a rainy day left him slightly depressed. Besides, the only good reading material up there was a complete set of Hardy Boys mysteries, and he'd already been so desperate for entertainment that he'd plowed through all of them.

He had planned to download some reading material at the coffee shop, but Pam had put the kibosh on that. And now the coffee shop was officially off-limits. Maybe he should rethink. Maybe he should hunt down Val and wring his neck.

Or maybe he should just buy a couple of books.

He spent the next twenty minutes browsing the store. He selected four books on various aspects of American history, a couple of John Grisham novels that he found in a box in a dusty corner, and a clothbound edition of *Walden* that was shelved with a bunch of philosophy.

He'd been thinking a lot about Henry David Thoreau. Thoreau had spent years living alone and off the grid. Maybe the long-dead author had some tips for surviving cabin life.

Jeff headed for the checkout, where he stumbled over a second cat—a long-haired calico—intent on winding itself around his ankles. This one was like a puffball with legs. Jeff put his books on the counter and scooped the animal into his arms.

It settled, purring like the engine of his vintage Porsche 911—the car he'd reluctantly left in Brooklyn. He'd "borrowed" Mom's Land Rover from its garage at the house on the Hudson. He'd left a note so Mom wouldn't worry, but she would worry anyway.

He stood there a moment, stroking the cat, waiting for someone to arrive at the checkout, when he realized that he'd been browsing for almost half an hour without seeing another soul.

"Hello?" he called.

Crickets. The silence was almost deafening.

"Is anyone here?" He shouted a little louder this time.

Footsteps sounded from the back of the store, and a moment later a girl appeared, heading slowly in his direction with her face buried in a paperback. Dark, horn-rimmed glasses perched on her nose. Thick, curly chestnut hair tumbled around her narrow face like an untamed mane. She wore a T-shirt with a vintage book illustration of Cinderella under a faded orange plaid flannel shirt and rust-colored skintight jeans that showed her slender figure.

She looked up with a puckish smile. "Hello," she said. "I heard you the first time. But I was at a particularly good part of the story." She closed the book, marking the place with her finger.

He had to return the smile. "What are you reading?" he asked.

The girl's pale cheeks colored. "Oh, just a paperback," she said in an I-just-got-caught-with-my-hand-in-the-cookie-jar voice. She hid the book behind her back.

Then, with catlike grace of her own, she climbed over the box of books that blocked her path to the cash register and quickly transferred the secret novel to a shelf under the counter where he couldn't see it.

"I'm sorry about the mess," she said in a rush, her face growing pinker still. "The books are from a large estate sale, and I haven't gotten around to cataloging and shelving them all."

No doubt because she'd been spending her time reading paperback novels. What had she been reading?

Mystery, suspense, *Fifty Shades of Grey*? He warmed at the thought.

Her eyes were the dark blue color of a fall sky, and the moment their gazes connected, he revised his estimation of her. She wasn't just some girl in colorful clothing. She was older than he'd first thought, and behind those smart-girl glasses, she was stunningly beautiful.

Awareness jolted him right behind his navel.

He had all day with nothing to do. A crazy, halfway desperate idea popped into his head. "I saw the sign in the window," he said as he gazed at the disorder around the checkout. "Guess you need some help, huh?"

She tilted her chin up a fraction. One eyebrow arched. "Do you know someone who loves books and is willing to work for nothing?" She had a low, sexy voice that did something strange and hot to his insides, while it erased his better judgment.

He rested his hip against the counter and, forgetting all about his recent troubles, he said, "How about me?"

Melissa Portman almost laughed in the man's face. He was most definitely not the teenager Grammy had been searching for when she'd put the "Help Wanted" sign in the window three months ago.

He was a grown man, probably her age or a little older, in his late twenties or early thirties. He wore clothes that branded him as someone who came from way, way out of town: a brown tweed jacket with elbow patches, a striped button-down shirt, and a pair of skinny jeans that showed off his muscular thighs. All in all, he gave the impression of a hot college professor.

He also had dark, soulful brown eyes, too-long black

hair that curled over his forehead like a sensitive poet's, and a well-groomed scruff of beard that Melissa found way too attractive for her own good. To top it all off, he held Hugo in his arms like a man who knew something about cats. In fact, just watching his long fingers stroke the cat was vaguely erotic.

No question about it. He was delicious eye candy. And she wasn't stupid enough to believe that he needed a job. The guy was flirting.

Wow, that hadn't happened in, like, forever.

She arched her eyebrow the way Grammy used to when faced with the utterly absurd and said, "You want to work here? Really?" She invested her voice with just the right tone of skepticism.

His mouth quirked and exposed adorable laugh lines that peeked through his *GQ*-style stubble. "Really," he said. "I appreciate literature."

His voice was low, deep, and had just the right hint of tease in it—like he might be calling her out for the book she'd hidden beneath the counter. Had he seen the title? She hoped not.

"Seriously," he said, "I'm interested in the job."

"It's minimum wage," she said.

"How much is that? I'm new around here."

No kidding. "Seven twenty-five an hour." She managed to say this with a straight face.

The professor's eyebrows lowered. "That's not very much, is it?"

Obviously Mr. Professor had been spending all his time in ivory towers or something. "Right," she said, nodding. "And that's why we only hire high school students. You're a little old for that."

He continued to stroke Hugo as he gazed at her out of those impossibly hot brown eyes. "I know, but I need the work. I recently lost my job."

Something in the set of his broad shoulders suggested that he was telling the truth, even if he was flirting at the same time. A momentary pang of sympathy swelled inside Melissa. She was in the same boat. She'd given up a good job with the Fairfax County Public Schools in order to take care of Grammy, and now she'd be out a full-time teaching job until next September. She didn't know how she'd pay her bills.

Unless she sold the historic building that housed Secondhand Prose. The Lyndons were willing to pay a fortune for it—enough to pay all of Melissa's bills, cover the property taxes, and give her something left over to invest. But selling out to the Lyndons was the last thing Melissa wanted to do. In her heart of hearts, she wanted to keep Secondhand Prose's doors open, which was just silly, wishful thinking.

"I could be very helpful," Mr. Professor said, breaking through Melissa's financial worries. "I'm good at organizing things, and I have other experience and qualifications that could be valuable to you."

She eyed the cat and then his handsome face. "Aside from charming killer cats?"

His mouth twitched again. "I'm an avid reader."

She rolled her eyes. "Aren't we all? But really, there is no job."

"But the sign. And you're clearly short—"

"The sign has been there for a while. My grandmother put it up before she died. I'm sorry, but there's no job available here."

"Oh. I'm so sorry about your grandmother."

For an uncomfortable moment, their gazes caught, and the kindness and concern in his eyes surprised her. "Grammy was pretty old," Melissa said, her voice barely hiding the sorrow that had hollowed out her insides. "So let me ring these books up for you, okay?"

Melissa picked up the books he'd laid on the counter while Mr. Hottie Professor continued to lean his hip into the counter, his mere presence disturbing the atmosphere and making Melissa adolescently self-conscious.

"That'll be twenty-five dollars for the books," she said in her best customer-service voice. She expected him to hand over a credit card, but instead the guy pulled out a money clip that held a big wad of bills. He sure wasn't a professor, not carrying cash like that. He had to thumb through several hundred-dollar bills to find a five and a twenty. So who was he? She was suddenly dying to know.

He put Hugo down, but the damn cat continued to circle his legs. "Nice cat," he said.

"His name is Hugo—well, his full name is Victor Hugo—and he's not friendly."

"Could have fooled me."

The cat meowed as if he knew they were talking about him. What was Hugo up to? He never made friends with strangers.

She handed the guy his bag. "So, where are you staying?" she asked, hoping she might prolong this conversation and get his name, e-mail address, or even his profile on Match.com.

He took his bag and broke eye contact. "I love your store. Next time I'm going to make friends with the cat in the window."

"Ha. I don't think so. Dickens is half wild."

"I already figured that out. Have a nice day."

And with that the guy turned and strolled down the aisle toward the door, looking amazingly like the hero in the romance novel she'd been reading when he'd first arrived.

Chapter
2

At six o'clock Melissa locked up the store and headed down Liberty Avenue with *The Lonesome Cowboy* tucked into her purse. She took her usual spot at the lunch counter and ordered the meat loaf blue-plate special and a glass of iced tea.

She'd been there for about ten minutes when Gracie Teague, the diner's owner and chief waitress, leaned over the counter, casting a shadow on page 183 of Melissa's book. "So what's it tonight, English aristocrats or down-home cowboys?" she asked.

"Cowboys," Melissa said, blinking up from the page. Gracie and Mom had been best friends in high school; maybe that's why Gracie had nominated herself as Melissa's keeper. Even before Grammy died, Gracie had been a fixture in Melissa's life. Their relationship started that summer when Mom and Dad had dropped Melissa off with Grammy while they'd pursued their lifetime dream of buying a sailboat and sailing from the Caribbean up the East Coast.

Even as an eight-year-old Melissa had loved books, but an eight-year-old wasn't patient enough to spend a whole day in a bookstore. So she'd come down to the diner and hung out with Gracie. Then the news had come that Mom and Dad had perished in a storm. The death of her parents had changed Melissa's life forever while simultaneously cementing her relationship with Gracie.

Gracie had attended Melissa's high school graduation. Gracie had made her prom dress. Gracie had driven Melissa down to Charlottesville to help her set up her freshman dorm room at the University of Virginia. Gracie had fed her ice cream when she'd broken up with Chris. And in the last three weeks, since Grammy had died, Gracie had provided the blue-plate special free of charge.

Gracie also made no bones about the fact that she intended to dance at Melissa's wedding—someday soon.

She gazed down at Melissa's book and shook her head. "Girl, it's Friday night, and here you are perched on your stool like you have been every night since Harriet died. You need to stop with the books and go find yourself a real man."

"I don't think so. I tried that once, and you know how it turned out. Besides, book boyfriends are much easier, and you don't have to clean up after them."

Gracie snorted. "You wouldn't clean up after anyone anyway."

Melissa nodded. "That's probably true. I love my dust bunnies. They're way sweeter than Grammy's cats."

"Exactly my point. You're too young to settle into the role of crazy cat-lady spinster. You should sell out, hon, and go somewhere exotic where rich, handsome bachelors hang out in droves."

Melissa gave Gracie one of Grammy's evil-eyed looks. "I could say the same for you."

"I don't have cats, and I don't want to sell out."

"So?"

"I guess you have a point," Gracie said as she scanned the diner, which had exactly one other customer this evening.

Several chain restaurants had opened up at the new strip mall down near the highway interchange. The new competition had siphoned off a lot of Gracie's evening business. Just like the online book retailers had siphoned off a lot of Secondhand Prose's business.

"I think I need to change my menu," Gracie continued on a long, sorrowful sigh.

"I like your menu just the way it is. People will get tired of the chain restaurants. I'm sure of it."

Gracie could give a look as well as she could take one. "Melissa, you are so stuck in your rut you can't even see the road in front of you anymore."

Melissa shrugged this off and turned back to her book.

Gracie freshened her tea, rang up the other customer, and returned to the lunch counter, where she sat down with a copy of *People* magazine. They sat together reading for a few minutes before Gracie asked, "Do you think he got her pregnant?"

"Huh?" Melissa looked up from her book, which just happened to have a plot line involving a secret baby. She was momentarily confused. "Who got pregnant?"

"Mia Paquet."

"Mia Paquet's pregnant? That's good news, if it makes her retire from reality television."

"Don't be superior, Melissa. A lot of people liked her in that show about Vegas pole dancers."

"So someone knocked her up?" Melissa glanced at Gracie's magazine. A big color photo of Mia Paquet and her cleavage dominated the page. A small black-and-white inset showed the reality star on the arm of some ridiculously cute guy wearing a tux and a bad-boy smile.

"Not just someone," Gracie said. "Daniel Lyndon."

"Oh, for crying out loud. Which Lyndon is he?"

"One of Charles's boys. Dropped out of college and seems to be intent on blowing his trust fund out in California."

"Give it a rest, Gracie. The Lyndons are not the saints and martyrs you seem to think they are."

"Danny is just young and misguided. He'll come around."

"If he got Mia Paquet pregnant, I certainly hope he marries her."

"I do, too. But you know how things go in Hollywood."

"Whatever." Melissa went back to reading.

"I'm much more worried about David," Gracie said, smoothing back her outrageously bright red hair.

When Gracie got on the subject of the Lyndons, she was like a pit bull with a bone. Melissa put her finger down at her place in the book and looked up again.

"He's not moving on with his life, bless his heart. He needs to find love again," Gracie continued.

Melissa closed her book. If she wanted to finish *The Lonesome Cowboy,* she would have to leave the diner. "Okay, I can see how David needs to move on, but please don't put me on your list of possible mates for him, okay? I mean, I feel for the guy. I knew Shelly a little bit. She used to come in the store all the time with Willow Petersen and buy romances by the dozens."

"See?" Gracie said. "You and David's late wife are a lot alike."

"No, we weren't. She was all about being a nice wife and fitting in with the Lyndon family's plans for David's political career. Can you see me doing that? Ever?"

"You could learn..."

"Gracie, please. I don't like Pam Lyndon, and I'm not interested in her son."

"Only because your grandmother carried a grudge. You know it's time to lay that to rest with her, don't you?"

"I guess."

"And you could do worse than hooking up with a Lyndon. If David isn't the one for you, he's got four or five cousins. They're all handsome as the devil."

Melissa ground her teeth. "Gracie, stop. I don't want anything to do with any of the Lyndons. Period. End of subject."

But of course it wasn't the end of the subject, because the way things were shaping up, she would be selling the Lyndons the one thing she held most dear.

Chapter
3

Mr. Hottie Professor made Melissa's Tuesday when he returned to Secondhand Prose. He walked through the door and almost bowled Melissa over in the front aisle, where she was shelving a few books on military history. In fact, she would have toppled right over if the guy hadn't snagged her shoulders and steadied her.

"Oh, hi," she said, taking a step back and shrugging off his touch, which had sent an electric shock down her backbone that woke up her girl parts. They had been dead to her for such a long time that she hardly even remembered she had them.

And now suddenly there they were, awake and aware and...well...aroused.

Whoa, wait one sec. She was not about to let her hormones take a dive into insanity. This guy was more than merely handsome. He was like Chris—an intellectual. And Chris was just the latest in a long line of attractive, brainy boyfriends, all of whom had broken her heart.

Mr. Professor looked utterly tempting today in his

skinny jeans, oxford cloth button-down, and a blue tweed sweater. The guy definitely had the urban casual vibe going for him—the kind that took a sizable clothing budget to achieve.

"Hi," she said. "How did you enjoy the Thoreau?"

"To be honest, it sucked."

"You didn't like *Walden*, really?" She blurted the words in surprise. He looked exactly like the type of guy who would not only enjoy Thoreau, but make a big deal of discussing it.

"No, I didn't. It doesn't work as a manual for living off the grid in the twenty-first century. And Thoreau is kind of preachy. I mean, it's depressing to discover that I'm living a life of quiet desperation caused by the weight of my personal possessions."

"Only if you're the type of person who values material things."

"I know. And that's why I'm here. I have a plan to improve myself."

"You do?" she asked. Was he flirting or trying to have a book discussion, or maybe both?

"Yes. I came to volunteer," he said.

"Volunteer?"

"Yeah. You need help, and I'm here to lend a hand."

"Doing what?" Several things came to mind, none of them involving books, unless he might consider reading poetry to her. Robert Browning would be perfect. She took another step back.

"I'm here to do whatever it is you need me to do. And I don't need the seven twenty-five an hour. According to Thoreau, working for nothing is more enlightening than working for peanuts."

He took another step forward, invading her space with impunity. He plucked the books from her hand.

"Ah," he said, studying their spines, "these are military history, so they get shelved here, right?"

She found herself nodding.

"By title or author?"

"Author."

He turned and started shelving the books.

"Look, you can't just—"

"What? Give you some help?" He finished shelving the books and turned back toward her.

"Um, I can't pay you."

"I know. And I have a plan for that, too. See, I've been trying to follow in Thoreau's footsteps—staying in a cabin that's way off the grid—but I've discovered that I can't survive without Internet. So I thought maybe we could work out an arrangement, you know? I'll give you a few hours a day doing whatever, and in return you can let me set up my laptop somewhere and borrow your Internet."

Something didn't add up. The guys who lived in those remote cabins usually wore camo vests or fishing shirts, not urban-hip tweed sweaters. She cleared her throat and tried to sound tough and decisive. "Uh, thanks, but I told you I don't need help."

"Then why do you keep the 'Help Wanted' poster on the front door?"

She shrugged, and they stood staring at each other for a long moment.

"Look," he finally said on a long breath, his eyes going even more soulful, "the truth is I'm a writer and—"

"Wait a sec. You're a writer?" Now she understood the

tweeds and the bulky sweaters and the Byronic hair and her fatal attraction. She loved writers. They were, in her opinion, practically gods. And here stood a particularly handsome specimen, right in the middle of her bookstore.

He nodded. "Yeah, I am a writer, and I—"

"Oh my God. What's your name?"

Damn. What now? If the bookshop girl stayed abreast of current events, she'd recognize his name, and he damn sure didn't want to have a discussion of his failings as a journalist. He also didn't want her blabbing her mouth around town. He just wanted something to occupy his time while he considered what he was going to do with the rest of his life. He'd discovered that brooding about the future, while spending endless days utterly alone in a cabin, was murder on his psyche.

He would have to lie.

"I'm not famous," he said. "I'm not even published."

"Oh," Melissa said in a disappointed tone.

He stuck out his hand. "I'm Jeff Talbert. Author in the making." This was only a half-truth. Like every journalist worth his salt, Jeff was sure he had a novel in him somewhere. He'd been talking about writing a book for years, but he'd done nothing about actually starting it.

He studied her face, waiting to see if she bought any of this, especially the abridged version of his Jefferson Talbert-Lyndon byline. She seemed to take him utterly at face value.

She took his hand, her palm warm and soft. "I'm Melissa Portman," she said. "I inherited this store from my grandmother."

"And I'm here to help you shelve books in return for

borrowing your Internet. Oh, and I also intend to make friends with your demon cat."

Melissa let go of a long breath. "I've told you, I don't need help. And forget about Dickens. He doesn't like people."

"I find that hard to believe."

She cocked her head, and Jeff swore her cheeks colored. She looked a lot like the vintage book illustration of Snow White on her pink T-shirt—pale skin, a round face with rosy cheeks, and a dark cloud of hair pulled away from her face with a plaid hairband. Her skinny jeans were green and hugged her curves, and she wasn't wearing any socks with her red Converse low-top lace-ups.

She eyed him from behind her black glasses, one eyebrow arched. "I'm not kidding. Dickens is a crazy cat. Don't try to pet him. You'll draw back a bloody nub."

"Okay. I'll stay away from the cats." He took another step forward in the narrow aisle, forcing her to retreat again. "I'll just head over to the checkout and start sorting the piles of books over there."

"I told you already, I don't need or want your help," Melissa said, crossing her arms over her Snow White T-shirt. She looked bad-ass, in a colorfully hip way.

He ignored her and simply took another step forward and then eased his way around her, brushing against her in the process. She smelled great, like a field of wildflowers.

He headed for the checkout, where he picked up the book on top of one lopsided pile—a hardback edition of *Robinson Crusoe*. "This is fiction," he said, laying the book aside and picking up the next one, a reference book on how to knit. "This goes in the how-to, reference area."

He laid that one down to start another subpile, then

glanced over his shoulder. The adorable Melissa Portman still had her arms crossed, only now there was a big rumple across her brow. He wanted to erase those lines.

"How am I doing so far?" he asked.

"I don't need your help."

"Of course you do." He turned away and sorted several more books, while Melissa's gaze burned a hole in his back between his shoulder blades.

The standoff lasted several minutes until Dickens, the demon cat, jumped down from his throne in the window and padded toward Jeff, his amber eyes dilated, his tail erect, ears perked. The body language seemed friendly enough, but Jeff could only see the cat out of the corner of his eye.

Jeff had had plenty of experience with feral cats in his day, so he avoided direct eye contact. He'd learned just about everything anyone ever needed to know about wild cats during his visits to Grandmother Talbert—a woman lovingly referred to as the Crazy Cat Lady on the Hudson.

So he braced for the cat to pounce, with claws extended.

But the attack never came. Instead Dickens gave a friendly sounding meow and then pussyfooted up against Jeff and gave him a little head butt that was a cat's classic request for attention.

He squatted down slowly and let Dickens get a good sniff of him before he carefully and gently rubbed his hands from the cat's head to his tail. The animal arched its hind end up to press against his touch.

Dickens's eyes closed to slits, and he started to purr as Jeff settled in to scratch him liberally behind his ears. When Jeff took his hand away, the cat moved forward and leaned his forehead against Jeff's knee.

He picked Dickens up and settled him in his arms. Then he turned toward Melissa. "See, I told you I would make friends with your cat."

Melissa's eyes had grown wide behind her glasses. "I'm seeing it, but I don't believe it," she said. "What are you, some kind of cat whisperer?"

Chapter
4

When Dickens came down from his tree and allowed Jeff to pick him up, Melissa had no choice, really, but to let Jeff stay and volunteer.

She relented for Dickens's sake. Since Grammy's death, Dickens had occupied the cat tree in the window almost twenty-four-seven, allowing no one to touch him, hardly eating, and leaving his perch only for litter-box calls.

She told herself that letting Jeff volunteer was about the cat, but having Jeff shelve the books that Grammy had purchased before she died gave Melissa a big dose of hope in a situation that was utterly hopeless. Having someone else around the store eased the loneliness that had settled into the deepest recesses of her heart.

Still, it was a fantasy, this idea of fixing up the store. She needed to end the charade. Tomorrow she would make an appointment with Walter Braden, the Realtor in town who handled commercial real estate sales. He'd already called a few times to let her know that the

Lyndons were anxious to make an offer on the building Grammy had owned for sixty years.

But Melissa's resolve disappeared on Wednesday morning, when Jeff showed up on her doorstep bright and early bearing gifts: a new, expensive-looking coffeemaker for the back room, a bag of cat treats for Hugo, and a catnip mouse for Dickens, who came down from his tree and played with it for a solid hour.

"So what's on today's agenda?" Jeff asked after he'd set up the coffeemaker and brewed the first pot of the day. Why the man didn't just get his coffee across the street was a mystery. But once she took her first sip of coffee from his new machine, she had to admit that the guy knew how to brew a good cup of coffee. Obviously Jeff was a master at winning lonely cat ladies over.

Plus she had a weakness for guys who wore tweed jackets... and formfitting white T-shirts and jeans, which was Wednesday's outfit.

Yup, he was as yummy as the coffee.

"Let's get the boxes behind the counter cleaned up and shelved," she said, casting aside her resolution about calling Walter Braden.

They went to work hauling books around the store while she attempted to give him the third degree. But he was slippery. Their conversations always left something to be desired.

"Where are you staying?" she asked.

"Up on the ridge." No specific address. And the Blue Ridge ran right through the middle of the state. Saying you were living in the Blue Ridge Mountains wasn't very informative.

"Where are you from?" she asked as they tidied up the history section.

"New York." Of course he was from New York. She could hear it in his accent.

"State? City?"

"Both." He was a master of the one-syllable response.

"Where did you learn to handle cats?" she asked as they reorganized the fiction department.

"My grandmother. She was a cat lady."

Two sentences. She was on a roll. "Mine too."

"I figured."

And that was the end of that conversation, unless she wanted to tell him all about Grammy, and at the moment conversations about Grammy tended to become overly emotional. She wasn't ready for Jeff to see her cry. And besides, she really ought to be calling Walter about selling the place. Tomorrow.

But on Thursday she forgot all about calling Walter. She'd had trouble sleeping that night, and she was all prepared with a bunch of book-related questions. Jeff seemed to know his literature.

So as they started dusting every inch of the store, she asked him if he'd ever read any Jack Kerouac. It was just the first question on her list of sneaky ones designed to see if he was a literature snob, like Chris.

He gave her a look from the measureless dark of his eyes. "Is that a trick question?"

Damn, he was onto her. "How could a simple question about a book be a trick question? Have you read *On the Road*?"

"Have you?"

"Of course I have."

"Did you read it because you thought it was hip?"

She blinked at him because the truth was she had read it because Chris had told her she needed to read it in order to be well rounded. She had not particularly enjoyed the book.

Jeff smiled before she could respond. "Don't worry. I won't tell the in crowd that you didn't much like it. The problem with reading Kerouac today is that everyone thinks he's cool, when the truth is, he was just the writer guy, you know, the dude with the journal keeping notes on the crazy stuff his friends did."

"I'm not worried about what people think," she said. "So, are you like him? I mean, are you the writer guy who keeps a journal and chronicles the crazy stuff your friends do?"

His smile faded. "No. Not really. But I have a question for you."

"Okay." She wasn't sure she wanted to be on the receiving end of any questions.

"What were you reading that day when I came in the store the first time?"

Oh, crap. She wasn't about to tell him she'd been reading a romance novel. How pathetic would that be? So she thought fast and lied. *"Oliver Twist."*

His mouth turned up adorably. He didn't believe her. "Good book. I wholeheartedly believe that we should all ask for more."

And that was the end of her attempt at using book talk to discover his secrets. It was, however, the beginning of several long conversations about the classics, where she discovered that Jeff Talbert had actually read *Jane Eyre*. He'd hated every minute of it, but he'd read it in high school.

He'd also read *The Call of the Wild* and *The Last of the Mohicans*. Those books he'd liked. She wasn't surprised.

All that book talk was tantalizing. So when Thursday came to a close, she took a leap and asked, "So, uh, you want to go down to the Jaybird for a drink or something?"

He gave her a soulful brown-eyed look and shook his head. "No. Maybe some other time." And then he left the store, but not before he glanced out the window as if checking to see who might be out there on the sidewalk, watching.

He should stop. Now. Going to Secondhand Prose on a daily basis was a dumb idea. Even though the store wasn't exactly the type of place Pam would frequent, he still risked being seen. He'd learned from the grapevine that Aunt Pam didn't spend much time with Uncle Mark in DC. She stayed at Charlotte's Grove and managed things. What things she managed were not precisely clear, but it wasn't unusual for Aunt Pam to be seen on Liberty Avenue shopping or visiting with merchants.

Maybe he should book a flight to the Bahamas or something.

He jettisoned the idea. For some reason, helping Melissa clean and organize her grandmother's bookstore had become the thing he wanted to do right now. It filled his days. It gave him purpose.

And maybe he was accomplishing something important—pulling Melissa out of her funk. She may not have shed a tear or said a word, but Melissa was grieving for her Grammy. Working to clean and organize the place seemed to have given her a purpose, too.

She obviously loved that store and wanted to keep it open. But she didn't have enough customers. That kept him up at night, worrying. And worrying about how to save Secondhand Prose seemed way more productive than worrying about his lost career in journalism.

So, despite his better judgment, he returned to the shop on Friday with a bag filled with color-coded adhesive tags.

"We're going to change your pricing system," he announced as he came through the door and gave Dickens a long head scratch.

"Why would we do that?" Melissa asked.

She must have been anticipating his arrival this morning, since she was standing in the history section at the front of the store, but she didn't seem to be shelving books or doing anything at all, except waiting for him. Today she greeted him wearing a bright yellow *Hansel and Gretel* T-shirt with red jeans.

He warmed at his first sight of her. What was she going to do today? Yesterday's book discussions had been way more fun than Wednesday's third degree. Last night she'd even asked him out for a drink. Saying no had been hard, but he needed to figure out where the Jaybird Café was located and whether Aunt Pam was a regular customer.

Scoping the place out was on his to-do list. But until he could fully define safe, Pam-free zones, he was sticking to his plan of mostly hiding out at Dad's cabin or here at the bookstore, where no one ever shopped.

"Change is good for the soul," he said, knowing full well that Secondhand Prose didn't really need a change in its pricing system. It basically needed a total makeover and an influx of lots of cash. Not to mention advertising and new merchandise. But she would probably get all freaked out if he said any of that. And besides, saying stuff like that might be offensive. After all, the bookshop had been owned and managed by Melissa's grandmother, and Melissa hadn't said one thing to suggest that she wanted to change things around here.

In fact, Melissa was resistant to change. Which was to be expected. So small steps were called for.

"I've got colored adhesive tags. I figure we could group books and price them accordingly. Like all hard-bound books at one price and all mass-market paperbacks at another."

"Uh, well, we sort of do that already."

"Yeah, but you have to handwrite a price sticker for every book in the store. Wouldn't it be easier to post signs with the color codes and then just put colored dots on each book?"

She nodded. "I guess, but it's a lot of work to do that for books that already have prices on them."

He shrugged. "I know, but I don't have anything better to do."

So he got to work, and before noon came around, Melissa was helping him while they had a lively discussion of *The Catcher in the Rye*, *The Color Purple,* and Ayn Rand's political philosophy.

When Friday came to a close, he didn't want to leave, but he didn't dare ask her out for a drink. So he reluctantly headed back up the ridge, but before he was out of cell phone range, his phone vibrated. It was his father, calling all the way from Japan.

He pulled the Land Rover over to the side of the road and punched the talk button on his phone. "Hello, Dad," he said.

"Where the hell are you?"

Jeff said nothing.

"Don't pull the silent treatment on me. Your mother is about to call the police and proclaim that you've been kidnapped."

He sighed. "I told her I was going away for a while. She knows I haven't been kidnapped."

"That's debatable. She's hysterical."

"You know, she wouldn't be hysterical if you hadn't allowed the White House to issue that statement in which you said I had no business being a journalist. I think that ticked her off. It sure ticked me off."

"Well, that's too bad. Because it's the truth. Go home, Jeff. Go manage your mother's money. She has so much of it, I doubt that you could screw things up the way you've screwed up the Durand nomination. But whatever you do, stay out of journalism and stay out of politics. Because you sure didn't inherit any of the Lyndon smarts when it comes to those things."

That was it. He'd had enough. "Ambassador Lyndon," he said in a tight voice, "I'm happy to comply with your request that I take myself out of the family. Tomorrow I'll be calling my lawyers and starting the formal process of removing your last name from mine." He pressed the disconnect button and sat there for several minutes breathing hard while his fury subsided. He hated his father. The feeling was clearly mutual.

He probably ought to move out of Dad's cabin. But what the heck. The guy was in Japan, and Jeff had the key. Besides, leaving Shenandoah Falls was the last thing he wanted to do right now.

On Saturday Melissa found herself anticipating Jeff's arrival, and the moment the front door opened with a

jingle, she and Dickens had almost the same reaction.
The cat sat up and meowed plaintively until Jeff stopped
and gave him a good scratch behind the ears and told
him what a beautiful feline he was. Melissa got hot and
bothered just watching him stroke the cat.

Hugo wasn't about to let Dickens get all the attention.
He waddled out from his lair in the back and demanded
equal time. Jeff lavished praise on him, too, allowing
Melissa to appreciate Jeff's manly but gentle hands, with
their long, patrician fingers.

Once Jeff satisfied the cats, he turned and strolled past
her toward the back room and the coffeemaker. "Can
I interest you in a cup of hazelnut coffee light on the
cream, heavy on the sugar?"

He pulled a package of coffee and a coffee grinder
from the sack he was carrying. "I stopped at the store on
the way in."

Wow. He'd been listening when she'd said that hazelnut coffee was her favorite. Boy, he was kind of terrific,
wasn't he?

He disappeared into the back room and emerged several minutes later with a mug of coffee, made exactly the
way she liked it. She was ready to melt right in front of
him. Where had this guy come from and why was he here?

"So what's it going to be today?" he asked.

The coffee warmed her hand. The spark in his brown
eyes warmed up every other part of her. "I don't know,
Jeff," she said. "I told you I didn't need help. Why don't
you tell me what I need?"

He grinned. "How about I fix the ladder?" He gestured
to the floor-to-ceiling shelves along the northwest wall.
"Then you could use the upper bookshelves again."

"I can't even remember the last time we had access to those shelves. I'm pretty sure the ladder is long gone."

"Actually, I found it in the back room when I was tidying up."

She was tempted to tell him to forget the ladder. She could use someone to tidy up the small apartment above the bookstore where she was living. But she held her tongue. She didn't want him to know what a slob she was. Her inability to keep things neat and tidy had been a serious bone of contention between her and Chris. "It's missing some pieces, I think," she said instead.

"Is it? Let's figure out what it needs and get it working again." He strolled past her, leaving his yummy scent—soap, coffee, and cedar—behind.

She settled into a comfy chair behind the checkout and watched him work. Today he was channeling his inner lumbersexual. His beard was impeccably groomed, and he wore a plaid flannel shirt and a chest-hugging black T-shirt. He'd left his skinny black jeans behind this morning and instead he wore a pair of faded blue ones that were almost threadbare in the seat and the knees.

Yummy.

He'd been impressive with his colored dots, but when he pulled out the old toolbox from the back room, along with the pieces of the broken library ladder, the show definitely took an erotic turn. What was it about a man in a flannel shirt and faded jeans using a screwdriver?

It took him two trips to the hardware store for parts, but by noon he had the ladder rolling along the rails the way it had when Melissa was eight years old and had first come to live with Grammy.

He was using the ladder to reorganize the books in the

children's area, near the back of the store, when the front door opened, jingling the bell. Pamela Lyndon—who Grammy always referred to as the Duchess of Charlotte's Grove—came gliding into the store wearing a designer dress in her signature shade of pale blue.

The duchess got about two steps into the bookshop before Dickens arched his back, fluffed out his fur, and yowled at her in a way that could only be called bloodcurdling.

Several things happened in quick succession after this.

First, the duchess said, "Goodness!" and retreated a step, clutching her purse in front of her like a shield. "Shoo, kitty," she said in a totally ineffective voice.

Second, Jeff, who was up on the ladder shelving fiction on the highest shelf, turned toward the cat and said several X-rated words. He must have thrown his weight to one side, because the ladder's rail (which he apparently hadn't checked earlier in the day) detached from the bookshelf. The ladder unexpectedly pivoted and slammed Jeff into the back wall of the store.

And that's when the unthinkable happened.

A long time ago, when the store had been more successful, Grammy had put up a bunch of coat hooks on the back wall, where she'd hung merchandise for kids. The coat hooks were empty at the moment. But when Jeff slammed against the wall, somehow his slightly threadbare jeans got snagged, so when the ladder pivoted again, Jeff didn't pivot with it. Instead, he was left behind, hanging there on the wall for a moment, suspended by the seat of his pants.

That didn't last very long. There was an audible *riiiiippp* as his jeans split. Jeff came down, dumped unceremoniously onto Melissa's favorite beanbag chair. His pants stayed put, snarled in the coat hook, his legs still caught in them.

"Good God," the duchess said.

Which was totally an understatement, because Jeff had started his day without underwear.

Melissa was momentarily stunned by the view, which probably explained why she was a little late in coming to Jeff's aid. But that was okay because the beanbag chair had cushioned his fall. He shucked off his shoes, disentangled his legs, and covered his private parts with those manly hands of his.

Even so, the view was stirring. Especially when he stood up and streaked into the back room, slamming the door behind his incredibly hot backside.

Chapter
5

Damn.

It was bad losing his pants. Although he still wasn't sure exactly how that had happened. One moment he'd been up on the ladder, and the next he'd been stuck to the wall and then falling.

A flush of embarrassment heated his body from head to toe. This was his penance for not doing his laundry. Although he had to admit he didn't mind Melissa seeing his junk, and in the nanosecond before he covered himself, she'd certainly been looking. With interest.

Being half naked in Melissa's presence didn't suck. Not so much with Aunt Pam though.

Why the hell was Pam here? Of all the places in Shenandoah Falls, this was the last place he'd ever expected his aunt to visit. Had she recognized him?

He eased the door open a crack, just large enough to see the checkout counter where Pam and Melissa were talking.

"So, Melissa," Pam said in her Tennessee drawl, "I

see you've been making improvements. I'm so glad. Maybe my visit is well timed." She cleared her throat, then glanced toward the scene of his disrobing. "Who was that man?"

He tensed. Pam would figure it out if Melissa said his name.

"Just the new helper," Melissa said, thank God.

"Uh-huh." Pam paused for a long moment as she swept her gaze over the store's interior before turning back toward Melissa. "Darlin', I know your grandmother had a blind spot about some things. But we both know her determination never to mortgage this property was old-fashioned."

"She had her reasons," Melissa said, crossing her arms over the *Sleeping Beauty* T-shirt she was wearing today.

"Well, yes, I suppose she did. But look, we need your help. The Town Council and the Liberty Avenue Property Owners Association have agreed to move forward with a request for a block grant to revitalize the historic structures downtown. That means we need every property owner between Lord Fairfax Highway and Sixth Street to agree to a special assessment that will provide the matching funds for the project."

"Every property owner? That means the Lyndon Companies and me, right? And when you say a special assessment, you mean a special tax, don't you?" Melissa sounded downright belligerent. Her body language said it all. She didn't like Aunt Pam.

Pam spoke again. "It's true that the Lyndon Companies owns more buildings than anyone else, but there are a total of five additional landowners, including yourself. And an assessment is not a tax."

"Oh, okay, how is it different?"

"To begin with, it's voluntary. But those who chip in will get matching funds to renovate their storefronts. By participating, you'll save a lot of money on the storefront renovations needed to get this building listed on the historic register. And, darlin', this building is worthy of that honor."

"I would love to see this building on the historic register, Mrs. Lyndon. But I can't afford your assessment without a mortgage. And if I mortgage the place, I'll probably have to close the store and find a more lucrative tenant."

"Darlin', that doesn't sound terrible to me. You could make money on this building. And while I know this is a difficult time for you, I really need your support. The deadline to submit our application is June fifteenth. That's just three weeks away. We'll have a better chance of winning this grant if we have unanimous participation."

"I need to think about it," Melissa said.

Aunt Pam leaned over the checkout, her body language aggressive. "In a few days you'll be officially in arrears on your property taxes. At that time the county will start proceedings to foreclose on this property, and Lyndon Properties is ready, willing, and able to buy this building. We'd prefer to pay full price if you're willing to sell. But you could finance this, Melissa, and make a lot of money. Rick Sharp down at the bank is ready to help you with the financing, and I know Walter Braden would help you find a well-paying commercial tenant."

"I need to think about it," Melissa repeated as she uncrossed her arms and stood toe to toe with Pam, staring her down.

Pam stepped back. "All right. I understand. But you don't have much time left, you hear?" She turned and headed toward the door. Dickens hissed at her on her way out.

Melissa was shaking when the bell above the door finally jangled and Pam Lyndon left the store. The time had come to make a decision. And, unfortunately, the decision would require her to close Secondhand Prose. Forever.

Her eyes filled with tears as she studied Dickens. "Maybe Jeff will take you," she whispered, then blew out a long breath. She stood there for a moment, collecting herself and wiping her cheeks.

When she'd regained control, she headed toward the back of the store to examine the damaged pants; then she headed toward the back room.

"Hey, are you okay in there?" she asked through the door.

"I'm good," Jeff replied. His voice eased her jangled nerves and soothed her aching heart. Just the sound of him calmed her down.

"I just checked your jeans. They're beyond repair."

Silence greeted her from the other side of the door, and her momentary melancholy was replaced by something else. It might be fun to open the door and have a good look at him. It would definitely distract her from her problems.

"Guess I picked the wrong day to go commando, huh?" he finally said. "Truth is, I need to do some laundry."

"Do you do laundry?"

"What does that mean?"

"Oh, nothing. It's just that your wardrobe is always so..."

"What?"

"I don't know. Together. I figured you took everything to the dry cleaner's."

"Well, yeah, I do."

"There's a good dry cleaner on South Third Street. Just sayin'."

"Thanks. But that doesn't exactly solve my current problem. Got any ideas?"

Melissa had a few, but they were all bad ones. The best thing would be to get him some pants so her libido would go back to sleep.

"Okay, look, hang loose..." She paused a moment because these words brought an image to her mind that was X-rated. "Uh...um, maybe that was the wrong choice of words. Just wait there for a minute, and I'll get you a pair of pants."

She checked the size of the shredded jeans and then headed down the street to the Haggle Shop, the local consignment store, where she scoured the rack for a pair of jeans with a thirty-four-inch waist and a thirty-six inseam.

The Haggle Shop had lots of cool vintage stuff, but you never knew what you'd find there, and the selection of guys' pants in a thirty-six inseam was limited to four pairs of ugly beige khakis and one pair of cool argyle golf pants in kelly green and pastel yellow.

The pants were loud. And fun. Wearing them was like being invited into Melissa's slightly weird, totally unique world of fashion. He opened the door to find her standing there with a naughty gleam in her too-blue eyes.

"I like the pants," he said. "I'm thinking I need more color in my life." He took a step forward. This time she didn't retreat, and he caught a whiff of her scent: a mountain meadow.

"Look, Melissa, I overheard what that woman said." He touched her shoulder, and she pressed herself in to his hand. Just like a cat hunting for a good scratch.

"I've been trying to tell you that the bookstore is a lost cause," she said. "I have to put it up for sale. I'm scheduling an appointment with Walter from Braden Realty on Monday." Melissa's voice was full of defeat.

His heart stumbled. "Won't that play right into that woman's hand?" His words came out in a rush.

"Maybe. But it's got to be done. Jeff, I'm sorry. I've been sitting here for a few weeks, unable to make a decision. That's why I left the 'Help Wanted' sign on the door. And then you arrived, and I got all caught up in the ridiculous fantasy that maybe I could keep the store going. But I can't. Taxes are due, and I have to mortgage the place to pay them. But I can't make mortgage payments by selling used books. There just isn't enough income in it." Her voice wobbled as she spoke, and then her eyes filled with tears.

He took her big black glasses off her face and pulled her into his arms. "It's okay. Just let it out. I'm thinking maybe you haven't even let yourself cry for your grandmother."

She didn't cry. But she leaned against him like Hugo did when he wanted attention. Jeff stroked the back of her head, her curly hair gliding under his palms, igniting a deep yearning. He had to admit the truth. It wasn't so much the bookstore that had him coming here every day as it was Melissa. He wanted to protect her. He wanted to be the comic book hero who swoops in and saves the world and gets the hot girl at the same time.

And why the hell not? He didn't need any superpowers to fix this problem. Money would do the trick, and if Jeff had anything, it was money—a gigantic and bothersome trust fund that made people think he didn't have any ambition or drive. A mother with so much money she needed someone to manage it all. Money was a big pain in the neck for Jeff, but it could solve all of Melissa's problems.

He could fix this for her and thwart Aunt Pam's plans at the same time. He just needed one day to make the arrangements.

Like changing his name, it would be the ultimate statement of rebellion.

Oh God. She was in Jeff's arms, and it felt like heaven, leaning up against his hard, male body. A girl could get used to leaning on a guy like Jeff. He was steady. Dependable. Sweet. Considerate. And he dressed well.

Also, his lips were warm and soft where they rested against her forehead. She wanted him to do something naughty with those lips.

She tilted her head, hoping he would get the message that she wanted to be kissed. He was all blurry since she wasn't wearing her glasses, so she couldn't read his expression. Was he just being kind? That would be so frustrating.

She wanted more from him than help with the store.

The store was irrelevant. It had to be closed and the building had to be sold.

And just like that she made the decision she'd been putting off. She would sell out, and she would stop waiting around for life to begin.

Today was the first day of the rest of her life, and she was going to seize control of it. Jeff Talbert might not be a forever love, but he was a nice guy and she was alone in the world. Besides, she'd been living like a nun for too long.

"So," she said, letting her voice drop into the husky range. "The store is closed tomorrow. You want to do something fun? I could take you up to the falls. It's a fun hike. Or are you opposed to long walks in the woods?"

"Are you asking me out on a date?"

"Uh, yeah, I guess."

"You guess? You don't know?"

Damn. The man was impossible.

"Yes, I'm asking you out on a date. Tomorrow."

She must have frowned at him or something because he started stroking her forehead with his thumb. The touch was comforting and arousing all at once. The cats loved it when he rubbed his thumb over their foreheads. Now she understood. She didn't purr, but her body definitely started to rev itself up for more. In fact, she closed her eyes and made a little moan of pleasure.

That obviously did it for him. He stopped stroking her, settled his hands on her hips, and pulled her in tight against his chest and thighs and all his other hard manly parts. His lips went back to her temple, but this time he kissed his way down the side of her face, over her cheek to the corner of her mouth. She moved into the kiss and opened up for him.

When their tongues finally met, she threw her arms around his neck and pulled him into the kiss. He was a virtuoso at this dance of tongues, doling out something sweet, carnal, mysterious, and addictive.

But when one of his hands left her hip and moved up toward her breast, she inadvertently stiffened. It happened like a reflex. She might fantasize about no-strings sex, but she was abysmally bad at actually having it. Her underlying caution always reared its head.

Damn.

And wouldn't you know it? Jeff was such a gentleman that he backed away a little. "Not okay?" he asked.

What was she supposed to do now? It was all so awkward. So she said nothing, even though she really wanted him to go back to kissing her and maybe even touching her.

Instead he relaxed his grip and put her in a safer zone without actually letting her go. "So," he said in a rough voice, "I'd love to take a hike with you up to the falls."

Oh, good. She'd have a second chance to get this right. "Great," she said.

"Cool," he replied. "Why don't we meet at Gracie's Diner for brunch or something?"

No, no, no. She backed out of his embrace. "Uh, no, not Gracie's. Let's meet at the Old Laurel Chapel. In the parking lot. At nine o'clock."

"The Old Laurel Chapel?"

"It's off Morgan Avenue, just north of State Road 606. There's a little gravel parking lot there and access to the Appalachian Trail, which connects to the trail that leads to the falls."

"What about brunch?"

"I'll pack a picnic."

There was a beat of silence before he said, "Are you ashamed to be seen in public with me?"

"Oh, no, that's not it. You see, Gracie is..." Her shoulders tensed and her voice stumbled.

"Gracie's what?"

"A busybody." And so much more. Gracie would grill Jeff because she saw it as her purpose in life to find Melissa the right husband, and Jeff was probably not that guy even if his kisses were amazing. He was probably just a guy passing through, looking for some fun.

"Oh, I see. Good thinking. I don't want any gossip," he said. Which seemed odd for a guy from out of town. But she let it slide.

Chapter

6

Melissa hardly slept a wink. She kept replaying the kiss in her mind, not to mention that moment when Jeff had scooted, butt-naked, into the back room. Hot. So hot.

She gave up trying to sleep at six a.m., when she got up and took a frigid shower, threw on some clothes, and headed to the Food Lion for the picnic stuff and a box of condoms.

Buying them was like burning the bridges to her past. Deciding to have a little fun with Jeff had become an important part of letting go of the store and moving on with her life.

A few hours later, with a backpack full of sandwiches and other goodies, she pulled off Morgan Avenue into the patchy gravel lot by the Old Laurel Chapel.

The stone ruin hadn't seen a congregation in more than a hundred years, and it had been sadly neglected during that time. Its roof had all but fallen in, leaving behind four stone walls with empty vaulted windows. Today the mountain laurel surrounding the building was in full, glorious bloom, edging the cemetery and dotting the woods with its pale pink blossoms.

Jeff hadn't arrived yet, so Melissa left her car and strolled through the ancient graveyard, where many of the headstones bore the surname of Lyndon or McNeil—families who had helped to found Shenandoah Falls almost three centuries ago.

The sound of tires crunching on gravel had her raising her head in time to see Jeff pull a late-model Land Rover into the lot. With a car like that, he wasn't hurting for money. But what did he do for a living besides being an unpublished author? Where did he come from? Why was he here?

Maybe she'd learn the answers today. Or maybe not. She'd decided that it didn't matter. Today was about not grieving, and not worrying, and just having a little bit of fun.

"Hey," she called, and waved. "I'm over here."

He locked his car and strolled toward her, wearing a pair of jeans and a black body-hugging T-shirt that showed off his shoulders and the wide, muscular expanse of his chest.

"Sorry I'm late," he said. "I had a few phone calls I needed to make. One of them took a while."

"Business?" she asked in a leading tone.

"No, just a personal call. Family stuff." He turned away from her to inspect the church. "Wow. That looks like it's been here three hundred years."

"So, you have a family?" she asked, ignoring his comments about the chapel.

"Yeah. A mother in New York. She's kind of overbearing and overprotective."

"Ah."

She wanted him to elaborate. Instead, he turned his gaze on her and then pulled her into a hot, sexy kiss that fogged her glasses and her brain. She wrapped her hands around the back of his head, running her fingers through his too-long hair, and tried to eat him up.

The kiss might have led to other things, but they were interrupted by a little girl who came skipping out of the woods like Little Red Riding Hood with a wicker basket on her arm. She wasn't wearing a red cloak, but her hair was certainly red. And tangled.

The child skidded to a noisy stop before she said, "Oh!"

Jeff and Melissa jumped apart like guilty teenagers caught in the act.

"Hello," the girl said.

Melissa adjusted her glasses. Oh, great. Nothing like being caught in the clinches by a Lyndon. The girl was Natalie, David Lyndon's daughter. A moment later Natalie's grandmother, Poppy Marchand, appeared at the forest's edge. Poppy was in her sixties, and Laurel Chapel was on the grounds of Eagle Hill Manor, which Poppy owned. Technically, Melissa and Jeff were trespassing.

Poppy eyed Melissa and then shifted her gaze to Jeff, where it remained for a long moment. "Hello," she said.

"Uh, hi, Mrs. Marchand. Good morning," Melissa said in a rush. "We're taking the shortcut to the Appalachian Trail. Is it okay to leave our cars in the lot?" She pointed with her thumb over her shoulder.

"You hiking up to the falls?" Poppy asked.

"Yeah."

"Nice day for it. The laurel is lovely this time of year.

It's no problem about the cars. No one ever comes up here anymore." Poppy paused for a moment as she continued to study Jeff. "Do I know you? Have you visited Eagle Hill Manor before?"

"No. I'm sure we've never met."

Poppy nodded. "I guess not. But you look very familiar for some reason."

Natalie tugged at Poppy's hand. "C'mon, Grammy, let's go." She pulled Poppy toward the old church. "Let's play princess, 'kay?"

"Y'all have a nice hike," Poppy said as the girl pulled her up the steps and into the ruined chapel.

"Let's go," Melissa said, pulling Jeff in the opposite direction. "There's a short path here that connects with the Appalachian Trail. We'll walk that for a couple of miles and then take the turnoff for the falls."

They found the main trail without much trouble, and Jeff took the lead as the ground began to rise. About half a mile before they reached the turnoff for the falls, they came to a break in the forest's cover that provided a view up a rise to a grand Georgian-style brick mansion. The house stood atop the hill, with the Blue Ridge Mountains at its back and its grand portico facing the Shenandoah Valley.

Jeff stopped in his tracks and stared at the house for a long, silent moment.

Melissa played tour guide. "That's Charlotte's Grove," she said. "The house you see was built after the Revolution. But the original cabin—"

"Save the history lesson. I know all about Charlotte's Grove."

"You do?"

"That's where the Lyndons live. The people who want to buy your store." There was no mistaking the enmity in his voice.

The big concrete bunker she'd built around her heart cracked a little bit. Jeff Talbert was on her side. She had an ally. "Yeah, they are. But the store has to be sold, you know."

He turned on her, his dark eyes suddenly intense. "No, it doesn't."

She laughed. "Jeff, it does. And I've finally made up my mind about it. So let's not talk about the store. Let's just have a fun day in the woods, okay?"

The sky got into Melissa's blue eyes somehow, and for a moment Jeff lost himself in that deep, limitless color. Looking into her eyes was almost like free-falling. He took her shoulders and drew her forward for another hard, needy kiss on her soft, open lips.

She tasted like the outdoors. Like springtime. He should have planned this better. He should have brought a couple of blankets. Maybe some condoms. She was sending up all kinds of signals that he was receiving loud and clear.

No. Just. No.

Not here, within sight of Charlotte's Grove. And not with her wearing that T-shirt with a truly gruesome illustration of innocent Little Red Riding Hood and a menacing wolf. Where did she get these T-shirts anyway? From the Brothers Grimm Department Store?

He broke the kiss. He owed her the truth about his background or he was no better than that ogling wolf on her T-shirt. He ought to say something right now, but that would ruin everything he'd put in motion yesterday afternoon. He needed one more day before he told her the truth. Once his plans were fully in place, he could tell her about his father, and she'd know right away whose side he was on.

She gazed up at him as wide-eyed as ever, even behind those glasses of hers, so innocent, so beautiful. She'd certainly found a place in his heart.

"Okay, you've got it. Today we'll pretend the Lyndons don't exist," he said.

"That sounds like the perfect plan," she said.

He gave her a quick kiss on the cheek and headed up the trail at a brisk pace, even though the path began to ascend steeply. By the time they arrived at the turnoff for the falls trail, Melissa was wheezing behind him. He turned. "I'm sorry. You should have told me to slow down."

"No, it's okay. I'm out of shape," she said on a puff of air. "This is what happens when you spend too much time in a beanbag chair reading genre fiction."

He laughed. "So you admit that you read genre fiction?"

She shrugged. "Yeah."

"So, what were you reading that day when I first came into the store and bought the Thoreau?"

She eyed him warily. "I'm not telling."

"Afraid to lose your credentials as a discerning reader?"

She laughed. "You're funny." She pointed to the trail that led off to the right. "C'mon. Let's go, but maybe a little slower. The falls are only two more miles."

The trail went up sharply for more than a mile, while

the rushing sound of a fast-moving stream met their ears. Then, abruptly, the path narrowed and headed downhill through lichen-covered rocks to a patch of sandy beach at the edge of a fast-moving freestone creek—Liberty Run.

Upstream, the run cascaded down a twenty-five-foot fall, sending water droplets into the air and filling the forest with its powerful roar. Eons of flowing water had cut a plunge pool at the base of the waterfall surrounded by tumbled rocks of various sizes.

They stood for a moment, under a canopy of red oaks and yellow poplars, interspersed with the occasional hemlock. It was green here. Green rocks, green canopy. Even the run had a brown-green tinge to it, created by the tannins in the water.

"It's magical here, isn't it?" he said.

"Magical?" Melissa stepped up onto the first stone of a rocky staircase that led to the top of the falls. She didn't climb all the way. Instead she sat down and started taking off her hiking shoes.

"Look around. Can't you imagine wood elves living here? Or maybe fairies?" he asked.

She cocked her head. "Have you been reading Tolkien on the sly?"

He laughed. "No. I haven't. I don't even like fantasy. It's just that this place seems enchanted somehow."

"Well, I've been up here to the falls at least a hundred times, and it's usually just like this. No fairies or elves. But you will encounter snakes and bugs. I can also attest that the falls are ghost-free. I know this because I spent one cold, wet night up here hoping to see Elakala's ghost."

"Who's Elakala?"

"She's supposed to have been an Iroquois princess whose father insisted that she marry the wealthy son of a rival chieftain. But Elakala loved a poor brave who didn't have much in the way of worldly goods. So on her wedding day she sneaked away and threw herself off the falls." Melissa gazed up at the cascades. "I find it hard to believe that she could actually accomplish that feat, to tell you the truth, since the water doesn't drop straight down. Some have speculated that she drowned herself in the plunge pool, which is also unlikely.

"Of course, you know how these Native American legends go. Every waterfall has a similar legend, and wherever there's a story of tragic death, there's also a ghost. And the legend grows bigger every time some foolish boy dives into the pool and comes up with a Native American relic."

"People dive for relics? Really?"

She stood up and scrunched her toes in the sand by the river's edge. "You'd be surprised by some of the stuff people have brought up from the bottom of the pool. Mostly junk, but every once in a while you find something cool."

"Oh." He took off the backpack and set it down on one of the rocks by the pool.

"To tell you the truth, teenage boys dive in the pool because it has the reputation of being dangerous. And also boys will be boys," she said, rolling her eyes in a way that was clearly a challenge.

"And that means...?"

"Every girl who grew up here in Jefferson County knows a boy who tried to impress her by diving into the pool, looking for Native American relics. It's a macho thing."

"Are you daring me to dive in the pool?"

"No. I wouldn't do any such thing," she said. He didn't believe her for one minute. Like every female, she gave off two messages at the same time. One with her words and another one with her gaze and her body.

Oh, yeah, her body. He hadn't forgotten about the feel of her hips beneath his hands or the pleasure of standing that close to her. Yeah, he had designs on her body, but he wanted her admiration, too.

Just then a purely adolescent idea popped into his brain. He didn't stop to think it through. He simply shucked his shoes, pulled his T-shirt over his head, and dropped trou. He streaked across the sandy beach and took a deep breath.

"Oh my God, no, Jeff. The water is—"

He didn't hear the rest of her admonition before the water closed over his head. Holy God, it was freezing cold. But then again, it was only May. The summer hadn't yet warmed the water, which was also dark and murky.

He frog kicked down, fighting the stream's current, until he reached the rocky riverbed. The pool wasn't all that deep—maybe eight or nine feet—but he was totally blind. He felt along the bottom, encountering mostly round river rocks and scree. But one of the stones had an oddly flat shape. He palmed it, and with lungs burning, he pushed off the bottom.

Melissa stood by the water's edge with her heart pounding in her ears. Her racing pulse had more to do with the magnificent sight of Jeff's naked bod than her fear for his safety, although this time of year the water was pretty cold. Good thing she'd brought a blanket and some beach towels. Not to mention the box of condoms.

Which just might come in handy after all.

She was pondering what came next when his head popped up above the water. He wore a big grin, like he'd proved something to someone. Such a guy.

"Guess you just discovered that it's probably too cold to go diving for relics this time of year." These were not exactly the first words her heart wanted to say. But they were what came out when she let her brain take over.

"I found something," he said as he swam toward her.

"You found something?" Her heart, already beating hard, began to race now in anticipation of him reaching the shallow water. Full-frontal nudity worked for her. Although she had to remind herself not to be disappointed. The water was probably no more than fifty-five degrees.

He stood up, water sluicing down his chest and abs and…other parts. He held out his treasure in his open palm, but Melissa's gaze was locked on his family jewels.

He seemed unaffected by her intimate study. "It's an arrowhead. Who knew?"

"What?" Her brain was starting to work again, sort of.

He raised his head and seemed to notice for the first time that she was totally ogling him.

"Enjoying the view?" He gave her a wolfish, predatory grin.

"Yes, I am, as a matter of fact."

He took a step forward. She stepped back. "Uh, look, um, you're all wet. And..."

Oh, bad move on her part, because he lunged and caught her in his cold, wet embrace. An embrace that immediately kindled an undeniable heat inside her.

"I could throw you in," he whispered in her ear, setting off hot, freezing shivers.

"Uh, please don't. I didn't bring a change of clothes."

"Oh, well, we can make sure your clothes don't get wet."

That was probably a challenge, but she wasn't getting naked to go swimming. She had other ideas in mind. So she wrapped her arms more tightly around his neck, pressed her mouth against his, and gave him a hungry kiss. Taking charge of it this time made her feel powerful, especially when Jeff let out a small, inarticulate growl and then kissed his way down her throat to a spot right by her earlobe that more or less set her on fire.

She tilted her head and let him have access to the sensitive flesh, groaning out loud while she snaked her hands up through his wet hair and pulled him closer, losing her glasses in the process.

Who knew where they fell? She didn't care as the world went out of focus, especially, a moment later, when Jeff snaked his hand under her T-shirt and cupped her breast. Blood pounded in her ears in a rhythm that echoed the rush of the stream at their feet.

"You're beautiful," he whispered wetly against her neck, and she drank him up like it was happy hour at the Jaybird Café and Music Hall and the margaritas were half price. She let him touch her, and she touched him right back, running her hands over the muscles of his chest and then down his spine, cupping his hard backside. And suddenly standing there was not nearly enough. She wanted to feel the weight of him. On her. In her.

"There's a blanket in the backpack," she whispered against the stubble on his chin. She was kissing her way down his neck when she spoke.

"You brought a blanket? Why?"

"We needed a place to sit. You know, for the picnic." She murmured the words across his collarbone. She was planning to take her mouth even lower, but he tilted her head up. His face was almost in focus even without her glasses. But it didn't matter because she closed her eyes while she was kissing him. Plus he smelled really good. She buried her nose in his skin and took a deep breath.

"You're a genius." His words rumbled in his chest. "Don't go anywhere. I'll be back."

He took his body and his fabulous smell away for a moment, leaving her standing there blind and almost deaf and totally dumb.

"Uh, wait," he said from across the beach. "You brought more than a blanket."

She didn't even blush when he started laughing. "I think we're going to be here for a while."

Thank goodness he returned a moment later, spreading the blanket on the sand and tossing himself and the box of condoms down onto it. Then he leaned back on his elbows, the condoms right beside him.

Even all blurry, a naked Jeff made her burn. So hot that she needed to take off her clothes. Now.

She pulled her T-shirt over her head and shucked out of her jeans with a little flourish, turned on by the fact that he was watching her every move. When she finally joined him on the blanket, he grabbed her by the shoulders and tilted her back. "You're killing me," he said in a gruff voice right before he covered her body with his own.

Finally they were skin to skin, chest to breast, sex to sex, heart to heart.

Chapter
7

Good God. She had actually carried through with her crazy plan to have sex with Jeff Talbert. In public, no less. She had wanted to be brave, but she'd never truly believed she could be *that* brave.

But why not? Jeff was delicious and erotic. And... well... lots of things that her heart shouldn't be thinking right now. Hearts had no business doing the thinking anyway. Brains were much better for that sort of thing.

She wanted more, but he hadn't invited her back to his cabin. She hadn't invited him up to the apartment above the bookstore either. But that was only because the apartment needed a total spring cleaning.

Knowing Jeff, he'd take one look at it and feel the need to reorganize before they could get naked. So she spent Sunday afternoon scrubbing her bathroom, straightening the living room, hosing down the kitchen, and putting fresh sheets on the bed.

Her mind was preoccupied reliving those moments by the plunge pool. But as evening approached, it wandered and became fixated on her phone. She expected him to call. She wanted him to call. In fact, she was stupidly hoping he would call so she could invite him over for a pizza or something else, with the emphasis on the something else.

Maybe she should call him? She was being brave, after all. She was taking charge. She was about to do just that when the doorbell at the back entrance to the apartment rang, sending her heart racing. She sprang to the door, threw it open...

And found her BFFs, Courtney Wallace and Arwen Jacobs, standing there looking concerned and positively grave.

"Uh, hi," Melissa said.

"Hi," Courtney answered, peeking around Melissa's shoulder at the freshly dusted surfaces in her living room. "Expecting company?"

"Uh, no. Come on in."

"No," Courtney said. "We're making an intervention."

"And taking you to the Jaybird for drinks and dinner," Arwen added.

"And we want to know who the hell this new guy is. Gracie called us both this afternoon. Apparently the Liberty Avenue Merchants Association has taken note that you've hired someone to redo Secondhand Prose. They've informed Gracie of this because, you know, Gracie is their fearless leader," Courtney said.

"And this afternoon Poppy Marchand came into the diner and told Gracie that she'd seen you this morning up at the Old Laurel Chapel, holding hands with someone," said Arwen.

Melissa's face began to burn.

Courtney turned toward Arwen. "Note the red face. The clean apartment. The fact that she's wearing a pair of common, ordinary blue jeans and a shirt that doesn't have one of those fairytale illustrations all over it. This is serious."

Arwen nodded. "Who is he?"

The answer to that question was so complex Melissa didn't even know where to start. So she changed the subject. "You know," she said, grabbing her purse from the hook beside the door, "margaritas sound great. Let's go."

Ten minutes later they strolled into the Jaybird Café and Music Hall, located in an old warehouse on the south side of town. Juni Petersen, whose family owned the Jaybird, had reserved a corner table in the back for Melissa and her friends, proving that Juni was also in on this intervention—a big problem, because if Juni knew about Jeff, then everyone would know about him by tomorrow morning.

The margaritas were also waiting for them when they arrived.

Melissa sank into a hard-backed chair and snagged her drink. She took a healthy swallow, the salt and sweet bursting on her tongue, just as Courtney said, "All right, we want all the details. Pippa Custis apparently told Gracie that your new assistant is 'the bomb.'"

Melissa put down her drink. "The bomb, really?"

"Well, you know, Pippa is sixty, and she's trying to be cool. She thinks he's cute."

"Is he?" Arwen asked.

"C'mon, guys, he's just a guy." Melissa turned away. "Who's singing tonight?"

"Earth to Melissa, it's Sunday, remember? Karaoke night."

"Oh, uh, yeah." Melissa's insides broiled. A girl in her situation—having just gotten all sweaty with a guy she didn't know that well—needed time for reflection, not the third degree from her friends. How much of what had happened today was plain garden-variety lust? And how much was something else?

Her heart said there was something else there, but her heart was so notoriously wrong about stuff like this. She probably shouldn't have done what she did today. It was foolish. Reckless even.

Oh, but it had felt like heaven.

"Oh my God, she's got a dreamy look on her face," Arwen said.

Courtney touched Melissa's hand where it rested on the table. "We're concerned about you. We all know about the financial mess your grandmother left you. So when it gets around town that you've hired some guy no one knows to help you fix up the store, it's natural for us to worry. Who is this guy? Where is he from? What kind of business plan have you come up with to deal with the mess Harriet left you?"

Melissa picked up her drink and drained it in several long gulps, but chugging her drink didn't make her friends disappear.

Oh hell. She wasn't going to be able to keep this secret. But she needed more fortification before she spilled the beans. She waggled her glass at Rory Ahearn, the bartender, indicating another round for all.

"Coming right up, luv," he said in his sexy Irish accent.

"You're stalling," Courtney said.

"Okay, it all started last week, with Hugo."

"Hugo? The cat?" Arwen's big brown eyes widened.

"Is there anyone else in my life named Hugo?" Melissa said.

"What does the cat have to do with this guy you've hired?" Courtney demanded.

"Last Friday a guy walked into the store, picked up Hugo, and bought a copy of *Walden*."

"No way," they said in unison.

"Yes way. He held Hugo for a long while, and the cat actually purred."

Juni Petersen overheard this because she was delivering their drinks. "Someone made friends with Hugo? Really?" she asked.

"Uh, yeah." Melissa snatched up her drink and took a big gulp.

"Who?" Juni asked.

"A guy. And it's not just Hugo. Dickens likes him, too."

There was a moment of silence around the table. Dickens didn't like anyone. It was a well-known fact.

"Oh," Juni said, "that's a sign for sure." She cocked her head and gave Melissa a goofy stare.

Meanwhile Courtney and Arwen nodded like a couple of bobblehead dolls. It was totally annoying the way her friends believed the stuff Juni said. Juni was into crystals and manifesting and reading people's auras.

"Okay, Melissa, stop beating around the bush," Courtney said. "We need a name."

"His name is Jeff Talbert."

"And…" Courtney pressed, as if she were cross-examining Melissa.

"And what?" Melissa said.

"And what else do you know about him?"

"Not much." Except he knew how to kiss, and he knew how to touch, and for a little while he'd made her believe there was a way to salvage the bookstore.

"And you hired him anyway?" Courtney asked. "What is he? A librarian? A contractor? An interior designer? What?"

Oh, crap. She searched for a handy lie and came up empty. "I didn't hire him," she finally admitted.

"You didn't?" Juni and her BFFs said more or less in unison.

She chugged down her second margarita. The tequila was starting to make her face feel a little numb. "He's a writer. Well, he's an unpublished writer who doesn't seem to do much writing. But, anyway, he just sort of volunteered to help. For free. But he's good at sorting books and color-coding price tags. Plus, he's widely read."

"He *volunteered?*" Arwen said this in a voice loud enough so that half a dozen other Jaybird patrons turned and stared.

Courtney leaned forward with real concern on her face. "Are you out of your mind? Don't you realize this guy could be a serial murderer, or a rapist, or something? You don't know anything about this guy."

Melissa didn't know if Jeff was a serial murderer, but he sure wasn't a rapist. That was good, wasn't it?

Arwen pulled her iPhone from her purse. "Let's just Google his name and see what comes up, okay?" Her thumbs got busy in an impressive way.

"Hmm, interesting. There are at least three Jeffrey Talberts who are professors, but they're—"

"No way. That's totally awesome." Melissa got all

warm and gooey inside as she grabbed Arwen's phone.
"Lemme see."

The letdown was kind of momentous when the first
photo—of Professor Jeffrey Talbert—was a balding
guy in his late fifties. The next photo wasn't much better. Melissa's pulse kicked up as she continued to scroll
through half a dozen Jeffrey Talberts, none of whom was
younger than forty-five.

And then, finally, there he was. Only she almost didn't
recognize him. The photo was a professional studio head
shot, and Jeff was wearing a dark, conservative suit jacket
and a red tie. His face was clean-shaven, and his hair was
a whole lot shorter.

"That's him," she said with a wistful sigh as she
pointed to his photo.

Arwen snatched her phone away. Her thumbs got busy
again, and then suddenly she said, "Oh my God, I can't
believe it."

"What? Is he really a professor, because he dresses
like—"

"No, honey, unfortunately not." She tilted her phone
so both Melissa and Courtney could see the screen. This
time it was a photo of Jeff wearing a tuxedo with a blond
bombshell on his arm. Jealousy pricked Melissa from the
inside. Oh boy, she was an idiot.

"His full legal name is Jefferson Talbert-Lyndon. That
should strike a familiar chord since the *New York Times*,
the *Washington Post*, the *Wall Street Journal*, and every
cable news network known to man have been dragging
him through the mud for the last three weeks. Honey, he's
a journalist. And he's also Nina Talbert's sole heir. When
she kicks the bucket, he gets her billions."

"What? Did you say Lyndon?" Melissa was confused. The margaritas had fogged her brain.

"Lemme see that," Courtney said, grabbing the phone out of Arwen's hand. "Oh my God. Melissa, he *is* a Lyndon."

"What?" Melissa's brain was having trouble processing her friends' words.

"He's that guy on the news. You know, the one who wrote that article that everyone is screaming about. About the Supreme Court."

Melissa shook her head. She had no idea what Courtney was talking about. She'd been hiding out in the store these last few weeks, reading genre fiction and letting the world pass her by. She wasn't up on current events.

"Honey, the Lyndon family is in a snit about him," Arwen said. "He's Pam Lyndon's nephew, and my boss at Lyndon, Lyndon & Kopp is his uncle. You didn't know this? He didn't tell you?"

"Well, at least he's not a serial killer," Courtney said brightly. "We can be thankful for that, even if he is a lying douche bag."

"A filthy rich and unbelievably cute douche bag," Arwen added.

How could this be? The duchess had been in the store yesterday and hadn't acknowledged Jeff at all. Why? Surely she'd recognized him, even if he hadn't been wearing pants.

And why hadn't he been honest about Pam? She'd told him everything. Trusted him. And he'd been lying from the start.

Melissa sank her head to the table and *thunk*ed it a

couple of times before the swearing started. The profanity didn't last all that long, because her vocabulary of bad words was limited, and also by the time she started to repeat herself, her throat had closed up, her eyes had overflowed, and talking had become impossible.

Chapter

8

Secondhand Prose wasn't open on Mondays, but Jeff found himself standing on the sidewalk staring through the windows. Dickens was keeping watch on his cat tree as always, but the place was dark.

He pounded on the door because he desperately needed to talk to Melissa and she'd been ignoring his phone messages and texts. He was just about to channel Stanley Kowalski, the character in *A Streetcar Named Desire* who stood outside the window and yelled his wife's name for all to hear, when a diminutive, fiftysomething woman wearing a big, brown tweed sweater tapped him on the shoulder and said, "You know, if you would just read the sign on the door, you'd realize the store isn't open today."

"I know that," he said as civilly as he could manage, considering his current state of mind. Why the hell was Melissa avoiding him? Yesterday had been amazing. Had he screwed up somehow? *Damn*.

"Good. I'm glad you can read," the woman said with

a nod. "And since the store is closed, it doesn't make any sense to be pounding on the door. You're disturbing my beginning knitters class." She waved in the direction of the adjacent storefront with the sign over the door that said EWE AND ME FINE YARNS AND KNITTING SUPPLIES. The women of the aforementioned knitting class were gathered around the yarn shop's window, trying to watch their instructor do battle with him.

"Do you know where I can find Melissa Portman?" he asked.

"I know who you are," the woman said. "And so does Melissa."

It was like the woman had just dumped a bucket of ice water over his head. "What?"

"You're Jefferson Talbert-Lyndon. And I heard at the Merchants Association meeting this morning that you lied to Melissa about your name and background. And everyone wants to know why."

The woman shook her finger in his direction as she continued. "Shame on you, lying to a nice girl like Melissa. What were you up to? Softening her up so that Pam Lyndon could buy her out on the cheap?"

The scorn in the woman's voice shamed him. "No. You have it all wrong."

"I don't believe you."

The knitting instructor gave him a cold stare that he was all too familiar with. He'd seen that look in his editor's eyes at the moment when George had lost faith in him, when the tide of public opinion had turned against him.

If the merchants were gossiping like this, then it wouldn't be long before his father's family heard all about it. And then things would get much, much worse.

He needed to do something fast if he ever wanted to regain Melissa's trust.

And not just talk. Talk was cheap, and apologies at this point would fall flat.

And not just writing a check. He'd already done that, and Melissa would be finding out about it soon. But paying her taxes had been easy, too. All it took was money—and not even a lot of it. For him, money might as well grow on trees. He had more than he'd ever be able to spend in several lifetimes. Money could buy a lot, but it couldn't buy trust and it couldn't buy love.

If he wanted Melissa in his life—and he did—he would have to earn back her trust. And then he might be lucky enough to earn her love, too.

Fifteen minutes later a maid ushered Jeff into Charlotte's Grove and left him waiting in a sitting room right off the main foyer. He'd visited Charlotte's Grove only once in his life, and his memories of the place were vague—just a sense of formality that left him cold. He'd expected the historic house to be filled with museum-quality Georgian furniture, but the room he was led to seemed surprisingly contemporary, with a couch and two well-used wing chairs.

"Oh my God, Jeff, I'm so glad you turned up." Aunt Pam entered the room from the hallway dressed for a day in the garden, in a pair of slacks and a long-sleeve cotton T-shirt that was slightly dirty. Her hair was pulled back in a haphazard ponytail, and she wasn't wearing makeup.

She hurried across the wide-plank wood floor and gave Jeff a fierce, motherly hug. She smelled of the garden. Like roses or lavender or something.

"I've called your mother," she said as she let him go. "She's so relieved. Honestly, Jeff, you should have called her. Where on earth have you been? And when did you grow a beard?"

Jeff steeled his resolve. He'd seen Aunt Pam in action; she certainly hadn't been this sweet to Melissa on Saturday. He took a step back. "I've been staying at Dad's fishing cabin, and I grew a beard so you wouldn't recognize me."

"But—"

"Look, Aunt Pam, I'm not here to reconnect with the family. I'm here to issue an ultimatum."

"What on earth...? About what?" A little V of puzzlement formed on her forehead.

"About Melissa Portman and Secondhand Prose."

The frown morphed into an expression of utter astonishment. "What in the...? Oh my goodness, you're the man who fell off the ladder." She chuckled. "I'm afraid I wasn't looking at your face that day."

His humiliation was utterly complete. But he wasn't going to let it get the best of him. It was well past time to go on the offensive.

"Yeah, I admit I managed to get disrobed by a coat hook. But that's beside the point. I'm here to let you know that I've paid Melissa's taxes. So you won't be getting your hands on that building."

"Oh, that's wonderful news, Jeff. I'm so pleased. I've been worried about Melissa. I know it's hard to let go of that bookstore, but once she realizes she can make money leasing out the space, I know she'll come around."

Wait a sec. What the hell was Pam saying? That she didn't want the building? That she cared about

Melissa's future? "Wait. I'm confused. You don't want her building?"

"Well, if she wants to sell it, I'm ready to buy it. But I'd rather see her join the rest of the property owners and participate in our downtown restoration project."

He stood there for a moment trying to figure out which Pam Lyndon was the real one, the woman who had threatened Melissa on Saturday or this sweet Southern lady.

"Sit down, Jeff. Lidia will bring us some tea, and we'll talk. I can see you're upset. But, truly, if you've paid her taxes, then that's good news." Her drawl was suddenly thick as a brick.

"I don't want any tea or talk, Aunt Pam. What I want is for you to call Melissa Portman and tell her you're sorry for the way you threatened her. I want you to make it clear that there is no truth to the rumors flying around town that you used me to soften her up so she'd sell out."

"What? Why are people saying that?"

"I don't really understand, except that when I introduced myself to her, I dropped the Lyndon from my last name. But now everyone in town thinks I lied because of some nefarious plan you set in motion. Honestly, you need to do some fence mending with some of the Liberty Avenue merchants."

Pam continued to look at him as if he'd blown in from Mars. "Why on earth did you drop the Lyndon from your last name?"

"Because I don't want anything to do with any of you, my father most of all. And just so we're clear, I've asked my attorney to begin the process of legally changing my name to Jefferson Talbert."

"Well, that's just ridiculous," she said. "Even if you

change your name, you'll still be family. Don't let Tom manipulate you, darlin'. We all know your father is a dick."

"What?" Her words left him breathless.

"You heard me. He's an idiot and a…Well, I've already used language I shouldn't have used, but in Thomas's case, it fits the bill. Thomas obviously hasn't said it recently, or maybe ever, but, Jeff, we're all so very proud of you."

Before he could collect himself, Pam stood up. "Wait right there, darlin'. Don't run away again, please. There's something you need to hear."

She left the room, and he started pacing. Had she even heard what he had to say? He didn't think so. Damn. He came to rest in front of a big window with old glass that gave a slightly wobbly view of the outside.

"Jeff?" an oddly familiar masculine voice said from behind him. Was his father here?

He turned. No. Not Dad. Uncle Mark.

The senator stood beside one of the comfortable easy chairs, wearing a pair of jeans and a golf shirt. The Senate was obviously not in session today.

"I'm so glad you came to find us," he said, resting his hand on the chair back. "Pam says you've been staying up at the fishing cabin. That's probably the last place any of us would have looked for you." He chuckled, his brown eyes dancing with some kind of merriment that eluded Jeff.

"What is it you want, Uncle Mark? I've already told Aunt—"

"I want to talk to you. First of all, I want you to know that the entire family was shocked by Tom's public statements about your story."

Jeff said nothing. His life had suddenly become theater of the absurd.

"I see I've surprised you," Uncle Mark said.

Jeff shrugged. "I don't give a flying fart what the family thinks about anything, really. I'm only here because Aunt Pam has gotten the Liberty Avenue merchants in an uproar. And they all think I'm part of some weird plan that she has to take over the real estate downtown. And, really, the only problem here is that I decided to drop the Lyndon from my name. And, you know, I'm not ever going to use that name again."

The senator's shoulders sagged a little. "I understand. And as for your aunt, she can sometimes be like a steamroller. I'll see what I can do to smooth things over with the merchants. It won't be the first time."

"Thanks. That's all I want. I'll be going now." Jeff turned and headed toward the door, but the senator blocked his way.

"Son," Uncle Mark said, "you have every right to be furious with your father. We're all furious with him. Family comes before politics, and Tom forgot that. So I just want you to think this through. If you want to strike back at your father, then you need to help me kill this nomination."

It took a moment for Uncle Mark's words to make it past Jeff's anger. "Wait a sec. Are you saying you believe the story I wrote about Joanna Durand?"

"Of course I do. Durand's family has a reputation for bending the rules when it comes to oil and gas. And her husband has more lobbying clients than a dog has fleas. I'm sure her husband and brother have been up to no good, and I could use your help in putting the kibosh on this nomination.

"By the way, I'm saying this not as your uncle but as a member of the Senate Judiciary Committee. Her confirmation hearing is set for this coming Thursday, and I have every intention of giving her a hard time."

"Oh." The adrenaline in Jeff's body began to dissipate.

Mark Lyndon continued. "I'm not letting Joanna Durand's nomination get out of committee. So, I'd like you to give my chief of staff a call and help him hunt down the smoking gun that will simultaneously clear your name and sink this nomination for good and all."

Jeff stood there frozen. He hadn't expected this. Not in a million years. "Okay, I'll help, of course, but—"

"Son, if you want to change your last name, go right ahead and do it. No one could blame you. But it won't change anything as far as I'm concerned, and I suspect you'll discover that resigning from the Lyndon family is a whole lot harder than you might expect."

Chapter
9

Hugo jumped on Melissa's bed and settled on her pillow, purring like a finely tuned engine. That was unusual, since the cat hadn't been upstairs since Grammy died. And never, in all the cat's twelve years on the planet, had he ever jumped up on Melissa's bed. So why had he chosen this morning, when her head was pounding like nobody's business?

She batted the cat away and pulled the pillow over her head, hoping that would quiet the pounding. But the cat meowed loudly and then opened his claws on her shoulder.

She sat up. Her stomach lurched as she groped for her glasses. She should never have had the third margarita. The world came into focus as she settled her glasses on her nose. She picked up her cell phone and checked the time. It was well past noon.

So much for getting an early start on the rest of her life. She had barely enough time to take a shower before her one o'clock meeting with Walter Braden. She was about to put the phone down when she noticed that she had new voice mail messages—twelve, in fact—all from Jeff. She'd missed his calls last night because she'd inadvertently left her cell phone at home.

Damn.

She listened to his voice mail. He'd actually called last night to invite her up to his cabin. And then he'd called again in the morning to invite her to breakfast.

Double damn.

Maybe she should return his calls.

No. He needed to come to her. Most definitely. And in the meantime, she needed to take a shower and move on with her life.

She got up, fed the cats, made some coffee, but instead of taking a shower, she called Walter and rescheduled her appointment for the next day. Then she set up her laptop on the kitchen table and started searching Jeff's name. Wow. He had lied about a lot of things, starting with the fact that he was, really and truly, a published writer.

An hour later she was still sitting there reading Jeff's articles—not just the one on Joanna Durand, but a dozen others. The man was a talented writer with a knack for writing profiles of the rich and famous. She was totally engrossed when someone tapped on her back door. Her heart took flight. Maybe Jeff had come to explain himself.

But it wasn't Jeff.

Gracie Teague stood on her landing wearing her waitress uniform and a determined expression. She didn't wait to be invited in. She just took the territory like General Patton rolling over France.

"I brought you a bacon and egg sandwich and some serious advice." She plunked a sandwich wrapped in wax paper onto the kitchen table and eyed the computer, the empty bag of M&M's, and the wastebasket filled with used tissues. "I should have come sooner."

"I'm all right. Really. I didn't make my appointment with Walter Braden, but I did reschedule for tomorrow. I've decided to take your advice and sell out, take the proceeds after taxes and find a beach somewhere with hot, gorgeous, rich men."

She'd expected Gracie to be overjoyed with this news, but instead her mother's BFF frowned. "You will do no such thing," she said. "Sit down. I have something you need to hear."

Melissa sat, and Gracie took the other chair. "There was an emergency meeting of the Liberty Avenue Merchants Association at oh dark thirty this morning. You know how everyone loved Harriet. And everyone remembers you as a little girl, and we're all just a little overprotective of you, I guess. So this Jefferson Lyndon situation has gotten everyone into an uproar. Half the shop owners think Pam Lyndon sent that man to soften you up. To convince you to sell out."

"But—"

Gracie held up a hand. "I know, hon. Why would a man help you fix up the store if he'd been sent to convince you that keeping it going was pointless?"

Melissa nodded. "Exactly."

"Well, not everyone is as logical as you and I. Anyway," Gracie said with a little gleam in her eye, "at the meeting this morning, some of the merchants took up a collection to help you with your taxes. It's not much, but we figured it might be enough to buy you some time. I was nominated to go down to the county clerk's office to make a payment on your behalf. But when I got there, I found out that someone had already paid your taxes in full."

"What?"

"That's right. Paid in full first thing this morning, just an hour before I got there. The clerk wouldn't tell me who. She said it was a privacy matter or something. As if there's any privacy in a town as small as Shenandoah Falls."

"You think Jeff paid my taxes?" The weight in Melissa's chest began to lift.

"That would be my guess. Now, why would a man do a thing like that?"

Melissa tried to think of a good business reason and drew a blank. "Because he believes in independent bookstores?" It was lame.

"Or maybe he believes in you?" Gracie said, covering one of Melissa's hands with hers.

Melissa's eyes filled up, but this time the tears weren't angry. "And I believe in him, Gracie," she whispered, her lips trembling. "I've been sitting here reading the things he's written, and I can't help myself. I think what he wrote in that story about the Durand nomination is true. I think he ran away from New York because even his father refused to stand by him."

"You know," Gracie said, "if my daddy had publicly disavowed me, I think I might return the favor. You know, by dropping the hyphenated part of my last name."

"Really? Because now that I'm sober and I've read his story and the reaction to it, I've come to the same conclusion."

Just then Dickens jumped up on the kitchen table, sat down facing Melissa, and proceeded to meow at her as if he were scolding her or something. Hugo followed suit, only he yowled in a way that was practically mournful.

"Mercy," Gracie said. "I've never seen them do anything like that before."

Melissa got up from the table. "It's a sign, Gracie. They've been trying to tell me for days that Jeff belongs here. I just wasn't listening."

Melissa called Walter Braden back and canceled her meeting. Without a tax bill looming over her, maybe she could make a go of keeping Secondhand Prose alive, saving Hugo and Dickens's home, and preserving a little piece of Grammy for a while.

And all because of Jeff, who had walked into her store and insisted on fixing it up. Not because he was paid to do it. Not because she'd asked him to do it. But because he had simply belonged there.

The cats knew it. And now Melissa did, too.

She needed to talk to him, so she decided the ball wasn't in his court after all. The ball was in hers. She texted him.

> **Melissa:** *We need to talk. Where are you?*
> **Jeff:** *I'm just leaving Charlotte's Grove. Expect an apology call from Pam. I'll be at the store in ten minutes.*
> **Melissa:** *No, not here. Too many busybodies. Where's your cabin?*
> **Jeff:** *:)*

His emoticon was followed by an address in the Blue Ridge off Scottish Heights Road. She told him she'd meet him there in twenty minutes.

The cabin turned out to be high up on the ridge off a dirt road. Jeff certainly hadn't been exaggerating when he'd said that he'd been living back in the woods.

It was an old place, built years before people had started putting up luxury vacation homes in the area. Its weathered logs and rustic stone chimney looked as if they'd been there for a century. It sat in a clearing, nestled between two gigantic oaks, on a ledge that provided a commanding view westward toward the Shenandoah Valley and the Allegheny Mountains beyond.

Jeff was waiting for her, sitting in an Adirondack chair on the covered porch. He stood up as she pulled her VW in behind his shiny Land Rover, and he was right there when she got out of the car.

"Let me explain," he said before she had a chance to say one word of the speech she'd been rehearsing in her head. "I never—"

"You didn't tell me the truth," she blurted.

"I'm sorry. I didn't mean to mislead you. I just—"

"I know you didn't. I get it. If I had a father who issued public statements about me, I'd want to divorce him, too. But you could have told me that. You could have trusted me."

Jeff's gaze intensified, his brown eyes full of emotion. "Are you telling me that you actually understand why I didn't give you my full name?"

"Well, duh. I read what your father said about you. And it was brutal. But more important, it was just wrong. I spent a lot of time today reading some of the things you've written for *New York, New York*. They were wonderful articles, Jeff. You have a gift for words. So what he said was just not true. You're a writer—a really good one. But the thing is, you should have been honest with me from the start."

He let go of a long breath and closed his eyes for a moment. "I'm sorry I wasn't honest, but I didn't know you at first. And then...Well, I wanted to take care of your taxes before I said anything. Please tell me you never believed that crap that's going around town about how Pam used me to set you up, because that's just not true."

"Of course I don't believe that. If that was your purpose, you had a funny way of going about it. All that dusting and organizing and color coding. It didn't make it easier to decide to sell the place, you know."

"You aren't going to sell it, are you? I'd hate to see that bookshop go out of business."

Tears filled her eyes, and a lump the size of a peach stone swelled in her throat. She shook her head. "I never wanted to sell. I just had to."

He took her by the shoulders and pulled her right into his arms. Her head hit his strong, steady shoulder, and she leaned on him like she'd never leaned on anyone in her life. The emotions she'd been denying finally found their way to the surface. She had to take off her glasses when the tears came. She cried for Grammy and her parents. She cried because, standing there in the circle of Jeff's arms, she didn't feel alone anymore. And finally, she cried because she didn't have to close her store.

He held her tight, stroked her head, and gave her a place to stand, a place to be. Leaning on him was like coming home.

When the tears had run their course, she tilted her head up, but it was no use. She couldn't see him because her vision was still smeared with tears. But it was all right, because he came toward her and started kissing away the tears that had run down her cheeks.

She started laughing then, which was weird because her heart had swelled to the point where breathing had become difficult. He ignored her laugh and continued to dispense little kisses all along her cheeks and over to her ear, where he whispered, "Listen to me, Melissa, for just one minute. I went up to Charlotte's Grove, and I told Mark and Pam Lyndon that I was changing my name. I've already taken the first steps to do that legally. I also told Pam that she needed to call you to apologize for the way she acted the other day."

She pushed him back and gazed into his eyes. He was a complete blur, but that didn't matter. "You told Pam Lyndon she needed to apologize? Oh my God, I don't think anyone has ever told Pam Lyndon that in her entire life."

He laughed a little and put his forehead against hers. "Well, there's a first time for everything."

They stood like that for a long moment as the tension of the last few days melted away. "So, I have a million questions," Melissa said.

"About what?"

"About you, Jeff. I want to know everything. I want to know what your favorite color is and what you like for breakfast, and lunch, and dinner. And which vegetable makes you want to yak. I want to know your birthday and the worst and best Christmas present you ever got. I want to know it all because, damn it, I crave your body, and when that happens, it means my heart is automatically involved. You know? I don't do the whole friends-with-benefits thing well. So if that's all this is, I'll just get in my car and go now, okay?"

She was prepared to have her heart crushed when he said, "Brussels sprouts."

"What?"

"I hate brussels sprouts. How about you?"

She took in a deep breath filled with the woodsy scent of him. "It's cauliflower that makes me want to hurl. And, for the record, my birthday is the sixteenth of March."

"Really? Mine's on the seventeenth. Next year we should throw a big party."

Next year. She closed her eyes and rested her head against his chest. His arms were still around her. She was safe here. She'd always be safe here. She may have met him only days ago, but he was "the One."

"I have something to seal this moment," he said, moving back a little bit. "I intended to present it to you last night. But you didn't answer my calls."

"I was getting drunk with the girls. Bad move on my part."

He laughed. "Put on your glasses."

She snagged them from her jeans pocket where she'd put them right before her crying jag. She slipped them on just in time to see him pull something from his pocket.

He held it out to her, nestled in his palm. "It's the arrowhead," he said. "Yesterday I bought a rawhide shoelace and made a necklace out of it. When I get a chance, I intend to take it to a jeweler for a proper gold chain. I thought you might like a little memento of our first time." He gave her a salacious grin. "Turn around. Let me put it on you."

She turned, and he pulled her hair aside and then fastened the necklace at her nape. He pressed his lips to the spot right below her ear, and she groaned out loud.

"Our first time, huh? That implies there will be a second time," she said.

"Yeah. And many, many more, I hope." And then he did the most romantic thing ever. He lifted her into his arms and carried her over the threshold of his cabin.

Epilogue

Three Months Later

Melissa was manning the checkout at Secondhand Prose and reading a murder mystery when the front door jangled. She looked up in time to see Jeff strolling through the door, carrying a cardboard box that looked as if it had come from an online bookseller.

Both cats immediately arrived on the scene and tried to trip him as he headed in Melissa's direction.

"Hey, you guys, give me a break," he said as he stepped over the felines with admirable grace—grace that hadn't yet failed to warm Melissa's insides.

"I bring gifts," he said, putting the carton on the counter and leaning across it to give her a kiss that left them both a little breathless.

"Hmm, nice. I like your gifts," she said.

He laughed. "I was talking about this," he said, nudging the box.

"This looks like a box of books," she said. "From the competition."

"Ah, but this isn't just any box of books. Look inside."

She opened the carton, and right on the top was a large-format paperback book titled *A Child's Book of Stories*. "Oh, how beautiful!" Melissa said in a rush as she opened the book and started browsing through. "I love Jessie Wilcox Smith's illustrations. She's my favorite illustrator of all time."

"Yes, I know. That was one of the first things I learned about you. All those fairytale T-shirts."

She looked up from the book and gave him another kiss.

"There's another book in the box," Jeff said after a very long, hot moment.

"Another Jessie Wilcox Smith book?"

"No, it's a hardbound copy of *Grimm's Complete Fairy Tales*."

She put her paperback on the counter and pulled the second book from the box. It was one of those leather reproduction books with a fancy embossed cover, gilt lettering, and a ribbon bookmark stitched into the binding. She wasn't fooled. The book probably retailed for less than ten dollars.

She glanced up at Jeff. There was a gleam in his eye, and the corner of his mouth was curling just a tiny bit, as if he knew a secret he was bursting to tell. Did he think he'd found her a special first edition or something?

"Oh, this is nice," she said, trying to sound super-enthusiastic, when she would much rather be hanging out on the beanbag chair drooling over Jessie Wilcox Smith's illustrations. Or, better yet, upstairs in bed drooling over Jeff.

"Open it," Jeff said, "to the marked page." Was there a tremor in his voice?

She opened the book to a three-paragraph story entitled "Brides on Trial." Right below the story's final paragraph, the book had been horribly defaced. Someone had cut a deep hole in the pages to create a secret hiding spot. And in the spot, with the ribbon bookmark threaded through it, was a sapphire and diamond ring.

Melissa's breath caught in her throat, and tears filled her eyes as she looked up at Jeff, the man who had become, in just a few short months, her best friend and the love of her life.

"Melissa," he said in his deep, quiet voice, "I walked into this enchanted place, and the minute I saw you, I knew I'd come home. I've patiently spent the last few months waiting for the right time to ask this question, and I don't want to wait anymore. I think I know enough about you to say that I never want to leave your side. You love Jessie Wilcox Smith, you know every story in *Grimm's Fairy Tales*, even the gruesome ones like the 'Heavenly Wedding.' You snore, you love margaritas, and you read romances when you think I'm not looking. Will you marry me?"

Like any fairytale prince, Jeff got down on his knee, took her hand, and kissed it.

"Oh my God, yes. Yes, yes." Melissa fell down onto her knees, too, and wrapped her arms around him. "I love you, Jefferson Talbert-Lyndon. And even though you are technically a member of the Lyndon family, I can't imagine spending my life with anyone else."

Jeff grabbed the *Grimm's Fairy Tales* off the counter and sat on the bookstore's floor. "Sorry about defacing a book, but I figured it was for a good cause. And we'll be keeping this book forever."

He pulled the ribbon bookmark through the ring. "Do you like it?" he asked. "It's a family heirloom, but from the Talbert side of the family. It's my grandmother's ring."

"The cat-lady-on-the-Hudson grandmother?"

Jeff grinned. "The very one." He took her left hand and slipped the ring on her finger. It fit perfectly. "Grandmother would have loved you, Melissa."

And just then, Dickens and Hugo joined the group hug on the bookstore floor, one cat in each lap, proving—at least to Melissa's satisfaction—that Grammy would have loved Jeff too.

Jenna Fossey's life is about to change. An unexpected inheritance and the chance to meet relatives she never knew existed have her heading to the charming little town of Magnolia Harbor. But as soon as she arrives, long-buried family secrets lead to even more questions, and the only person who can help her find the answers is her sexy-as-sin sailing instructor.

Please turn the page to read an excerpt from Hope Ramsay's *The Cottage on Rose Lane*.

Available now.

Chapter One————————————

Was this her father's boat? The one he'd been sailing the day he died?

Jenna Fossey stood on the sidewalk, shading her eyes against the early-September sun, studying the boat. It was small, maybe fifteen feet from end to end. It sat on cinder blocks, hull up in the South Carolina sunshine, its paint blistered and cracked. Much of the color had faded or peeled away, leaving long gray planks of wood. Even the boat's name had bleached away; only the shadow of a capital *I* on the boat's stern remained. Some kind of vine—was that kudzu?—had twisted up the cinder blocks and crawled across the boat's hull, setting suckers into the wood and giving the impression that only the overgrown vegetation held the pieces together.

A thick, hard knot formed in Jenna's chest. She held her breath and closed her eyes, imagining the father she'd never known. In her thirty years on this planet, she'd imagined him so many times. In her fantasies, he'd been a fireman, a detective, a handsome prince, a super-hero, a scoundrel, a bastard, and an asshole. That last role had stuck for most of her life because, before she died of breast cancer three years ago, Mom had refused to talk about him. In fact, by her omission, Mom had made it plain that Jenna's father had been a mistake, or a one-night stand, or someone Mom had met in college but hardly knew.

And then, one day out of the blue, Milo Stracham, the executor of her grandfather's will, arrived at her front door and told Jenna the truth. Her father had been the son of a wealthy man, a passionate sailor, and he'd died before she was born.

She took another breath, redolent with the tropical scents of the South Carolina Low Country. Musty and mossy and salty. This was an alien place to a girl who'd grown up in Boston. It was too lush here. Too hot for September.

She shifted her gaze to the house where Uncle Harry lived. It was a white clapboard building bristling with dormer windows and a square cupola on top. Its wrap-around veranda, shaded by a grove of palmettos at the corner, epitomized the architecture of the South. She stood there listening to the buzz of cicadas as she studied the house, as if it would tell her something about the man who owned it.

At least Uncle Harry didn't live in a big, pretentious monstrosity like her grandfather's house on the Hudson. She would never live in her grandfather's house. She'd told Milo, who had become the sole trustee of her trust fund, to sell the place. But, of course, her grandfather's will restricted such a sale, just as it had restricted her ability to sell her grandfather's stock in iWear, Inc., the company he had founded and which now was the largest manufacturer and retailer of optics in the world, including sunglasses that regularly retailed for two hundred dollars or more a pair.

The *Wall Street Journal* may have dubbed Jenna the Sunglass Heiress once the details of Robert Bauman's will had become public, but that was so not who she was.

She'd been raised in Dorchester, a neighborhood in Boston, the daughter of a single mother who'd worked two jobs to keep her in shoes and school uniforms. She'd been a good student, but even with scholarships, Jenna had taken out huge loans for college and graduate school. But she'd earned her MBA from Harvard, and landed a job in business development with Aviation Engineering, a Fortune 500 company.

But her inheritance had cost her the job she loved, because iWear was a direct competitor in the advanced heads-up optics market that was so important to Aviation Engineering's bottom line.

The company she'd devoted eight years of her life to had made her sign a nondisclosure agreement and had booted her out within a day of learning of her good fortune. It was as if the universe were sending her a message that just ignoring the money or refusing to accept it was not sufficient.

So she did what she'd been thinking about doing for years—she took a year-long trip to the Near and Far East, intent on deepening her understanding of meditation and Buddhism. Her goal had been to learn how to handle the karmic consequence of the inheritance her stranger of a grandfather had given her.

She needed something meaningful to do. But what? She needed a cause. Or a reason. Or something.

After a year spent mostly in India, she'd come to the conclusion that she could never build a new life for herself without confronting the secrets of the old one.

Which was why she'd come to Magnolia Harbor, South Carolina, with a million questions about her father, seeking the one person who might be able to answer them—her uncle Harry, Robert Bauman's younger brother.

She crossed the street and leaned on the picket fence. It would be so easy to ascend the porch steps, knock on the door, and explain herself to the uncle she had never known. But it wasn't that simple. The rift between Robert and Harry had been decades wide and deep, and she didn't understand the pitfalls. She couldn't afford to screw this up. She'd have to gain Harry's trust before she told him who she was.

She walked away from the house and continued down Harbor Drive until she reached downtown Magnolia Harbor. The business district comprised a four-block area with upscale gift shops, restaurants, and a half-mile boardwalk lined with floating docks.

On the south side of town, an open-air fish market bustled with customers lining up to buy shrimp right off the trawlers that had gone out that morning. On the north side stood a marina catering to a fleet of deep-sea fishing boats and yachts. In between was a public fishing pier and a boat launch accessed from a dry dock filled with small boat trailers.

Presiding over this central activity stood Rafferty's Raw Bar, a building with weathered siding and a shed roof clad in galvanized metal. Jenna found a seat on the restaurant's terrace, where the scent of fried shrimp hung heavy on the air. She ordered a glass of chardonnay and some spinach dip and settled in to watch the sailboats out on the bay.

"The Buccaneers are always fun to watch," the waitress said as she placed Jenna's chardonnay in front of her.

"Buccaneers? You mean like pirates?"

"Well, they're obviously not pirates, but they do pretend sometimes. Some of them love to say *arrrgh* at appropriate moments. They also regard Talk Like a Pirate Day as a holy day of obligation."

Jenna must have let her confusion show because the waitress winked and rolled her eyes. "Oh, don't mind me. I'm a sailing nerd. Those sailboats are all Buccaneer Eighteens, a kind of racing dinghy. The Bucc fleet always goes out on Tuesday afternoons for practice races."

"So, sailing is a big thing here, huh?"

"It always has been. Jonquil Island used to be a hangout for pirates back in the day. And the yacht club is, like, a hundred and fifty years old."

Had her father belonged to the yacht club? Probably. It was the sort of thing the son of a rich man would do.

"Oh, look," the waitress said, pointing. "They're done for the day, and *Bonney Rose* is leading them in. Her skipper is a crazy man, but so cute. He's got a chest to die for." She giggled. "My friends and I sometimes refer to it as 'the Treasure Chest.'" The waitress pointed at the lead boat with a navy-blue hull and crisp white sails.

The boat was heading toward the floating dock with the others behind it. The two sailors sat with their legs extended and their bodies leaning hard over the water in an impressive display of core strength. The guy in the back of the boat was shirtless with his life vest open to expose an impressive six-pack. His skin was berry brown, and his curly dark hair riffled in the wind.

Jenna caught her breath as a deep, visceral longing clutched her core. He resembled a marauding pirate. Dark and handsome with a swath of masculine brow, high cheekbones, and a full mouth. Like someone with Spanish blood and a little Native American or Creole mixed in. Or maybe African too.

Had they met before? Perhaps in a past life?

She watched in rapt attention as the boat came toward the dock at a sharp angle. He was going to crash. But at the last moment, the boat turned away, stalling in the water, allowing the second sailor, a man with a salt-and-pepper beard, to step onto the dock in one fluid motion, carrying a mooring line. The big sail flapped noisily in the wind as the shirtless sailor began pulling it down into the boat, his biceps flexing in the late-afternoon sun.

Five more sailboats arrived in the same noisy manner, and for the next few minutes, an orderly chaos ensued as boats arrived and dropped sail and got in line for the launch. Jenna had trouble keeping her eyes off the man with the too-curly hair and the dark skin.

It was probably because she'd spent the day thinking about her father and the way he'd sailed here, and died here. Had her father been like a dashing pirate ready to buckle some swash? She pulled her gaze away and allowed a wistful smile. She was doing it again. Inventing a father for herself instead of seeking the real one.

"Can I get you anything else?" the waitress, whose name tag said Abigail, asked.

"Yes. What's his name? And why is the name of his boat misspelled?" She pointed to the man and the boat, where BONNEY ROSE was painted in gold letters along the stern.

"That's Jude St. Pierre. And the boat's name is a tribute to Anne Bonney, a female pirate from back in the day. It's also a tribute to Gentleman Bill Teel's boat, which broke up over near the inlet back in the 1700s. That boat was named the *Bonnie Rose*, after Rose Howland."

"And who is that?"

"She's the lady who planted jonquils all over the island in memory of Gentleman Bill, the pirate."

"I sense a story."

"It's basically the town myth. Explains all the pirate stores in town. You can pick up a free Historical Society pamphlet almost anywhere. I'd give you one, but we're out of them. It's the end of the summer, you know. Things are starting to wind down here."

"Do many boats go down in the inlet?" Jenna asked, a little shiver running up her spine. Is that what had happened to her father?

Abigail nodded. "The currents can be treacherous there if you don't know what you're doing or you get caught in a squall. Can I get you anything else?"

Jenna shook her head. "Just the check."

As Abigail walked away, Jenna turned to study the man named Jude St. Pierre. Her skin puckered up, and her mouth went bone dry. She pushed the attraction aside. That was not what she wanted from him.

She wanted a sailboat ride to the place where her father had died. But since she didn't know where that might be in the vastness of Moonlight Bay, maybe the best she could do was a sailing lesson so she could find it later herself.

"You've got an admirer," Tim Meyer said, nodding in the general direction of Rafferty's terrace. "Easy on the eyes, dirty blond, with big brown eyes."

Jude didn't follow Tim's glance. Instead, he concentrated on the job of securing the mast to its cradle with a couple of bungee cords. He didn't have time to flirt with tourists.

"She's a cutie. Aren't you even going to look?" Tim, newly divorced and constantly on the make, had spent the entire summer chasing female tourists who were too young for him, so this comment rolled right off Jude's back.

He'd learned the hard way that tourists always went home. Besides, he had a rule about blondes. His mother had been a white woman with blond hair, and she'd abandoned the family when Jude was fourteen. He could do better than a blonde. He wanted a Clair Huxtable who could also speak Gullah, the Creole language of his ancestors.

"I can't believe you aren't even going to check her out," Tim said. "She's got a hungry look in her big brown eyes."

Jude raised his head without meaning to.

Big mistake. The woman's gaze wasn't hungry exactly. It was steady and direct and measuring. It knocked him back, especially when her mouth quirked up on one side to reveal a hint of a dimple, or maybe a laugh line. And she wasn't blond. Not exactly. It was more cinnamon than brown with streaks of honey that dazzled in the late-afternoon sun. Her hair spilled over her shoulders, slightly messy and windblown, as if she'd spent the day sailing. She was cute and fresh, and he had this eerie feeling that he'd met her before.

Her stare burned a hole in his chest, and he turned away slightly breathless. Damn. He was too busy for a fling. And never with a woman like that.

"See what I mean? She's maybe a little skinny but... kind of hot," Tim said.

Jude ignored the sudden rushing of blood in his head and focused on snapping up the boat's canvas cover. "Stop objectifying. Haven't you heard? It's no longer PC."

Tim chuckled. "Objectifying is a scientific fact."

"So says the science teacher. If the parents of your students could hear you now, they'd—"

"Come on. Let's go get a drink and say hey," Tim interrupted.

"No. I have a meeting tonight."

Tim rolled his eyes. "With that group of history nuts again?"

"They aren't nuts. Dr. Rushford is a history professor." And he'd donated his time and that of his grad students to help Jude get several old homes listed on the historic register. Jude's last chance to preserve those buildings was the petition he and several of his cousins and relatives had made to the town council, asking for a rezoning of the land north of town that white folks called "Gullah Town." The area wasn't really a town at all, but a collection of small farms out in the scrub pine and live oak that had been settled by his ancestors right after the Civil War. Jude's people never used the term "Gullah Town." To them, the land north of Magnolia Harbor was just simply home.

The council was having a hearing this week. Jude had been working on this issue for more than a year with the professor's help. He wasn't about to miss a meeting to flirt with a tourist. An almost-blond tourist at that.

"Okay. It's your loss." Tim slapped him on the back. "But thanks for leaving the field of play. You're hard to compete with, dude." Tim strode off while Jude finished securing the last bungee cord. When he glanced up again, the woman with the honey hair was still staring at him, even as Tim moved in.

Tim was going to crash and burn. Again.

Jude turned away. He wanted nothing to do with another one of Tim's failed pickup attempts. Instead, he headed down the boardwalk toward the offices of Barrier Island Charters, his father's company, where Jude had parked his truck. He needed to get on home and take a shower before the meeting.

"Can I have a minute of your time, Mr. St. Pierre?" someone asked from behind him.

Jude turned. Damn. It was the woman with the honey hair. She had a low, sexy voice that vibrated inside his core in a weird, but not unpleasant, way. "Do I know you?" he asked.

"Um, no. Abigail. The waitress? At the raw bar? She told me your name."

"Can I help you with something?" he asked.

"Well," she said, rolling her eyes in a surprisingly awkward way. Almost as if she was shy or something. Which she was not, since she'd chased him down the boardwalk. "I was wondering if you might be willing to give me sailing lessons."

"What?" That had to be the oddest request he'd gotten in a long time. He was not a sailing instructor.

"I'd like to learn how to sail a small boat."

"Did Abby put you up to this?"

She shook her head. "No. Of course not. I was watching you sail, and, well, you seem to know what you're doing out there." A telltale blush crawled up her cheeks as she talked a mile a minute. She was a Yankee, all right, from Boston. He didn't need the Red Sox T-shirt to tell him that either. She had a broad Boston accent. She must be here soaking up the last of the summer sun before going back north.

She'd be gone in a week.

"I don't give sailing lessons," he said in a curt tone and then checked his watch. He really needed to go.

"Oh. Okay. I'm sorry I bothered you," the woman said in an oddly wounded tone. Her shoulders slumped a little as she started to turn away.

Damn.

He'd been rude. And stupid too. If she really wanted sailing lessons, it was an opportunity to earn a few extra bucks doing the thing he loved most. Barrier Island Charters could use all the income it could get this time of year. "No, uh, wait," he said. "How many sailing lessons do you want?"

She stopped, midturn. "I don't know. How many would it take?"

"To do what?"

"Learn how to sail? On my own, you know."

"No one sails by themselves. I mean, even in a small boat like *Bonney Rose* you need a crew."

"Oh?" She frowned.

"Unless you're learning on an Opti or a Laser. But I don't have an Opti or a Laser."

The frown deepened. "Oh."

"Optis and Lasers are one-person boats. They capsize. A lot."

"Oh."

"If you want to learn on a bigger boat, you know, with a keel, you should check out the group courses in Georgetown."

"What's a keel?" she asked, cocking her head a little like an adorable brown-eyed puppy.

He fought against the urge to roll his eyes. "A keel boat has a...Never mind. It's bigger and more comfortable. And safer."

"Okay, then I want to learn how to sail the other kind. Does *Bonney Rose* have a keel?"

"No. She has a centerboard."

"Perfect." Her mouth broadened.

"I'm not a certified teacher. In Georgetown, you can—"

"So you've already said. But I'm not interested in group classes in Georgetown. I don't want that kind of thing. I want to learn how to take risks. Live on the edge. Sail fast."

"Look, sailing can be dangerous, and I don't do thrill rides."

She folded her arms across her chest, her eyebrows lowering a little and her hip jutting out, the picture of a ticked-off female. "I'm not looking for a thrill ride."

"No?" He gave her his best levelheaded stare.

She blushed a little. "Okay. I know nothing about sailing. But I want to learn."

"Go to the sailing school in Georgetown."

"Is that where you learned?"

Damn. She had him there. He'd learned from one of the best sailors on the island. He shook his head.

"Okay. So, can you give me the name of your teacher?"

"No. My teacher is retired now."

"Oh." She seemed crestfallen. Damn.

He checked his watch again and huffed out a breath. He was going to be late to the meeting. "Okay, look, I don't know if I'd be any good teaching you how to sail, but if you want to charter *Bonney Rose* for a couple of hours, the going rate is two hundred fifty an hour." That should shut her up. Judging by her worn-out flip-flops and threadbare camp pants, she didn't look like someone who could afford that kind of rate.

Her face brightened. "Okay."

"Okay?"

She nodded. "Tomorrow?"

Damn. "Yeah. I guess. At the public pier. Four o'clock." He turned away before she could argue.

"Hey. Wait," she called as he scooted down the boardwalk.

He didn't wait.

"Hey. Don't you even want to know my name?" she hollered at his back.

He turned around and backpedaled. "Why? I'll recognize you if you show up tomorrow. Oh, and bring cash."

About the Author

Hope Ramsay is a *USA Today* bestselling author of heart-warming contemporary romances set below the Mason-Dixon Line and inspired by the summers she spent with her large family in South Carolina. She has two grown children, a demanding lap cat named Simba who was born in Uganda, and a precious cockapoo puppy named Daisy. She lives in Virginia, where, when she's not writing, she's knitting or playing her forty-year-old Martin guitar.

You can learn more at:
HopeRamsay.com
Twitter: @HopeRamsay
Facebook.com/Hope.Ramsay

*Fall in love with these charming
small-town romances!*

BAREFOOT BEACH
By Debbie Mason

Theia Lawson and Marco DiRossi are determined to beat the match-makers of Harmony Harbor at their own game. Both lone wolves, the two conspire to pretend that they've already fallen in love. But just when they want to make their relationship real, a secret is revealed that puts everything Marco and Theia have fought for in jeopardy.

Discover exclusive content and more on
read-forever.com.

SPRINGTIME AT HOPE COTTAGE
By Annie Rains

In Sweetwater Springs, love has a way of mending even the most damaged heart. When Josie Kellum is sidelined in a small town, she focuses on her rehab to get back to the big city ASAP. But that becomes awfully difficult when she falls for her hunky physical therapist. Includes a bonus story by Hope Ramsay!

Find more great reads on Instagram with @ReadForeverPub.

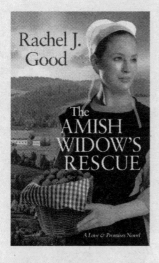

THE AMISH WIDOW'S RESCUE
By Rachel J. Good

Pregnant and recently widowed, Grace Fisher is determined to provide for her family on her own. Elijah Beiler has always admired his neighbor Grace, so standing by while she struggles to support her family isn't an option. Determined to help, Elijah finds it difficult to remain detached. Can he overcome past hurts and open his heart to this ready-made family?

WELCOME TO LAST CHANCE (REISSUE)
By Hope Ramsay

When Wanda Jane Coblentz arrives in Last Chance with five dollars in her pocket, all she wants is a hot meal and a fresh start. But when she falls for sexy musician Clay Rhodes, she never expects a bad boy like Clay to rescue a damsel in distress. Thank goodness Jane plans on rescuing herself. Includes a bonus story!

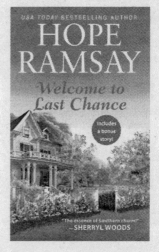

Follow @ReadForeverPub on Twitter and join the conversation using #ReadForever.

THE WAY YOU LOVE ME
By Miranda Liasson

Gabby Langdon secretly dreams of being a writer, so for once she does something for herself—she signs up for a writing class taught by bestselling novelist Caden Marshall. There's only one problem: Her brooding, sexy professor is a distraction she can't afford if she's finally going to get the life she truly wants. Includes a bonus story by Alison Bliss!

THREE LITTLE WORDS
By Jenny Holiday

Stranded in New York with her best friend's wedding dress, Gia Gallo has six days to make it to Florida in time for the ceremony. And oh-so-charming best man Bennett Buchanan has taken the last available rental car. Looks like she's in for one long road trip with the sexiest—and most irritating—Southern gentleman she's ever met.

Connect with us at Facebook.com/ReadForeverPub.

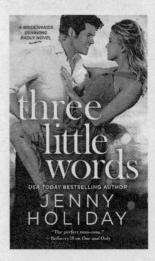